Tainted with

Undone by

Can he truly w

A *Wayward* Woman

Helen Dickson

and

Anne Herries

bring you two sparkling and sensational
all-new historical romances

Helen Dickson was born and lives in South Yorkshire with her retired farm manager husband. Having moved out of the busy farmhouse where she raised their two sons, she has more time to indulge in her favourite pastimes. She enjoys being outdoors, travelling, reading and music. An incurable romantic, she writes for pleasure. It was a love of history that led her to write historical fiction.

Anne Herries is an award-winning author who lives in Cambridgeshire. She is fond of watching wildlife and spoils the birds and squirrels that are frequent visitors to her garden. Anne loves to write about the beauty of nature and sometimes puts a little into her books—although they are mostly about love and romance. She writes for her own enjoyment and to give pleasure to her readers.

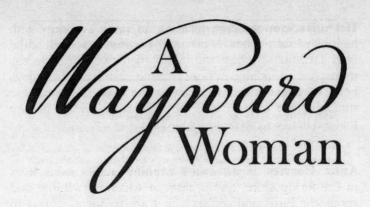

A *Wayward* Woman

HELEN DICKSON
ANNE HERRIES

MILLS & BOON

Harlequin Mills & Boon Limited, Eton House,
18-24 Paradise Road, Richmond, Surrey TW9 1SR

ISBN: 978 0 263 88723 5

10-0311

Harlequin Mills & Boon policy is to use papers that are natural,
renewable and recyclable products and made from wood grown in
sustainable forests. The logging and manufacturing processes conform to
the legal environmental regulations of the country of origin.

Printed in Great Britain
by Clays Ltd, St Ives plc

CONTENTS

Diamonds, Deception
and the Debutante

HELEN DICKSON

Author Note

Diamonds, Deception and the Debutante is set in the Regency period. It is one of the most turbulent, glittering and romantic times in our history, when rakes and dandies, outrageous gambling and scandals abounded. It is a period enjoyed by both readers and writers alike. I am no exception.

Every one of my books is special to me, but the one I am working on at the time is always the most important. When I finish a book I always intend having a break from writing to catch up on things I set aside until the story is finished before embarking on another, but invariably my imagination begins to stir and in no time at all I'm off again.

History has always held a fascination for me—it was one of my best subjects at school. I am interested in how people lived, how different everything was from today and how much one can learn from the past. My inspiration is drawn from many things. I am an avid reader and I enjoy music and walking. My characters are not based in any direct way on anyone in particular and I use my own brush to paint things in a fictional way. I do home in on certain traits and embody them in the characters in my books. I love seeing the people I create come to life and develop personalities of their own.

Writing is something I enjoy tremendously and it gives me a great deal of personal satisfaction. I hope you enjoy reading *Diamonds, Deception and the Debutante* as much as I enjoyed writing it.

Prologue

June 1815

As the rain lashed down to compound the misery of the troops, the scene was set for battle. The British troops had been engaged by the French and forced to retire after a sharp engagement lasting the afternoon and they had to struggle to hold their position. The following morning Wellington drew back, establishing himself at the posting inn at the village of Waterloo.

It was here that one of Colonel Lance Bingham's staff officers brought him a note. It was crumpled and stained, as if it had passed through many hands.

'A lad brought it, sir,' the staff officer said. 'It's urgent, and he said I had to deliver it to you personally.'

Colonel Bingham tore the missive open and read it quickly. He spoke one word, 'Delphine.' Apart from a tightening of his jaw, his expression did not betray even a flicker of reaction. 'There is something I have to do.'

'But, sir, what if General Bonaparte…'

'Don't worry. I'll be back. Take me to the lad.'

Knowing he risked being court-marshalled for leaving his post on the eve of battle, Colonel Bingham rode away from the encampment. With rain beating at his face, following the lad on a small but swift-footed nag, he prayed to God that he was right and that Bonaparte wouldn't attack before dawn, for it was his way to fly at his opponents without waiting to be attacked.

The farmhouse to which he had been summoned was down a dirt track. It was a humble dwelling, the stench of animals and their dung as strong inside the house as it was in the farm-yard. The lad, who was the son of the farmer and his wife, hung back, pointing to a room at the top of a rickety staircase. Climbing up, Colonel Bingham paused in the doorway. It was dimly lit, hot and fetid with the stench of childbirth. A man stood next to the bed on which a woman lay, and in a corner of the room a young woman nursed an infant.

The man turned to look at the stranger, who seemed to fill the room with his presence. He saw an officer in military uniform, tall and with broad, muscular shoulders, deep chest and narrow waist, his handsome features ruggedly hewn.

'Colonel Bingham?'

He nodded, removing his hat, his face set and grim.

'I am Reverend Hugh Watson—attached to His Majesty's army,' he said, stepping back from the bed to allow him to ap-proach. 'Thank goodness you have come. Miss Jenkins hasn't much time left. When the midwife who attended the young woman at the birth of her child realised she would not pull through, when Miss Jenkins requested a clergyman to be ab-solved of her sins, she summoned me.'

Giving the clergyman, who had a prayer book open in his hands, a cool glance, taking note of his crumpled dark suit and grimy neck linen and that he was in need of a shave, never had Colonel Lance Bingham seen a man who looked less like a clergyman.

Seeming reluctant to approach the bed, his face hardened

into an expressionless mask, Lance observed the woman from where he stood. Not having seen her these seven months gone, he did not recognise her as the attractive, vivacious young woman who had kept him happily entertained throughout most of his years as a soldier in Spain. Drenched in sour sweat, she was lying beneath the covers, her lank brown hair trailed over the pillow. Her face was waxen and thinner than it had been, and dark rings circled her deep brown eyes.

As if she sensed he was there they fluttered open and settled on his face. Her heart beat softly inside her with love and wonderment that he had come. A smile lifted her tiredly drooping mouth. 'Lance—you came.' She tried to raise a hand to him, but sapped of strength it remained where it was.

Dropping to his knees beside the bed, Lance took her hand and raised it to his lips. 'Delphine, what in God's name are you doing here? I told you to go back to England.'

'I did, but then I followed you to Belgium—as I followed you to Spain, remember? I—haven't been well. I didn't think I would survive the birth. I did, but I know I haven't much time, Lance—but it gladdens my heart to see you again.'

'Miss Jenkins has just been delivered of your child,' the clergyman informed him.

Colonel Bingham stiffened and for the briefest of moments, shock registered in his eyes. 'My child? Is this true, Delphine?'

She nodded. 'A girl. You have a daughter, Lance. A beautiful daughter.'

Lance knew he would never again feel the shame, the guilt, the absolute wretchedness that seized him then, as he looked at what he believed to be the dying spirit of the woman who had taken his fancy when he had seen her perform on the London stage, this woman who had followed him to Spain, from one battlefield to the next, without complaint, without demanding anything from him, and was now slipping away.

When they had met, her freshness and vivacity were something his jaded spirits had badly needed. Delphine had proved to be a thoroughly delightful mistress. She had been there to satisfy his craving for carnal appeasement. They had talked and laughed and kissed and shared sweet intimacies. But knowing nothing could come of their affair, he couldn't let her waste one moment of her precious life loving him or waiting for him, and so he had ended it, telling himself that he had done the right thing, the noble thing. But nothing had prepared him for the days and nights of missing her, of the sweet softness of her in his arms.

'Delphine, I have to ask…'

'The child is yours,' she uttered forcefully. 'Never doubt it. There has been no one else. No one was good enough—after you.'

He bent his head over her hand. 'Dear sweet Lord, this is the cruellest thing you have ever done to me. Why did you not write and tell me? I would have come to you, Delphine. I would not have let you endure this alone.'

'I am sorry. I didn't know what else to do. I—I thought you might hate me—that you would turn me away—but I had nowhere else to go. I couldn't go home and I had to do something, which was why I came to Belgium—to find you.'

'You were afraid of me?' His voice was soft with compassion. 'You were afraid to tell me? Am I such an ogre, Delphine?'

'No…' She trembled and clutched his hand, a great wash of tears brimming in her eyes.

Lance felt his heart jolt for her pain. He would give anything to know how to comfort her, to reassure her that he would not leave her. He was an arrogant bastard, he knew that himself, a man who liked, demanded, his own determined way, but the emotion this woman aroused in him, the sweetness that flowed through him from her, could be matched by nothing he had ever known before.

'Don't cry, my love,' he murmured. 'I'm here now. You're safe with me and always will be.'

'Go and look at your daughter, Lance. You will see she is yours.'

Lance did as she bade and went to look at the flesh-and-blood evidence of the result of their loving. His heart began to beat against his chest wall. The wet nurse pushed away the cover shielding the infant's face. This was his child and he was almost too afraid to look at her because he did not know how he would feel when he did. He forced himself to look at the babe's face, compelled by some force he did not recognise. As he looked she yawned and turned her face towards him, before settling herself to sleep against the woman's breast.

It was his mother's face and his own he saw, the line of her brow with the distinctive widow's peak, the way in which her eyes were set in her skull, the black winging eyebrows, and the tiny cleft in her round chin. On her head her hair swirled against her skull, a clump of curls, coal black like his own, on her crown.

Turning from her, he went back to the bed. 'She is a fine girl, Delphine.'

'Yes, a fine baby girl. I've named her Charlotte—after my mother. As her father you will—look after her, won't you, Lance, be responsible for her—care for her and protect her? She has no one else.'

Lance nodded, a terrible constriction in his throat, for she was so weak, so defenceless against what was to happen to her. He damned all the fates that prevented him from righting the wrong he had done her by casting her from him, the cruel fates that prevented him from having this warm and lovely girl in his life once more.

'You have my guarantee that she will be supported in a manner suitable to her upbringing. But—is there anything I can do to ease your suffering? Anything at all?'

'You could do the honourable, gentlemanly thing and marry

Miss Jenkins, sir,' the clergyman suggested stoutly, almost forcefully. 'The child is a bastard and the stigma of being born out of wedlock will follow her all the days of her life. As your legitimate daughter her future will be secure.'

Lance was momentarily lost for words. Before this it would have been impossible, unthinkable to take her for his wife for he had a position to consider and a wife such as Delphine would not have been tolerated, but, by heaven, this changed everything. Lance knew a man's rightful claim to being a gentleman was not something one could inherit. Compassion, honour and integrity were just three of the characteristics. Certainly a man had a responsibility and an obligation to protect those who were close to him, those who depended on him, from the cruelties of the world. Looking from Delphine to the child, never had he felt the weight of that responsibility as he did now. He could not in all conscience and honour cast Delphine aside along with their child like something worthless.

Without any visible emotion, he said, 'Is this what you want, Delphine?'

She nodded, a tear trickling out of the corner of her eye and quickly becoming soaked up in the pillow. 'For our daughter's sake. I am dying, Lance, so I will not be a burden to you and you will be free to go on as before. It won't be long. Will you do this—for me?'

'I shall be proud to make you my wife, Delphine,' Lance said hoarsely. He looked at the clergyman. 'Very well. Get on with it.'

After summoning the farmer and his wife to bear witness to the proceedings, they spoke their vows, the infant beginning to wail lustily when the clergyman pronounced them man and wife.

Delphine smiled and closed her eyes. 'You can go now, Lance. There is nothing more to be done.'

That seemed to be so. With a final sigh her head rolled to one side.

Lance stared at her, unable to believe this dear, sweet girl—his wife for such a short time—was dead. Oh, sweet, sweet Jesus, he prayed as he bent his head, the agony he felt slicing his heart to the core.

The clergyman went to Delphine and placed his head to her chest. Straightening up, he shook his head solemnly. When he was about to pull the sheet over her face, Lance stayed his hand.

'Wait.' He looked at her face one last time, as if to absorb her image for all time. It had taken on a serenity absent before death, so calm and untroubled he felt his throat ache. The eyes were closed, the lashes long and dark in a fan on her cheek. The skin, no longer the almost grey look of the dead, had taken on a soft honey cream.

Not one to show his emotions, after taking a moment to compose himself, Lance signed some papers and then handed the clergyman some money for the burial, telling him to have Delphine interred in the graveyard of the local church. His face stony, his eyes empty, he turned his attention to the woman holding his child.

'You are English?'

'Yes, sir.'

'What are you called?'

'Mary Grey, sir. My own baby died—six days now—and the midwife who attended your wife asked if I would wet nurse your daughter.'

'And your husband?'

'I have no husband, sir. My man died before I gave birth.'

'I see.' He thought for a moment, considering her. At least she was clean and quietly spoken. 'Will you continue to wet nurse the child and take her to an address in England? You will be well paid for your trouble. I will send someone to accompany you—along with a letter for you to give to my mother.'

'Yes, sir.'

The clergyman moved from the bed. 'Don't feel you have to remain, Colonel. I will take care of things.'

'Thank you. I do have to return to my regiment. Battle is imminent. Tomorrow many will die. Your services as a priest will be needed, too.'

The child began to whimper. He looked at it and quickly looked away as if he couldn't bear to look at her, trying to defend himself against the rising and violent tide of anger directed against this tiny being—this infant whose entry into the world had taken the life of its mother. Angry, relentlessly so and unable to understand why he should feel like this, his face absolute and without expression, without a backward glance Colonel Bingham left the farmhouse.

Mary Grey had noted the look on his face and recognised it for what it was. He blamed the child for its mother's death, this she understood, but she was confident it was a problem that would solve itself. But in this she was to be proved wrong.

In silence the clergyman watched him go. What could he say? How could anyone—man or woman—recover from such pain and the agony of such grief?

Lance rode back to his regiment, eager for the battle to begin so that he could lose himself in the fray and forget what had just transpired—and the fact that he had a daughter.

Chapter One

'Miss Belle, I simply do not know what to do with you. Your grandmother is waiting for you in the dining room, and she doesn't like to be kept waiting. Now hurry. You look fine, you really do.'

Isabelle 'Belle' Ainsley spun round from the mirror, the bright green of her eyes flashing brilliantly as her temper rose. 'For heaven's sake, Daisy. I am nineteen years old and will not be hurried. And I will not look fine until *I* am satisfied with how I look.' She twisted back to the mirror, scowling petulantly at her hair, which, as usual, refused to be confined. Daisy had arranged it in twists and curls about her head, but a curl as wayward as the girl herself had sprung free and no matter how she tried to tuck it away, it defiantly sprang back.

Daisy shook her head in amusement, unperturbed by her new mistress's outburst of temper. 'We both know that could take all night and that would never do. You certainly have your grandmother's temper, but she's older and if I were you I wouldn't delay any longer or you'll feel the rough edge of her tongue.'

Belle groaned with exasperation and then in a fit of pique

she grabbed a pair of scissors and cut off the offending curl. In a swirl of satin and lace she flounced across the room and out of the door, not deigning to look at Daisy's bemused face.

Belle's descent of the grand staircase was not in the least ladylike and brought a combination of smiles, raised eyebrows and frowns of concern from the footmen who paused in their duties to watch her. She was certainly a wondrous sight to behold, was Lady Isabelle. In the tomb-like silence of the Dowager Countess of Harworth's stately home, the arrival of her granddaughter from America ranked as an uproar and had not only the servants scratching their heads, but the countess as well. And now the countess was in high dudgeon over being kept waiting.

Entering the dining room, Belle steeled herself for the unpleasant scene that was bound to occur. Her grandmother rose stiffly from the chair where she was reclining, her hand gripping the gold knob of her cane. At seventy-two she was still a handsome woman with white hair, elegant, regal bearing, and the aloof, unshakeable confidence and poise that comes from living a thoroughly privileged life. Despite the stiff dignity and rigid self-control that characterised her every gesture, she had known her share of grief, having outlived her husband and two sons.

'Good evening, Isabelle,' she said, looking with disapproval over her granddaughter's choice of dress, which had seen much wear and was not in the least the kind a young lady of breeding would wear in a respectable English drawing room. The sooner her dressmaker arrived to begin fitting her out for a new wardrobe the better. 'You are inordinately tardy. What do you have to say for yourself?'

'I'm so sorry, Grandmother. I did not mean to upset you. I simply could not decide which dress to wear. I chose this because it is such a pretty colour and looks well on me. You could have started dinner without me. You didn't have to wait.'

The Dowager gave her an icy look. 'In this house we dine

together, Isabelle, and I do not like being kept waiting. How many times must I tell you that I demand punctuality at all times? Thank goodness we do not have guests. You have grieved cook, who has been trying unsuccessfully to keep our dinner warm and palatable.'

'Then I shall make a point of apologising to cook,' Belle said, unable to understand why her grandmother was making such a fuss about nothing. 'I have no wish to put anyone out. I could quite easily fetch my own food from the kitchen.'

'And that is another thing. You will not do work that is best left to the servants.' She sighed, shaking her head wearily. 'You have so much to learn I hardly know where to begin.'

'But I like to be kept busy,' Belle answered, smiling across at the agitated lady.

'I shall see that you are—with matters concerning your future role in life, although I realised from the start how difficult and unyielding is your nature.'

'Papa would doubtless have agreed with you. He ever despaired of me.' Thinking of her father, dead these two months, a lump appeared in Belle's throat and the lovely eyes were shadowed momentarily. 'I miss him very much.'

'As I do.' The faded blue eyes never wavered, but there was a hoarseness in the countess's voice that told Belle of her grandmother's inner grief over the death of her second son. 'It was his wish that you come to England, where you will be taught the finer points of being a lady—and I shall see that you do if I expire in the attempt.'

Belle swallowed down the lump in her throat. How difficult her life had suddenly become and how difficult the transition had been for her to leave her beloved Charleston and come to London. She missed it so much. Would she ever fit in here? she wondered. How she hated having to live by her grandmother's strict rules when her father had allowed her to roam as free as a bird back home. The task of learning to be the lady her grandmother intended her to become was both daunting and seemingly impossible.

She looked at her grandmother, her green eyes wide and vulnerable. 'I'm sure I must be a terrible disappointment to you, Grandmother, but I will try not to let you down. Despite what you think, I am only foolish, not stupid. I am ignorant of your ways, but I will learn.'

'Then you will have to work very hard.'

The countess knew she had her work cut out with her grand-daughter. Her manners were unrefined and she knew nothing about genteel behaviour. She was a wild child, as wild as they come. At first sight they had regarded each other, two fiercely indomitable wills clashing in silence. That her granddaughter was proud and strong and followed her own rules was obvious, but the countess would not concede defeat.

Belle crossed to the long table and waited until Gosforth, the butler—who had a habit of appearing and disappearing seemingly from nowhere—had seated her grandmother prop-erly, before pulling out her own chair and seating herself, which earned her another condemning frown from the elderly lady.

The dowager looked at Gosforth. 'We are ready to start, Gosforth, now my granddaughter has deigned to join me. I suppose we might as well see how cold the beef has grown.'

Belle sighed, folding her hands demurely in her lap. The evening was definitely off to a bad start. If only there was some distraction. Anything would be preferable to an evening at home alone with her grandmother, who would endeavour to teach her unsophisticated American granddaughter how young English ladies behaved. All Belle's attempts to try to curb her restlessness and be demure were unsuccessful.

Already—and unbeknown to her grandmother—on her daily rides across Hampstead Heath, Belle had garnered the favours of several curious local young beaux—one with raff-ish good looks and much sought after, apparently. His name was Carlton Robinson. On occasion he had watched for her when she rode out, and when she had managed to shake off her accompanying groom—who despaired of trying to keep up with her since she could ride like the wind with the devil on her tail—he had joined her.

Carlton Robinson had never met anyone quite like this American girl and he had soon turned to putty under the assault of her big green eyes and stunning looks. Out of boredom it was all a game to Belle, and when she had captured him completely, the game had soured and she had sent the young man packing—blissfully unaware of the consequences of her liaison with this particular gentleman.

She sighed, taking a large, unladylike gulp of her wine, already wishing the evening would end so she could escape to her room—and to make matters worse the beef was overdone.

The following morning, standing at her bedroom window overlooking the gardens, the countess watched her granddaughter as she cantered up the drive—hatless and astride, her long legs gripping her mount, her hair blowing loose in the wind, and having left the groom somewhere on the Heath.

That very morning one of the countess's acquaintances had hastened to inform her of a scandal that was beginning to unfold concerning Isabelle—a scandal that was entirely of Isabelle's making, if it was to be believed. The countess was incensed by her granddaughter's behaviour. Not in her wildest dreams had she imagined that the lovely, inexperienced young woman would form a liaison with a young man whose exploits were the talk of London as soon she arrived. And Carlton Robinson! No man but he would dare, would have the temerity, the sheer effrontery to interfere with the granddaughter of the Dowager Countess of Harworth. She summoned Isabelle to the salon immediately.

Daisy had heard the gossip and told Belle she could expect no mercy from her grandmother. Belle's naïvety and inexperience had not prepared her for a young man of Carlton

Robinson's reputation. Not to be made a fool of by an ignorant American girl, he had let his tongue loose to do its worst and turned the tables on Belle. He had laughingly told his friends that the American girl was an amusingly peculiar, pathetic little thing from the backwoods of America, and when she was launched, he had no intention of plying his suit.

An inexplicable premonition of dread mounted the closer Belle got to the salon. After listening to what her grandmother had to say, making no attempt to conceal her anger and disappointment, Belle was swamped with remorse and shame.

'Well? What have you to say for yourself?' the countess demanded of the wretched girl.

'I'm so sorry, Grandmother. It was nothing, please believe me. We—met when I was riding on the Heath. We only met three times. He—said he liked my company. I didn't like him, so I ended it. Daisy has told me that the odious man has said some dreadful, wicked things about me that simply are not true.'

'Carlton Robinson says objectionable things about people all the time,' the countess answered drily.

'I never meant for this to happen. I didn't know.'

'There's a great deal you don't know. A girl newly arrived from America—ignorant to our ways—he saw you as easy prey.' She shook her head wearily, blaming herself for allowing Isabelle too much freedom. 'I accept that you are ignorant of how things are done in England, Isabelle. Carlton Robinson is a conceited braggart and the most lascivious reprobate in town. Resentful of your rejection, he has tried to destroy your reputation in the most alarming manner—to make you a hopeless social outcast before you have even made your début.'

'I'm sorry, Grandmother,' Belle whispered brokenly, truly repentant. 'You risked a great deal taking me into your home. Little did you know you would be risking disgrace.' She looked at her grandmother, her eyes wide and vulnerable and shining with tears. 'I've a hideous disposition and I haven't a feminine accomplishment to my name. What is to be done?'

The countess's heart melted for the lovely, spirited, bewildered girl her younger son had borne, and in a moment her old loyal heart had her fighting in defence of her granddaughter, at whose door the blame had been unfairly laid. 'We shall do as the Ainsleys have always done, Isabelle,' she said on a gentler note, 'and weather the scandal. By the time you make your début, hopefully it will have blown over.'

And so the Dowager Countess of Harworth began to shape the artless, unsophisticated girl from America into a respectable English young lady. Isabelle hadn't a grain of sense or propriety in her, but her determination not to be restricted or confined had to be curbed. She knew nothing of fashion and cared even less, but Isabelle had been well tutored in most subjects. She spoke perfect French, read Latin and Greek, and she had a good head for numbers.

Miss Bertram, a woman of unimpeachable character, was to arrive today to begin instructing her on the refinements of etiquette. No one would dare to question the acceptability and character of any young lady in her charge. The Season would begin in just a few short weeks. Hopefully it would be enough time for Isabelle to learn everything she needed to know to make a full-fledged début and to outfit her for the full Season. Until then the countess would begin by taking her to the theatre, where she could be seen but not approached, but apart from that, she must be kept locked away from everyone.

Her grandmother's house, situated close to Hampstead Heath, was unlike anything Belle had imagined. She had been mesmerised by its splendour—imposing without being austere. This was where her grandmother lived when she came to London, preferring the relative peace and quiet of living just outside the city, where the air was cleaner. The ancestral home, Harworth Hall, was in a place called Wiltshire.

On her arrival in England, at first Belle had objected and

fought against all her grandmother's efforts to make her conform. Her grandmother was hard to please, overbearing and possessive, whereas Belle was a free spirit and used to doing as she wished, and she wasn't ready to be buried alive by protocol and the traditional English customs. But now her 'hysterics', as her grandmother called it, had cooled to an acceptance of her situation and a steely determination. Admitting her lack of knowledge about English protocol, Belle was sensitive enough to realise that she was lacking in certain social skills—and she was her own harshest critic. She accepted that her grandmother was the only family she had, and, like it or not, this was now her home, so she had best conform and make the best of it.

Miss Bertram had the formidable task of teaching her social graces, and under her relentless and exacting tutelage, Belle began to settle down and worked diligently to learn anything that might help her win favour in her grandmother's eyes.

Madame Hamelin, her grandmother's personal dressmaker, arrived, accompanied by two seamstresses to fit her for an extensive wardrobe, and Madame Hamelin was full of praise for the beautiful American girl, complimenting her on her natural grace and excellent posture. Belle allowed herself to be pushed, prodded and poked and scolded if she did not stand still for the fittings, and sometimes praised—for she was excited, and what girl would not be?—the centre of attention, admired and exclaimed over.

Next came the dancing instructor, who had her whirling around the room to the imaginary strains of a waltz and to the countess's relief announced that her granddaughter had a natural ability and was far from hopeless.

And so Belle learned how walk properly, how to curtsy, how to open and close a fan, and learned that it had other uses—for flirting and to occupy the hands—other than for cooling oneself. By the time of her début, although she still had much to learn and her wilfulness was far from curbed, her grandmother was confident that she would be ready to be introduced into society. Hopefully the scandal of her brief and completely innocent association with Carlton Robinson would be completely forgotten.

Lance Bingham groaned and pushed himself out of the bed. Reaching for the water pitcher he poured the contents over his hair before raising his dripping head and looking at his face in the mirror. He felt terrible and he looked it. His eyes were bleary, and dark stubble covered his chin. He forced himself to breathe deeply in an attempt to clear the alcoholic fog from his head. Towelling his head dry, he went to the window, shoving it open and breathing deeply the sharp air of a Paris morning.

Today, his life with the army over, he was to return to his home in England, an event he viewed with little joy when he thought what awaited him there. When Delphine had died part of him had died too. Never again would he let his emotions get the better of him. His heart was closed to all women—including his daughter, whose birth had taken away the only woman who had touched his inner being.

Throughout the years with his regiment, he had been motivated by the adventure of being a soldier and driven by the excitement of battle, but the battles' images and the loss of his friends had left their scars. It was going to be no easy matter settling down to life as a civilian. He had everything—breeding, looks and wealth—and however much he would regret its passing, his military career and the manner of Delphine's death and the guilt that would hound him all the days of his life, had made him world weary, restrained and guarded.

The voluptuous French redhead in the bed stirred and lifted herself upon an elbow, her body stiff and aching deliciously from her companion's prolonged and energetic lovemaking. She studied the darkly handsome man, his brooding looks marred by cynicism. He was standing with his shoulder propped against the window frame, looking out. Gazing with admiration and a fresh stirring of desire at the lean, hard lines of his body, her eyes roving down past the rigid muscles of his chest and flat stomach, every inch of him positively radiated raw power and unleashed sensuality.

His latent animal sensuality swept over her. 'Come back to bed,' she murmured huskily, aching for fulfilment, hoping he would, but Lance Bingham seemed not to hear. 'Please,' she persisted, slowly, languidly, running her hands through her hair.

He turned and looked at her dispassionately. 'Get dressed and go.'

'What? Did I not satisfy you, my lord?' She smiled seductively, letting the sheet slip to reveal her swelling orbs, hoping the sight of them would entice him back into her arms. 'You enjoyed yourself, didn't you?'

The voice was lazy and full of promise. A soft smile played about her mouth, inviting him to her, but he remained unmoved. He hated loose women, but she exuded a rich aura of passion and the full, ripe figure and smouldering eyes promised an obvious knowledge of the art of exciting men. Last night he had invited her to his room and she had come gladly. Now the mere sight of her sickened him and he was coldly telling her to get out.

'That was last night. I was drunk and now I'm sober and not bored enough to want to sleep with you again.'

The woman scowled at him. 'You don't have a very high opinion of women, do you?'

'No. I do not believe in the inherent goodness in anyone— including myself. If you don't mind, I would like you to go.'

The woman's eyes narrowed and anger kindled in their depths. 'Why—you—you bastard,' she hissed.

The look he gave her was one of mild cynicism. 'If calling me names makes you feel better, I'll let it go. For my part I apologise if I've given you grief. I could put it down to your being an attractive woman and me being a long way from home and pretty damn lonely. Whatever it was, it's over. Now get out.'

About to argue, the look on his face made the woman afraid of him for the first time since she had come to his room. Strange and explosive emotions lurked in the hard eyes glittering in the dim light of the room and rendered her speechless. Last night under the effects of drink and full of lust, she had thought him completely malleable, but she now read a hardness of purpose and coldness of manner beyond any previous experience.

Paying no more attention to her, Lance turned away to watch the teeming mass of humanity scurrying along the wide, rain-swept boulevards. The woman threw back the covers and reached for her clothes. Even before she had flounced out of the room he had put her from his mind as if she had never been.

Having sat for what seemed to be hours before her dressing-table mirror, watching as Daisy had painstakingly arranged her heavy hair into an elegant coiffure, deftly twisting it into elaborate curls and teasing soft tendrils over her ears, Belle now fingered the diamonds Daisy had just fastened around her throat—drop diamonds that danced in her lobes and a double row of diamonds with a single, enormous oval-shaped diamond pendant that rested just above her breasts. They were hard and cold and absolutely exquisite in their beauty. They belonged to her grandmother and were famous for their chequered history, and had not been worn for fifty years.

Belle smiled at her reflection in the mirror, a mischievous, calculating smile, a smile those who knew Isabelle Ainsley would know to be wary of.

'Shall I take them off now, miss?' Daisy asked. The countess had agreed to her granddaughter looking at the famed jewels. After handing them over to Miss Belle, the countess had been called away, telling her to put them back in the box and return them to her before they left for the Prince Regent's party at Carlton House.

'No, Daisy.' Belle's eyes were sparkling with defiance, her concentration unbroken as she continued to finger the diamonds. 'I think I shall wear them for the party tonight. After all, what is the point of having beautiful things if they are to be kept hidden away? A necklace of such beauty should be seen and appreciated, and tonight is such a grand occasion, don't you agree?'

'Oh, yes, miss. But your grandmother… Oh, miss,' she said, shaking her mob-capped head, 'she'll have my hide if I don't take them back—and her with one of her heads coming on.'

The anxiety in the maid's voice broke Belle's reverie, and she looked at the terrified girl as she wrung her hands nervously. 'And you will, Daisy. I can promise you that. But not until after the banquet at Carlton House—and if Grandmother is suffering one of her headaches, then she may be so preoccupied that she won't notice.'

'But she will see them when it is time for you to leave. She will never allow—'

'What my grandmother sees and what she will allow is neither here nor there, Daisy,' Belle said sharply, standing up, the transparency of the material of her chemise making no pretence of hiding the softly veiled peaks of her firm breasts. 'The necklace will be concealed beneath my cloak, and not until we reach Carlton House will she see them. By which time it will be too late to do anything about it.' Seeing Daisy's anxiety, she smiled confidently. 'Trust me, Daisy. Everything will be all right.'

She looked at the bed where the gown she was to wear had been carefully spread to await its donning, thinking how the vibrant turquoise silk would enhance the jewels and bring out the lights in her rich, mahogany-coloured hair. 'Now, please help me into my gown.'

With the gown setting off her figure to perfection, Belle

turned this way and that in front of the dressing mirror to survey her reflection. 'There, what do you think, Daisy? Will I do?'

Daisy stood back, taking pride in her handiwork—although Miss Belle was already beautiful. She looked positively breathtaking, daring, elegant and special. 'Indeed you will, Miss Belle. Any man, even one in his dotage, who sees you tonight, looking as you do, will surely find his heart going into its final palpitations—as will Prince George himself.'

Belle laughed happily. 'I don't think so, Daisy. The Prince has so many ladies buzzing about him, he will fail to notice an unknown American girl.'

'Don't be too sure about that, miss. Prince George may not be as handsome as he once was—his gargantuan appetite has seen to that—but he cuts a fine figure in his military uniforms and the sumptuous clothes he wears. He is still charming and amusing and has an eye for a pretty face.'

The preparations complete, when the summons came from her grandmother and Daisy had carefully folded her velvet cloak about her shoulders, concealing the necklace, Belle proceeded down the stairs where her grandmother awaited her.

Belle was excited about going to Carlton House and meeting English royalty. Prince George was a splendid host, at his happiest when entertaining on a grand scale. The whole of society aspired to be invited to his fêtes. According to Belle's grandmother, the banquets were always glittering occasions, the point of the proceedings to admire, for the Prince, who spent weeks planning the setting of his next event, liked to show off his aesthetic taste and imagination.

Feeling decidedly gay and definitely light-hearted, Belle had been looking forward to the party for days, and she intended to enjoy every minute of it.

Having arrived early and trying to work up some enthusiasm to attend Prince George's banquet, which he imagined would be tedious and infinitely dull, Lord Lance Bingham lounged in the shade against the wall to await his good friend, Sir Rowland Gibbon. He idly watched the long line of carriages—a solid block of elegant equipages stretching all the way to St James's Street, depositing the glittering cream of London society at the door.

Raising a lazy brow on seeing a sleek black coach with the Ainsley coat of arms emblazoned on its door come to a halt, his interest sharpened as the coachman lowered the steps to allow the occupants to alight. First of all came the Dowager Countess of Harworth, followed by a young woman. The woman took the coachman's hand and allowed him to assist her.

'Thank you, Denis,' she said.

'My pleasure, Miss Isabelle.'

Miss Isabelle! So, Lord Bingham thought, that was Isabelle Ainsley, recently come from America. Who else could it be? This was the girl whom London society talked about, a young woman who had lost no time in creating a scandal by forming a most unfortunate liaison with young Carlton Robinson—one of London's most notorious rakes and a despair to his father.

Intrigued, Lance stared quite openly, unable to do anything else. A cool vision of poised womanhood, she was undeniably the most magnificent woman he had ever seen, though it was not the way she looked that drew his eye, since the distance between them was too great for him to see her features clearly. It was the way she tossed her imperious head, the challenging set to her shoulders and the defiant stare that did not see the lowlier beings about her.

He stood and watched her as she walked a few steps behind the countess—though walked hardly described the way she moved, for she seemed to glide effortlessly, her body eternally female in its fluid movements, her expensively shod feet barely touching the ground.

As they disappeared through a portico of Corinthian columns that led to the foyer, with a frown Lord Bingham resumed his pose, propping his shoulder against the wall. Where the devil had Rowland got to? he wondered, his patience beginning to wear a trifle thin. He stared into the verdant depths of the ruby on his finger. Gleaming with a regal fire, it seemed to motivate him into action. Slowly drawing himself upright, straightening the folds of his bright red officer's coat, he walked with deliberate strides towards the portico.

Having discarded her cloak, Belle prepared herself for her grandmother's wrath. The countess regarded her granddaughter with an attentive expression in her eyes. For a moment Belle regretted her impulsive action to wear the necklace and quailed at the storm that she knew was coming. She did not have to wait long. Her grandmother advanced on her, her expression turning to stone as she saw for the first time the necklace.

The countess's eyes narrowed dangerously, for it seemed to her that her granddaughter had overstepped the mark. Isabelle's green eyes, so like her own, were fearful and yet at the same time her face wore an expression of defiance.

'Well?' Her voice, which she kept low so as not to be overheard, was as cold as her face. 'I left the necklace with you in good faith, Isabelle—that you would return it to me as I instructed you to do. I did not intend for you to wear it. How dare you disobey me? How dare you?'

'Grandmother—I—I am sorry...'

'It is most unseemly that you should embarrass me before so many.'

'That was not my intention. I saw no harm in wearing it—it is so beautiful and the occasion seemed fitting.' She raised her hands to the back of her neck. 'Of course if it upsets you, I'll remove it—'

'Leave it,' the countess snapped, her tone causing Belle to lower her arms. 'It's too late for that. Its removal—now it has

been seen by all and sundry—will only give rise to unwel-
come speculation. You may keep it on. This is not one of your
finest performances. I am most displeased with you, Isabelle,
most displeased.' She turned away to speak to an acquaintance, pinning a smile to her face, but inside she continued to
seethe at her granddaughter's disobedience.

Relieved that the moment had passed and the necklace was
still in place, Belle was very much aware that the moment
she appeared all eyes turned to her. As usual the whispering
began and she was surrounded by dozens of people, most of
them young men, who obviously thought they might have a
chance with the Dowager Countess of Harworth's American
granddaughter.

Belle always became the focus of everyone's scrutiny, male
or female, when she entered any room. The early scandal of
her brief liaison with Carlton Robinson had given her a certain
notoriety. Ever since she had made her début, she had become
accustomed to the admiring looks of the young bucks, either
at some society event or on those occasions when, having
taken account of her customary rides with her grandmother
through Hyde Park, they often waited for her somewhere along
the route with the hope of gaining an introduction from her
guardian.

It was quite a distinction to have been named as the most
beautiful débutante of the London Season, and the most desirable to join the marriage mart, which was quite an achievement for a girl newly arrived in London from the Carolinas.
She wished she weren't so beautiful, because people, especially the young bucks, behaved like complete idiots around
her.

But an interesting fact to some was, upon her marriage, the
man who married her would become the recipient of a dowry
generous enough to elevate his status considerably. Hardly a
day passed without some new request for her hand being addressed to her grandmother.

Belle had met rich men, she had met handsome men, but she had not fallen in love. Disheartened and thoroughly disenchanted with the opposite sex, she scorned them all, much to her grandmother's dismay, for she was eager for her to make a good marriage, and with so many eager young males of good families posturing about, she could have the pick of the bunch.

Adjusting one of her gloves that had slipped down her arm slightly, Belle looked up and found herself looking straight into the eyes of a stranger. There was an expression of utter boredom on his indecently handsome face, an expression that altered dramatically when his eyes met hers, half-startled, half-amused, and something else—something slightly carnal that stirred unfamiliar things inside her and brought heat to her cheeks. She was struck by two things: the man's obvious good looks and some kind of arrogance in those eyes, an arrogance that told her he knew who she was, knew everything about her, which unnerved her slightly.

He was dark, dark as the American natives who roamed the plains. The expression on his face was calm and controlled—he was obviously a man much used to being looked at. His close cropped hair was black, like the smooth wing of a raven, but it was his eyes that held her attention. In a face burnt brown by a hot tropical sun, they shone vivid and startling, and as blue as the speedwell that carpeted the summer meadows. They were heavily fringed with thick black lashes above which his eyebrows swooped fiercely. His broad shoulders were adorned with gold epaulettes affixed to the bright red fabric of his military tunic, and narrow-fitting white breeches encased his legs.

Lance gave her the same inspection. Closer now he could see that this was no ordinary girl. He was drawn to the freshness and vitality with which she carried herself, looking at the setting with brilliant eyes and a playful tilt to her mouth. She was exceptionally beautiful, so beautiful that it was impossible not to stand and stare at her.

Her eyes were wide set and accentuated by wing-swept black brows; the patrician nose, the heart-shaped face, the fine texture of her skin, the haughty set of the queenly head crowned with a glorious mahogany mane, upswept and sporting a silk flower matching the vibrant turquoise of her gown, all bespoke aristocratic blood. In her low-cut bodice, revealing the top curve of her firm breasts and the satin smoothness of her bare shoulders, she was a beauty, he decided, simply beautiful—and the light from the chandeliers sparked the diamonds around her neck with a cold fire. His eyes narrowed as they settled on the jewels. Suddenly she had all his attention.

Belle stood in shock beneath his leisurely perusal, and was she mistaken or did his gaze actually linger on her breasts, or was it only her imagination? His close study of her feminine assets left her feeling as if she'd just been stripped stark naked. Indeed, she could almost swear from the way he was looking at her that he had designs on her person and was already deciding on the areas where he would begin his seducing. She was bewildered, embarrassed and insulted, all at the same time. The gall of the man, she thought with rising ire. He conveyed an air of arrogance and uncompromising authority which no doubt stemmed from a haughty attitude or perhaps even his military rank. Whatever it was, it was not to her liking.

Sensing her granddaughter's distraction, the countess turned and looked at her, following the direction of her gaze. Her expression became one of severe displeasure when she saw the object of her attention.

Belle saw an odd, awed expression cross her grandmother's face as she scrutinised the dark-haired man in military uniform and was both puzzled and troubled by the look in her eyes. She had no way of discerning what thoughts were being formed behind that hard mask of concern.

'Isabelle,' she reproached severely, her gaze swinging

sharply to her granddaughter, 'you look too long at that particular gentleman. Pull yourself together. We have an audience, if you hadn't noticed.'

Belle had and she couldn't suppress her amusement when
the stranger gave her grandmother a mocking smile and affected an exaggerated bow.

The dowager countess was relieved to move on, away from
the man who had looked at Isabelle with the hungry admiration of a wolf calmly contemplating its next meal. Lance
Bingham was one gentleman she would prefer not to show an
interest in her granddaughter. She had planned for too long
to see Isabelle become just another conquest of the notorious Lord Lance Bingham, fifteenth Earl of Ryhill in a line
that stretched back into the dim and distant days of the early
Tudors, and whose reputation left very much to be desired.

For years gossip had linked him with every beautiful female
of suitable lineage in Europe, and before he had gone to Spain
to fight Napoleon's forces, wherever he went he left a trail of
broken hearts, for marriage was not what he offered. She was
not at all happy to see him back in England. He was the last
man in the entire world she wanted her granddaughter to associate with—but there were other reasons too, reasons that
went far back in time, and when she glanced at the necklace
adorning Isabelle's neck, glittering in the light of the chandeliers, she shuddered at the painful memories it evoked.

It was all a long time ago now. The young people wouldn't
know what a fool she had made of herself over Stuart Bingham,
the only man she had ever loved, but the older generation
remembered and any kind of association between Stuart's
grandson and Isabelle would resurrect the old scandal.

'Who was that gentleman, Grandmother?' Belle ventured
to ask as they passed into another room, where great arrangements of flowers filled the air with their fragrance.

The countess turned and gave her a baleful look. 'His
name is Colonel Lance Bingham—the Earl of Ryhill, or Lord

Bingham as he is now addressed since the death of his uncle over a year ago—and I am amazed that a man could ignore his duties as prime heir for so long a period of time. He is only recently returned to London—not that it concerns you, since I would rather you did not have anything to do with him. I saw the way you looked at him, Isabelle; it is true enough that he is a handsome devil, but he's a cold one.'

Belle remembered the warmth of those vivid blue orbs and doubted the truth of her grandmother's observation. There was a vibrant life and intensity in Lance Bingham's eyes that no one could deny.

The countess went on. 'I remember him for his arrogance. I pity the woman who marries him. He may be a revered soldier, but before he went to Spain he was a rake of the first order, which young ladies such as yourself should be wary of, for I doubt things have changed now he has returned. I don't want you to have anything to do with him, is that understood?'

Belle nodded. 'Yes, Grandmother,' she answered dutifully, shaking her head to banish the vision of the man who continued to occupy her mind, and hinted at what the strong, straight lips had not spoken. The memory of the way he had looked at her sent a dizzying thrill through her. Her face flamed at the meanderings of her mind and angrily she cast him out.

'Sorry I'm late, Lance,' a calm voice said beside him. 'Had the deuce of a job getting away from my club—interesting game of dice kept me.' He took a deep breath. 'Ye Gods, just look at this place. I think the Regent must have invited half of London.'

Recognising the voice of his good friend Rowland Gibbon, grateful for the distraction, Lance tore his gaze from the delectable Isabelle Ainsley and turned to the man next to him. 'I see that you have still not had a shave,' he commented casually, drawing his friend to a quiet spot beside a rather large exotic oriental plant. 'How long is this rebellion against the fashionable world going to last?'

Rowland grinned, proudly rubbing his whiskers. 'As to that, I've not yet decided. My valet chastises me about it daily. I fear that one night when I crawl into bed deep in my cups, he will take a razor to it and shave it off. If he does I shall have to get rid of him, for I am determined to bring back the fashion for beards. Damn it, Lance, the London beaux need someone to keep them in check.'

Rowland, tall and lank and seeming rather disjointed in his gangling limberness, was too untidy to be described as a beau. His mane of light brown hair looked forever in need of a brush and his clothes often looked as though they had been slept in—which they often had on the occasions when he was too drunk to remove them and his valet had gone to bed. Wild, disreputable and outrageous, he was also warm hearted and possessed an enormous amount of charm, which endeared him to everyone and was the reason why he was invited to every fashionable party. The two had been close friends since their days at Oxford.

'It's good to have you back, Lance, and that you've assumed your earldom. Have you been to Ryhill?'

'I've just got back.'

'Your mother will be relieved you're back. Is she well?'

He nodded. 'She visited me at Ryhill prior to leaving for Ireland to visit Sophie. My sister is expecting her first child and naturally Mother insisted on going over to be with her.'

'And your daughter—Charlotte?' Rowland enquired cautiously. 'You have seen the child, I take it?'

Lance's face was devoid of expression as he avoided his friend's probing gaze. 'No, but I have it on good authority that she is thriving and being thoroughly spoilt. She is with Mother in Ireland.'

Rowland knew not to pursue the matter of Lance's daughter.

It was a subject he would never discuss. 'And you're finished with the army for good?'

Lance nodded, looking down at his uniform. 'The old uniform will have to go, but it's the best I have until my tailor provides me with new clothes—tomorrow, I hope. After Waterloo I had intended carrying on with my military career, but on learning of the death of my uncle, as his heir I had a change of heart. So I left the army, casting my sights towards home. I swore an oath to do my duty to my newly acquired title. Even to think of the estate being bestowed upon another went against everything I hold dear.'

'Well, you've certainly set tongues a wagging since you got back, with every mama with daughters of marriageable age setting their sights your way. There's one right now,' he said, indicating a young woman standing close by with her mother.

Lance casually glanced their way and acknowledged first the older, then the younger woman with a slight inclination of his head. The mother smiled stiffly and the daughter blushed and giggled behind her fan.

'There you are. You always did have women falling over themselves,' Rowland remarked casually. 'You were always viewed as the biggest fish in a very small pond. Every time you're in town they begin casting nets in hopes of scooping you up.'

'I'm particular as to which bait I nibble at, Rowland, and that particular morsel is not tasty enough for me.' Lance withdrew his gaze from the young woman and fixed his eyes once more on Isabelle Ainsley, who wandered back and forth in admiration of her surroundings.

Rowland followed his gaze to the source of his distraction. 'You look at that particular young lady with a good deal of interest.'

'You are too observant, Rowland,' Lance replied shortly.

Rowland raised one eyebrow. 'Well, out with it, man. Am I to know the identity of the lady?'

'Isabelle Ainsley, the granddaughter of the Dowager Countess of Harworth, recently come from America.' Lance didn't turn to look at Rowland, but he could sense his surprise.

Rowland made a sound of disbelief. 'You have been involved too long in the wars, my friend. See a pretty face and you lose your wits over her. Good Lord! You've only recently returned from France, and already you know who she is.'

Lance grinned. 'You know me, Rowland—always one to keep ahead of the rest.'

'You know how to live dangerously, I'll say that.'

'Who said anything about living dangerously? I have not laid eyes on her until tonight.'

'You wouldn't since you've been out of the country fighting those damn Frenchies. The American girl has certainly hit the London scene by storm and is no nitwit, that's for sure. Wherever she goes men are dazzled by her. She received countless marriage proposals before she came out, and countless since. The dowager countess is aiming high—the greater the title the greater the chance for the suitor.'

'Now why does that not surprise me?' Lance murmured drily. 'Nothing but the best for the great lady.'

'Yes, only the best. The real test for any man is fairly simple. All he has to do is win the lady's heart, for by winning it, he will then gain her grandmother's approval—maybe. Foolish logic indeed, for they will soon learn that many a pompous lord, after striving to gain the young lady's favour, has toppled from their plinth with scarcely an excuse from the young lady herself. As a consequence she has been dubbed the Ice Maiden and I have to wonder if she is as cold and haughty as those rejected suitors have claimed. I'd say her beauty is unparalleled. I wonder if she's as beautiful on the inside.'

'That, my friend, is immaterial to me,' Lance said quietly. 'It's what she has around her neck that counts.'

'I did notice that she had some rather pretty sparklers adorning her equally pretty neck.'

'The famous diamonds.'

Rowland looked at Lance, realisation dawning on him. 'Ah, how interesting—*those* diamonds. I think this needs further examination, old chap. I thought they were under lock and key, never to see the light of day again. Now I understand. It certainly explains the attraction—although after all that has happened in the past between your two families, I doubt the Dowager Countess of Harworth would consider a Bingham suitable for the hand of her granddaughter.'

'Who said anything about wedding her?'

'Then it's time you gave it some thought. Besides, you do realise that not a woman in town will spare the rest of us a glance until you have been claimed. You're not getting any younger, you know. If you intend to sire a dynasty, then you'd better get started.'

'I have already started, Rowland, and after my tragic marriage to Delphine I am not looking for another wife, and won't be doing so for a good many years.' Lance grinned, a hint of the old wickedness in his eyes that Roland had not seen in a long time. 'I have a few more years of grand debauchery to enjoy before I settle for one woman.'

If he had thought to convince his friend he failed, for although society thought otherwise, Lance's days as a debauchee were long and truly behind him. Lance was the stuff ladies' dreams were made of, fatally handsome and with the devil's own charm. Having spent several years as a soldier, his daring and courage in the face of the enemy had won him praise from the highest—from Wellington himself. His skill and knowledge in numerous bloody battles added to his reputation as a clever strategist and an invincible opponent.

The Lance Bingham who had returned to England was

very different from the one who had left. The changes were startling. In contrast to the idle young men who lounged about the clubs and ballrooms with bored languor, Lance was full of energy, deeply tanned, muscular and extremely fit, sharp and authoritative, and although he laughed and charmed his way back into society, there was an aura about him of a man who had done and seen all there was to see and do, a man who had confronted danger and enjoyed it. It was an aura that women couldn't resist and which added to his attraction.

'I wonder why the old girl's suddenly decided to show the diamonds off,' Rowland mused.

Lance shrugged. 'I have wondered myself.'

'Have you never tried to get them back? After all they are rightfully yours.'

'No—at least not lately.'

'And now you're back in England, will you attempt to get them back? Although I don't see how you can. Getting the great lady to part with those precious diamonds will be like getting blood out of the proverbial stone. I'd stake my life on it.'

'I wouldn't want your life for a gold pot, but I am always game for a friendly bet. A hundred pounds says you're wrong. I will have the diamonds in my possession by dawn tomorrow.'

Rowland chuckled, happy to pick up the gauntlet. 'Make it two hundred and you're on. I love a sure bet. But the fascinating young lady will be returning to Hampstead after the ball, so how will you be settling this bet?'

Lance shrugged nonchalantly. 'You'll have to wait and see.'

Rowland smiled smugly. 'I doubt you'll succeed. I'll call on you tomorrow to claim my winnings. Now, as much as I would like to stay and chat, right now I see the delectable Amanda, the daughter of Viscount Grenville, has just arrived. If you'll excuse me, I'll go and secure a dance or two before her card is full.'

Left alone, Lance considered the amazing bet he had made, and he knew he would have to act quickly if he were to see it through. Normally he would have kept his money in his pocket, but there were reasons why he'd impulsively made the bet. There were benefits to be obtained from securing the diamonds, for not only were they were worth a fortune, by rights they belonged to him.

Lance continued to watch the two Ainsley women as the dowager countess greeted those she knew. There was insolence and arrogance written into every line of Belle Ainsely's taut young body, but its symmetry was spellbinding. She was exquisite and he had already made up his mind to be formally presented to her. If her dragon of a grandmother objected, then with the inbred arrogance and pride of a man who is not accustomed to being denied, which of course he did not expect to be, he would find a way of introducing himself.

At some point during the evening he was confident that he would succeed in separating her from the laughing, chattering throng and whisk her away to some quiet arbour, where they would drink champagne and engage in the dalliance that was the stuff of life to him.

Chapter Two

Nothing had prepared Belle for the splendour that was Carlton House, which faced the south side of Pall Mall; its gardens abutted St James's Park.

Following her grandmother past the graceful staircase and through the spacious, opulent residence, which was packed with hundreds of people—nobility, politicians, the influential, the wealthy, the elite of London society—admiring the superb collection of works of art hung on the walls of every room, ornate fireplaces, crystal chandeliers—dripping with hundreds of thousands of crystals and ablaze with blinding light, marble busts in niches, mirrors and gold leaf—Belle, finding it all magically impressive, absorbed every detail.

The dowager countess smiled at her mixture of fascination and bemusement. 'Wait until you see the rest of the house— and the table. The food will be delicious—even though it does have so far to travel from the kitchens that it invariably arrives cold. The Prince shows great imagination in planning these parties and one always enjoys his hospitality.'

Belle stopped and closed her eyes, dizzy with the incomprehensible sights of so much dazzling splendour. Quickly recovering, she snapped open her fan and briskly fanned herself. 'It would be impossible not to. I've never seen anything like it,' the dazzled girl said. 'How can all these people not be struck blind by all this beauty?'

'The Prince stresses there is nothing in Europe that can compare with Carlton House. As for being struck blind, why, these people have seen it for so long that it's lost all meaning to them.'

'You mean they don't appreciate it?'

'Not as much as you evidently do. The Prince would be well pleased.'

Belle said not a word, merely drinking in every sight as though she had never before in her life seen such beauty. The supper table was covered with linen cloths and laden with delicacies far more numerous than Belle could ever have imagined. It glittered and sparkled and gleamed gold and silver on both sides, running the length of the dining room and into the conservatory beyond. The oriental theme the Prince had chosen for the table decorations was exquisite in every minute detail. At equal distances elaborate crystal fountains bubbled musically, the liquid in them not water but wine.

The atmosphere became electrified when the Prince arrived, looking larger than life and extremely grand in a military uniform heavily trimmed with gold braid. His eyes twinkled good-humouredly as he welcomed everyone and there was a great deal of bowing and dipping of curtsies.

While waiting to be seated, Belle looked about her, her eyes drawn to Lord Bingham, who stood across the room conversing with a group of young bucks. She studied him surreptitiously. His blue eyes glinted with a sardonic expression. Broad shouldered, narrow of waist, with a muscular leg, he gave the appearance of an athlete, a man who fenced and hunted. Yet, she thought, with that determined, clefted chin there was a certain air of masculinity, something attractive, almost compelling, about him, and certainly dangerous.

As Lance became tired of standing around, his eyes sought out the delectable Belle Ainsley, which, despite the house being almost full to capacity, wasn't too difficult. He saw her surrounded by doting swains enthralled by her uncommon beauty, a premise that, curiously, strangely nettled his mood on finding himself observing her audience of aristocratic suitors. She was enjoying herself, laughing and at ease, a natural temptress, he thought, alluring and provocative and with the body of a goddess. He had to fight the insane impulse to disperse her personal entourage of admirers, carry her to a quiet place, take hold of that lithe, warm, breathing form, crush it beneath him and kiss the irreverent laughter from her soft, inviting lips.

Belle was seated next to her grandmother, Lord Bingham several places away from her on the opposite side of the table. She tried hard not to look at him, but found her eyes turned constantly in his direction. At one point he caught her glance and held her eyes with his warmly glowing blue orbs. His lips widened leisurely into a rakish grin as his gaze ranged over her, and he inclined his head to her in the merest mockery of a bow and raised his glass.

Considering the perusals she had been subjected to so far, Belle deemed his perusal far too bold. At least other men had the decency to size her up with discretion, but Lord Bingham made no attempt to hide his penchant for studying and caressing and feeding on every aspect of her person so that she felt she was being devoured.

Hot with embarrassment over being caught staring and the smug manner in which he'd acknowledged her, Belle curled her lips in derision and, lifting her chin in an attitude of haughty displeasure, looked away, aware that if she didn't stop it and take more interest in the general conversation that was going on around her, her grandmother would notice.

It proved to be an especially fine banquet and, continuing to find herself the recipient of Lord Bingham's careful perusal and feeling the dire need of its numbing effects, Belle imbibed more wine than she normally would have done. There was no protection from that rogue's hungering eyes, and at times the warm glow she saw in them made her feel quite naked. She was not at all surprised when she realised her nerves were taut enough to be plucked.

Three hours later when the banquet had ended, Belle strolled through the lantern-lit gardens with her grandmother, who had become overcome with the heat and thought some fresh air might help alleviate her headache, which had become quite intense. She also strove to keep Isabelle in her sights.

People collected in groups to gossip while high-spirited young couples sought privacy among the shrubs. After she had excused herself to go to the ladies' retiring room when her grandmother stopped to acknowledge an acquaintance, on returning and finding herself alone for the first time since she had entered Carlton House, Belle followed the sound of music and stood in the ballroom, watching dancers attired in satins and silks swirling around the floor in time to a lilting waltz.

Suddenly she got that unnerving feeling she got when some-one was staring at her. The sensation was so strong she could almost feel the eyes on her, and then a deep voice seemed to leap out from behind her, and said, 'Dance with me.'

Belle turned in astonishment as the officer materialised from the shadows. Belle recognised that mocking smile—it was identical to the one he had given her across the table, when he'd caught her inadvertently staring at him. His voice was deep and throaty, like thick honey. It was a seductive voice that made her think of highly improper things. It seemed to caress each word he uttered, and she knew there couldn't be many women who could resist a voice like that, not if the man speaking looked like Lord Bingham. But she told herself she needn't worry, for she was completely immune to that potent masculine allure.

'That would not be appropriate. I don't know you.'

Lance laughed at her. 'Well, my fine lady, you should indeed know me—and if you don't, I will tell you that I am Lance Bingham, at your service. Now does my name sound familiar?'

'My grandmother has already told me who you are,' Belle replied coolly.

'I thought she might.'

She looked at him directly. 'Why does she not like you?'

Instead of reacting with offence, he merely chuckled. 'You should ask your grandmother. You may find what she has to tell you—interesting.' He grinned, his mouth curving up at one corner. Beneath his heavy, drooping lids his eyes were filled with amusement, and idle speculation. 'What's the matter? Cat got your tongue?'

She cocked a dark, finely arched brow above a baleful glare, which, with the chillingly beautiful smile, could have frozen the heart of the fiercest opponent. Woe to the man this woman unleashed her wrath upon.

'I'm minding my own business. I suggest you mind yours.'

He grinned. 'You're outspoken.'

'None of your business. Why don't you just go away?'

'Hostile, too. I don't often encounter hostility from young ladies.'

'I'm surprised.'

'You're not impressed?'

'Not a bit.'

Those seductive blue eyes settled on her. 'Well, Miss Isabelle, I find you quite challenging.'

'You do?'

'Did anyone ever tell you you're quite lovely?'

'All the time.'

'And you've got lovely hair. You're got a provocative mouth, too.'

'Save your breath. I am not interested.'

'No?' He arched a brow.

'Not in the slightest.'

'I find that hard to believe.'

'You are very convincing. You actually make a woman believe you are speaking the truth—but then you have undoubtedly had a great deal of practice.'

He grinned. 'True, but I am sincere.'

Belle could feel her cheeks warming as she met those smiling blue eyes. 'You seem terribly sure of yourself, my lord.'

'And I can see you're not easily taken in, but can you not understand what a man like myself experiences in the presence of such a beautiful woman?'

Belle peered at him frostily. 'And I can see you're all talk.'

Leaning forwards, Lance ensnared her gaze and carefully probed those dark green eyes as a slow smile curved his lips. 'You've got me all wrong. You've awakened emotions within me that I was sure I was incapable of feeling—some of which are appreciative—others I'm simply struggling to restrain.'

'Then you will just have to curb your emotions, my lord, for I am not interested.'

He cocked a sleek black brow. 'No?'

'Conceited, aren't you? Conceited and arrogant.'

He pretended offence. 'You do me a terrible injustice. In fact, you make me feel quite downcast and disconsolate. Here I am, complimenting you on your beauty, and you start casting aspersions on my character. You think I'm insufferable?'

'Quite,' she agreed heatedly.

'That's quite a temper you have,' he said, shaking his head in teasing, chiding reproof. 'And here I was thinking that you wanted me to ask you to dance.'

Her eyes flared. 'Do you actually think I was waiting for you to ask me?'

Her show of outrage bestirred his hearty laughter. Thoroughly incensed, Belle glowered at him until his amusement dwindled to nothing more than a slanted grin. 'You can't fault a soldier recently returned from the wars for hoping that such would be the case. You really are quite the most enticing female I've met. So, what do you say? Will you dance with me?'

'No. Like I said, you are insufferable. I don't think I like you very much.'

'A little would do. Actually, I'm quite delightful once you get to know me. I do have a reputation, I admit it frankly—but I've been dreadfully maligned. You shouldn't believe all you hear about me.'

Belle gazed at him with a cool hauteur. After a moment he smiled a devilishly engaging smile, offended demeanour gone.

'Are you sure you don't want to dance?'

'Quite sure,' she retorted.

'You don't know what you're missing.'

'Sore feet, probably.'

'It's a long time since I trod on a lady's toes, Belle.'

Her heart lurched at his familiar use of her name. 'Maybe so, but I will not risk it. I did not invite you to ask me to dance.'

He grinned unrepentantly. 'I know. I took it upon myself. Always was impetuous.'

'Now why doesn't that surprise me? If you will excuse me, I see my grandmother beckoning to me.'

Lance Bingham gave her a mock-polite nod, eyelids drooping, a half-smile playing on his mouth. Lowering his head, he spoke softly into her ear, his warm breath fanning her neck. Mingled with an underlying essence of soap, the pleasantly aromatic bouquet of his cologne drifted into her nostrils and twined amazingly through her senses, and she found the manly fragrance intoxicating.

'Go if you must, but I will not give up.'

True to his word, Lance Bingham didn't. His mind never wandering far from the diamonds around her neck, Belle

Ainsley's delectable form fully visible to his hungry eyes was an inducement he was unable to resist.

The Dowager Countess of Harworth had watched him throughout the evening carefully. She had seen him approach Isabelle and noted her rejection. However she was unsettled by it. Countless young women surrounded him all the time, all vying for his attention. Lord Bingham, she noted, treated them with amused tolerance, for his attention was on the only female at Carlton House who seemed immune to his magnetism—her granddaughter.

Having serious cause to doubt that he had never seen such perfection before and tempted to dally with the lady to his heart's content, half an hour after he had spoken to her, Lance threw caution to the four winds and approached Belle once more.

From where she sat conversing with two elderly ladies who were friends of her grandmother, glancing up, Belle saw his head above the crowd and instinctively knew he was looking for her. When he turned his imperious head his eyes locked on to hers and he smiled, a lazy cocksure smile. When he strode arrogantly towards her, she was not in the least surprised when the crowd parted before him like the Red Sea before Moses.

Belle lifted her eyes to look into his face. He was smiling down at her, the bright blueness of his eyes catching her breath. She was used to male admiration, but this one was the first to rouse her hostility while at the same time stirring her senses and capturing her imagination. Not that she'd let him see it, for that was not her way, but she had never reacted like this before to any man.

'As you do not appear to be taken for this dance, I wonder if I might—'

Belle raised her chin haughtily. 'Thank you, but I am not dancing at the moment.'

'I can see that, which is why I am here. Now, if the ladies will excuse us…'

Bowing in the direction of the open-mouthed ladies, Lance took Belle's hand, pulled her out of the chair and whisked her into the middle of the swirling dancers where he took her into his arms. Belle was so unused to anyone forcing her to do something against her will that she went with him, automatically falling into the right steps of the waltz before she realised what she was doing.

Her astonishment at his outrageous audacity was short lived and anger took over. For two pins she would walk off the floor and leave him standing, but she was acutely aware that almost everyone was watching them and she could not do that. To do so would be a slight to him, and she could not do such a thing to him in front of all these people. Nor could she shame her grandmother by creating a scene, even though she did not hold a high opinion of Lord Bingham and had told her in no uncertain terms that she must have nothing to do with him. So she made up her mind not to speak to him and leave when the dance ended

They danced in silence for a few moments, a silence in which Lance noted the strange lights dancing in her shining hair, and her slender shoulders gleaming with a soft, creamy lustre. 'This is pleasant, is it not?' he said at length, and there was a touch of irony in his mocking tone.

Feeling his arm tighten about her, Belle stiffened and for an incredulous moment she was speechless. Looking into his eyes, she forgot her intention not to engage in conversation with him. 'I would be obliged if you would not hold me so tightly. I am only dancing with you because you dragged me on to the floor,' she said with an effort, in the coldest and most condescending manner. 'Do you usually snatch your partners away from their chaperons so ungallantly?'

He raised one thick, well-defined eyebrow, looking down at her. A faint half-smile played on his lips as if he knew exactly what was going on in her mind. 'Only when I think they might refuse to dance with me—or need rescuing.'

'I did not need rescuing, as you well know, Lord Bingham,' she retorted, resenting his effect on her, the masculine assurance of his bearing. But she was conscious of an unwilling excitement, seeing him arrogantly mocking, and recklessly attractive. Here they were, together in the middle of the dance floor, in an atmosphere bristling with tension. 'I was perfectly happy where I was.'

'I don't believe you. Besides, it's not every day I get to dance with an American girl.'

Belle looked at him condescendingly and gritted out a menacing smile. 'Lord Bingham, I am curious about your name. You see, I knew some Binghams in Charleston. Scurvy lot they were—thieves and cutthroats. Are you perhaps related, sir?'

The sweetness of her tone did not hide the sneer she intended. He met it with a flicker of amusement showing upon his lips. 'It's not impossible. I have distant family scattered all over the place. Who knows? Some of them may quite possibly have settled in the Carolinas. You dance divinely, by the way,' he murmured, spinning her in an exaggerated whirl that made her catch her breath.

'Will you please behave yourself?' She spoke sharply, jerking away from him.

'I do,' he murmured, his warm breath fanning her cheek as he pulled her back to him. 'We are partners. How else should I behave?'

'Do not hold me so tightly. Be a gentleman—if that is not too difficult for you.'

'A gentleman?' he said, flashing his white teeth in a lazy grin, his gaze dipping lingeringly to her soft lips. 'How can I do that? I am but an ignorant soldier, unschooled in the postures of the court, trained only to fire a gun and fight the enemy.'

'Do not play the simpleton with me. It won't work. Why have you singled me out from all the other ladies to dance?'

'Is it so very strange for a man to want to dance with the most beautiful woman in the room? You are a very beautiful—enough to drive a man to madness.'

'I really had no idea,' she apologised sarcastically. 'Perhaps you would like to prove your words.'

'Prove?'

Calmly Belle met his gaze. How she yearned to erase that smirking grin from his lips. 'Your madness!' She sounded flippant and casual. 'But you need not burden me. A few flecks of foam about your mouth would serve as well to prove the claim.' She ignored the amusement that shone from his eyes and was sure her remark would have had him laughing out loud had they not been in the middle of a crowded dance floor. 'Am I the first female you've ever met who didn't want to dance with you?'

'I confess to being somewhat spoiled by women who seemed to enjoy dancing with me. And you,' he added, knocking back her momentary sense of triumph, 'have been too long surrounded by besotted beaux who would willingly kiss the ground on which you walk, begging your permission to be your lord and master.'

'Heaven forbid! I will never call any man my lord and nor will I allow a man to be my master. When I marry it will be a partnership. I will not be a dutiful little wife expected to behave like an obedient servant.'

Lance glanced down at her with an odd combination of humorous scepticism and certainty. 'No I don't suppose you will. You have quite a following of admirers,' he commented, his eyes skimming over the bachelors who had been among her audience earlier. They were now eyeing him enviously and with keen attention. 'I must say that I'm relieved you didn't walk off the floor and leave me standing.'

'Had I done so, I would have put my own reputation in jeopardy.'

His eyes, sweeping over her face and coming to rest on the

sparkling gems around her throat, narrowed. 'Even so. You should know that if I want something I take it, whatever the consequences.' He lowered his head as he spun her round, his lips close to her ear. 'I've never seduced a girl from Charleston before.'

Deeply shocked by his remark, Belle had the urge to kick his shin and leave him standing, regardless of the consequences, but instead she controlled her expression and met his look head on. 'No? Then might I suggest you go there and find one. I am not so easily seduced,' she retorted, too angry to be humiliated.

'No?'

'A very *definite* no. I wouldn't let you touch me to save me from drowning.'

He looked down at her with mock disappointment. 'I am mortified to hear that—but it's early days. I always enjoy the chase. You will think differently when you get to know me.'

Belle looked at him with withering scorn. 'Why, of all the conceited, arrogant—what a thoroughly selfish, insufferable individual you are, Lord Bingham. Do you make lewd remarks to all the women you dance with?'

'And do you treat every gentleman who dances with you with such animosity—or only me?'

'Lord Bingham, in the first place, you are no gentleman—which I have already pointed out. In the second, I don't like you. And in the third, you should not be speaking to me at all.'

'I shouldn't?' Her hostility didn't offend him in the slightest. In fact, it added to his determination to get to know her better.

'We have not been properly introduced.'

'Do you mind?'

'No—not really,' she confessed honestly, hating the protocol that now ruled her every waking moment, tying her in knots lest she do or say the wrong thing.

'Good. Neither do I. I would like it if you would call me Lance,' he said, his gaze settling on her face, 'since I intend for us to become better acquainted.'

'Forgive me, but that would go against the basics my grandmother has tried to teach me since coming to this country. I have been taught to show proper respect for gentleman of any standing.'

Lance considered her at length and had to wonder why she refused to be so informal with him after he had invited her to be. 'I must assume by your answer that you're averse to the familiarity.'

'It is what my grandmother would demand of me.'

'Does that mean you insist on me addressing you in like manner?'

'Whether you adhere to the strict code of gentlemanly conduct is entirely your affair.'

His eyebrow quirked with some amusement. 'Come now, Belle—and in case you're wondering, I know that is what you are called since I have made enquiries—'

'I wasn't,' she cut in crossly.

'—but your grandmother is stuck in the past,' he continued. 'Times are changing—at least I hope they are.'

Belle had never known her name could sound so very different, so warmly evocative when spoken by a man, or that she could feel as if she were dissolving inside when those soft, mellow tones caressed her senses.

'Can you not agree that if we are to get to know each other on more intimate terms,' Lance went on, lowering his head so that his mouth was very close to her ear, 'it should allow us privileges above the usual stilted decorum of strangers?'

His husky voice and the closeness of his mouth so that she could feel his warm breath on her cheek was almost her undoing. She blushed scarlet. There was still so much of the girl in her at war with the young woman, and this man had the knack of bringing it quickly to the surface. Yet for all her annoyance with him, she was aware of everything about him—of the handsome face above the scarlet jacket, tanned and healthy. She was surprised to see, at close quarters, faint lines of weariness about his face as silently, reluctantly, she felt drawn once more towards him. Recollecting herself, she tried to change her thoughts, finding her emotions distasteful.

'But that is precisely what we are, Lord Bingham, strangers—and I intend for us to remain that way. I am convinced you have plied many light o' loves with similar persuasive reasoning. I can well imagine that you have become quite adept at swaying besotted young girls from the path their parents have urged them to follow.'

His eyes twinkled down at her. She was right. Apart from Delphine, there had been temporary light o' loves—and one or two had lasted longer than others—but he had never considered his involvement with them of any consequence. 'You are very astute, Belle, but if you think you have the measure of me, then you are very much mistaken. I saw you the moment you arrived and I've wanted to speak to you all evening.'

'And now you have,' she said, staring into those eyes that had ensnared her own. 'And don't get any high-minded ideas that you're any better than the other gentleman I have partnered tonight, because if you do you will be wrong.'

Belle thought he was too much aware of her physically, and that the banter was leading to something. He made her uneasy and yet at the same time he stimulated and excited her. He did seem to have a way about him and she could not fault any woman for falling under his spell, for she found to her amazement that her heart was not so distantly detached as she had imagined it to be. To her amazement his voice and the way he looked at her evoked a strangely pleasurable disturbance in areas far too private for an untried virgin even to consider, much less invite, and she didn't quite know what to make of them. They seemed almost wanton. But she didn't intend making it easy for him.

'Clearly I didn't make my aversion to conversing with you plain enough,' she retorted hotly.

He chuckled low. 'I thought you were merely playing hard to get.'

'I don't play those sorts of games,' she retorted hotly. 'My pleasure would be to walk off the floor and leave you standing, so be thankful that I've let you retain some of your pride. My grandmother will reproach me most severely for dancing with you.'

'That is for you to deal with, Belle, but heed my warning. I do not run from fierce old ladies, no matter how hard or how loud they huff and puff. Her dislike of me is quite unfounded.'

'My grandmother has never said that she dislikes you, and she never says anything about anyone without good reason. And, of course, you're the poor innocent and undeserving of any condemnation.'

His eyes glowed in the warm light as he gave her a lazy smile. 'I never claimed to be an innocent—in fact, I am far from it.'

'I would hardly expect you to admit it if you were,' she retorted crisply.

'I could show you if you like.' His eyes seemed to glow, laughing at her, mocking her.

'Not a chance.'

'Are you enjoying the Prince's hospitality?'

She looked at him boldly from beneath her long eyelashes, her lips parted, her tongue visible between the perfect white of her teeth, and a tell-tale flush having turned her cheeks a becoming pink. 'Very much, and Prince George seems very charming—unlike some of his guests.'

'Oh? Anyone in particular?'

'I don't think I need spell it out, do you? The Prince is awfully good at giving wonderful parties.'

He gave her a penetrating look through narrowed eyes. 'So, Belle Ainsley, your grandmother has warned you about me?'

Belle leaned back in his arms and looked up at him. His taunting grin made her realise the folly of baiting him. He had all but stated he was no gentleman and did exactly what he chose to do. She felt a perverse desire to shatter a little of his arrogant self-assurance.

'If she has, it's because you have a certain reputation. She cannot bear me out of her sight, for in her opinion every male in London has designs on me. Not that she would object to it being the right man, you understand, since she's forever reminding me that the Season is for young ladies to find husbands.'

'Which is true. Otherwise what is the point of it all?'

'Indeed, and I'm afraid that at present I have more suitors than I know what to do with. Grandmother sets great store by propriety and everything must be done according to the rules of courtship.'

'And you? Did you want to leave America?'

'No. It was my home, where I wanted to remain, but on my father's demise my grandmother—who had become my guardian—insisted I come to England.'

'Well, I for one am very glad she did.'

'I don't see why you should be, for since my grandmother seems to have an aversion to you she will see to it that we are never in the same company.'

The brief shake of his head dismissed her remark. 'If I have a mind to get to know you better, Belle, your grandmother won't be able to do a thing about it,' he said in a deep, velvety voice.

Belle saw the look in his eyes, and her heart began to hammer uncontrollably while a warning screamed along her nerves, a warning she knew she should take heed of if she was to retain her sanity. He had set her at odds with his insolent perusal of her earlier, but she had to admit that he was the most exciting man she had met—and the most infuriating.

As the dance progressed, couples dipped and swayed, but Lance Bingham and Belle Ainsley were unaware of them. They made a striking couple. There was a glow of energy, a powerful magnetism that emanated from the beautiful, charismatic pair, he so handsome, she so lovely—so everyone thought, everyone, that is, but the Dowager Countess of Harworth. Sitting with a group of elegant men and women who composed her personal retinue, as she watched her wilful, headstrong granddaughter skim the ballroom floor in the arms of and in perfect unison with the notorious Lord Bingham, her expression was ferociously condemning.

Even the other dancers turned their heads to watch, making way for them as they circled the room. Guests, who had been chatting and laughing and drinking champagne, aware of the enmity that existed between the Ainselys and the Binghams— that there had been much strife and that emotions were still raw—grew watchful and quiet, glancing now and then at the dowager countess, so enormous was her consequence among the *ton*, to see what she would do.

The countess observed through narrowed eyes that the famous diamonds had created a lot of interest and drew a good deal of comment and envious glances—not least that of Lance Bingham. Already the air was buzzing with whispered conjectures and she knew the word would spread like wildfire that, by singling Isabelle out to dance, Lord Bingham was sending out the message that the age-old feud was over. This thought the countess found most displeasing and was not to be borne. The last thing in the world she wanted was for her granddaughter to capture the interest of this particular aristocrat, but it would appear she had done just that. By breakfast the affair would be being discussed in every household in London.

Belle was whirled around in time to the sweeping music by a man who danced with the easy grace of someone who has waltzed a million times and more. Lance was a good dancer, light on his feet, keeping in time to the rhythm of the music. Belle could feel the muscles of his broad shoulders beneath the fabric of his coat, and her fingers tingled from the contact.

And then the dance was over and he released her, but he was reluctant to part from her. Belle Ainsley intrigued him. She was the only woman who had dared stand up to him, and flaunting the diamonds that by rights belonged to the Binghams—the sheer injustice of it—was tantamount to a challenge to him.

'Would you defy your grandmother and dance with me again?'

'Why? Are you asking?'

'Would you like me to?'

'Yes, just to give me the satisfaction of saying no.'

He grinned. 'Don't cut off your nose to spite your face, Belle.'

'Don't flatter yourself. One dance with you is quite enough. Please excuse me. I think this brief encounter has gone on long enough.'

She turned from him, about to walk away, but he caught her arm. 'Wait.'

She spun round. 'What?'

'Protocol dictates that I escort you back to your grandmother—or do you forget so easily what you have been taught?'

'Are you sure you want to? Do you have the courage?'

'After confronting Napoleon on the battle field, confronting your grandmother is mere child's play.'

Belle elevated her brows in question. 'You think so? Would you like to tell her—or shall I?'

'I wouldn't bother. Your grandmother might take offence to being compared to the mighty emperor.'

'I don't think so. Both are stoic and determined people, and unafraid of the enemy. I think they would get on remarkably well.' She tossed her head haughtily. 'I suppose you must return me to my grandmother—it will be interesting to observe the outcome.'

Taking her hand, Lance led her off the dance floor. He sensed that, in her belief she could do whatever she fancied, there was an air of danger about her. Nothing will ever beat her, he thought. He would wager she had teeth and claws. Determined too. What she wants she'll go after—a girl after his own heart. But she was still young, still impressionable—trembling on the edge of ripe womanhood. Isabelle Ainsley would not be long without a husband. The Regent's court possessed many handsome beaux, who would be willing to wed the beautiful granddaughter of the Dowager Countess of Harworth. She thought she had his measure. He smiled, confident in his own power over the female sex. She was only an apprentice compared to him.

He liked his women to be experienced, experienced in the ways of pleasing his own sexually mature body, and there was no doubt Belle Ainsley would make a perfect bed mate. But she must be shown that it was Lance Bingham who called the tune. However, Lance knew full well that though it was not in his nature to care what people thought of him—especially the Dowager Countess of Harworth—he must, for the time being, do the right thing and return this beautiful baggage with her reputation intact.

Lance bowed to the countess, his smile courteous. 'Your granddaughter dances divinely, Countess. I hope you will forgive me for stealing her away. I was somewhat precipitate in rushing her on to the floor as I did.'

The dowager countess regarded him with an expression of acid tolerance for which she was known—and feared—by all the *ton*. A deep shudder passed through her and she felt as if she were being taken back in time, for Lance Bingham, with his lean, noble features, stunning good looks and tall, broad-shouldered frame, was so much like his grandfather. She was shocked by the likeness. He had the same mocking smile that she had always found so confusing. It had promised so much and yet meant so little.

'Yes, you were. So, Colonel Bingham, you are back from France.'

'As you see, Countess. I am especially honoured by this opportunity to renew our acquaintance.'

The countess considered it prudent to ignore his remark. 'You are back for good?'

'Indeed.'

'You have been to Ryhill?'

'I have, but pressing matters of business brought me back to London for the present.'

'Wellington and Prince George have sung your praises often during your campaigns. From all reports, your regiment was a shining example of a well-disciplined force, which proved itself as valiant in battle as any in the British Army—in particular the battle at Waterloo. You are to be congratulated, Lord Bingham.'

'No more than any other. Waterloo was a great victory for Wellington. Any officer would have deemed it a privilege to serve under his leadership. You kept up with what was happening?'

'I read the newspapers,' the countess replied, her tone stilted.

'Of course you do.' Lance's eyes flicked to Belle. 'I should be honoured if you would permit me to partner your grand-daughter in another dance, Countess.'

'I imagine you would be. However, I believe her dance card is full. I'm sure you will find some other young lady willing to partner you.'

Her face became alarmingly shuttered and without expression and her eyes darkened until they were almost black. That this impertinent man, whose family had done her so much harm in the past, should have the effrontery to try to ingratiate himself with her granddaughter was insupportable.

Lance nodded, understanding perfectly, but he was quite ready to be summarily dismissed. 'I'm sure I shall, Countess.' He looked at Belle and bowed his torso in a courtly gesture. 'I enjoyed dancing with you, Miss Ainsley. Should one of your partners be unavailable, I am at your service. The night is still young. Who knows? Anything might happen.' Without another word or so much as a glance at Belle, he bowed and walked away.

Determined to dedicate herself to keeping Lance Bingham away from Isabelle, and having planned to leave for the Ainsleys' ancestral home in Wiltshire at the end of the Season, the countess considered it might be as well to leave in the next few days. Although even in Wiltshire it couldn't be guaranteed that Isabelle would be safe from the officer if the wily rascal had a mind to see her.

She was pleased with the way Isabelle had turned out—even if she had enjoyed frustrating all her tutors' efforts to correct any part of her like some precocious child out to tease her elders. However, her demeanour was much improved. She was at ease and content fraternising with affluent aristocrats with lofty titles and well respected. But there were still times—like tonight and her disagreeable and defiant behaviour over the necklace, and her refusal to send Lance Bingham packing when he'd asked her to dance—when the old Isabelle surfaced to remind her that the spirited, wilful hoyden was still present.

'If Lord Bingham approaches you again, you will have nothing to do with him, Isabelle. The man believes he can talk his way into, or out of, any situation and I have no wish to see him do you harm. He has charm in abundance, but you will have nothing more to do with him. Do you understand?'

'Yes, Grandmother,' Belle replied dutifully, knowing that

if Lord Bingham had a mind to approach her again, there wasn't a thing she could do about it.

As the evening progressed, from a distance Lance watched Belle Ainsley, making no attempt to approach her for the present, though this had nothing to do with her grandmother's displeasure. No matter how he tried to clear his mind of her, the more difficult it became, for the woman was entangling him in desire and he hadn't even kissed her yet, never mind possessed her. But he would. Yes, he would. Although Lance considered himself an experienced ladies' man, with justification he knew when to take a step back. His senses were giving him that message right now.

However, his attention never wavered from the provocative sensuality of her as she danced with more men than she would be able to remember. There was a natural, unaffected sophistication and exhilarating liveliness that drew men to her, and he took pleasure in looking at her, at the vibrancy of her, her laughing face, his gaze shifting now and then to the glittering diamonds resting against her creamy flesh that brought a quiet, secretive smile to his lips.

The festivities were drawing to a close when he saw her standing by a pillar alone. He lazily regarded her, his eyes following her, snapping sharply. Going to stand behind her, he lightly trailed his skilled fingers down the soft nape of her neck, reassured when she did not move away.

Belle recognised the scent of his cologne. She gasped and quivered, a warmth suffusing her cheeks. Though she commanded herself to move, her legs refused to budge. She felt it so strongly, it was as if her whole body was throbbing suddenly and in her head her thoughts were not orderly—just odd, strong responses. And in her breasts—how could a touch, a caress, reach her breasts? Yet it had; it was making them desperate to be touched and it was all she could do not to reach for one of his hands and place it there.

And the sensation moved on, lower, sweetly soft and liquid; small darts of pleasure travelled as if on silken threads to her stomach and inner thighs as the infuriating man continued his rhythmic stroking, with Belle unaware as he did so that he was giving particular attention to the clasp of her necklace. The heat of his hand seemed to scorch her cool flesh and she licked her dry lips. Re-collecting herself, she shrugged away from his caress, but not too forcefully.

'You overstep yourself, sir,' she murmured, a little breathless.

'But you enjoy me touching you, Belle, do you not?' Lance breathed in a tight, strained voice. 'Would you deny either of us the pleasures of being together?'

Oddly feeling no grudge against him, Belle turned and looked at him surreptitiously. His bold gaze stirred something deep within her, and the sensation was not unpleasant. 'You go too fast. I hardly know you at all.'

Lance's eyes gleamed with devilish humour, and his lips drew slowly into a delicate smile. 'You're quite right. You must allow us to get to know each other. You could be the light of my life. Have mercy on me.'

Belle lifted her chin. 'I am hardly the first or the only one. It passes through my thoughts that you are a rake, Lord Bingham, and have probably said those very words to so many women you have lost count.'

'I cannot deny any of what you say—but then I had not met you. You impress me. You attract me. It is a long time since I said that to a woman.'

Confused by the gentle warmth of his gaze and the directness of his words, Belle was moved by what he said. It was impossible to determine whether he mocked her or told the truth. He was not like any man she had ever met. When she had spoken to hurt him, to insult him, he had taken it in

his stride or with humour, with patience, and still he complimented her.

'You must forgive me if I appear confused. *You* confuse
me.'

The softening in her manner enhanced her beauty, and
Lance boldly and appreciatively stared, encouraged by it. He
leaned closer so that his mouth was close to her ear. 'At least
we have something in common.'

His warm breath stirred shivers along her flesh, and a curious excitement tingled in her breast. She had to fight to keep
her world upright. What was the matter with her? Had she
consumed too much wine and was now feeling its effect?

'Is it too hard to imagine that we could become lovers?'
he asked softly. 'I find you absolutely fascinating, and yet
you suddenly seem afraid. Is it me you fear—or something
else?'

The endearment spoken in his rich, deep voice had the
same stirring effect on her as his finger on the back of her
neck. 'I am not afraid,' she said, trying to control herself and
the situation, 'and nor do your words sway me. I realise that
this is merely a dalliance to you.'

'Liar.' A seductive grin swept across his handsome face.
'Admit it. You are afraid—afraid of the things I make you
feel.'

'Lord Bingham,' she gasped breathlessly, 'I am not a
woman of easy virtue and certainly do not intend giving
myself to you. Now please go away before my grandmother
sees us together. You have no idea how angry she can be.'

'Yes, I do.'

'Then you should take heed and leave me alone.'

He moved round her to stand in front of her, his eyes hooded
and seductive. 'Come now, you don't mean that.'

With trembling effort Belle collected herself, and, as he
stared at her, she drew a deep, ragged breach. 'She says I must

have nothing to do with you. I'm beginning to think she's right.'

He chuckled softly. 'Is she afraid I will lead you astray? Is that it, Belle?'

She gave him a level look. 'I believe she does, but that isn't the only reason, is it? My sixth sense tells me there is some other reason why she dislikes you.'

'Your sixth sense does you credit.'

'So I am right.

He looked at her, his eyes amused, a smile curving his full mouth, and when Belle met his gaze she was struck by the sheer male beauty of him. And then she was struck by something else, very strongly indeed—it shocked her with its violence, a great blow of emotion, emotion for him.

She wasn't quite sure what it was even, but she acknowledged it—it was startling and unexpected and absolutely new. The evening—the privilege of being at Carlton House, the build up to it, of being with so many people, the music, the laughter, the champagne, all far removed from what she knew—had heightened her emotions, made them raw, even a little reckless and dangerous. She knew quite clearly—they both did, for she could see in his eyes that he acknowledged it too—that this was a new and important thing, only just beginning. And yet she knew she must not accept it, not let it happen. That she must fight it.

Chapter Three

When their coach finally arrived at the front of Carlton House, Belle was glad to climb in. Her feet ached and she was tired and couldn't wait to get into her bed. She was travelling alone in the protection of the grooms, for her grandmother's headache had become much worse. She was feeling so poorly that Lady Canning, a close friend, had invited her to spend the night at her house in town. She was expected to return home the following afternoon.

With two armed footmen travelling at the back of the coach, the coachman urged the horses forwards. The Dowager Countess of Harworth took no chances when travelling after dark.

Not only did one have to beware of highwaymen, but discontented soldiers—soldiers once loyal to the country, who had been cashiered from their regiments to eke out a miserable existence in the slums. Many of them took out their spite on the gentry as they travelled the quiet roads after dark to their elegant residences, robbing them of valuables before retreating back into the dark city streets.

A light wind blew, sending heavy rain clouds scudding

across the sky, veiling the moon so that it shone through in a pale, diffused glow. The Ainsley conveyance lurched through the London streets and headed north. The house was close to the picturesque suburb of Hampstead. It stood high outside London, where the air was fresher. Beyond the orange glow of the carriage lamps, the trees all around them seemed to have taken on strange, moving shapes.

Suddenly a gunshot sounded ahead of them, startling the occupants of the coach. The coachman was heard to shout, 'Robbers up ahead.'

Belle leaned out of the window, but could see no assailant, and in an urgent voice ordered the coachman to set the horses to a faster pace. But it was too late. The footmen had no time to load and cock their pistols. There was a sudden movement to the side of them, as if the trees had come to life, and they found themselves confronted by a menacing, ominously cloaked rider who called upon the driver to bring the coach to a halt.

The driver pulled on the brake lever and hauled at the reins to bring the team to a halt. Belle heard a muffled voice ordering the footmen and the coachman to climb down. Belle was beset with alarm. After what seemed like an eternity, but could not have been longer than a minute, the door was pulled open and the muzzle of a pistol appeared in the doorway held by a man in full cape and a tricorn low over his brow.

'What do you want?' she demanded. 'If you mean to rob me, I have no money on me.'

'Step outside, if you please,' the man said from behind a concealing scarf half-covering his face, his voice low and rough sounding. 'I will see for myself. I will be on my way when you've handed over your valuables. Be kind enough to oblige without causing me any trouble.'

Struggling to gather her wits about her and trying to quell the fear that threatened to overwhelm her, with great indignation, Belle said courageously, 'I most certainly will not! You'll get nothing from me, you thieving rogue.'

The pistol was raised, its single black eye settling on Belle where it stared unblinkingly for a long moment. Beneath the threat, even that brave young woman froze, as the man growled, 'Then I'll just have to take it. Get out of the coach— if you please, my lady,' he added with mock sweetness.

With the pistol levelled on her, she knew there was nothing for it but to comply with the thief's demands. He was ominously calm and there was an air of deadliness about him. Stepping down, she gasped with concern on seeing the footmen and the coachman all bound helplessly together. Unconcerned for her own safety, she turned her wrath on their assailant. The cold fire in her eyes bespoke the fury churning within her. She held herself in tight rein until the rage cooled. What was left was a gnawing wish to see this highway robber at the end of a rope.

'How dare you do this? Please God you haven't harmed them. What is the meaning of this?' she demanded.

The robber scorned the words and would heed no argument. 'Quiet, lady,' the tall, shadowy figure rasped.

Belle's eyes were glued to him. This was not how she had imagined highwaymen to be—fearless cavaliers, carefree, chivalrous, romantic knights, in masks and three-cornered hats, adventurers, 'Gentleman of the Road'. Reluctant to submit to this footpad's searching hands, she stepped back and looked around her, considering the idea that she might be able to disappear into the confines of the trees.

He read her thoughts. 'Don't even think about it,' he rasped. 'It would be foolish to think you could get away. You could not escape me if you tried.' He swaggered closer. 'What have you got, pretty lady, hidden beneath your cloak? A well-heeled lady like yourself must have something. Show me. Come now,' he said when she shrank back, 'it's not worth dying for, no matter how much your valuables are worth. Are they so concealed that my fingers may have to forage?'

She shook her head, taking another step away from him. 'Keep away from me. You are nothing but a thieving, unmitigated rogue out for easy money.'

'True,' he agreed almost pleasantly. 'Come now—a bracelet, a brooch, a pretty necklace—a rich lady like yourself will not miss a bauble or two. I must ask you to hurry. I find myself getting impatient and that causes my finger to twitch on the trigger of my pistol.'

When he reached out to her with his free hand, incensed with his boldness and at the same time terrified of what he might do to her, Belle slapped his hand away. 'Get away from me, you lout.'

He uttered a soft curse. 'For a wench who has no help at hand, you're mighty high minded. Do you think you can stand against me with your impudence? You'll come to heel if I kill you first.'

'I'll shred your hand if you dare to touch me. I swear I will. Leave me alone,' she cried, her body trembling with fear. 'You have no right to touch me.'

'Stop your blustering.' In the blink of an eye he had reached out and flicked open the frogging securing the front of her cloak, which slid from her shoulders to her feet. Catching the light of the carriage lamps, the necklace sparkled. The man emitted a low whistle of admiration.

'So, milady, you say you have nothing of value. Those sparklers look pretty expensive to me. Remove it.' When she made no move to do so, he bowed his head in mock politeness. 'If you please.'

'You can go to hell,' she hissed.

'I shall—and very soon, I don't doubt, for my chosen profession usually includes death at an early age.'

'And well deserved,' she retorted indignantly. 'Hanging's too good for the likes of you.'

He chuckled low in his throat, the sound feeding Belle's anger. 'You think you're not afraid of me, don't you?' he said. 'You sneer at me with your pretty face and big monkey eyes. When I take to the road I feel like a king and I'd like to think tonight is to be my lucky night and come daybreak I shall be as rich as one. Now turn around,' he ordered, 'if you value your life. If you try anything rash, I have no qualms about shooting your coachman.'

Afraid that he might carry out his threat, Belle reluctantly turned her back to the robber, who moved to stand directly behind her and, using one hand, his fingers reached to the back of her neck. A deadly sickness came upon her and she flinched when she felt the cool contact on her flesh. It only took him a second to unclasp and whip the necklace away.

Shoving the precious gems inside a pocket of his cape, the thief backed away, keeping the pistol levelled at her. 'There, that wasn't too painful, was it?'

'You have what you want,' Belle uttered scornfully. 'Now what do you mean to do with us? Shoot us?'

'Nothing so dramatic.'

'Then you can leave us. I have nothing else to give.'

The man laughed. ''Twill be more than your jewels I'll be having my fun with, your ladyship.'

When he moved closer Belle took a step back. Reaching out, he caressed her cheek with the back of his hand, amused when she drew back. Tiny shards of fear pricked Belle's spine while a coldness congealed in the pit of her stomach. She was wary of angering him and bringing him to a level of violence that would destroy her. She had heard tales of how highwaymen sometimes killed those they waylaid—and a lone woman wouldn't stand a chance against the strength of such a powerful man.

'You wouldn't dare,' she whispered, almost choking on the words.

'Wouldn't I?'

'And don't look at me like that.' She could feel his eyes devouring her, and could well imagine the lascivious smile on his lips behind the scarf. A shudder ran through her, and it was not because it was cold. 'You'll hang for sure.'

He placed the pistol beneath her chin so that the barrel touched her throat and tipped her face up to his. 'Madam, if looking is a hanging offence, then I'd rather fulfil every aspect of my desire and be strung up for a lion than a lamb.'

She stared back at him in horror—the colour drained from her face. After a moment, which seemed like an eternity to Belle, he removed the pistol and stepped back.

'Please don't touch me again.'

He cocked a brow. 'Please, is it? So the lady has remembered her manners. But worry not. I have neither the time nor the inclination, lady. I have what I want—you have been most generous. I thank you for your co-operation.'

'Don't think you'll get away with this—you—you devil.' Belle cried, unable to contain her fury. 'I'll find out who you are and see you hang. I swear I will.'

The thief laughed in the face of her ire. 'Dear me, little lady. You have a strange preoccupation with seeing me hang. I'd dearly like to see you try.'

Having got what he wanted, without more ado the man took the reins of his horse and leapt into the saddle with the agility of an athlete. Turning about and giving her a farewell salute and a cheeky, knowing wink—a playful, frivolous gesture that infuriated Belle further—he galloped off into the night.

Seething with rage, her heart pounding in her chest, Belle watched the animal speed along, matching the wind over the narrow road. His hooves flashed like quicksilver in a brief spot of light, and his coat glistened as the muscles beneath it rolled and heaved. She did not move or utter a sound until the thief's muffled laughter and the hoofbeats could be heard no more.

Quickly releasing the footmen and the coachman and

assured that they had not been molested in any way—while concealing her anger at their incompetence, for to her mind their pistols should have been loaded and cocked in the likelihood of such an event occurring—her face as hard and expressionless as a mask, she ordered them to take their positions on the coach.

Picking up her cloak, quivering with outrage and deeply shock by what had happened—and slightly bewildered, for something about the robbery and the highwayman did not make sense—Belle climbed inside the coach. The consequences of the theft of the jewels were too dreadful to contemplate.

How was she to tell her grandmother? They meant so much to her, not to mention their value. Dear Lord, this was a calamity—a disaster. Her grandmother would be livid, and rightly so. She should not have been wearing them in the first place. Even if the robbery was reported first thing in the morning, the thief would be far away by then so it would be difficult to apprehend him. And if he was apprehended, he would already have disposed of them.

They arrived home without further incident. Not until Belle was in bed did she give free rein to her thoughts. She was relieved her grandmother was still in town and had not been party to the ordeal she had suffered. Grandmother didn't intend returning until the following afternoon, so she had a reprieve until then. But she would have to be told eventually. There was no way of escaping that.

Tossing and turning and unable to sleep, she went over and over in her mind what had happened. There had been something about the thief that was familiar. But what? It bothered her and she couldn't shake it off. Then a strangled gasp emitted from her and she shot bolt upright as a multitude of thoughts chased themselves inside her head—a pair of familiar blue eyes glinted down at her as he danced her about the floor. A deep voice tinged with laughter as he lowered his eyes to her neck and said *if I want something, I take it*.

In the space of five seconds, all these memories collided head on with the reality of what had happened on the road. And something else. The scent the thief wore—the faint smell of his cologne when he had stood directly behind her to remove the necklace—was the same scent that had assailed her earlier, when she had been dancing with Lance Bingham.

Flinging herself out of bed in a tempestuous fury, she paced the carpet, unable to believe what she was thinking, unable to contain it. She remembered the moment when he had stood behind her and caressed her neck, when she had thought… What? What had she thought? That he wanted to touch her, that he desired her?

Oh, fool, fool that she was. Why, that arrogant lord had merely been checking the clasp on the necklace, familiarising himself with it, to make it easier for him to remove. He had set out to use her to get the necklace. Why he should want to eluded her for the moment, but she would find out.

The blackguard! The audacity and the gentlemanly courtesy with which he had demanded that she part with her valuables was astounding. There was no doubt in her mind that he was the thief. The man she had met at Carlton House had turned into the Devil when determination to steal the necklace had removed all semblance of civility from him, frightening her half to death. But he wouldn't get away with it. Oh, no. She would see to that.

Every nerve in her body clenched against the onslaught of bitter rage. She continued to pace restlessly. After allowing the tide of emotion to carry her to the limit, nature took command of her again and she was strengthened, something of the old courage and force returning. She stewed. She seethed. Never had she been this angry before in her life. She had to decide on what course of action to take, ways she could make him pay for this outrage, how she could retrieve the stolen necklace before her grandmother returned—and she would, even if she expired in the attempt. Nothing could stop her doing anything once her mind was made up.

But beneath it all was the hurt when she remembered the tender words Lord Bingham had spoken to her on their parting at Carlton House, words she now knew to be empty, without meaning. How could he have said all those things to her and then do what he did—terrify and threaten her at the point of a gun?

The man was cold and heartless and without a shred of decency. She wanted to hurt him, to hurt him badly, and she would find a way to do it without letting him see how much he had hurt her—without letting him see how much she cared.

But why had he taken the necklace? She was utterly bewildered by his actions. And why did bad feeling exist between the Ainsleys and the Binghams? Whatever it was, she suspected it had something to do with the past.

Belle had always been self-willed, energetic and passionate, with a fierce and undisciplined temper, but her charm, her wit and her beauty had more than made up for the deficiencies in her character. She hadn't a bad bone in her body, was just proud and spirited, so determined to have her own way that she had always been prepared to plough straight through any hurdle that stood in her path—just as she was about to do now.

But what was she to say to her grandmother?

As it turned out she was granted a welcome reprieve. The following morning a note was delivered to the house from Lady Channing, informing her that the countess had taken a turn for the worse and that the doctor advised her it would be unwise for her to leave her bed to make the journey to Hampstead until she was feeling better.

Later that day, with a groom in attendance, Belle rode from Hampstead to visit her grandmother. She did indeed look very ill when Lady Channing showed her to her room—too ill to be told about the theft of the necklace. Before returning to Hampstead, she joined a large gathering of fashionable people riding in Hyde Park, struck forcibly by the noise and colour and movement and wanting to feel a part of it. It was a glorious day, hot and sunny. Roses bloomed profusely and she could hear a band playing a jolly tune.

Serene and elegant atop her horse, she looked striking and stood out in her scarlet riding habit. Daisy had brushed her hair up on her head in an intricate arrangement of glossy curls, upon which a matching hat sat at a jaunty angle. She was greeted and stopped to speak to those who recognised her, who expressed their distress when told the dowager countess was unwell.

Suddenly she felt a small *frisson* of alarm as all her senses became heightened. Ahead of her a man atop a dark brown stallion had stopped to speak to an acquaintance. She did not need to see his face to know his identity. He was dressed in a tan jacket and buff-coloured breeches. He sported a tall hat and a snowy white cravat fitted snug about his throat.

As he turned slightly, and not wanting to be found looking at him, Belle averted her gaze, but not before she had seen a world of feelings flash across his set face—surprise, disbelief, admiration—but only for an instant.

Lance nudged his horse forwards, eager to introduce Rowland to this vision in scarlet.

Watching them ride towards her through the press of people, Belle braced herself for the encounter.

Lance bowed very coolly before her, his gaze calmly searching her face. 'Miss Ainsley. I had hoped to have the pleasure of seeing you, but I did not think to find you here. Allow me to compliment you. You are exquisite.'

Aware that every person in the park seemed to be watching them, Belle straightened her back and lifted her head, unaware that she had been holding herself stiffly, her shoulders slightly hunched, as though to defend something vulnerable. She stared at him uncomprehendingly.

'Why—I—thank you,' she said, having decided to be tact and patience personified. She had also decided to play him at his own game and give him no reason to suspect she had identified him as her highwayman of the night before. 'For myself, your presence took me wholly by surprise. I did not expect to see you again so soon.'

Belle studied his features, looking for something that would give her some hint of what had happened on her way back to Hampstead last night, but there was nothing to suggest he had been the thief. But there was something different in him today. His manner was subdued and his tone of voice made her look more closely at him. She detected some indefinable, underlying emotion in it as his brilliant blue eyes gleamed beneath the well-defined brows. Belle was not shaken from her resolve that he was the one, and before she had finished she would prove it.

'May I introduce you to this gentleman?' Lance gestured to his companion. 'This is Sir Rowland Gibbon, an old and valued friend of mine. Rowland, this is Miss Ainsley—the Dowager Countess of Harworth's granddaughter. Rowland wanted to meet you, Miss Ainsley, having recently returned from America, where he travelled extensively.'

'You exaggerate, Lance.' Rowland bowed to her. 'Although I did find the country interesting and exciting and hope very much to return there one day. I believe you are from America, Miss Ainsley.'

'Indeed,' she answered, liking his easy manner and trying not to look at Lord Bingham. Sir Rowland was not a handsome man by any means, but he had obviously spent a goodly amount of coin on his attire, for, completely devoid of prudence, he was garbed in a flamboyant fashion in dark-green velvet coat with a high stiff collar, frothing neck linen and skintight white trouser that clung to the line of his long legs above his black riding boots. He sat his horse with an easy swagger and the dashing air of a romantic highwayman.

Highwayman? Belle sighed. Highwaymen were very much at the forefront of her mind just now. 'I was born there—in Charleston. And you are right to say it is exciting. I too wish to return there one day, but I can't see that happening in the foreseeable future.'

At that moment someone caught Rowland's eye and he excused himself to go and speak to them.

Lance's unfathomable eyes locked on to Belle's. 'Ride with me a while, will you, Belle? I should like to hear more about America,' he said, reverting to a quiet informality.

Belle hesitated. She was aware of the curious stares and of a hushed expectancy from those around them.

'Is it my imagination, or is everyone watching us?'

'It is not your imagination. In the light of the bad feeling that exists between our two families, it is hardly surprising. Ride with me and I will show you just how inflamed the gossip is.'

'You are extremely impertinent and I do not think I should. The last thing I want to do is to create a scandal that will upset my grandmother.'

Lance's eyes darkened and his gaze was challenging. 'What's the matter, Belle? Afraid of a little gossip? Your grandmother isn't here to see—and by the time she hears of it it will be too late.'

Something of the man she had met at Carlton House resurrected itself when he suddenly grinned wickedly, and despite Belle's resolve to remain unaffected by him, she could not quell the small shiver of delight that ran through her. His teasing eyes were so lovely and blue, so blissfully familiar and admiring.

'Very well,' she murmured, forcing an uninterested politeness into her voice. 'But instead of riding in the park, perhaps you would care to ride with me a little way back to Hampstead.'

'Gladly.'

Together they rode out of the park, her groom following at a discreet distance. Belle could feel the fascinated stares of everyone in the park as they left. As they rode up Park Lane, the steady pace of their mounts eased their tensions and they began to unbend, each filled with the other's presence.

Just like the night before when they had danced together, they drew attention from passers-by. Isabelle's beauty and Lord Bingham's tall, lean handsomeness made them unique. And he was handsome, perhaps the most handsome man Belle had ever seen, so there was little wonder he attracted attention, she thought, smiling to herself as she quietly admired her partner. In his broadcloth jacket, which fit his wide shoulders perfectly, his dark hair beneath his hat shimmering in the sunlight, he was devastating. She had to keep her eyes away from his, or at least she tried to, because it was so easy to get lost in his gaze and forget what he had done.

Lance turned his head and looked at Belle. She was like a magnet to his eyes, and now he felt an odd kind of possessiveness. Not the kind one felt on owning material things, but something else. There were different types of possessiveness, and he didn't even want to think of the more common form, which had no place in his emotions.

'I see you've dispensed with your military attire, my lord,' Belle commented airily at length, the cut and seam of his coat evidence of the tailoring only noblemen could afford. 'Your tailor must delight in the opportunity to clothe such an illustrious hero of the wars with Napoleon. Why, a gentleman with such expensive and stylish apparel will be the envy of every roué in London.'

Lance met her cool stare. From all indications it seemed she was none too pleased with him, which did much to heighten his curiosity. 'I count myself fortunate in my tailor, who has made my wardrobe for a good many years—military uniforms, mainly. Now I have retired from army life he is delighted at the opportunity to finally outfit me with all the clothes of a gentleman.'

'Indeed, I think even that master of style and fashion Mr Brummell will have to sit up and take notice.'

'My tailor is a man of sober tastes and it would go against the grain to kit me out in garish garb—and I have no desire to emulate the overdressed Beau Brummell. Besides, that particular gentleman has fallen out of favour with Prince George and it is rumoured that he is heavily in debt and no longer as stylishly garbed as he once was.' He frowned across at her. 'Was your comment about my attire because you find it flawed in some way?'

'Not in the slightest. In fact, I must commend your tailor's abilities, although I imagine you must feel strange in civilian attire after wearing a uniform for so long.'

'It will be something I shall have to get used to—even to tying my own cravat. Thankfully my valet is a master.' After falling silent while they negotiated a congested part of the thoroughfare, he said, 'Your grandmother is well?'

Belle glanced at him, wondering what had prompted the question. Was he curious as to how she had reacted on being told about the theft of the necklace? She answered carefully. 'No—as a matter of fact my grandmother is not feeling herself.'

He glanced at her sharply. 'She is ill?'

'Indisposed,' Belle provided, not wishing to divulge too much. If he thought her grandmother was so distressed over the loss of the diamonds that she had taken to her bed, so much the better—although if a man as cunning as he could rob people at gunpoint and scare them witless, then she doubted he would be moved over the plight of an old woman grieving her loss.

'I am sorry to hear it,' he sympathised, his gaze searching. 'I hope she will soon recover.'

'I doubt it—that she will recover soon, I mean. She really is quite distraught over the loss of something that was close to her heart.' Apart from a narrowing of his eyes, Lord Bingham's expression did not change.

'She is? And was this item—valuable?'

'You might say that—but then—' she smiled, tossing her head and urging her mount to a faster pace '—it is a family matter and I am sure it will be resolved very soon.'

Although she hadn't objected to riding with him, Lance was a little taken aback by the courteous, but impersonal smiles she was giving him. He decided it prudent to let the matter of her grandmother drop.

'I am giving a supper party tonight. There will be a large gathering. I would very much like you to come, but I realise you would encounter difficulties with your grandmother.'

'Yes, I would. You know she would never allow it—but I thank you for the invitation all the same.' They had been riding for some time and on reaching the place where she had been accosted last night, she drew her horse to a halt and faced him. If he thought there was any significance in her stopping in the exact spot, he didn't show it. 'I can manage quite well from here. I'm sure you have more important things to do than play escort to me, Lord Bingham. I shall be quite safe with my groom.'

Lance frowned across at her. 'What's wrong, Belle? You weren't like this when you almost melted in my arms before we parted at Carlton House last night. '

Belle's green eyes widened in apparent bewilderment. 'Did I really almost do that? Goodness, I must have imbibed more champagne than I thought. I danced so many dances with so many different beaux, I forget. I recall dancing with you and you were hardly the soul of amiability—unlike my other partners—and some of them were much more desirable than you.'

'Really?' he said frostily. 'In what way?'

'For one thing, they were younger than you,' she replied, trying to seem cool and unemotional. She longed to slap this insufferable, arrogant lord down to size. 'I have decided that you are much too old for me.'

Lance's eyes darkened very nearly to black. 'What the hell are you saying?' he hissed. 'Don't play games with me, Belle, because you'll find you are well out of your league.'

She looked at him in all innocence and said breezily, 'Games, my lord? I don't play games. If I said anything to mislead you, then I apologise most sincerely.'

Lance's eyes hardened and his jaw tightened ominously. When he spoke it was with a cold savage contempt, his voice dangerously low. 'You're nothing but a common little flirt. Take care how you try to bait me,' he murmured softly. 'I'm not one of the besotted fools who dance attendance on you night after night. I might want more from you than you are ready to grant—and when I want something, I do not give up until I have it.'

Drawing her horse away from him slightly, reminding herself not to let him annoy her and that she must carry out the charade to the end, Belle feigned innocence. 'But—surely you have what you wanted?'

She saw something move behind his eyes and for a split second his gaze went to her unadorned neck before rising to her face. She waited, her eyes holding his, challenging him, aware of the sudden tension inside him, the stirring of suspicion behind his gaze.

'I have?' he answered, not without caution. 'What are you talking about?'

'Why, you asked me to ride with you—and here I am.' She tilted her head to one side and smiled, her eyes questioning. 'Why, were you referring to something else?'

He studied her carefully before saying coldly, 'I think this unpleasant encounter has gone on long enough. I bid you good day.' With that he rode away.

Without a backward glance, Belle headed for home, a sense of triumphant jubilation in her heart, for Lord Bingham's invitation to his supper party had given her an excellent idea as to how she might recover the diamonds.

At nine o'clock Belle, dressed in breeches and a jacket and a low-brimmed hat, with no time to lose and with much chiding from Daisy, who knew all about the missing necklace and what her mistress had in mind, left the house and climbed into the waiting coach.

The driver knew it was not his place to ask questions—although he did look startled at Miss Isabelle's male form of attire. She gave him the address of Lord Bingham's London residence, which had not been too difficult to procure, since he was so well known that the servants had been able to provide her with the address. Settling into the upholstery, in an attempt to still her wildly beating heart she took a deep breath. There was so much depending on this night. She could not expect everything to go well and doubt thwarted her attempt at calm.

By the time she reached her destination—a fine Palladian mansion located close to Hyde Park on Park Lane—she had worked herself up into such a knot of anticipation and foreboding that she was tempted to tell the driver to return to Hampstead. Quickly she recollected herself and, sternly determined, fought to bring her rioting panic under control, thinking of the immense satisfaction and triumph she would feel if her plan succeeded, which would have very little to do with retrieving the necklace, and everything to do with outwitting Lord Bingham.

Belle left the coach some distance from the house, telling

the driver to wait, that she hoped not to be long. She avoided the front of the house, where several smart equipages were lined up. Quickly becoming lost in the dark, she found her way to the back of the house and into a yard with buildings that housed Lord Bingham's carriages and horses. Standing in the shadows she carefully surveyed his town residence.

Lights shone from the windows and people could be seen strolling about the rooms and sitting about. Thankfully several of the upstairs rooms were in darkness and it seemed quiet enough. Suddenly she was overcome with a sense of urgency, for there was a need for haste if she was to find what she was looking for without being seen. Letting herself in by a door that led into a passageway, she paused and listened. Sounds of domesticity and cook issuing orders to the kitchenmaids could be heard from a room on her right—the kitchen, she thought. Fortunately the door was only slightly ajar and she managed to creep by. A narrow staircase rose from the passageway and gingerly she made her way upwards. With a stroke of luck she found herself on a landing, on the top floor of the house, off which were several rooms.

With her ears attuned to every sound—conversation and laughter from Lord Bingham's guests and the clink of glasses—she went from door to door, pressing her ear to it before opening it a crack and peering inside. They were bedrooms mostly—though not one of them gave the impression of belonging to the master of the house. Undeterred, she crept along another landing, peering into each room until eventually she found it. Looking through the slightly open door she waited, afraid Lord Bingham's valet might be in an adjacent room. After a few moments when nothing happened she stepped inside and closed the door.

Only one lamp was lit, giving off a dim light. She could have done with more, but decided she would have to manage. She set to work, starting on a tall bureau beside the door. Thankfully the drawers slid open soundlessly. After rummaging inside and being careful to leave things as she found them, she went on to the next piece of furniture, working quietly, admiring the expensive quality of everything her fingers touched.

She glanced at a rather ornate clock on the mantelpiece as it delicately chimed ten o'clock. Wondering where the time had flown and disappointed that her search had produced nothing as yet, she knew she would have to hurry. Looking about her, she saw a door that she assumed must lead into a dressing room. Slipping inside, she searched the chests of drawers and among racks of clothing, but all to no avail.

Feeling crushed and extremely disappointed, she emerged into the bedroom once more. She was about to admit defeat when her eyes lighted on the bedside tables. She paused to listen. Had she heard a noise on the landing, or was it the noise of the wind that had risen? Whatever it might have been, she decided to get on with it. She had no wish to be caught red-handed.

With one last desperate attempt to locate the jewels, she looked inside the first bedside table, almost shouting out in triumph when, on opening a small velvet pouch and seeing its sparkling contents, she realised she had found what she was looking for.

'Got you, you thieving rogue,' she whispered, pocketing the pouch. Quickly she closed the drawer and then halted abruptly. This time she could not mistake the footfall on the landing as someone came towards the bedroom. Her heart thumping wildly in her chest, Belle flew to the lamp and blew out the flame, placing it on the floor so it could not be lit in a hurry—although there were others in the room to light, so she needn't have bothered. The room was now in almost total darkness. Belle stood in the middle, turning about indecisively. She had to find a place to hide. Her eyes lit on the dressing screen and she flew behind it just as the door handle turned.

Lance came in, uttering an oath under his breath when he

found his room in darkness, and an even louder oath when his foot made contact with the lamp and it toppled over.

'What the devil has happened to the light?' His voice bore an edge of sharpness that bespoke of vexation. Without more ado he picked up the lamp and, striking a sulphur match, soon had it lit. He stood for a moment in puzzlement. His eyes did a quick sweep of the room. Seeing that everything appeared to be in place, he removed his jacket and threw it on to the bed.

From behind the screen Belle listened to him moving about, wondering why he had come to his room and how she was going to get out without being seen. Her heart racing in confused fright, she took a deep breath, trying to calm her rapid pulse and to peer through a crack in the screen. She saw him loosen his neck linen and remove his waistcoat—and what was that dark stain? It looked like wine. So that was it. He'd clearly spilled some on his clothes and come up to change. Hopefully he would do it quickly and go. Seeing him disappear into his dressing room, she waited in trembling disquiet, horrified when, having changed his clothes, he came back into the bedroom and approached the screen.

Lance was just reaching to fold it back when it was shoved towards him by a decisive force. He was almost toppled over by its weight and was momentarily stunned as a shape leapt past him and ran towards the door, pausing for a split second to blow out the lamp. Angrily Lance tossed the screen aside and with quick long strides reached the intruder before he could escape, snatching a handful of his coat and pulling him back.

A rending tear preceded a startled cry and then a booted foot kicked at his shins.

'Dammit, who the hell are you, and what do you think you're doing in my house?' Lance ignored the hands that flailed the air, hitting out at him, and jerked the figure around roughly.

Belle stumbled against the bed and in great trepidation scrambled across it to the other side.

Angered beyond bearing, Lance lunged after what he thought to be a man, since the figure was wearing breeches and the face was concealed by a low-brimmed hat.

Making a concerted effort to escape, Belle picked up his jacket and threw it at him, but swinging round the bedpost, Lance tossed it aside, his fingers again reaching out to ensnare the shadowy figure. Belle side-stepped and darted about the room, but the vague blur of bodies in the dark room gave away their movements. When he was near her, Belle abruptly changed directions and scurried to the door. Lance was faster and leapt after her in time to catch her full against him, clamping a hand over her mouth when she opened it to scream.

'Be still. If you continue to fight me, I'll knock you senseless. Do you understand me?' His captive nodded, in which case he began loosening his grip slightly.

The moment he did, Belle sank her teeth into the fleshy part of his palm and flung herself away from him. He grabbed her before she had taken two steps and held her prisoner in his arms.

'So, you want to draw my blood, eh?'

The sudden contact of their bodies brought a gasp to Belle's lips.

Lance continued to hold her, finding the form too slender, too light to be that of a man. A youth, perhaps?

Taking her with him to the door, he turned the key before releasing her and lighting the lamp. Giving all his attention to his captive, who continued to squirm against him, he reached out and tore the hat away, his mind rebelling in disbelief at what he saw—the dark brown hair, with highlights of red and gold, framing a creamy-skinned visage. The lips were soft and sensuous, the eyes a clear, sparkling shade of green.

'What the hell… Good Lord!' he cried. 'Belle!'

Belle turned from him, but he caught her wrist. Blindly,

insanely, she fought him, wildly twisting and writhing and clawing at him in an attempt to get away from him.

'Will you be still?' he growled, pressing her back against the wall and trying to still her frantic threshing with the weight of his own body. When she wouldn't he increased the pressure of his grip upon the delicately boned wrist. Stubbornly Belle resisted the pain until Lance finally loosed his hold, not wishing to hurt her unduly. Feeling what little fight she had left drain away, slowly she quieted, breathing heavily, very much aware that his thighs were crushing her own quaking limbs.

'Stop fighting me, Belle, and I'll step away. Then I will listen to what you have to say. You owe me that much at least.'

'I owe you nothing,' she hissed through clenched teeth, open mutiny in her tone, her eyes hurling daggers at him. She sidled away from him, rubbing her wrist. 'I swear I'll break your hands if you dare touch me again.'

Lance stepped away from her. A wave of anger that she could be so reckless, that she had put herself in danger like this, washed over him. 'Do you realise I could have killed you, you stupid girl?'

Belle tossed her head in defiance, her expression indignant. 'Desperation leads me to do stupid things.'

'Desperate? You? Don't make me laugh,' he uttered sarcastically. 'How nice of you to drop in to my party. Do you mind telling how you got past my butler—looking like that?'

'I came in through a door at the back of the house. It wasn't difficult.'

'Are you going to tell me what the hell you think you're playing at?'

'Do I really have to tell you—thief?' she hissed accusingly, looking at him with withering scorn.

He looked at her very calmly now, everything beginning to fall into place. 'Thief? Now, that's debatable.'

'Not to me.'

'You know, if you're going to take this defensive attitude, we're not going to get anywhere. I take it that you have found what you were looking for?'

She nodded.

'So, you saw behind my disguise.'

'That wasn't too difficult when I had time to piece things together. It was your cologne that gave you away.'

His lips twitched with the hint of a smile. 'How astute of you. Trust a woman to notice that—and it certainly explains your attitude towards me at the party.'

'What you did, holding up a coach on the King's highway and forcing—at gunpoint, I might add—a woman to part with her valuables, is a criminal offence—one you could be hanged for.'

'As you took great pleasure in informing me last night. Please don't go on,' Lance drawled in exaggerated horror. 'You will give me nightmares.'

His ability to mock his fate and ignore his crime was more than Belle could bear. Her voice shook with angry emotion, and she stared at him as if he were something inhuman and beyond her comprehension.

'And my grandmother? Did you not spare a thought to how your actions might have affected her had she been in the coach? She might have suffered a seizure on being confronted by a violent highwayman.'

'I doubt it. Your grandmother is made of sterner stuff than that. However, I heard it mentioned that she wasn't feeling well and was to remain in town with Lady Channing.'

'And if she had been in the coach?'

'I would not have held you up.'

'How perfectly noble of you,' she scoffed. 'My grandmother could bring charges against you for what you did.'

'And who would believe a high-ranking lord of the realm—as well as being a highly respected and decorated officer in

Wellington's army—would stoop so low as to take to the road as a highwayman?'

Belle glowered at him. 'Is there no limit to what you will dare?'

'No,' he said. 'No limit whatsoever. If you suspected it was me who took your necklace, didn't it occur to you to simply ask me about it when we met earlier today, instead of taking matters into your own hands and sneaking into my home to look for them?'

Belle shrugged. 'It's no worse than what you did to me—you—you wretch. Besides, what was the point in asking you? You would have denied it.'

'And you know that, do you?'

'Don't you feel any guilt at all about stealing the diamonds?'

'No. Should I?'

'I don't suppose you would. One has to have a conscience to feel guilt,' she said, shrugging out of her coat to examine the tear in the back.

'If I were guilty of taking something that didn't belong to me, maybe I would deny it. But I didn't.'

'What are you saying?'

'The diamonds belong to me—to my family. I was merely retrieving them.'

Belle stared at him, surprised by his revelation and clearly shocked. 'To you? But—they are Ainsley diamonds—my grandmother—'

'Told you they belonged to your family, I know. Maybe after all these years she has come to believe that. Is the loss of the diamonds the reason why she has taken to her bed?'

'No. You were right. She wasn't feeling too well at Carlton House last night and stayed with Lady Channing. She is still not well, so I thought it wise to wait until she is feeling better before I tell her the diamonds were stolen.'

'One cannot steal something that legitimately belongs to them.'

'But why go to all that trouble of pretending to be a highwayman?' Belle demanded.

At that moment Lance preferred not to think about the bet he had made with Rowland. 'Because I wanted you to think the person who took your valuables was nothing more than an ordinary thief. Would you have given them to me if I'd asked?'

'Of course not.'

'There you are, then. You have your answer, but I cannot believe you planned this—to come here dressed as…you are,' he said, contemplating her attire, thinking that in her white silk blouse, long and shapely legs encased in buff-coloured breeches, she really was a wonderful sight to behold, 'and that you were foolish enough to come to my house to steal them back.'

Suddenly Belle felt suffocated by his nearness. Her whole being throbbed with an awareness of him, but she knew that if she gave any hint of her weakness, it would only lead to disaster. She saw where his gaze was directed and, glancing down, realised the twin peaks of her breasts were standing taut and high beneath her blouse. Her cheeks grew suddenly hot with embarrassment, and she folded her arms across her chest, glowering at him.

'I never would have, if not for the fury I was beset with at the time—and there's a confession for you. I have a temper—I can't help it, and I'm rarely able to control it once it snaps.'

'I'd already figured that out for myself,' Lance said drily. By his actions he had woken a sleeping dragon.

'Then perhaps you'll think twice about provoking it in future.'

His eyes narrowed dangerously. 'I, too, have a temper, Belle. You would do well to remember that.' He stared at her for a moment, his jaw tight and hard, and then he sauntered to the fireplace, resting his arm on the mantelpiece.

'If I were a man, I'd call you out for what you did to me last night.'

'That would not be wise, Belle.'

'No? After threatening my life and the men whose duty it was to protect me, nothing would satisfy me more that to put a bullet between your eyes.'

'What? You can use a gun?'

'Of course I can—I'm a very good shot, as it happens. Where I come from it is not unusual for women to learn how to shoot. I can hit a target with the best of them.' She smiled wryly. 'I suppose you will say my vanity is showing itself.'

'No, I'm impressed. Not one of the ladies of my acquaintance would know which end of a gun to fire.'

'Then you should become more selective in the ladies you associate with.'

'I don't think so,' he replied drily. 'To become intimately acquainted with a woman whose skill with any weapon might exceed my own, could prove to be dangerous.'

'Then that lets me off the hook,' Belle retorted flippantly.

'How so?'

'Last night you let me believe you were as enamoured of me as the rest—just to get your hands on my grandmother's diamonds. You certainly know how to dent a girl's pride.'

Lance would like to have told her that she had jumped to the wrong conclusion, and that he was enamoured with both her and the necklace. The truth was that she was too beautiful, too sensational for a man not to be enamoured of her. But he refused to feed her vanity more than it already was by the doting swains who trailed in her wake.

'I have every confidence that your pride will soon recover.'

Belle was disappointed that he wasn't attracted by her, but didn't show it. Why had she to say that? How absolutely embarrassing. He probably thought she'd been making advances toward him, fishing for compliments. She should have known that her remark would be pointless. But damn it all, why did he have to point it out?

Chapter Four

For the first time since the diamonds had been taken, Belle had a feeling of self-doubt. Carrying her jacket, she moved towards Lord Bingham, confused as to what she should do. If the diamonds really did belong to him, then by rights she should give them back.

'So, Belle. What are we to do? You have the jewels. Will you return them to me?'

'I think I should wait and see what my grandmother has to say about that.'

'Belle, they really do belong to me. If you don't give them to me voluntarily, then I shall have to take them from you. Is that what you want?'

'What?' she uttered, her eyes flashing with scorn. 'Will you threaten to shoot me like you did last night—and I seem to recall there was a moment when you implied that you would. What kind of man are you, Lord Bingham? What was it that drove you to play such a despicable game? Is there some quirk in your nature that you enjoy doing that to people? Why should I believe anything you say?'

'Because I am a fairly honest person. Trust me. Something

happened between our families concerning the diamonds when our grandmothers were in their prime. My grandmother kept a journal. Everything explaining proof of ownership and what happened at that time is written there. I will show it to you if you like, but there isn't time now. I have to return to my guests.'

Belle turned to the door. 'I think I should go. I told the coach driver to wait for me at the corner of the street.'

'Belle…' She turned and looked at him. His eyes were steadfast. 'The diamonds.' Slowly he walked towards her, holding out his hand.

Belle knew he wouldn't let her out of that room unless she gave them to him. Reluctantly she fumbled in the pocket of her coat and took out the pouch and handed it to Lord Bingham.

'Thank you,' he said, taking it.

'What do you advise me to tell my grandmother?'

'The truth. She'll understand. Come, I'll take you back to the coach—although I can't think what your driver was thinking of bringing you here, dressed like that, in the first place.'

'I can be quite persuasive when I want to be—even with coach drivers when I use my best smile on them.'

She didn't need to elaborate. The effect of her smile was highly predictable. Lance could well imagine the driver's dilemma, how dumbstruck and willing to do her bidding he had been when she had flashed her pearly white teeth and fluttered her eyelashes.

'What a truly vain creature you are, Belle Ainsley.'

'You may see it as a flaw, but at times it can be useful.'

Lance shook his head. The way the female mind worked sometimes was beyond his comprehension. 'There are some things that would tempt a man beyond good sense. Your smile is one of them. However, the ease with which you have managed to get into my house tells me that I must have a word with my butler about increasing the security. Any miscreant from the street could enter. You encountered no one?'

'No—and I can find my own way to the coach.'

'I'll make sure you leave the house without being seen. I insist. I certainly don't want any of my guests confronting you looking like that.' Taking her jacket from her, he held it while she thrust her arms into the sleeves. 'I apologise for the rip. A good seamstress should be able to repair it.' Placing his hands on her shoulders, he turned her round to face him. 'I would like to apologise for last night,' he said calmly. 'I can't remember the last time I apologised for anything, so you must forgive me if I appear awkward.'

Belle was not to be so easily mollified. 'What an arrogant man you are to think that after what you did to me last night and the violence that you threatened, I can be placated with a few words of apology. You can apologise all you like, but it still does not absolve you or solve the problem I shall have explaining what you have done to my grandmother.'

His face darkened with annoyance, and Belle could almost feel his struggle to hold his temper in check. 'I could say that your own behaviour—by coming here tonight and breaking into my home, is not beyond reproach either. However, I am truly sorry if I frightened you last night. Despite how it looked, it was never my intention to hurt you.'

'You didn't hurt me. I was simply furious that you should have the audacity to do what you did. And now if you don't mind I would like to leave.'

Turning on her heel, she went to the door. Lance followed, halting her by catching hold of her arm and speaking close to her ear from behind. 'Of course you must go, but before you do, Belle, I will give you a warning. Just one,' he enunciated coldly. 'Call it advice, if you prefer.'

'If I wanted advice,' Belle retorted, spinning round, her eyes sparking green fire, 'I would not come to you.'

'I don't normally receive guests in my bedroom—but then, you are not my guest, are you? If you break into my house again and come to my room and search through my personal belongings, I will lock you in and not release you until you are well and truly ruined. Do you understand me?'

Belle felt a sudden stillness envelope them. Vividly aware of the heat of his body and the spicy scent of his cologne, she was overwhelmingly conscious of the man behind her. She was irritated by the way in which he had skilfully cut through her superior attitude. She knew she had asked for it, but the magnetic attraction still remained beneath all the irritation.

'I'm sure you would like nothing more, but I will not give you that satisfaction. Now, can we go?' He was far too close and Belle was beginning to feel distinctly uncomfortable. The tight tension of regret was beginning to form in her chest that she had dared to come here.

Lance continued to hold her arm. Now the issue of the necklace was out of the way he was reluctant to let her go, and to his way of thinking it was time she received her come-uppance and realised the danger of coming uninvited to a man's bedroom.

'Not yet. I have not quite finished with you.'

'Are you saying I am in danger?'

Black brows arched above gleaming blue eyes. 'Of the worst kind, I fear. Tell me, Belle, have you ever been kissed?'

The tension in her chest was tightening. 'No man kisses me except the man I want.'

An almost lecherous smile tempted his lips as his eyes did a slow perusal of her lips before travelling to the slim, erect column of her neck, to the beckoning fullness of her breasts straining beneath her blouse. The all-too-apparent woman-liness of her and the heady scent of her perfume evoked a strong stirring of desire, and he felt a familiar stirring in his loins.

'Then I will have to *make* you want me, Belle.'

He moved closer, close enough so that she was trapped and could not move without coming into contact with him. He braced his forearms against the door and gazed down at her face. He ached to caress the womanly softness of her, to hold her close, and ease the lusting ache that gnawed at the pit of his belly.

His nearness threatened to destroy Belle's confidence and composure, but only threatened. This man was far too bold to allow even a small measure of comfort. She lifted her head imperiously, and her eyes glinted as they glared into his.

'I don't want you to show me. I don't want you to touch me, so kindly step back and let me go at once.'

'Not a chance,' he drawled. Gripping both her upper arms, he pulled her to him, holding her tightly against his chest, his fingers digging cruelly into her soft flesh.

Resolutely she squirmed against him. She saw his eyes darken in the dim light, his lean and handsome features starkly etched. A strange feeling, until this moment unknown to her, fluttered within her breast, and she was halted for a brief passing of time by the flood of excitement that surged through her. With renewed determination she forced it down.

'I asked you to release me. I really must go.'

'What's the rush?' he murmured against her ear and brushed warm kisses along her throat. 'I'd like to show you that I in no way resemble those fancy bucks who dance attendance on you night after night, pouring flatteries and endearments into your ears they do not mean.'

'Leave me be. And don't get any high-handed ideas that you are any better than they,' she stated shortly.

'Say what you like, Belle, but I suspect that you'd prefer a real man to warm your bed than any of them.'

His statement brought a bright hue creeping into Belle's cheeks. 'I find that remark extremely insulting and uncalled for. The conduct of the men I meet at the affairs I attend has been exemplary and I have no complaints. You speak as if you are some great gift to womankind, whereas you could learn a lot from them. And now I wish to leave. Anything is preferable to this. At least they are gentlemen and wouldn't take advantage of a woman as you are doing.'

'Don't you bet on it, but relax, Belle. I'm not going to hurt you.'

An iron-thewed arm slipped about her waist and brought her against that broad chest. Belle thought to remain passive in his embrace and did not struggle as his mouth lowered upon hers, but they flamed with a fiery heat that warmed her whole body. That was when she realised the idea was ludicrous and a gross miscalculation of her power to deny him, for the kiss went through her with the impact of a broadside.

Her eyes closed and the strength of his embrace and the hard pressure of his loins made her all too aware of the danger she was in, that he was a strong, determined man, and that he was treating her as he would any woman he had desire for. Her head swam and she was unable to still the violent tremor of delight that seized her, touching every nerve until they were aflame with desire. Her world began to tilt, and she was lost in a dreamy limbo where nothing mattered but the closeness of his body and the circling protection of his arms.

Moments before she had thought herself knowledgeable about men, but now, as Lance slid one hand down to her buttock and pressed her to him, she became acutely conscious of her innocence.

His lips caressed and clung to hers, finding them moist and honey sweet, and for a slow beat in time, hers responded, parting under his mounting fervour. She leaned against him, melting more closely to him, as though the strength had gone from her. Aware of her weakening, he raised his head and lifted her in his arms.

'Put me down,' Belle panted breathlessly, panic rising. 'This is not at all what I want.'

'To hell with what you want, lady,' Lance muttered thickly. 'I can feel your need, Belle. It is the same as my own.'

'Please,' she cried. 'This game has gone on long enough.'

'Games are for children. But this is something more between a man and a woman.' His eyes burned into hers as he strode purposefully to the bed with her. Kneeling on the mattress, he lowered her to its softness and before she could move his arms came down on either side, trapping her between them.

'You beast,' she hissed. 'You filthy beast. How dare you lay your hands on me…?'

He silenced her with his lips, kissing her long and deep and hard. She struggled, but her physical resistance was useless against his strength and his unswerving seduction. Lowering his weight on to her body, he cradled her head between his arms. He was strong, muscular, savage even and very determined, and for a moment Belle felt her insides lurch—she didn't know why—and in the pit of her stomach flared a spark of something, and again she didn't know what or why.

'Don't be afraid,' he breathed against her throat. 'I won't hurt you. Let yourself enjoy it.'

'I can't,' she argued.

'Yes, you can.'

Again he found her lips and parted them. Shuddering excitement passed through her, and the strength ebbed from her limbs. Not for a moment did Lance break the kiss that was inciting her. His mouth was hungering, turning to a heated, crushing demand. Her anger had become raw hunger, cindered beneath the white heat of their mutual desires. It was sudden, the awakened fires, the hungering lust, the bittersweet ache of passion such as Belle could never have imagined.

His position gave him full access to her body. Pulling her shirt out of the waistband of her breeches, his hand slowly snaked its way up to the tantalising fullness of her naked breast, cupping it, teasing her nipple until it was a hard bud. She made a sound deep in her throat. She wasn't sure if it was a protest or merely a sound of pleasure she couldn't contain, so wonderful did it feel. She was kissing him voraciously as the pleasure swiftly escalated, her entire body trembling with desire. She moaned again and wrapped her arms around his neck, shoving her fingers in his hair without even thinking about it, for she couldn't seem to help herself and it seemed the most natural thing to do.

Lance closed his eyes, intense desire for this woman torturing him and making him acutely conscious of the celibate life he had led for some time now. As he caressed the sweet, young body, his flesh betrayed his need, rising up against his will. He was hungry for her and could hardly restrain himself to free her from her garments, possibly even tearing them if they resisted his fingers.

His hands slid from her breast and Belle felt him fumbling with the fastenings of her breeches. Instantly her sanity returned and with a horrified gasp, she broke away from him, her whole manner conveying her fury, which reappeared with shocking speed. With a tremendous effort of will she flung herself away from him and rolled off the bed. She stood glaring at him, breathing hard, her hair tangled in disarray about her shoulders, her green eyes burning, completely unaware of the vision she presented to his hungering eyes.

'How dare you?' she hissed. 'How dare you do that to me? I will not be forced.'

Struggling for control, finding it with effort, getting off the bed, Lance straightened his clothes. 'Come now, Belle,' he managed to say, smiling, though he himself was shaken by the moment. 'It was only a kiss—an innocent kiss, nothing more sordid than that.' But he was not convinced by his words. With her long sleek legs encased in breeches, he was led to think that he had never caressed any that had evoked his imagination as much as those. The lingering impression of those trim thighs entangled with his own had done much to awaken a manly craving that had gone unappeased for some months.

He cursed himself for letting Belle Ainsley affect him in

this way. He went from hot to cold, a sensation not normal for him, a man who had always had a woman at his whim, had enjoyed a woman casually and made love to her for his pleasure. Now this young woman needed to be taught a lesson and he could hardly keep his hands off her.

Belle's anger was boiling. Every single word she uttered seemed to make it worse, as if it were feeding upon itself. And having no other outlet for this anger, it would continue to grow and fester.

'A kiss that would have led to other things—which was what you had in mind you—you lecher—had I not had the presence of mind to end it,' she flared, furious with herself for not only responding to it, but *liking* what he had done to her. 'You forced your will on me, forced me to kiss you. I did not invite you to do that.'

'I forced nothing,' he said, raking his fingers through his hair. 'You brought it on yourself when you decided to invade my bedchamber, don't forget.'

He sounded entirely too smug in saying that. 'Only because I thought it wouldn't have you in it. I am here because I had no choice if I was to retrieve the necklace.'

'Choice? Yes, indeed.' He turned her angry words aside as he walked round the bed to stand before her, the burning heat back in his eyes. 'Choice you are, my love.' He ran his fingers down the soft curve of her cheek. 'The very cream of the lot.'

His soft answer and soothing caress awoke once again tingling answers in places Belle tried to ignore. This betrayal by her own body aroused an impatient vexation. She had foolishly thought that all the quickening fires she had just felt in his arms had been thoroughly quenched by her anger. But she was becoming increasingly aware of the folly of that conclusion. Where his finger touched, she burned. It was a hard fact for her pride to accept. He was capable of scattering her wits in a thousand different directions. She wished she could deny it, for she realised he had a way of affecting her that made her uneasy of future encounters.

He stood before her, his wide shoulders narrowing her world to a dark, limited space. She glanced past him, but quickly dismissed the idea of darting for the door, for she strongly suspected he was as quick as he was strong. Shaking her head, Belle stepped back from him and pressed a trembling hand to his chest to hold him away.

'You have been too long with the military and got too comfortable with the camp-followers to know how to treat a lady. I've heard how soldiers like to dally here and there at their leisure—I can't imagine officers being any different.'

'In some cases your imagination is correct, Belle. After years of soldiering, adjusting to civilian life is not an easy matter, and I, for one, intend to try.'

'And I am not gullible enough to believe in miracles,' she bit back. 'I am not one of your common women. I will not be tumbled between the sheets and left to bear a child in shame. This was a mistake, a mistake you will have cause to regret.' She walked past him, heading for the door.

'A mistake for you, maybe, but not for me. You see, I know you now, Belle. I know how you react to my kiss, to being in my arms. The next time you may not be so eager to leave.'

She whirled in a flare of rage. 'Why, you conceited—buffoon. There won't be a next time. I would see you in hell first.'

Striding towards her, he bent his head, his laughing breath touching her brow as he chucked her playfully under the chin. 'Your endearments intrigue me, but I did not fight with every measure of skill and wit at my command to preserve my life as well as my company of men on the battlefields of Spain and Waterloo, to have it taken away in peacetime by a mere slip of a girl.'

'The slip of a girl you speak of I left behind in America, my lord.'

'My eyes confirm what you say, Belle,' he murmured, his eyes probing with flaming warmth into hers. 'You are what any man would desire—softly rounded in all the right places, yet slender and long of limb. You have whet my imagination to such a degree that my pleasure would be to throw you back on to the bed and make love to you.'

She stepped back. Behind the pattern of her beautiful face, she was outraged. The red blushes on her cheeks had settled into a dark glow, the flush of sudden battle in her face. Her retreat was necessary to cool her burning cheeks, and to ease to some degree the unruly pacing of her heart. 'Stop it. You should not be saying such things.'

'Come now, Belle, believe me, after surrendering your virginity you will be amazed at the pleasures to be found in the arms of a lover.'

'Lover? Ha!' she scoffed. 'The man I surrender my virtue to will be my husband. It is not something I shall give away in the weakness of a moment in the bed of the vilest of rakes.'

Lance did not seem surprised or insulted. Undaunted, he lifted his brows quizzically, a twist of humour about his beautifully moulded lips. But never had he looked more challenging. 'This is indeed a crushing moment, Belle! I have been called some names in my life, but I must confess never to have been called—the vilest of rakes.'

Belle saw him struggling to hold back his deep amusement. Then, to her rising dismay, he threw back his head, letting out rich, infectious laughter. 'This has really made my day—"the vilest of rakes".'

'You are insufferable,' Belle cried angrily, her rage pouring out. 'Let me out of this room this instant.'

'You needn't be distressed by what has just happened between us,' he said, no longer laughing, but still quietly amused. 'Making love can be just as pleasurable for a woman as for a man. Are you so fearful of losing your virtue, Belle?'

She thrust her face forwards to deliver her own angry re-

joinder. 'With you? Yes!' she answered with a finality that
brooked no discussion. 'I will not allow myself to be sullied
and then tossed aside by you, leaving me little hope of attract-
ing a respectable husband. Rumours have a way of shattering
lives, my lord. No man wants spoiled goods.'

Lance offered her a cajoling smile, appealing to her with
all the charm he was capable of putting into play. He had not
got to where he was in life without becoming aware that many
women he had known had been intrigued and captivated by
the smile on his lips.

'I'll have you know that right now you're presenting a definite challenge to me,' he accused, amusement gleaming in his
eyes. 'I've never before known a woman who seems to loathe
me one minute and the next accept my attentions as you did
just now on the bed. Can I not persuade you to relent?'

'You certainly know the right words to entangle a gullible
maid's mind, my lord. But I am not gullible and certainly
know the risks I would encounter if I allowed myself to be
taken in by the likes of you. What woman would willingly
invite such disgrace?'

Cocking a magnificent brow enquiringly, Lance peered
down his noble nose at her. 'Not all women who know me
would consider it a disgrace.'

'Just how many women have you addled with comments
of that sort, my lord?' Belle asked snidely. 'If any of them
believe you then they must be simple minded. You can say
what you like, but any *lady* would be upset to be involved in
a conversation such as this. It is hardly a topic to soothe one's
nerves.'

His eyes danced as he probed the bright green orbs. 'I'll
allow the subject itself wouldn't soothe your nerves, Belle,
but the joining of our bodies in the ritual of making love
would do wonders for relaxing you. I'd be more than willing
to show you.'

'I'm sure you would, but I'm not going to give you the

chance. Now please stop it. You are far too persistent for my peace of mind.'

'When I see something I want, I go for it.' He shrugged nonchalantly. 'It's in my nature. At least the men under my command thought so.'

'I'm not one of your men,' she retorted, and had cause to wonder what would follow as his eyes gleamed tauntingly into hers.

'Believe me, my lovely Belle, looking as you do, I would never mistake you for one of them—not even for an instant. None of my men ever looked even remotely appealing to me.' Lance chuckled softly. Devilment shone in his blue eyes as he placed a finger beneath her chin and tilted her face to his. 'Don't be alarmed. Relax. I'm not going to kiss you again. At least not yet.'

Suddenly Belle found herself trying to gather the shattered pieces of her aplomb. His persuasive voice seemed to bombard her very being.

'Just be thankful I've decided to let you leave.'

She met his warmly alluring eyes with a cool stare as she warned him crisply, 'I should jolly well hope so. If you lay one hand upon me, my lord, I'll scream the house down. That much I promise you.'

'In which case, I shall comply with your wishes. Your presence in my bedchamber would take some explaining to my guests.'

Belle now had cause to regret her impulsive decision to come to his house. It was the kind of bad behaviour she had indulged in when she was a child—too hasty to jump in, too stubborn to draw back before it was too late, and suffering regret afterwards. There was more than just regret this time, however, much more.

She flung her head backwards so that more of her hair was loosed from its pins, coiling down her spine, so gloriously a shade of rich brown, now as dark as night. Her chin jutted dangerously and her eyes flashed.

'How noble of you,' she uttered sarcastically. 'If you know what's good for you, you will never lay hands on me again.'

Her lips curled back over her teeth in a snarl, and Lance thought she was like an animal on the defensive. Dear God, she was a magnificent creature, but heaven help the poor devil who got landed with her as a wife. He liked his women quick-tempered, spirited and with fire in their veins. It made for a satisfying and exciting relationship, but Belle Ainsley with her bull-headed stubbornness would not only need a husband as strong-willed as herself, but with the patience of a saint.

'As to that, Belle, I shall make no promises. Who knows what will come from our association? I will tell you now that I consider my independence of great importance. I am not necessarily anxious to give it up immediately now I have returned home, but I may just decide to forget the promise I made to myself to remain a bachelor and take you to wife just to show you what delights can be had between a married couple.'

Belle glowered at him and spoke with derision. 'What subtle ploys you practise, Lord Bingham. If you think to get me into your bed with your liberal use of the word *marriage,* you will find I am not as gullible as you think.'

Lance laughed outright. 'I get the message, Belle, so continue with your parties and concentrate on finding a husband—which is what the Season is all about. I've seen the many smitten swains following at your heels. I would think you'd find it difficult to choose among them. Although I can almost pity the man you eventually settle on. The poor man won't have a moment's peace.'

'Like you I am in no hurry to wed, and Grandmother is not putting pressure on me to do so. I have only recently come to England and I am testing the water, so to speak. I am quite happy with my single state.'

'Ah, but you will be caught and settle down to connubial bliss with one of your suitors ere long.'

Angry and humiliated beyond anything she had known in her life, as she watched him turn to retrieve his discarded jacket, Belle vowed to make him regret in a thousand different ways that he'd tampered with her. Her eyes settled on a small table where he had put the pouch and the smile that tempted her lips was one of cunning. Starting with the necklace.

So, he thought he had outwitted her, did he, by telling her some lame story about it belonging to his own grandmother? How easily she had swallowed it. How gullible she had been, but no more. She would not give him his victory. While picking up the pouch, which she slipped into her pocket, she grabbed hold of her hat, dropping it. She bent to retrieve it, and, turning round, Lance halted abruptly, for he found himself confronting a very fetching derrière stuck up in the air.

He emited a low groan with the gnawing hunger she aroused in him, for he had never seen anything quite so stimulating as those snugly bound buttocks, for the tight trousers left nothing to the imagination. Tempted to go to her and slide his arm around her waist and pull her back to him, to forget all logic and again sweep her down on to his bed, he halted, prone to wonder if he was having another lewd fantasy involving this precocious young woman, and it came as no surprise to him that she had sharply awakened his manly cravings like none other before. He stepped back as she straightened up, having retrieved her hat.

Aware of the pouch in her pocket, unaware of Lance's lewd thoughts, her smile turned to one of triumph at her own cleverness. It was the perfect payback. Pulling her hat down over her ears, tucking her wayward locks beneath it, she turned to the door.

They were descending the stairs when Belle's worst nightmare was realised. Rowland Gibbon emerged from the dining room without bothering to close the doors behind him. Some of Lance's guests followed him into the hall. Cursing softly, Lance immediately took Belle's arm and was already pulling her back up the stairs in an attempt to forestall a calamity, but too late. Rowland had seen them. He let out a loud gusto and started towards the bottom of the stairs, his heels clicking on the black-and-white tiled floor.

'Ha! What's this, Lance? Trying to hide from your guests. I won't have it. Already Lady Marlow and the other ladies are feeling quite bereft and have sent me to find you.'

Realising the futility of trying to escape, Lance and Belle made a final descent of the stairs.

Rowland's eyes shifted to Lance's companion, whom he thought to be a youth hanging back. Rowland raised an enquiring eyebrow. 'And who have we here?' he asked, bending over to peruse the face under the hat. He turned to Lance with a grin. 'So, you had another engagement. Are you not going to introduce me?'

'You've already had that pleasure.'

'I don't think so—although the lad does seem somewhat familiar.' Without more ado he snatched the hat from Belle's head, drawing a shocked gasp of furious indignation from her. Rowland uttered a soft whistle when her hair cascaded about her shoulders. His exclamation was one of disbelief and he chuckled softly. 'Why, 'tis no lad I see before me.'

The guests let out a collective gasp, and a few giggles came from the maids of the house, who had stopped in their tracks to gawp at the youth who had a definite feminine air about him, only to be shooed away by an irate butler.

'Leave it, Rowland,' Lance uttered through his teeth.

Rowland wasn't going to let it drop. With Belle's identity revealed, he turned his incredulous look on Lance and back to the slender, black garbed figure. 'Good Lord! If it isn't Miss Ainsley!'

Belle felt physically ill and glanced towards Lord Bingham's guests. She recognised several of them as being elite members of the *ton*. The expressions on their faces ranged from amusement to icy condemnation. Knowing there was no help for it but to brazen it out, in a defiant gesture she thrust out her chin and squared her shoulders.

'As you see, sir,' she replied coolly. 'Please don't ask me to explain what I am doing here dressed like this. You would not believe it.'

Smiling broadly, Rowland laughed. 'I might. I shall certainly enjoy hearing it.'

'Miss Ainsley took the opportunity of me being otherwise engaged to steal into my house to retrieve the necklace I took from her last night,' Lance told him, careful to keep his voice low. It was bad enough that his guests had witnessed Belle coming down his stairs with him attired as she was, without providing them with her reason for being in his house.

Comprehension dawned in Rowland's eyes, quickly followed by astonishment. 'Ah, she did?'

'Indeed. My disguise didn't deceive this clever young lady and she must be complimented on her success. She was about to walk off with the necklace when I returned home unexpectedly and took it back.'

'Did she, now? Then she is to be congratulated, but I'm sorry you got it back. I would have been in order to demand my money back, for I would have considered I'd won the bet.'

Belle frowned, but what Sir Rowland was implying didn't sink in immediately. Until she saw Lance cringe.

'Take no notice of what Rowland says, Belle.'

But as if he hadn't spoken, she said, 'A bet? Am I to understand last night, when you posed as a highwayman and put me through hell, was all about a bet?'

'It wasn't like that.'

'It wasn't?'

'No,' Lance assured her. 'I told you, I was simply retrieving my own property.'

'That's what you told me,' she flared. 'But now I am not inclined to believe you.'

'It's true. Believe me.'

'And the bet?'

'Was merely a reaction to Rowland's scepticism.'

Belle glanced at Sir Rowland to see him somewhat shame-faced now. 'You mean he didn't believe you would succeed?'

'I didn't,' Rowland said. 'Not for a minute.'

Belle didn't reply immediately. All she could think of was Lord Bingham and his friend laughing together at her when they'd made their bet. As the colour mounted high in her cheeks and warmed her ears, the people crowding in the doorway became a blur.

'Well, I'm glad you had some fun at my expense—enjoying yourselves enormously, I don't doubt.' The look she turned on Lance was murderous. 'You accost me in the early hours—at gunpoint, I might add—you steal my grandmother's neck-lace, scare me half out of my wits by threatening to shoot me—and all because you had money riding on it.' Moving to stand before him, she thrust her face close to his. 'My God! My breaking into your house was nothing compared to that, you—you animal. I hope you enjoy your winnings.'

Turning on her heel, she strode past him, past a stupefied butler, who was standing with his mouth agape, her only thought being to get out and away from her tormentor and his astonished guests as quickly as she could.

'Belle, wait. Your grandmother?'

She spun round. 'What about her?'

'She will have to be told.'

'I don't think so—you see, there is nothing to tell.'

'Wait.'

'Go to hell,' she bit back, whirling round and hurrying to the door, unable to say more because she couldn't get any more words past the lump in her throat.

Lance followed, but she rushed out of the door before he

could stop her. With her coach waiting down the street, she was inside and on her way home within moments.

Lance stood in the doorway, watching her coach disappear.

After ushering the guests who had watched the whole scene back into the dining room and closing the door, Rowland came to stand beside him and casually remarked, 'I take it she didn't know about the bet?'

'Of course not.' Lance spun round. 'Do you see *stupid idiot* written on my face, Rowland?'

He shrugged. 'Why should it matter to her if we made a bet? You won, don't forget—and besides, Miss Ainsley's intrusion into your house was not the action of a respectably reared young lady, now, was it?'

'She came here for all the right reasons.'

'Well, I think you've come out of it pretty well. You have the necklace and two hundred pounds.'

Frowning, Lance closed the door. Something puzzled him—Belle's parting remark about her grandmother. She had nothing to tell her, she had said. Why would she say that—unless…?

Lance looked at Rowland. 'Wait here.'

'Lance—what…?'

'Wait.'

Rowland watched his friend bound up the stairs two at a time. Not a minute passed and he was back.

'Well?' Rowland asked, unable to hide his curiosity.

'She's taken them.'

'Taken what?'

'The diamonds.'

Rowland smiled, his face almost comical in its disbelief. 'Do you mean to tell me that the delectable Miss Isabelle Ainsley has outwitted you?'

'This time, Rowland—and it will be the last. When I get my hands on that green-eyed witch, I'll…'

Rowland could clearly see that Lance's pride had suffered a grievous blow. 'You'll what?'

A smile flickered into Lance's eyes as he shot a wry look at his friend. 'I haven't made up my mind yet. But whatever I decide, she won't like it.'

He stood and looked at the closed door through which Belle had disappeared, thinking of her in his arms, of her soft warm body curving to him, of her long, lovely limbs entwining with his. The hot blood surged through him and he chuckled to himself, amazed that one young woman could make him feel like this. He was worse than any rutting stag in her company.

In helpless misery Belle leaned back against the upholstery inside the coach, her heart filled with dread in anticipation of the condemnation she would ultimately receive from her grandmother. Had her departure from Lord Bingham's house not been witnessed by his guests, she could have returned the diamonds to their rightful place and her grandmother would have been none the wiser.

She was confident the coach driver and the two footmen wouldn't say anything about being held up. They were terrified she would accuse them of being irresponsible. After all, they were supposed to be taking care of her granddaughter. They were armed and should have been prepared for such a thing happening.

As it was there was nothing for it but to tell her grandmother everything. There would be no redemption for her, she knew that. People were too quick to judge and condemn. She had already tarnished her reputation with her liaison with Carlton Robinson when she had known no better, and there were those among the *ton*—ladies mostly, who saw her as an American upstart who outshone their own daughters, and deeply resented her popularity among London's eligible bachelors and therefore reducing their chances of making a good match—who would take vindictive delight in her down-fall. In their eyes she was a shameless wanton.

As for Lord Bingham, she could not see her actions reflect-ing on him, she thought bitterly. If there was a scandal, she doubted he would be embarrassed by it. The man was a com-plete and utter scoundrel and she hoped never to set eyes on him again—and yet she did wonder how he would react when he discovered she had taken back the necklace. She could only hope that he would concede defeat and not pursue it, but deep down she knew he wasn't the kind of man to let it drop.

Her grandmother arrived home the following afternoon feeling much better, but insisted on going to her room to lie down, summoning Belle to follow her up.

From her bed where she was sitting propped up against a mountain of pillows, the dowager countess looked at her granddaughter perched on the edge of a chair next to the bed. 'Did you enjoy yourself at Carlton House the other night, Isabelle?'

'Yes, very much,' Belle answered, putting off the moment to tell her of the awful thing she had done. 'I always enjoy parties and the Prince Regent excelled himself.

The countess's gaze became pointed. 'Are you feeling well, Isabelle? You are very pale.'

'Yes—I am quite well. I—I didn't sleep very well last night.'

'Then you must have an early night. I must say that I would have preferred you not to have had anything to do with Lord Bingham. I sincerely hope he has not approached you since?' The countess noticed that a bright pink had swept into her granddaughter's cheeks, a sure sign that the girl was guilty about something. 'He has, hasn't he—the scoundrel.'

'I—I happened to encounter him yesterday after visiting you. He—he rode part of the way home with me.' She quailed at the look that entered her grandmother's eyes—a mixture of disappointment, hurt and anger. 'I'm sorry, Grandmother. I know you asked me not to have anything to do with him, but I—I couldn't avoid him.'

The countess rested her head against the pillows and closed her eyes, deep in thought. 'That man is too persistent,' she murmured at length. 'I have decided we shall leave for Wiltshire earlier than I intended. I would like to think that at Harworth Hall you will not be so easily available to him. Unfortunately that may not be the case. The Ryhill estate borders Harworth Hall, so unless our neighbour remains in London—as I sincerely hope he will—then there is every chance that the two of you will meet some time. Hopefully it will be later rather than sooner, and in the meantime Lord Bingham will have found himself a wife.'

Belle fell silent. As relentlessly as she had tried to thrust that blue-eyed devil from her mind, regretfully he was still very much in residence. She remembered what it had felt like to be in his arms, how his kiss had made her forget everything but the two of them, how he had sent her emotions spiralling upwards, her passion mounting until she feared for her sanity. In fact, it was something of a shock to her that she was just as susceptible to his absence as she was to his presence.

It seemed far fetched to think that one man could move her to such extremes, yet when she compared her joy at the feelings he had awakened in her to the strange, inexplicable yearning that presently thwarted her mood, what else could she put it down to?

Anger stirred inside her, anger at her response to his seduction, at the betrayal of her body. Damn him, she thought. How dare he do this to her? And now her grandmother had told her his home in Wiltshire adjoined Harworth Hall, and she found herself in the vexing position of how to avoid him in the future. What could she possibly do to save herself now that he looked like some godly being sent to earth to play havoc with her mind and her heart?

Unable to stop her mind running off in a dozen different directions, she got up and went to the window and stood looking out. Her back was ramrod straight, her hands clenched by her sides.

'Isabelle? What is it?'

With a worried, haunted look, as though she carried a burden too heavy to bear on her young shoulders, she turned and looked at her grandmother, meeting her questioning eyes. She would have to tell her everything. It could not be avoided.

Chapter Five

Belle thought her grandmother was going to have an apoplectic fit as she hesitantly told her of everything that had transpired from the night Lord Bingham had played highwayman. Her eyes never moved from her granddaughter's face. She seemed unable to speak, to form any words, from between her rigidly clamped lips. When Belle had finished speaking she remained for a while in contemplation of her clasped hands. Belle respected her silence, stifling her painful anxiety.

At last the older woman raised her eyelids and looked at her and Belle shivered at the anger and disappointment in her eyes.

'I am deeply shocked, Isabelle. Deeply so.'

'Grandmother, I am so sorry.'

'Sorry? Isabelle, what you have done is outrageous. Among other things, to enter the house and the bedchamber of any man, never mind a practised seducer, was disgraceful. Do you know what you have done? No decent man will have you now. Did he touch you?'

Growing increasingly alarmed by her grandmother's anger

and distress, Belle actually considered telling a lie, but the increased colour in her face told its own story.

'So, he did.' The Countess's voice was low and shaking. 'You foolish, foolish girl. The answer is written all over your face.'

'Grandmother, please don't upset yourself. It was my fault. I—I should not have been there.'

'At least you have got that right. You may not understand the enormity of what you have done, but he knows. He is just like his grandfather—uses women for his own amusement and then discards them. I will not let Lance Bingham do that to you. He has to do what is right.'

'Oh, please,' Belle burst out, having no idea what her grandmother meant by that. 'He did nothing so terrible. It was just a kiss, nothing more than that.'

'It was enough,' she said, with biting, icy calm. 'Do not forget that you are already treading on thin ice in society's eyes because of your liaison with Carlton Robinson. Another scandal will ruin you completely. Your reputation was shattered the minute you entered Lord Bingham's house, destroying any chance of your making a decent marriage—and to add to the shame your wantonness was witnessed by the elite of London society. You were seen coming down the stairs together, so everyone will have correctly surmised that you were with him in his bedchamber. No other man will have you now. As soon as the scandal breaks—indeed, I shall be surprised if it hasn't already—you will be blacklisted. We have to go and see him, you do realise that, don't you?'

'I would rather not see Lord Bingham ever again,' Belle mumbled miserably.

Her grandmother smiled thinly. 'You have no choice— wretched girl. I'm surprised that after all the trouble he went to to get the diamonds, he could be persuaded to part with them.'

'He wasn't. I mean—I took them back when he wasn't

looking. He told me they belonged to him—but I didn't believe him. Is it true, Grandmother?'

'Yes, it is true, and if I had been aware of what had occurred, I would have let him keep them. You should have let
me deal with it. What were you thinking?'

'What is the story behind the diamonds?' Belle asked.
'Will you not tell me?'

'Never mind that now. What is important is how we are
going to extricate you from this sordid affair without complete
ruin to your reputation.'

The countess knew the lengths the *ton* would go to os-
tracise Isabelle—and there were many who, regarding her
as an American upstart who gathered men around her like
flies, would enjoy slating her. Those who were anxious for
their own daughters to make good marriages were jealous of
Isabelle's burst into society, putting their own darling daughters in the shade. It wasn't just her beauty that drew the attention of single males. There was a vibrancy about her, a sparkle
that was absent in many of the newly launched débutantes.
Now they would have enough fuel to cinder Isabelle and turn
to ashes any infatuation that London's bachelors might have
felt for the girl.

The countess prided herself on being realistic and a moment's thought made her understand that what she was about
to do was the right thing for Belle—and it was borne out of the
fact that she refused to let history repeat itself. The countess
had been treated very badly by Lance Bingham's grandfather,
Stuart Bingham. She still felt the pain of being jilted and the
humiliation that almost ruined her reputation that followed,
and she didn't want this to happen to her granddaughter. The
diamonds—a Bingham family heirloom—had been given to
her on her betrothal to Stuart Bingham. When he had broken
the engagement and asked for them to be returned, as a form
of punishment she had refused and had kept them to this day.
Perhaps now was the time to give them back.

Lance Bingham was handsome and so well mannered that resorting to posing as a highwayman to get back something that by rights belonged to him, one could hardly believe that in doing so he had done anything wicked. He was so like his grandfather with that merry twinkle in his eye, that soft smiling curl to his mouth, the way he spoke. She had noticed the way he had taken Belle on to the floor at Carlton House, the way he had looked at her. Who could help it, and the idle thought occurred to her that here was a man whom Belle could not get the better of. He might be the one person who could tame her wild and rebellious granddaughter. Perhaps it was time to forget all the old grievances after all.

Lance was in his study when the butler came to inform him that the Dowager Countess of Harworth and Miss Isabelle Ainsley had arrived and that the countess insisted on seeing him.

The word *insist* caused Lance's eyebrows to snap together into a frown. 'Show them into the drawing room,' he said shortly. 'I'll see them in there.'

Keeping her eyes straight ahead of her, Belle followed reluctantly in the wake of her grandmother. The butler swept open a pair of carved oaken doors and stepped aside to admit them into the drawing room, a comfortable, tastefully furnished room.

Belle's entire being was engulfed in mortification, her misery increasing a thousandfold as she sat stiffly on the edge of her chair across from her grandmother and facing the fireplace. She couldn't help remembering the last time she had been in this house, and knowing how furious Lord Bingham must have been on discovering she had taken the diamonds when his back was turned, she dreaded the moment when she would have to confront him and see what she knew would surely be contempt written all over his features.

She was not wrong. The man who strode in moments later,

his tall frame clad in impeccably tailored dark blue trousers and coat and white shirt and neckcloth at the throat, bore little resemblance to the laughing man she had met at Carlton House only four days ago. Today he was an aloof, icy stranger who gave her no more than a cursory glance before focusing all his attention on the stately woman who was watching him closely.

'This is an unusual occurrence, Countess, for an Ainsley to step over the Bingham threshold,' Lance remarked coolly. 'Not that I don't welcome it, you understand. In my opinion it is high time that whatever grievances there have been between our families in the past were left there. However, you could have spared yourselves the embarrassment of this visit. I had every intention of calling on you later.'

'Then I have saved you the trouble,' the countess replied stiffly, her purple turbaned head erect and her gloved hands folded upon the jewelled head of her cane. Having lived with her dislike of the Binghams for many years, she was too carefully schooled in good manners to show it.

'Nevertheless it is good of you to take the time to call at this unfortunate time. Can I offer you refreshment?'

'No, thank you. I have not come here to make polite conversation,' she stated ominously, looking at Lord Bingham intently.

He crossed to the fireplace, draped his arm across the mantel and turned, regarding his visitors with a cool and speculative gaze. His gaze lingered on Belle, who was watching him with a cool reticence. He could not help but admire the way she looked. Her overall appearance was flawless and he was quickly coming to the conclusion that she would set the standard by which all other women would have to be judged, at least in his mind.

Her garments were in the height of fashion, and her slender form complemented them perfectly. The high-standing collar and the waist of her short, cropped jacket gave something of a military flare to the dark blue creation of soft wool. A dove-grey silk stock flecked with darker threads was wound about her slender throat and the skirt was in a contrasting paler blue to the jacket. Her glorious hair had been smoothed back from her face and caught up at the crown in a heavy coil, upon which sat a dark blue hat, which matched her jacket. Several feathery curls had escaped the confines of the style, lending a charming softness to her creamy skin, and the appeal in her large, silkily lashed green eyes was so strong that he had to mentally shake himself free of their spell.

'No, I thought not,' he replied in reply to the countess's remark.

'I recognise that I must lend all my support to my grand-daughter at this time,' the countess went on. 'She has told me of everything that has transpired since the two of you met at Carlton House and how you forcibly removed some valuables from her person and terrified my servants. I don't like primi-tive behaviour, Lord Bingham—especially when it threatens a member of my family.'

'I saw something that belonged to me and I took it back.' He flicked his brows upwards mockingly. 'Primitive behav-iour,' he stated quietly. 'However, it proved to be a pointless exercise since your granddaughter took them back.' His eyes swung to Belle. 'Is that not so, miss?'

Belle stiffened her shoulders and met his gaze direct. 'Yes. I saw the opportunity and I took it.'

'I expected better of you, Lord Bingham,' the countess re-marked. 'Your actions were those of a feckless youth—not a distinguished military officer.'

'I agree absolutely. And for what it's worth I regret what I did. I should have approached you over the matter.'

'Yes, you should. However, it's too late for that, which is most unfortunate. I am not here to question what prompted a man of your standing and experience to behave like a halfwit. It is done now and we have to try to make the best of it.'

Lance ignored her reference of him being a halfwit. To argue the point would be stupid and serve no purpose. 'Why are you here, Countess?'

'Because by your actions you have compromised my grand-daughter.'

'I disagree. Your granddaughter compromised herself the moment she entered my house,' he said, not in the least per-turbed. 'So,' he said, going to sit in a large winged chair, prop-ping his right ankle on his left knee and steepling his fingers in front of him, 'am I to believe that your conscience smote you and you have come here to do the right thing and apologise for breaking into my home?'

'My conscience has nothing to do with it,' Belle snapped, clamping her lips together when her grandmother shot her a stern look of displeasure.

'Then do you mind telling me why you are here?' he de-manded, his dagger gaze pinning Belle to her chair.

'My granddaughter in her naïvety came to your house to retrieve something you took from her by force—at the point of a gun, I understand—something valuable she believed was mine. In return you ruined her.'

Abandoning his nonchalant manner and sitting forwards, Lance sounded ready to explode. 'I did what?' he ground out ominously.

'You attempted to seduce a young lady of good breeding in your bedchamber.'

'I did not invite her into my bedchamber. She came of her own volition,' Lance reminded her forcefully, preferring to ignore what she said about seduction since it was true.

'When you found her you should have seen to it that she left your house discreetly and not under the watchful eyes of soci-ety and your servants. I have a moral code, Lord Bingham, and you publicly breached that code by exposing her to scandal.'

'If anyone can make a scandal out of a woman leaving my house—although I feel that I must point out that at the time your granddaughter far more resembled a youth than a respectable young lady—then they need their minds examining.'

'Not when that young lady is my granddaughter.' The countess gave Belle a withering look. 'Lord Bingham's remark leads me to assume you were wearing those appalling breeches you brought with you from America. This is worse than I thought. You have given society enough bait to feed off until the next Season. I recall telling you to dispose of those wretched clothes when you arrived.'

The severe rebuke caused Belle to lower her eyes and mumble, 'I'm sorry, Grandmother. I forgot.'

'What she was wearing is insignificant,' Lance remarked.

'Insignificant! A respectable young lady wearing breeches may seem insignificant to a practised seducer like yourself, Lord Bingham, but Isabelle is nineteen years old with high hopes of making a good marriage and you have ruined her.'

'You know, Countess, I find it amazing,' Lance drawled with some amusement, 'that nearly everyone who knows me is half-afraid of me, except a handful of my friends, you, madam, and your granddaughter. I can only surmise that courage— or recklessness, call it what you will—is passed through the bloodline to her. So,' he finished with a mocking grin, 'I will give you leave to take me to task in my own home if it will make you feel better. What is it you want from me?'

The countess looked at him, her piercing eyes alive with anticipation. 'You may not like what I have to suggest—indeed, I don't like it myself, yet I can think of no other way at present to stop the gossip that will surely ruin Isabelle.'

'Say what's on your mind, Countess. I am listening.'

'There are many kinds of persecution that are not readily apparent, such as the whispered conjectures, the gossip and subtle innuendoes that can destroy a reputation and inflict a lifetime of damage. I can think of only one possible arrangement that can hold sway over that to be adequate enough to protect her. I am suggesting that you marry my grand-daughter.'

Lance was taken aback; his face became livid with anger. 'What? Marry your granddaughter! Have you gone mad?'

'I can assure you that I am not,' the countess stated firmly.

Lance struggled to calm his temper. The suggestion that he marry Belle Ainsley was almost too much to bear. When he next spoke his face was a taut mask of controlled fury. 'Forgive me, Countess. Since your suggestion is not what I expected,' he uttered drily, 'I must take a moment and consider the possible repercussions that may occur because of it.'

Pushed beyond the bounds of reason by her grandmother's words and shamed to the depths of her being, Belle sprang from her chair. 'No,' she cried, managing to drag her voice through the strangling mortification in her chest. This was worse, much worse than she had dreamed it could be. Her glance skidded from her grandmother to Lord Bingham. 'Please believe me, I knew nothing of this. The idea of our marrying is ludicrous. I don't want to marry you.'

Lance's eyes jerked to Belle's and his face became a cynical mask. 'You're absolutely right,' he mocked sarcastically, remembering another time and another face—Delphine's face, a face that still wrenched his damaged heart. Also that of a child he couldn't bear to look at because it reminded him of the woman its arrival into this world had taken from him, reminding him of the guilt that continued to torture him and would not let him be—the guilt of abandoning Delphine in her hour of need. 'It is ludicrous and I don't want to marry you either. And yet all this time I've been harbouring the delusion that all girls yearn to snare wealthy and titled husbands.'

'I am not like other girls,' Belle bit back.

'I sensed that from the moment I met you,' Lance remarked in a bland drawl.

Belle heard the insult in his smoothly worded agreement,

and she almost choked on her chagrin. 'Then that's it. We won't wed.'

'Sit down, Isabelle,' her grandmother ordered with icy calm, turning her determined gaze on Lord Bingham once more when her granddaughter, humiliated to the very core of her being by his unkind words, had obeyed. 'And I would appreciate you addressing my granddaughter with more respect, Lord Bingham.'

Lance allowed a meagre smile to convey his apology. 'After many years as a soldier, Countess, I'm afraid I shall have to relearn the art of gallantry.'

'I dare say there was not much call for it in your encampments. It is with considerable distaste that I feel I must ask this of you. I am doing it for Isabelle's sake. If it were not for the slur you have placed on her virtue, I would put the matter from me and have done with it. Since no decent man will want to marry her now, you will have to do the honourable thing and marry her yourself. I think it's the least you can do. Her birth is as exceptional as yours. She is your equal, so you can have no objections to her suitability.'

A muscle twitched in Lance's cheek as his angry glare took in the two people staring at him. Why did he have this feeling that he was caught in a trap? 'No objections?' he bit back, his face turning positively glacial. 'I have plenty.'

'Yes,' the countess scathingly replied. 'I thought you might.'

'And so has your granddaughter if the look she is giving me is an indication of how she feels.'

'Isabelle will fulfil her part of the bargain.'

'Even though she might thoroughly loathe me?'

'She will do the honourable thing. She may be as averse to marriage as you are just now, but I believe that will change when she realises the seriousness of the situation—and she does not loathe you.'

'No?' Lance questioned, glancing at the beauty who looked

fit to burst with fury. 'We have just listened to her vehement protests. If I discerned anything in her manner, then I'm willing to wager that you would never get her to the altar.'

'You are too free with your wagers, Lord Bingham,' Belle broke in scornfully, 'and I do not care for them. I shall no doubt suffer from the wager you made with your friend Sir Rowland Gibbon for a long time to come.'

'In case your granddaughter didn't give you the full facts, Countess, I shall enlighten you. The reason why I decided to retrieve the diamonds was due to a wager laid down by my good friend,' Lance explained. 'He did not believe I would succeed. I am happy to say that I won the wager, before your granddaughter took it into her mind to enter my house to steal them back. What will you do if I refuse to marry her?'

'Then I shall have to consider having you charged with armed robbery and even go so far as to include attempted seduction.'

'That is ridiculous,' Lance responded with cold sarcasm. 'To openly accuse me would only broadcast throughout London the very scandal you find so damaging to your granddaughter. I will not marry her and that is that.'

'For that I thank you,' Belle retorted with angry sarcasm, ignoring her grandmother's sharp eyes that were telling her to be quiet. 'I think I would rather be ruined in the eyes of the *ton* before consenting to be your wife.'

The eyes he turned on her were hard and a jeering grin showed startling white teeth against the swarthy skin. 'I am glad we are of accord, Belle. *If* I ever decide to take a wife it will be in my own way, with the woman of my choosing, and not when a woman is holding an axe over my head, which is precisely where all my manly instincts rebel.'

'An axe,' she repeated innocently.

His mood was mocking, cruel and angry. 'You know perfectly well what I mean. I don't like being forced. It goes against the grain—my grain.'

'So you intend to go merrily upon your way and not right the wrong you did,' the countess said coldly. 'You should have known what the consequences would be of dallying with an innocent, respectable young woman in your bedroom—that it could affect your life in a most permanent fashion.'

Lance looked at her long and hard, refusing to be moved. He was a man who had made his own choices for most of his life, and as much as he yearned to appease his manly appetites with Belle Ainsley, how could he, like some lapdog, blandly accept this elderly woman's will without yielding his mind?

'As far as I am concerned, Countess, I have done no wrong. Had I done so, I might have even married your granddaughter if she had acted as if she desired marriage to me. It is an unfortunate occurrence, I grant you.

'I do not feel committed to marry her, and to come here and threaten me was most unwise. Do exactly as you have threatened and have me publicly charged and brought up before the Court for armed robbery if it will make you feel better. But do not forget that in order to punish me you will destroy your granddaughter and your own good name. Is that what you want?'

'What I want is fair play, Lord Bingham.'

'In that we are in accord. I am certain that when your society has chewed over the incident, in time, when another scandal hits the scene, it will blow over and be forgotten as they get on with slating someone else.'

His arrogant calm and the recollections of her own ill use at his grandfather's hands brought the countess to her feet, shaking with wrath. 'How dare you refuse to give the respectability of your name to Isabelle—to take advantage of her and then to simply cast her off the way your grandfather...' She halted, breathing heavily as she struggled to bring her anger and her emotions under control. When she next spoke her voice had lost its strength under the strain and at the possibility of opening old wounds.

'Forgive me. This has nothing to do with the past. It is about Isabelle and saving her from ruin. You kissed her—and, yes, I know you found her in your bedchamber, but that did not give you the right to lay your hands on her.'

Suddenly Belle, who had remained a silent observer during her grandmother's outburst, went to her and took her arm with concern. 'Please do not upset yourself, Grandmother. I am sure all this can be sorted out in a calm and reasonable manner.' Drawing herself up straight and squaring her shoulders, looking more like Miss Isabelle Ainsley than she ever had, she fixed Lord Bingham with a level stare.

'I can understand your reticence to marry me, Lord Bingham, and you know I have no more desire to marry you than you have to marry me. We will take our leave of you now, but before we do so I feel that I must say that your behaviour from the very beginning has not been what I would expect from a man of your standing.'

'You are absolutely right and I apologise for any distress I may have caused to you and the servants who were with you that night on the road. For what it's worth, I had no intention of harming any of you.'

'Faced with a masked highwayman with a pistol pointed at us, we weren't to know that. As far as I am concerned the matter is closed.'

'Not quite,' her grandmother said. Taking a velvet box from her reticule, she placed it carefully on a table to the side of Lord Bingham. Slightly puzzled, he looked from the box to her. 'The diamonds, Lord Bingham. The time has come to return them. It will be a relief to be rid of them after all these years. They have been a permanent reminder of a time that is painful for me to remember.'

'You didn't have to hold on to them, Countess.'

'Pride, Lord Bingham. It was pride that made me hold on to them—which you should know all about. I will ask you for the last time. Will you reconsider your decision and marry my granddaughter?'

In the same tone of voice in which he would have shoved away a hand offering a box of sweetmeats to him, he said, 'No, Countess, certainly not.'

The countess understood that his decision was irrevocable. She had lost. 'Then if you will excuse us, I will not waste any more of my time. Come, Isabelle.'

The countess swept out of the room, followed by her granddaughter. A deadly calm had settled over Belle, banishing everything but her shame and humiliation. There was nothing she could do. Her grandmother's arguments had slid off him like a smooth, frozen block of ice. Her grandmother could not compel a man to marry her granddaughter when he neither loved nor desired her and when his self-interest could be served as well by some other solution. Pride alone might perhaps constrain him.

She looked squarely at Lord Bingham as he held the door open for her to pass through, and as she met his gaze her small chin lifted and her spine stiffened. Lance saw her put up a valiant fight for control—a fight she won—and she looked as regally erect as a proud young queen as she followed after her grandmother, a dark blue hat on her head instead of a crown.

Only the ragged pulse that had leapt to life in his throat attested to Lance's own disquiet as he stared after her with mingled feelings of regret and concern. However, he was relieved he had escaped from the dilemma and seized on his own instinct that the dowager countess was not serious in her threat to have him charged. He had also mentally listed all the reasons why he was reluctant to marry again—why he should not sacrifice himself on the altar of matrimony with Belle Ainsley.

But as he had stared at the proud young beauty before him, he could not put from his mind that by his own actions, if the scandal did indeed hit society like the explosion of a thousand guns, he would have inadvertently, but effectively, destroyed her future. If not for his damnable pride, he might have broken his guise of stoic reticence and agreed to marry her. He'd be wiser by far to test the susceptibility of his own heart where she was concerned before he severed his association with her completely.

The simple truth was that he was strongly attracted to Belle Ainsley and she was far too beautiful for any man to turn his back on. Though his eyes saw the door through which she had just passed through, her face was imprinted all over it and the force of his feelings astounded him. He was quite bewildered by the emotion he felt in his heart. He couldn't really describe what he felt for her because he didn't have any words. All he knew was that he felt strange, wonderful, different from anything he had ever expected to feel or would ever feel again. It was as if he had spent his whole life waiting for her to be there, but marriage to her was out of the question.

On leaving Lord Bingham's house, something inside Belle, some bright and hopeful light that shone brighter whenever she thought of him, faded and winked out of existence. But out of sheer pride she held herself tightly together around the emptiness, not wanting to betray the desolation she felt.

Belle thought she could not feel any more humiliated than she had on her last encounter with Lord Bingham at his house, but she soon discovered she was mistaken. He continued to remain a popular figure at any event. This was not so for Belle. In every well-to-do house—above and below stairs—there was a hunger for a bit of scandal. Those that had been present to witness her disgraceful escapade gossiped, and what they had to divulge about her visit to Lord Bingham's house and the time she must have spent in his bedchamber, was liberally embroidered and flew like a forest fire from house to house.

From that time onwards no callers, no entertaining billet doux which she usually received from her admirers, and which she generally enjoyed reading as a flattering diversion, arrived at the house in Hampstead. Belle could not have imagined the effect it would have. Reluctant to go out, for the first few days she remained secluded within the house, needing somehow the security of the solid walls around her. But despite her self-imposed seclusion she had no doubt the whole of society knew what she had done and that she would have to face everyone soon.

Having abandoned her decision to go to Wiltshire, for she had no wish to be seen to running away from a situation that would confirm what everyone believed, the Dowager Countess of Harworth decided to sit it out. To Belle's surprise her grandmother was sympathetic to the way she was being treated and not even her influence could persuade people to change their minds. In the eyes of the *ton* she had broken all the rules governing moral conduct. She was unfit company for virtuous young ladies and gullible heirs, a shameless wanton soiled and used.

Belle dragged her thoughts from the memories of the handsome, blue-eyed man who haunted every moment of her days and nights, and despite the despicable way he had treated her, she was unable to dismiss her hungering guilt at having actually enjoyed the things he had done to her. She was unable to blot out of her mind the exquisite sweetness of the moments she'd spent in his arms, the memory of his passionate kisses, of his whispered words of passion, for they kept returning to torment her, and she couldn't prevent it.

Not to be defeated—and by no means having given up on Lord Bingham doing the honourable thing by Isabelle—the countess persuaded Belle to attend a function she had been invited to before the scandal became public—a ball at Lord and Lady Schofield's house in Mayfair.

Belle shuddered at the thought of what might happen. 'I cannot do it. I cannot face everyone.'

'Yes, you can. You won't be alone. I shall be with you and you have spirit enough to withstand what everyone will put you through. If you are seen out and about, it will help stem the gossip until the next unfortunate young lady falls from grace and they will lose all interest in you.'

And so Belle gave in.

Less than half an hour in the crowded ballroom, she was painfully aware of the extent of her disgrace. It was the first time since she had come out into society when she was not surrounded by admiring beaux. Those friends and acquaintances who did not wish to distance themselves from the influential Dowager Countess of Harworth were polite and courteous, but didn't hesitate to cast scathing glances at Belle. She responded mechanically to the few cold greetings addressed to her. It seemed to her that the sun had gone out and that life tasted of ashes.

Heads turned, and she couldn't fail to notice the censorious way people looked at her and whispered behind their fans. They had plenty of reasons to criticise her and she hated them all, loathed every prying eye. They were all strangers, brittle, sophisticated strangers, who resented her intrusion into their select society and who were relishing the mortifying situation in which she now found herself.

Determined to put on a brave face and keeping her head high, in a state of consuming misery Belle stood on the side of the dance floor, watching the dancers whirl by, while drowning in humiliation and making a magnificent effort to pin a smile on her face and avoid the malicious eyes that made her skin burn. Nothing of what she saw penetrated her thoughts, for her mind moved like a disembodied wraith through everything but the quandaries she faced. Afraid she would lose her slender thread of control and the tears shining in her eyes would find their way down her cheeks, her grandmother never left her side.

From a distance, witnessing Belle's humiliation at first hand, believing he had had a hand in her downfall by exposing her at Lance's house and mortified by it, Sir Rowland Gibbon left to seek out his friend at his club, to take him to task for feeding a beautiful young woman to the wolves, for in his opinion that stupid wager had been the beginning of her fall from grace.

Striding into the gaming room of the dimly lit exclusive gentleman's club, which was not lacking for wealthy occupants willing to wager enormous sums of money on the turn of a card, Rowland found Lance just finishing an unsuccessful game of faro. On seeing his friend he stood up, the expression on his face dour.

Rowland laughed lightly. 'For a man who is usually lucky at cards, Lance, you have a remarkably sour look on your face.'

An ironic smile twisted Lance's lips. 'Tonight isn't a good night. As you know I normally find cards a pleasurable occupation, but tonight my concentration is elsewhere. Come and join me in a drink.'

The two men left the card room and seated themselves in two comfortable armchairs. Lance nodded to a footman to bring two drinks to their table.

After a few minutes of companionable silence, Rowland said, 'I've just come from the Schofields' ball in Mayfair—a splendid affair as usual.'

'Then why aren't you still there?'

'I came to seek you out. The Dowager Countess of Harworth has taken it upon herself to defy the whole *ton* and introduce Miss Ainsley back into the ranks, which, considering what I witnessed tonight, is no mean feat. The object is to try to brave it out, but I don't envy the beautiful Belle.'

With a grimace of annoyance, Lance leaned back in his chair and picked up his glass. 'What has this got to do with me, Rowland?'

'It has everything to do with you,' he pointed out, trying unsuccessfully to keep his voice blank as he crossed his legs in front of him.

Lance stared icily at his friend. 'In what way?'

'Belle Ainsley has been given the cut direct from half the *ton*. It seems grossly unfair to me that while she is being ostracised so severely, the unprincipled reprobate who brought so much unhappiness into her life should be enjoying such good fortune when her future looks so bleak.'

The glass in Lance's hand froze halfway to his lips. 'You exaggerate, Rowland. Miss Isabelle Ainsley is a beautiful young woman who is proving to be the biggest success of the Season.'

'That was before she encountered you. Ever since it became known that she spent some time alone with you in your bed-chamber, it's been public knowledge that she's used goods.' Rowland watched with grim satisfaction as a muscle began to twitch in Lance's rigid jaw. 'It is a brave thing she is doing— showing herself in the face of so much hostility. Think yourself fortunate that the countess didn't bring a charge against you for highway robbery. As a result of everything you have done, Miss Ainsley is at the mercy of the *ton* and will probably have to leave London and live in shamed seclusion in Wiltshire.'

'Come, Rowland, you exaggerate.'

Rowland looked at him askance. 'You really have no idea, do you, Lance?'

'With the Season winding to a close, in the two weeks since I last saw her, apart from going to my club, I've immersed myself in business matters, for I fully intend leaving for Ryhill within days. And also,' he added with contempt, 'among what is amusingly called polite society, matters that concern you personally are never discussed openly—only behind one's back. How is she bearing up?'

'She isn't—if what I have just witnessed is anything to go by. The first time I saw her, her sparkle almost knocked me off my feet—but now that sparkle lacks lustre and she is just going through the motions. She will undoubtedly find it hard to forgive you for the transgression against her.'

Lance had given little thought to how Belle must be suffering the *ton*'s rejection. Silently cursing himself, he tossed down the contents of his glass as if he wanted to wash away the bitterness of his friend's verbal attack. He didn't try to defend himself. How could he? What Rowland said was true and it brought home to him his own cruel treatment of that beautiful young woman.

Thoughts of his father came to mind. As his only male offspring, his father had sought to share his wisdom he had gleaned from his own experiences, teaching his son not merely with words but through example. Above all he had shown him the true meaning of duty and honour, which Lance had put into practice many times in his military career and his daily life—the same duty and honour that had been absent in his treatment of Delphine, but which he must apply to dealing with this situation of Belle.

As so often of late and to his absolute chagrin, he found himself once more beset by visions of her. He remembered how she had looked when he had come upon her in his room, the golden candlelight on her creamy skin, her softly curling hair about her face, and his thoughts brought to mind how those sweet and gentle arms had felt about his neck, and how her subtle body had curved into his own.

Though he had once thought himself immune to the subtle ploys of women, even though he had known her for such a short time, he had begun to think he would never be free of

Belle. From the very beginning she had stirred his baser instincts. Yet much as she ensnared his thoughts, he found his dreams daunting to his manly pride, for whenever she flitted through them like some puckish sprite, he felt more like a slave than a conqueror. Although he'd have greatly preferred to limit her constant assaults on his thoughts and his poorly depleted restraint, he was beginning to suspect that, in comparison, standing firm against Napoleon's forces had been child's play.

He was caught in a trap, and unable to think of a means of escape from this dilemma that had presented itself, he felt the noose of matrimony tighten inexorably around his neck. If he married Belle, he would not come out too badly. But for now he was furious that by his own behaviour he was being forced into making a decision that was thoroughly distasteful to him, and not having the upper hand.

'The way I see it,' Rowland went on, 'you have done her a great disservice. You have no choice except to rescue her from what she is suffering now. There is no lack of beaux at the ball, but not one will partner her. Good Lord, Lance, the lady could not be blamed if she took it into her head to hate you for this.'

An indescribable expression flashed across Lance's face as he slammed his glass down and surged out of his chair. 'I don't intend to give her the opportunity,' he replied in an implacable voice.

'Now what?'

'To the Schofields' ball, but before that I shall recruit as many unattached males from the club who will be utterly delighted to partner Miss Isabelle Ainsley at the ball. I must also stop at my house to change into my evening clothes, and arriving at the ball I will speak to the Dowager Countess of Harworth. '

'Really?' This would be worth seeing and Rowland, determined not to miss such a momentous occurrence, shot after him. 'I'm coming with you.'

Latecomers to the Schofields' ball were still coming through the door, the butler's monotone rhythmic tones rising above the noise. *Lord and Lady Hazelwood. Sir Thomas and Lady Mortimer. The Earl of Ryhill...*

Belle's eyes opened wide and she blanched, not daring to look at the man who was the architect of all her troubles. There was a dread, sick feeling in the pit of her stomach, yet in her heart, pounding heavily, bloomed an odd sense of elation.

'I would like to leave,' she said to her grandmother in a furious voice.

An odd quiet was sweeping over the room as heads turned to stare at the new arrival, and after they had had a good look, turned to look at Belle with raised brows. She knew exactly how their collective minds worked. They were eager to see what would happen next. Would Lord Bingham acknowledge her—or would he cut her dead?

Having no wish to wait and find out, she said, 'I cannot possibly stay now.'

The countess read what was written on her granddaughter's face. 'Don't even consider leaving,' she stated quietly but firmly. 'Get a grip on yourself and see it out.'

Looking towards the door, Belle felt her legs begin to tremble and a gasp rose in her throat, for clad in black evening clothes and wearing an expression of mild amusement, was Lord Bingham, the Earl of Ryhill. Her shock was superseded by a feeling of unreality as she watched him prowl the outer limits of the dance floor like some sleek, powerful panther.

Lance stood on the sidelines, a solitary, brooding man looking with a bored expression on his handsome face at the scene before him, and then he saw the tawny-haired goddess and his heart lurched. Though he made every effort to resist her appeal, he could feel the meagre store of his resolve waning. At times like these, he had cause to wonder why he had refused the Dowager Countess of Harworth's offer of her granddaughter's hand in marriage, for the only person he was punishing was himself. He couldn't imagine the virtuous Belle being tormented by cravings of the magnitude he had recently been suffering. But marriage? God damn it! He didn't want to get married, not to anyone. Never again.

Belle was looking at him, pale and stricken and very lovely—and furious. Seeing how the fashionable set shunned her and whispered about her, he was angry, but managed to appear superbly relaxed and smiled slightly before turning to speak to an acquaintance.

It was difficult for him not to cut a way to her side, but if he was going to make things right for her it was important to play out a charade and appear casual. Since he couldn't stop the gossip about his relationship with her, he had set out to turn it about, to ensure the attention was directed in a way he wanted it directed. He knew everyone was watching them both, positively bursting for a firsthand *on dit* about his relationship with her and what actually had happened between them when they had been alone together in his bedroom.

He mingled with the throng, giving a nod here and pausing now and then to shake hands and speak with an acquaintance, but all the while never losing sight of Belle. His eyes followed the undulating sway of her gown that flowed and shimmered in glistening waves about her long legs.

Another waltz was starting when Sir Rowland Gibbon suddenly appeared by Belle's side.

'Come, Miss Ainsley, dance with me.'

He led her on to the floor and danced her into the midst of the twirling couples, and the fact that Sir Rowland Gibbon was championing her was immediately remarked upon. Swallowed up by other dancers, Belle breathed a sigh of relief. She was safe for the time being, but then a humiliating thought occurred to her and she scowled up at her partner.

'I have been an outcast all night and suddenly you ask me to dance. Did you want to dance with me by any chance, or did Lord Bingham tell you to?'

Rowland grinned down at her, his face very boyish and amiable now he had bowed to Lance's pressure and shaved off his beard. 'Lance has much to thank you for. He regrets what has happened to you and wishes to make amends. He has asked me to tell you not to worry and that everything will turn out right.'

Belle's eyes widened with shock. 'Amends?' She shook her head at the sheer absurdity of what he was saying. 'He can make as many *amends* as her likes, but he cannot escape the fact that because of him I am well and truly ruined. As far as I am concerned, I want nothing more to do with that arrogant Earl. I would appreciate it if he would keep as far away from me as it's possible for the time we are here.'

Chapter Six

Of course Lance had no intention of doing any such thing. A flamboyant young lord who had been drinking heavily latched on to him, and following his gaze as he watched Sir Rowland Gibbon dancing with Belle, he remarked, 'Miss Isabelle Ainsley is a beauty, is she not? But then you would know, wouldn't you,' he uttered with a leering grin, 'having had her all to yourself—in your bedchamber. You must have come to know the lady—intimately.' Showing his lack of polish—and also his inability to hold his drink—he gave Lance a nudge and a knowing wink.

Lance nodded without changing his expression, and taking a glass of wine from a tray raised it to his lips. 'Do I?' he said in an amused tone.

The gentleman snorted with surprise and disappointment. 'You mean you don't?'

'That is precisely what I mean.' Then he automatically added a proviso to forestall further gossip. 'However, I count myself fortunate to be on friendly terms with all the Ainsleys.'

The gentleman heard that with some surprise. 'You don't say? But I thought your two families were...'

Lance lifted his eyebrows with some amusement. 'What? At daggers drawn? It is nothing but lamentable nonsense and people should learn to separate the rubbish from the truth. Over the years there has been a gross lack of understanding. Don't believe a word of it.'

'But you were alone together, and you did compromise the lady?'

Unable to deny it since everyone knew Belle had spent time with him alone, instead of throwing a punch as he was sorely tempted to do, Lance said, 'The whole of London knows it to be true—but it was a ruse of mine to get her alone.'

'And?'

'And nothing. I lured her to my house with the promise of returning some property I had taken from her. It was not through want of trying on my part. Miss Ainsley—who is a paragon of virtue and a finer example of refinement you couldn't hope to meet—would have none of it. I succeeded in getting her alone, but she soon gave me my come-uppance and left. I'm here tonight in the hope that she'll accept my apology and look on me with more favour.'

'Perhaps she will,' the lord chuckled. 'Nothing as fickle as women, eh?'

And so saying he left to impart this new bit of information to his friends, that the beautiful Miss Isabelle Ainsley had repulsed the powerful Earl of Ryhill and that particular bit of information was far more interesting than that he had seduced her.

Standing aside, Lance watched with satisfaction as the story was circulated and within no time at all male heads turned to look at Belle with renewed interest and speculation, and several hesitantly presented themselves to the dowager countess and requested she introduce them to her granddaughter. While remaining curious at this change in direction, she was more than happy to oblige.

However, everything was explained when Lord Bingham had arrived and requested to speak with her alone, telling her that he had come to stem the gossip about Miss Ainsley. Seeing the sense of his words, that they combine forces to dispel this nonsense that was in danger of ruining her granddaughter completely, she had agreed. When he had left her she had been a quiet observer of his movements.

It was with a sense of unreality that Belle danced with these gentlemen who had lost their aversion to her. She smiled politely and listened to their comments, but her only real feeling was that she was no longer ostracised. She even danced again with Sir Rowland, and was not aware when he looked at Lance or of the moment when Lance tipped his head that Rowland danced her on to the wide stone terrace, where he left her with the excuse of going to get two glasses of champagne.

A man came on to the dimly lit terrace and a voice said, 'At last. I was beginning to think I would never get you alone.'

Shock stiffened Belle's body. For a split second, her feet rooted to the ground, then abruptly she turned away from him. 'Go away. I have no wish to speak to you.'

He moved slowly towards her and took her arm.

Belle could feel fury bubbling up inside her. 'Let go,' she snapped and jerked her arm. She would have fled back inside, but he held her fast. Her voice broke with the anger she felt. 'I said let go.'

'Easy, Belle,' he said, releasing her arm. 'You and I have a matter to discuss.'

Spinning round, she glared at the handsome, forceful, dynamic man standing before her. He looked powerful, aloof and disgustingly self-assured. 'Anything we have to say has been said. After everything that has happened, how dare you feel you have the right to approach me? How dare you try to manipulate me as if I am yours to direct—just as though you have a perfect right to? Now go away.'

Even in the meagre light, her unparalleled beauty proved a strong lodestone from which Lance could not drag his gaze. Quietly, he said, 'Will you calm down and listen to what I have to say?'

Belle did her best to hold in the resentment she felt, to be dignified, as a lady of her class would be, but it was very hard and her expression was icy. 'Nothing you can say can undo what you have done to me.'

'I would like to try.'

'And I suppose this was your doing—getting your friend to bring me out here?'

'There is nothing untoward in that, Belle. I merely wanted to talk with you privately for a few moments. After all that has happened, I thought it especially needful tonight.'

'Why tonight?'

Lance bent his head, considering how best to approach the subject. 'Personally I don't care a damn what people think of me, but no matter what you think, it is not my wish to cause more gossip that will hurt you.'

Her face working with the strength of her emotions, which had, for the moment, got the better of her, reluctantly Belle gazed up at him. In the dim light his eyes shone softly down into hers. His words, spoken quietly and with gravity, made her wary. 'It's a little late for that. You must have seen how I am being treated in there. They might as well have tarred and feathered me and tied me to a lamppost.'

At any other time Lance would have laughed at the image her words conjured up in his mind, but now he would not insult her by doing so, for the strain of what she had gone through—was still going through—was there on her lovely, troubled face for him to see.

'You have been treated harshly. You did not deserve that. For what it's worth I'm sorry and would like to put it right.'

'Ha,' she scoffed. 'What are you all of a sudden—some kind of wizard? All those partners. You made them dance with me, didn't you?'

'They were easily manipulated.'

Belle was so humiliated by his answer that it took her a moment to reply. 'Have you any idea how humiliating it is for me to know that?' she fumed.

He shrugged nonchalantly. 'It needn't be. Those men wanted to dance with you. They are not nearly as malicious as their female counterparts and were looking for any excuse to lead you on to the floor. I provided them with the answer.'

Gazing at the cool, dispassionate man standing before her, looking so powerful, aloof and completely self-assured, Belle managed a nervous little laugh and said sarcastically, 'Not only are you an accomplished soldier on the field of battle, my lord. You also appear to have a gift for strategy and subtlety on the dance floor, too.'

'I do my best,' he replied, ignoring her sarcasm. 'There is also a rumour circulating that I was the one who pursued you, that I was responsible for you being in my bedchamber, and that you evaded my advances.'

'And who started this rumour?'

'I did. So far most people in there are starting to think you might have been wrongly maligned.'

'I can't argue with that.'

Lance's eyes glowed with the reflected light of the lanterns as he watched her unrelentingly for a lengthy space, heightening Belle's tensions until she could hardly stand the suspense. Rather than leave herself open to his unyielding stare, she turned her head away.

'I think I should go back inside. Grandmother will be wondering where I've got to.'

'Come and dance with me. I have no doubt the tongues will wag even harder, but let them. This time they will wag to a different tune.'

'I'm supposed to be evading you, remember,' Belle retorted cuttingly. 'What will everyone say when we suddenly appear and take to the floor?'

He grinned. 'They'll see how weak you are and can no longer resist my manly charms.'

She looked at him coolly. 'Don't flatter yourself—and don't you think you should seek my grandmother's favour first?'

'Somehow I don't think your grandmother will raise any objections, and will be happy to combine forces if it stills the gossip.'

'You mean I'm not completely ruined?'

'Not if you marry me.'

Belle paled, unable to believe what he had said. Her anger stirred. 'Marry? I think you've taken leave of your senses. I recall you telling me in no uncertain terms that you didn't want to marry me,' she said with cold, quiet dignity, lifting her chin and stiffening her spine. 'In fact, you made it bitingly clear that you didn't want me for your wife.'

'That was then. This is now. I've changed my mind,' he said flatly.

She frowned, giving a hard, sceptical look. 'Changed your mind? As easy as that? Why? Is it pity or guilt that has prompted you to ask me—that has prompted you to do the honourable thing?' she demanded.

He shook his head, knowing she would suspect this—and as proud as she was, her pride would make her oppose him. 'Neither. I care enough about you to be hurt by the dreadful way you have been treated by society. You do not deserve that.'

'No, I don't—and I thank you for your concern,' she remarked with heavily laden sarcasm. 'Whether it is genuine or not means little to me. Your honourable nature is to be applauded, but you don't have to feel under any obligation to marry me.'

'I don't.'

Belle's chin lifted even higher at his suddenly chilling tone. 'I told you I didn't want to marry you. Have you, in your arrogance, assumed that I have changed my mind?'

'It has been known for some women to do so,' he stated rudely.

'And I recall telling you I am not like most women.'

'I know that too.'

'So we won't marry.'

Lance stared at the scornful young woman who was regarding him down the length of her pert nose and felt a glimmer of respect that she would dare to take him to task over what he was offering, which was to her advantage. 'On the contrary. I have already spoken to your grandmother. It is settled.'

His smoothly worded statement made Belle almost choke on her chagrin. 'You have done this without consulting me first? How dare you do that? You had no right. None whatsoever.'

'I had every right,' he said coldly. 'Your grandmother was the one who approached me, remember. Do not forget that in order to punish me she threatened to have me publicly charged with highway robbery and attempted seduction.'

'She would not do that. She was bluffing.'

'Maybe she was, but it is a risk I am not prepared to take. Do me the justice to admit that we were both responsible for the circumstances to bring about a union between the two of us, so that now it's a question of that union being a success. It is in both our interests. It is obvious that in marrying me—'

'It is not obvious at all,' Belle cut in irately. 'In marrying you I do not make a love match or even one I could possibly approve of. I might even say I make a forced marriage. Would it be a great surprise to you if I told you that the feelings you inspire in me, far from resembling love, rather approach a feeling of anger?'

Lance did not seem surprised or insulted. Undaunted, he lifted his brows quizzically, a twist of humour about his beautifully moulded lips. 'I can imagine,' he said, shrugging his shoulders in a way that Belle hoped was casual, but at the same time she was filled with pain. But why should she care whether he loved her or not? He was offering her a life line, to enable her to hold up her head in society and not have to listen to the slights and slurs, the whispers and jeers. Why should she care about the rest?

'I ask you to put aside your feelings and see marriage to me as a way forwards. Otherwise...'

'Otherwise?'

'You'll be dreadfully unhappy.'

Belle's face hardened, and she said through clenched teeth, 'Because of you, I have already been unhappy. I have no intention of starting all over again.'

'It needn't be like that. You won't find me a cruel husband—and you'll find me generous, I promise you.'

'That is not what I mean,' Belle burst out a little hysterically. 'You expect me to be grateful for your generosity and that I should submit to you accordingly. You speak of marrying me as if you're discussing a—a business arrangement—without any feeling or emotion, without even a pretence of...'

'Of what, Belle? Of love?' As he held her gaze his features noticeably hardened. 'You have just told me that a union between the two of us will not be a love match, so I assume you have no illusions about that,' he sneered at her coldly. 'Love is a word that is so over-used it loses its meaning and force. It is a word used to manipulate idiots. I am sure you will agree.'

Hearing her words quoted back at her with such frankness, Belle stepped back and turned away from him, wrapping her arms around her waist as she thought about what to do, knowing he was waiting for her answer. He obviously didn't want to marry her—in fact, she suspected he must have thought hard for some way out of marrying her, for he seemed to dislike her intensely, but as he had shown when they had been alone together, he desired her too. Then again, perhaps she was only trying to fool herself into believing it.

Unable to see her face, Lance moved to stand behind her. Now he had made up his mind to marry her, he could not understand her reticence. Was he not doing her an honour by consenting to make her his wife? How dare she argue and defy him? How dare she challenge him?

'Well? How far have you got in making your decision?' he asked harshly.

Belle stirred and seemed to wake from a bad dream. 'It's agreed. I will marry you.' She turned and faced him. 'But I want to say that after what you have done and my own aversion to you, I was wounded by your harsh refusal to consider my grandmother's suggestion that you do the honourable thing and consider me for your future wife. Have you any idea how difficult and humiliating that was for her? The fact that it was you who started the whole thing by taking the diamonds, and that disgusting wager with your friend, made your rejection all the more painful.'

'But you do agree to the marriage?'

'Yes. I respect your decision, but I know this is not what you planned or even what you want.'

'No, it isn't,' he stated frankly, 'and I won't pretend otherwise. I made that plain enough when your grandmother came to see me and I take nothing back. My freedom has always been important to me, and I am averse to relinquishing it.'

For a lengthy moment, Lance's deep blue eyes probed the dark depths of hers. He was profoundly aware of the enchanting young woman's body standing close to him and her intoxicating perfume. His entire personality was pervaded by a shrewdness that had never taken principles into account, but only the fluctuations of human nature. He was clever, and he knew that when he held a woman in his arms he was very powerful. There was always a moment when the woman's self-defence yielded before the lure of sensual rapture and he knew how to turn that moment to his advantage. If Belle was to be his wife, then perhaps he didn't have to wait for the wedding night to enslave her. It was a pleasing thought, one he intended to act upon.

'However,' he went on, his eyes suddenly teasing as his hands went to her shoulders and he drew her near, his voice low and seductive, 'I do find myself attracted to you. It just so happens that I want you, Belle—you cannot condemn me for that—and I know you want me. We have wanted each other every time we have been together. You are beautiful, innocent and courageous, passionate and stubborn—and I hope you will forgive my wrongdoings and get to like me.'

Feeling perilously close to tears, Belle dropped her gaze, unable to absorb the amazing revelation that he was actually attracted to her. 'I liked Carlton Robinson when we first met,' she whispered. 'After a couple of days I couldn't stand the sight of him and couldn't wait to be rid of him. It would seem that I have poor judgement in the matter of men. Maybe I should change my mind about marrying you.'

'Belle,' he said softly, 'you have no choice if you want come out of this with your reputation intact. Come, let me look at you,' he cajoled gently, but when she complied by raising her head, his brows gathered in perplexity. The tears glistening in the long, silken lashes were hard to ignore. Laying a hand alongside her cheek, he gently wiped away a droplet with his thumb. 'What has happened is not so bad that you should feel a need to cry.'

Embarrassed because she couldn't contain her emotions, Belle responded with a shake of her head. 'I'm not.'

'Come now, your lashes are wet. If they aren't tears, then I would have to think it is raining, and yet I cannot feel it.'

Belle recognised the threat of her emotions were about to get the better of her once more and she stepped away from him, away from the gentle touch of his hand on her cheek. It certainly didn't help her composure now to feel a resurgence of the various sensations she had experienced when they had been alone together in his bedchamber. Though sorely lacking experience in the realms of desire, instinct assured her the wanton yearnings gnawing away inside her were nothing less than cravings that Lance Bingham had elicited with what he had done to her that night she had crept into his bedroom.

'I'm all right. It was just a moment of weakness, that's all. It has passed.'

'And you're sure of that, are you, Belle?'

Before she could prepare herself, his arms rose and dragged her to him. And then he was kissing her hair, her cheek, and caressing her lips with his own. His lips moved on hers, the fierceness changing to softness, to the velvet touch of intoxication. An eternity later he pulled his mouth from hers and looked down into her eyes, which were warm and velvety soft.

'That was a mistake,' Belle said desperately.

His lips quirked in a faint smile. 'Then let's make another one.'

As he spoke he took her hand and led her down the terrace steps into the darkness of the garden beyond and away from prying eyes. His tall figure dark against the shadows, with just enough light from the house to see her by, he reached out and pulled her to him. His eyes were like flames of fire, scorching her.

Belle was astounded at her body's reaction to this man. A touch, a kiss, a look, and he could rouse her, and something rose and shouted for the joy of it. Her heart was pounding in her breast and she could feel his beating against hers to the same rapid rhythm. She pressed herself close to him, not with fury but with delight, with something she had felt before when he had kissed her, which she knew was the female in her responding to the male in him. It was madness. She made a sound in her throat and she threw back her head in the exultation of the moment.

'You do want me, don't you, Belle?' Lance triumphed softly, her breath sweet and warm against his mouth as she still clung to him. 'Say it. Your heart beats far too quickly for you to claim uninterest, my love.'

She was dazed, her eyes unfocused with that soft loveliness that comes when a woman is deep in the pleasures of love, her senses completely overruled by this magic that had sprung up between them. Cupping her chin, he began to kiss her face, her eyelids, her cheeks. Her lips trembled as he again claimed them fiercely with his own.

'My God,' he whispered hoarsely, his blue eyes smouldering as he gazed at her upturned face. 'You are the most direct, self-willed woman I have ever met, traits I admire in any woman, but you are also so damn lovely and desirable.' Pulling her down on to a bench, in the semi-darkness, where the light of the moon contended with the glow from the occasional lantern, the sight of her white shoulders, the fragile neck, aroused in him a violent but unfamiliar desire, such as no woman had ever aroused in him. It was not just blind and bestial lust. There was about it a somewhat mysterious, almost sweet and gentle allure.

Covering her mouth with his own once more, his lips moved against hers, his breath on her mouth. His hand caressed her hard nippled breasts and seemed not to want to stop, before sliding carelessly under her gown and over her thighs as he kissed her passionately. His lips touched her cheeks and moved to her throat and Belle shivered involuntarily at their burning intensity and the touch of his hand on her bare flesh. Her conscience told her to fight him, but there was no fight in her and her senses staggered with ecstasy. Her whole being seemed to burst into flame, while delicious sensations overwhelmed her. The feel of him, the smell of him, all combined to transfix her. She hardly noticed the moment when he lifted her off the hard bench and placed her on the cool, soft, sweet-smelling grass.

Clinging together, their world became one of passion and

incoherent sound and heat. From the ballroom the strains of
music and voices floated on the night air, and overhead an owl
screeched, but the lovers were deaf and blind to everything but
each other. When Lance raised her skirts Belle caught a flash
of her own rounded thighs, pale and lustrous, above her silk
stockings. She became aware that she was holding her breath,
that her face and breasts were hot as if a fire had burned them.
Drawing her breast from her bodice, Lance cupped it in his
hand and kissed and sucked it with his mouth. Belle had never
been touched there by a man before, and the sensations he
created drove her almost out of her mind.

She was conscious of a trembling throughout her body and
desired, above all things, to feel his hard, lean body pressed
to hers. He carried on kissing her and caressing her, arousing her until thought and feeling, heart and head became a
liquid flame. He drew out all her suppressed longings, freeing
her passion until she could deny him nothing. She obeyed the
passions of her body, caught up in an agonisingly sweet, yet
terrible intensity. Lance lay on her and she felt the strength of
him as he held her unresisting body close and took her, penetrating deeply. She held him to her as he took his pleasure of
her, moaning with pleasure and pain of her own. Entwined,
Belle was conscious of nothing but a wild ecstasy as they
merged together, each fulfilling the other in the most sublime
act of making love.

Lance gloried in the feel of Belle's pliant, firm young
body straining against his. It was like a yielding, living substance as she gave all her desire and passion, responding to
his inner heat. Her slender arms wrapped around his neck as
their mouths fastened hungrily on one another, hers moist and
warm. A man well used to the lusty pleasures that were always
available to him, Lance had not until he had met Belle held
a woman in his arms who was not only young but innocent,
untouched and pure, with a serene beauty that delighted him.

Then it was over and for a time Belle had no immediate

thoughts. She had nothing but the memory of incredible joy, of something immense that had happened to her, beyond which nothing was comparable. Opening her eyes, she saw Lance's face bent over her. Wanting to hold the moment and feel him close to her, she was disappointed when he moved away and stood up, calmly adjusting his clothing. Belle sat upright, confused, her body still pulsating with heat and the feel of his body joined to hers. She couldn't believe that she had given herself to him because of deeper feelings she did not fully understand.

Lance took her hand and pulled her to her feet. He smiled as she struggled to compose herself, relieved that they were alone in the garden and no one had come to find them.

'Are you all right?' he asked, raising his hand and gently caressing her cheek. He was looking down at her, his gaze penetrating. Her eyes were dark and huge in her pale face, and her skin gleamed like soft silk in the dim light. She was as bewitching as any pagan statue, and she had responded to him not as a girl but as a woman. He was not disappointed. However, his body's almost uncontrollable desire for her had amazed, unnerved and thoroughly displeased him. He would not touch her again until she was his wife.

Belle nodded, lowering her eyes and smoothing her skirts, suddenly shy of him. Even on the brink of surrender she had realised that she was on the point of giving something to him which by rights belonged only to a husband, and yet since Lance was to be her husband, oddly, she found neither shame nor scruples and felt no will to resist. Why not give him what he so boldly demanded, she had thought, what no woman could be sure of keeping once a man had made up his mind to take her by force or cunning?

'Do you feel any regrets?' he asked.

'Yes,' she confessed. 'I—I wish you had waited until—until we are married before you did that. I have been told a woman's virginity should be a highly valued gift to her husband. Should you decide not to marry me, who else will have me now?'

'Once I give my word about something, Belle, I never retract it. We will be married, and the fact that you are no longer the chaste virgin of a moment ago matters little to me. Personally, I have never particularly prized virginity.' He shrugged with complete indifference. 'It doesn't matter.' He took her hand. 'Are you ready to go back inside?'

'Yes, I think we should.'

As he led her back to the ballroom, Belle wished he hadn't been so cavalier about her lost virginity. She wished it had been more important to him.

Word had spread of Lord Bingham's public defence of Miss Isabelle Ainsley. When she appeared on the dance floor with him, whatever had taken place between the two of them that had created the scandal seemed to have vanished. Observing the Dowager Countess of Harworth's expression of approval as she watched them dance together, those present concluded that a betrothal might be imminent after all. It was a possibility that distressed the lady's other suitors, and no matter how they vied with each other for her attention and argued amongst themselves, it was plain to see that Lord Bingham had prior claim.

On the day the betrothal of the Earl of Ryhill and Miss Isabelle Ainsley was announced in the newspaper, as arranged, Lance rode to Hampstead to discuss arrangements for the wedding with Belle's grandmother.

The dowager countess always kept her emotions under rigid control and in this instance she was feeling a grim and angry resignation towards the marriage of Isabelle to Lance Bingham. Entering the salon where he was waiting for her, as she regarded him she contemplated with bitter amusement this unexpected twist of fate. How had things come to this—her granddaughter marrying into the family she had distanced herself from for fifty years, and all because Lance Bingham's grandfather had rejected her love?

But this was no time to argue over former grievances. The brutal fact was that if this marriage didn't go ahead, then her granddaughter's chances of making a suitable marriage were negligible.

Seating herself in her favourite high-winged chair beside the hearth, with a nod of her head she indicated the chair opposite. She sat quite still, her back ramrod straight, her white head high, but the bitter disappointment of the last weeks had added a decade to her face.

'Isabelle will be in shortly. She's been riding on the Heath and has just returned.' She gave Lance a piercing look as he sat across from her and crossed his long, booted legs, thinking him a handsome devil despite everything. In fact, he was exactly the man she would have picked for her granddaughter, for he was a vigorous, forceful man to keep Isabelle well guarded and safe, especially now. She was a girl who needed firmness, a strong hand to guide her, but with care. 'Of course I would rather it hadn't come to this—you must know that.'

'I do—and no doubt my mother will be uneasy about it when I tell her, although she cannot fail to be taken with your granddaughter. When she has been made aware of the circumstances that have brought our betrothal about, she will agree that I am doing the right thing.'

'I understand your mother does not live at Ryhill?'

'No. She resides at Bilton House—which is where I was raised. As you know—since you are as familiar with the area as I am, it's a mere three miles from Ryhill—not too far to visit. At present she is in Ireland—County Cork—which is where my sister Sophie lives with her husband's family. Sophie is expecting her first child and my mother travelled over to be with her. When we have arranged a date for the wedding, I shall write informing her of the event. Unfortunately she may not be able to get back in time.'

'Like you say, that is unfortunate. You are quite certain about marrying Isabelle?'

'When I left the army I confess that marriage was not in my immediate plans. However, what is done is done and let me assure you that when Isabelle is my wife, I will take care of her and do my utmost to make her happy.'

For the next fifteen minutes they discussed the terms of the betrothal and the dowry, until the door was flung open and Belle appeared, drawing their attention.

Belle's cheeks were still flushed from her ride and her eyes glowed. She marvelled at the tingling rush of excitement that affirmed Lance's presence, even before she glanced in his direction. She was aware in that instant of a sudden pang in her breast, a familiar, wild, uncontrollable beat. Something in the brilliance of his eyes made her catch her breath, and her flush deepened when she remembered how wantonly she had given herself to him at the Schofields' ball. She felt her body heat with passion, and for once she did not care.

As she looked at him, the rush of familiar excitement caused her to become tongue-tied, affected strongly as she was by the force of his presence. She was all too aware of the strong body that had pressed down on to her own. Emotions swept over her and two spots of high colour touched her cheeks as she remembered the intense passion they had shared. Sometimes, at night, she imagined him in her bed, and her skin would perspire, and a flame would flicker through her to gather in the deep recesses of her body, between her thighs, much to her disgust and rising passion. Her thoughts now were in disarray, desire and reason conflicting.

Warily she watched him rise to his feet with that panther's grace of his that seemed so much a part of him. At this shift in their relationship to that of an engaged couple, she found herself decidedly disarmed and equally aghast at her own shy response to him. But she was not so naïve as to believe his character had reformed in the three days since the ball when she had last seen him.

It didn't help her composure at all knowing that behind that charming mask of refined masculinity there lurked a disreputable rake bereft of any concern for how he used besotted young women for his own ease and pleasure. His kisses and caresses had been lethal in stripping away her resolve, and she realised she had cause to fear for she had become just as susceptible. He had aroused a yearning inside her for a repeat of his attentions, and she fervently wished she could banish the weeks until their wedding to the four winds.

With a growing sense of unreality she watched him move away from her grandmother and start toward her with long, purposeful strides. He grew larger as he neared, his broad shoulders blocking her view of the room, his blue eyes searching her face, the slight smile curving his lips one of arrogance and self-assurance.

'Good morning,' Lance said, his eyes running over her slender figure, clad in the sensuous softness of shimmering green velvet. Recalling the way he had made love to her at the ball, he dragged his eyes from the vee of her bodice and scanned her face for signs that she might have come to regret her decision, but there was no sign of it. Having given her time to reconsider her decision, would she have done so, he wondered, had he not taken her virtue?

'Good morning, Lance,' Belle said, unsure how engaged couples greeted each other. His expression was guarded, his eyes sharp and almost unfriendly as he looked at her. She was the only one who noted it, however, for he had his back to her grandmother. 'I'm sorry I wasn't here when you arrived. I've been riding on the Heath. It's such a lovely day I lost all track of the time.'

'I think some refreshment is in order,' the countess said. 'Ring the bell, will you, Isabelle?'

One of the servants appeared in answer to Belle's summons, then left to fetch a tray of drinks and food.

Cupping her elbow in the palm of his hand, Lance led Belle to a sofa and sat beside her. 'Your grandmother and I have just been discussing the terms of the betrothal.'

'Have you?' Belle found it incredible that he still intended going ahead with the wedding. He had told her he was attracted to her, that he cared for her. At least, she thought cynically, he didn't mouth words of love he didn't feel. Neither had he proposed to her with any show of affection, so she had accepted his proposal in the same unemotional way it had been offered.

'Will it be a large wedding?' she asked; considering Lance's title, his family and her own, she couldn't imagine it being anything else.

'You are the bride,' Lance answered. 'What would you prefer?'

'That it's not too large—if that's all right. I'm afraid I'd find it all rather daunting and would prefer a small affair.'

'Then that is how it will be.' He looked at her grandmother. 'Are you in agreement, Countess?'

The dowager countess acquiesced with a regal nod of her head. 'Like you said, Isabelle is the bride—although I would prefer the wedding to take place at Harworth rather than here in town. The ceremony would be at the local church—where generations of Ainsleys are interred—the wedding celebrations at Harworth.'

'How long must we be betrothed?' Belle asked. 'A year? Six months?'

'Absolutely not,' Lance said irrevocably. Having already come firmly to the awareness that being within close proximity of Belle aroused every mating instinct he was capable of feeling, despite his aversion to the marriage itself, he was determined their betrothal would be of short duration. 'I wish to proceed with the courtship with all possible haste.' He glanced at his fiancée sitting rigidly beside him. 'What say you, Belle? Do you have any objections as to the date upon which the testing of our emotions should begin? If you have none, then may I suggest that we start as from today?'

'No, I have no objections—that would be perfect.'

'You have to get to know each other,' the countess countered. 'The rules are strict. At the ball the other night you went to a great deal of trouble to make it seem there had been little but flirtation between the two of you. Unless you go through the appropriate courtship rituals, which Isabelle has every right to expect, no one will ever believe it. Although I am of the opinion that you conquered the highest hurdle that night and everyone will move on to talk about something else.'

'What do you have in mind?' Lance demanded shortly.

'A courtship never takes less than a year, but I will concede and say six months,' the countess offered, compromising, 'of calling on her properly, escorting her to the normal functions, and so on.'

'Two,' Lance announced flatly.

His imperious tone didn't daunt the countess in the slightest. 'I suppose if it isn't to be a large wedding, it could be arranged in two months,' she conceded. 'Now the betrothal has been announced,' she said briskly, looking at the newspaper beside her where she had been reading the announcement before Lord Bingham's arrival, 'I would like to return to Harworth very soon—next week at the latest—which should give us enough time to begin preparations for Isabelle's wedding gown. Then your courtship can be conducted away from the prying eyes of the *ton*,' she said, reaching for the tea the servant had just put in front of her.

'I would be honoured if you would both dine with me this evening,' Lance offered amiably. 'Afterwards I will be your escort to the Earl and Countess of Sidmouth's party at Sidmouth House.' His gaze slid to Belle. 'After all, it is the evening of our engagement and everyone will expect to see us together. We can use the occasion to set a pattern for our future—and enjoy everyone's surprise when they realise you really are to be the next Countess of Ryhill.'

After they had drunk their tea and nibbled on cakes, with the countess's permission, Lance took his future wife for a turn about the garden.

After a few moments of strolling along the walkways in an amiable but somewhat nervous silence, Belle said, 'None of this is easy for my grandmother. Despite her haughty manner and plain speaking, she is finding it difficult to come to terms with my betrothal to you—as I am myself.'

'I am very much aware of that, Belle.'

'The reason why she is finding it difficult is stuck firmly in the past. I know that much. You said your grandmother kept a journal. I take it you have read it?'

He nodded. 'It certainly makes for interesting reading.'

'Will you tell me what you know?'

'Certainly. Your grandmother and my grandfather knew each other for many years—the families were good friends and she and my grandfather's sister were close. She always believed they would marry. They became engaged—the necklace was his gift to her, but then my grandfather met my grandmother and fell hopelessly in love with her.'

Belle stared at him aghast. 'Did he jilt my grandmother? Is that what happened?'

Lance nodded. 'I'm afraid he did. Your grandmother tried everything to get him back, but to no avail. In the end she gave up, but refused to return the necklace when my grandfather requested it for sentimental reasons. It was a family heirloom and meant a great deal to the Binghams.'

'Poor Grandmother. Your grandfather must have hurt her terribly.'

'I imagine he did. When she realised it was hopeless, since my grandfather's love for my grandmother was very much in evidence wherever they went, she married the Earl of Harworth, your grandfather, and went to live at Harworth Hall—which was as close as she could get to my grandfather.'

'Are you telling me she didn't love my grandfather?'

'I'm sure she was fond of him and held him in high esteem, but I think she still carries a candle for my grandfather to this day.'

'I'm glad she decided to give the jewels back—although had she done so sooner, we would not be where we are now.'

Lance looked at her sharply. 'What's this I hear, Belle? Regret?'

'It would certainly cast a different light on everything. There would have been no scandal. You wouldn't have asked me to marry you and we certainly wouldn't be planning our wedding. Admit it, Lance. It's the truth, isn't it?'

'I suppose it is. And would you have turned me down had I asked you anyway?'

'Yes. I'm sorry. Do you mind?'

He looked at her with grudging admiration. This situation must be devastating for her, he realised suddenly, having to support a solution to her predicament without much enthusiasm. 'You've no need to apologise or look so despondent. Don't ever fear telling me the truth—no matter how bad it is. I can accept it and even admire you for having the courage to say it.'

'Thank you.'

'You are correct in saying that we wouldn't be thinking of our future together if you hadn't taken it into your head to wear the necklace to the Prince's party at Carlton House.'

'Yes. Little wonder Grandmother was angry with me. I had no idea how upset she would be, because I didn't know the story behind them. I merely thought they were too beautiful to be kept locked away all the time. At least she returned them to their rightful owner.'

He gave her a wry smile. 'After fifty years, I suppose one could say better late than never. Do you think she would have done so, had you not brought the matter back into the public eye?'

'I don't know that. I cannot speak for my grandmother. What I do know is that from what you have told me and knowing her as much as I am able to do after such a short acquaintance, she must have loved your grandfather very much.'

'I believe she did, which accounts for her actions and for which—as anyone who has been in love will understand—she can be forgiven.'

'Being aware of your own perceptions on love, which you explained to me so frankly the other night, I am surprised that you have even a modicum of understanding. But I thank you for saying that.'

'Maybe that is why she is so protective of you, and why, after the humiliation she suffered herself all those yours ago, she wanted to save you from the same fate.'

'She is not a devious person and I can imagine the torment that lies beneath her façade of stiff dignity, which is her nature, and none of us can help our nature. Nor is she an ogre. I have full confidence in her ability to be fair minded when it's deserving—which was the case when she returned the diamonds to you—and equally harsh when circumstances compel her to be so—as when she insisted that you should do the honourable thing and marry me. I sense that she very much regrets what happened and her part in it. I can also understand how resentful you must have felt when you saw me wearing the necklace at Carlton House.'

'Yes, I confess I was resentful—and angry—but I also knew that my resentment had nothing to do with you.'

'I have to ask you this, Lance—what of your family? How will they react when they realise you are to wed a woman from a family they must despise?'

'My mother does not despise anyone. What happened

between our grandparents had nothing to do with her. She is fair minded and will not turn her back on you because of who you are. After she has weighed everything up, she will see that we are doing the right thing and accept you as my future wife. To be honest, I think she'll be relieved to end the feud and move on.'

Belle paused and turned to look at him. 'And you, Lance? Will you be glad to move on?'

He frowned, his expression becoming tense, causing Belle to regret having asked the question. It was as though Delphine's ghost stood between them. The picture of the woman who was the mother of his child continued to haunt him, those well-remembered brown eyes daring him to fall into the same dangerous trap in which he had allowed himself to be ensnared not so very long ago, causing him to lose his self-respect and his sanity.

'I accept that things will change when we wed, but as for moving on—well—we shall see.'

Chapter Seven

Lance glanced at her. 'As my wife, you know what will be expected of you?'

'Of course, but I hope you won't expect too much too soon.'

He scanned her upturned face, finally broaching what was on his mind. 'I gather, then, that you didn't enjoy it when I made love to you.'

Belle flushed to the roots of her hair and she averted her eyes, feeling a profound embarrassment. She appeared to consider his question before saying hesitantly, 'It—it was not what I expected—although I found it most—illuminating.'

His eyes narrowed on hers. 'Illuminating? I was hoping for something better than that. Have you ever been kissed before, Belle?'

'That is a secret I'd rather not confess. It is for me to know and for you to wonder about.'

'Few confidences can remain untold between husband and wife. Couples share the most *intimate* secrets—as well as other things.' He gave her a sharp, knowing look. 'And by that you know what I mean, so do not play the innocent.'

Finding it increasingly difficult to meet his gaze, Belle proceeded to walk on, trailing her hands over the flower heads as she went. 'Intimate? Are we to be *intimate* again then, Lance?'

Following in her wake, Lance scowled, watching her skirts swaying jauntily ahead of him. He had the greatest temptation to drag her off the path and into the confines of the shrubs and do more than kiss her, yet he was intrigued by her enquiry. Gently taking hold of her arm, he turned her to face him.

'We were intimate at the ball. Would you like to be intimate with me again?'

Beneath his closely attentive stare, a soft flush heightened on Belle's cheeks. She knew how quickly his passions could be inflamed, and how eager he must be to repeat his actions of that particular occasion, and she also knew she must be wary. Even so, she kept her composure well enough to say, 'I'm sure your disposition will be tested enough during the two months of our betrothal for us to ascertain our compatibility with just the minimal amount of physical contact, so if you intend using your manly charms to weaken my defences again, Lance Bingham, perhaps you should consider that I will not succumb to you again without the lasting commitment of marriage.'

'You will have to get used to it when you are my wife,' he warned, moving to stand dangerously close to her. 'You will have to be available to me whenever I want you.'

Acutely aware of the nearness of his tall, wickedly muscular body, a blaze of excitement and tension leaped through Belle, her reaction a purely primitive response. She could almost feel its heat and vibrancy through her clothes. Helplessly, she stared up at him, two bright spots of colour staining her cheeks.

His eyes smouldering, Lance stared back at her. 'Consider it, Belle. As my wife you will be at my beck and call day and night. I will take my pleasure of you at my leisure, whenever I want.'

If he was trying to destroy her resistance, he was succeeding. His voice had suddenly grown husky with sensuality, slicing through her like a hot knife through butter. She believed him—the fire streaking through her loins was so fierce it made her tremble.

'Do you enjoy provoking me—and teasing me?' she remarked. 'Are you trying to persuade me to change my mind about marrying you? Is that it?'

He gave her a hard look, his mouth tightening as he stared at the softly heaving bosom and the tantalising mouth. Belle Ainsley might look fragile, but he was beginning to suspect she was as strong as steel inside, and that behind that sweet, beautiful exterior of a genteel lady lurked an impish vixen who was every bit a match for the animal in him. He wouldn't persuade her to change her mind.

'I am merely pointing out to you what you can expect. I would waken all the passion in that lovely, untutored body of yours and make you moan with pleasure—' He broke off, realising his mistake. His strategy had backfired with a vengeance. He had begun by trying to threaten and frighten her into backing out of this marriage he had grudgingly agreed to, and had finished up with his own resolutions threatened instead.

He could feel his body reacting to the image his own words were arousing. Mentally flaying his thoughts into obedience, he made a fierce effort to control himself and stepped back, looking down at her standing there, wide-eyed and vulnerable and trembling. And lovely. Dear Lord, she was lovely. He wanted her with a fierceness that took his breath away.

The fact was undeniable. He did not want to keep himself in restraint for the next eight weeks. How would he be able to endure having her near without making love to her? He told himself that she was just a woman, and women were all alike, and he had never known one who couldn't be driven from his mind. But Belle was different. She was to be his wife and bear his children. That alone made her different. His inner turmoil turned to self-scorn. He should never have got so close to her. He should have kept his distance.

'I told you, Lance,' Belle said quietly. 'As your wife I shall know perfectly well what is expected of me. I will try not to give you reason to regret marrying me. I promise you.'

'No, you won't,' he stated. 'Don't be concerned that my barbaric display with words will be repeated. Despite my attempts to banish the tantalising memory of making love to you, I find I cannot.' A devilish smile twisted his lips. 'You're presenting a definite challenge to me, so before I weaken and forget myself and sweep you off into the bushes from which you will not emerge without yielding to my animal desire once more, I think I should return you to your grandmother.'

Focusing her gaze ahead of her, Belle was beset with so many conflicting emotions: anger, humiliation, wounded pride, regret. Was it possible to make this ill-fated marriage work when her feelings were so nebulous and chaotic? Yet one stood out clearly—her desire for this man.

She wondered how she was going to get through the weeks of her betrothal, how she was going to withstand this powerful man walking beside her. She knew it would prove far more difficult than she imagined. When she was with him she couldn't breathe without feeling his presence with every heightened sense of her female perception. It would be so easy to allow herself to yield to those provocatively stirring memories he had created when his hands had moved boldly over her body and he had invaded her in the most intimate way, that even now brought blood rushing to her cheeks and a feeling of molten heat flowing through her and into her loins so that she could think of nothing else.

Later, extremely nervous about appearing in society for the first time as Lance's fiancée, Belle was suffering from a severe fit of nerves. She took special pains with her appearance, knowing she'd be dashing the hopes once and for all of others who might have had their hopeful sights on Lance as a possible husband.

A pale pink taffeta creation that bared her shoulders sublimely was what she chose to wear. It was bejewelled with tiny seed pearls and other diminutive beads that shimmered in the light. She wore no adornment at her throat, for the garment needed none. Her hair was drawn back smoothly from her face, the shining tresses intricately woven into a weighty mass above her nape. The fact that she had spent so much time fashioning her coiffure attested to her desire to win her future husband's approval.

She tried to tell herself she was marrying Lance because she had no choice, that it was the only way out of an impossible situation, but as she closed the door of her bedroom to go downstairs, she admitted that wasn't entirely true. Part of her *wanted* to marry him. She loved his handsome looks and his lazy smile. She even liked the brisk authority in his voice and the confidence in his long, athletic strides and the way his eyes gleamed when he laughed, and the way his lips felt on hers.

There were so many things she liked about him, she thought bleakly, and there were so many things about him that she had yet to find out. She had no illusions about what Lance felt about her. He was attracted to her, she knew, but beyond that he felt nothing for her. She, on the other hand, was in serious danger of falling in love with him. But he had told her he didn't want her love and would scorn her for it.

When they arrived at Lance's house, for a moment he stood before her drinking in her beauty in quiet appreciation. Belle accepted his slow, exacting scrutiny as an unspoken compliment, for the warmth of those deep blue eyes had intensified significantly by the time they reached her shining head. She gazed at the dangerously impressive figure of the unpredictable Lance Bingham, attired in evening black and white that made him look overwhelmingly male.

Lance favoured them with a glinting smile, but Belle noted his manner was guarded and reserved. 'Good evening,' he said briskly. 'Welcome to my home.' He looked at Belle. 'Spare me just a moment, will you, Belle?' He looked at his butler. 'Show the dowager countess into the drawing room. We won't be a moment.'

Excusing herself, Belle followed him into his study.

'I won't keep you long,' he promised, reaching into a drawer of his large carved desk and taking out a small velvet box. Without another word, he took her hand in his and slid a ring on to her finger. Belle gazed at it in wonder. A cluster of large emeralds were surrounded by shimmering diamonds.

'Lance, I—I never expected... It is the most incredible, beautiful ring. Thank you.'

'It is an engagement ring—what a man gives to his future bride. It is customary.' His lips curved in a smile as his gaze settled on her lips. 'You can thank me with a kiss.'

He stepped closer, forcing Belle into nerve-racking proximity with his powerful body, and slowly lowered his lips to hers. He saw her mouth part to welcome his, which captured hers in a long, hungry, thorough kiss, crushing her hard against him. Leaning up on her toes, she slid her hands up along his hard chest and twined them around his neck, letting her fingers slide through the soft hairs at his nape, while he explored her mouth with heady delight, his kiss attesting to his ravenous greed, draining Belle's mind by his ardour and her body's helpless response to it.

When he finally lifted his head, she stared into his smoky deep blue eyes, trying to understand why his kisses always had this shattering effect on her.

Lance stared down at her with an odd expression of bemusement and self-mockery on his chiselled features. 'I can see I shall have to give you jewels more often to get a response like that from you. But for now my gift comes with a dire warning, Belle. Do not kiss me again like that until after we are married, otherwise I will not be held responsible for the consequences.'

Belle already knew how easily he could be carried away by his ardour, which would lead him to behave in an unspecified way. He was telling her he had no wish to lose his head and she was feminine enough to feel a surge of satisfaction because her nearness and her kiss could so affect this extremely experienced man. She also knew of the dangers of getting too close to him, for she would be unable to resist him if he plied her again with his persuasive wooing. He could steal her will away with no more than a gentle kiss.

She smiled coyly up at him. 'I have your meaning, Lance, and will be only too happy to oblige.'

He scowled down at her. 'Eight weeks, Belle, for eight weeks, and then you can prepare yourself for my assault.'

At dinner the three of them conversed amiably. No one seeing them would believe that theses two families had been anything but friends for the past fifty years.

Afterwards they attended the Earl and Countess of Sidmouth's ball in Mayfair. It seemed as if everyone in London was there, and every pair of eyes seemed to shift to them as their names were announced. Having read the announcement of the betrothal in the newspaper, heads turned, fans fluttered and whispers began.

No one looking at Belle would have guessed how nervous she was. For a moment while Lance paused to greet an acquaintance, she stood beside her grandmother at the top of the steps leading down into the ballroom, looking down into the sea of nameless faces. Then Lance suddenly appeared by her side and held out his hand. Belle placed her hand in his and he tucked it possessively in the crook of his arm.

Lance felt it tremble, and, bending over her, murmured, 'You're nervous, aren't you? I can tell.'

'Terrified,' she amended, pinning a smile to her lips. 'Everyone is looking at us.'

'Belle,' he said severely, but with a dazzling smile for the benefit of the onlookers, 'you are the young woman who brazenly entered my bedchamber and threatened to break my hands if I dared to touch you.'

Belle stared at him askance. 'Did I really say that?'

He grinning down at her. 'Every word. So do not dare turn cowardly now.'

Her mouth suddenly dry, Belle glanced around at the curious faces, some craning their necks better to see her. 'I'll try not to,' she replied, 'but it won't be easy. Don't they know that it's impolite to stare?'

'Probably not. Ignore them,' Lance quipped, unlike her completely impervious to the stir they were creating. When the countess was approached by an acquaintance and invited to sit with her, he took two glances of champagne from the tray of a passing footman. His bold admiring gaze swept over Belle's face, and then he lifted his glass and gave her a subtle toast.

It was all sweetly poignant, and Belle, beginning to relax, no longer cared a whit about any other reason for being there other than it was to celebrate their engagement. It seemed to take an age for them to reach the dance floor, because they were interrupted at every step by someone insisting on a friendly word.

They partnered only each other, waltzing with effortless ease, and in his arms Belle glowed and sparkled and reigned like a young queen. Lance's recent kiss, the husky sound of his voice, the way he held her in the dance, they were like sweet music playing through her heart. He was daring and bold and passionate, and Belle had no objections, but through it all she felt a certain amount of unease, for she sensed Lance was being like this for her benefit, and that behind that smiling façade he remained guarded and resentful of being drawn into a situation he might have cause to regret.

'You look radiant tonight, and very beautiful,' he said, studying her upturned face closely. 'You appear to be happy with the situation, Belle.'

'I am—very happy—but I am also apprehensive,' she confessed.

'You are? Why?'

'Because I'm afraid it might all go terribly wrong.'

'And why should it do that?'

Her gaze fell from his and she looked at his frilled white shirt front. 'I'm being silly, I know, but it's a feeling I have.'

'This is what you want, isn't it—marriage to me?'

She raised her eyes to his. 'Yes—of course.' She meant what she said, but the apprehension that occupied a small corner of her mind would not go away. 'But—is it what you want, Lance?'

He looked away from her, his face guarded. 'Of course,' he replied, his answer brusque, as the strains of the waltz died. 'This is the last social event we will attend before I have to leave for Ryhill and you for Harworth. Will you mind leaving all the glamour and sparkle of the Season behind for the solitude of the country?'

'Not really,' Belle replied quietly, disappointed by his unconvincing response to her question, but in no mood to take him to task over it just then. 'I shall be happy to go. Besides I am looking forward to seeing Harworth.'

'And Ryhill—of which you shall be mistress of very soon.'

'I know—and thank you, Lance.'

His broad shoulders lifted in a shrug. 'Then since the dance has ended, I think it is time for us to leave.'

'Yes,' Belle replied, realising he was uncomfortable with her gratitude.

'Might I suggest that, if your grandmother would care to leave for Harworth earlier than planned, we could travel to Wiltshire together?'

'You needn't put yourself to so much trouble. Besides we have things to do for the wedding before we can leave for Harworth.'

'As you wish.'

After he escorted Belle and the countess back to Hampstead, when her grandmother went inside the house Belle said a quiet goodnight to Lance. He stood looking down at her a long moment, and after kissing her lightly on the lips—which was more like a duty kiss than of the passionate kind she was becoming accustomed to, Belle thought with a surge of disappointment—he turned on his heel, walking with long strides back to the carriage.

Belle followed his tall, powerful form with her gaze until he had climbed in and told the driver to move on. Her expression was wistful, her yearning for him written on her face. Tears welled in her eyes and a tight ache in her heart. Deep down she knew Lance didn't want to marry her, but she hoped, with all her heart, that all that would change when they reached Wiltshire and they had the time to get to know each other better.

At present it would appear that the passionate interlude they had shared had done nothing to change their relationship. What had been a devastating experience for her had meant nothing to him at all. She blinked back the tears. She had had been stupid to confuse physical desire with love. Just because a man made love to a woman with such fierce intensity didn't mean his heart was engaged.

In the days that followed, Belle had little time to think of Lance as she was swept into preparations for the wedding, her wedding gown being of prominence to all else. Her grandmother took charge of everything, and Belle couldn't help smiling at the return of her grandmother's familiar autocratic manner—it was vastly preferable to the wounded and worried woman the scandal had made of her.

In the midst of all the preparations, Belle did take a moment to consider her situation. How had it come to this? she wondered. At the beginning of the Season she had made her début on the London scene with no other thought in her head than to enjoy herself, and if she met a man she fell in love with then so be it. And because she had no experience of men like Lance Bingham, being gullible and blind to everything but the devastatingly handsome man she'd met at Carlton House, she had been drawn to him in the most inexplicable way, but not in the way she had imagined it.

The truth was that before he had taken up his military career, Lance Bingham had the reputation of being a notorious rake with a well-deserved reputation for profligacy. Did men change all that much? she wondered. Countless women fell in love with him all the time, and she was just another one of his victims to fall prey to his fatal attraction. He was twelve years her senior, which in the beginning had made her even more wary of his appeal. What could a naïve young woman do to fortify herself against the persuasive charm of a man of experience? Certainly a few moments in his presence could make her flustered despite the handsome young aristocrats who gathered around her, each vying for her attention. But in retrospect these eager gallants seemed hopelessly immature when she had met a more worthy subject with whom to compare them.

However, she must not forget that Lance was not marrying her from choice and that their marriage was one of great inconvenience to him. He did want her—at least physically—his lustful wooing left her in no doubt of that. And the whispered overtures he had had plied her with when he had found her in his bedchamber, coaxing her to yield to the delights to be found in his bed, of how he would like to introduce her to the more erotic rudiments of being a full-fledged wife, quickened her own hunger now that he had given her a taste of what to expect. But was it any different to what he would say and do to any other attractive woman?

In the days that preceded her wedding, Belle was content to settle down at Harworth. It was an extensive, splendid estate, the Tudor house with additions in various styles added through the years. There was a constant stream of friends and neighbours of her grandmother, who came to call to wish her well. Only Lance stayed away and she was deeply hurt and disappointed by this. On the odd occasions when he did escort her to formal events in the neighbourhood, his polite attentiveness could not be faulted, but beneath his handsome façade he was cool and guarded and she felt she could not reach him. It gave Belle the uneasy feeling that she was marrying an absentee stranger.

He was a man any woman would be proud to have for her husband—or lover. Belle fought the memory that thought aroused. She tried not to think of when he had made love to her. Sometimes she forgot for a while the incredible wanton things they had done, and the mention of his name would send them rushing back. Yet he seemed to have dismissed their moment of shared passion so easily. If it had meant anything at all to him he wouldn't be avoiding her like this.

She tried to appear unconcerned about his absence, even going so far as to make excuses for him, saying how busy he must be at Ryhill, having only recently taken on his inheritance and the heavy responsibilities this must entail. But deep inside her she was profoundly hurt and more than a little angry by his absence during these days before their wedding, which they should be spending together and getting to know each other better.

The closer it got to the wedding, more often her heart

seemed torn asunder by two choices, both of which at different times seemed rational. One was driven by a growing desire to become Lance's wife in actuality, the other, based on the fear of entering into a loveless marriage, to abscond. Yet when she mused on the latter option, knowing she was soiled goods and no other man would want her, a miserable emptiness settled on her heart, leaving her feeling drained, and she'd find herself struggling against an assault of tears, both strong indications of his effect on her and her reluctance to leave him. In spite of the precautions with which she had sought to fortify herself, it was a hard fact for her to face knowing that her fascination with this man had deepened in the short span of time she had known him.

Despite the reticence he felt toward his forthcoming marriage to Belle, she would have been surprised to know how Lance, who was determined to hold her at bay for as long as possible, found his gentlemanly forbearance surely strained. Belle was far too beautiful and alluring for him to nonchalantly endure her nearness and not make love to her.

In a quest to put some distance between them, he limited the time he spent with her. Even when he was forced by the demands of protocol to conduct himself in social good manner and escort his fiancée to functions that required their attendance as a couple, he sought to remain distantly detached. He conversed with her when compelled, and then briefly, a contrivance which allowed him by dint of will to maintain his gentlemanly forbearance.

On the morning of her wedding day Belle was unable to dispel her feeling of despondency. Today she was going to commit her entire life into the keeping of a man who did not love her. Every instinct for self-preservation that she possessed warned her not to go through with it, not to marry Lance. She couldn't help comparing her own situation with that of her grandmother, how she had been forced to live without the love of her life and had married someone else—her grandfather. Had they been happy? She hoped so, but all her life she must have felt she had settled for second best.

Second best! This was where the difference lay. Second best did not apply to her, for there had been no one else before Lance. He was the first man to stir her emotions and set her body aflame with desire. She wasn't sure she liked the way her heart was inclined to race when she recalled the occasion when they had made love, when he had spoken smooth endearments into her ear, for it made her realise how vulnerable she was to his charm. The powerful persuasiveness that he was capable to launch against her womanly being could reap devastating results, for what defence had she against a man adeptly skilled in the art of seducing women?

It was these thoughts that persuaded her that she wanted Lance to be her husband. She wanted to be made complete by him, to become a part of him, to know him as she had never known a man before—and perhaps with the knowing, for both of them, would come love.

The weather was warm and heady with the intoxicating scents of flowers wafting on the gentlest of breezes. With the sun's radiance in evidence, it was perfect. With time to spare before they were to leave for the church, alone with her grandmother, Belle hesitantly brought up the subject of the diamonds—the diamonds Lance had given her to wear on this special day—believing that if they did not speak of it, there would always be some unease about it.

'Lance told me about the necklace, Grandmother. Why did you not tell me that you were engaged to his grandfather?'

The countess turned her head away, gazing out of the window, and Belle said quickly, 'I am sorry. You needn't tell me if it will upset you to speak of it.'

'It's not that,' she said, slowly returning her gaze to Belle's face. 'I know how very sensible and understanding you are, but it was all so long ago now that I often wonder if I understand it myself. '

'But you loved him.'

'Oh, yes. I loved him with all my heart and soul. We were to be married and I loved him and he cut me out of his life for someone else when he was the only thing worth living for. He had given me the diamonds on our betrothal. You know the rest.'

'That you did not return them.'

'Afterwards I hated myself more than I hated those diamonds. I wanted to give them back, but I felt if I were to do that, my humiliation would be total. So they remained in the box until you took it upon yourself to wear them.'

'I should not have done that. It was unforgivable of me. My stupidity hurt you, and for that I am sorry.'

'Don't be. It's too late for self-recrimination now.' She smiled softly, reaching out and gently fingering the diamonds that had been the cause of so much controversy. 'They are exquisite, are they not? I'm glad Lance thought you should wear them today. There could not be a more fitting occasion. You—are quite taken with Lance Bingham, are you not, Isabelle?'

She sighed. 'He is handsome and manly, with the most persuasive smile.' Her eyes suddenly clouded. 'However, I—confess that I have had my doubts about marrying him. Why, on waking this morning I asked myself if I was ready for all of this. I almost got cold feet and considered calling the whole thing off—but—when I weighed everything up, I realised that marrying him was the sensible thing to do.'

'Have you fallen in love with him?'

'In all honesty I don't know how I feel. He—he makes me feel things I have never felt before. I like being with him. I like it when he smiles and laughs and tells me I look nice. I—have come to care for him deeply.'

The countess smiled and, taking Belle's hand, squeezed it gently. 'There you are, then. If it isn't love you feel now, it soon will be. I believe Lord Bingham is quite taken with you, too.'

Belle had no idea what Lance's feelings were where she was concerned, for she still felt a profound disappointment and hurt that he had not come to see her as often as she would have liked. When he kissed her he made her feel that he wanted her, but that was desire, and desire and love were worlds apart.

'How can you know that? Has he said so?'

The countess chuckled softly. 'No, not in so many words, but I have eyes in my head and I have seen the way he looks at you. If he felt nothing for you he would never have bowed to propriety and agreed to marry you. I can see you are like me after all—and he is so like his grandfather. And who knows? There may come a time when we shall have cause to bless those diamonds that have been the cause of so much discord.' She got to her feet and straightened her spine, smiling at the young woman she had come to care for very much. 'Now come along, Isabelle. I think we've dawdled long enough. We have a wedding to go to—or has it slipped your mind?'

The roads around the village church were snarled with curricles and carriages that had disgorged their passengers. The little church was full to overflowing with the local aristocracy garbed in silks and fine brocades, and friendly villagers lined both sides of the path, all come to witness this union between two of the most notable—if not always friendly to each other in the past—families in Wiltshire.

More nervous than she cared to show, in an ice-blue gown of incredible beauty and extravagant expense, Belle took a footman's hand to be helped from the carriage. There were so many people, all strangers, yet they were all wishing her well.

In the vestibule Daisy fussed about straightening her train and adjusting her veil. When all was as it should be, Belle placed her trembling fingers on Rowland's arm, glad that he had agreed to give her away, there being no male influence in her life.

When she paused before she began the endless walk down the aisle, where all eyes were focused on her, that was the moment when the enormity of what she was about to do hit her. Panic shot through her and she asked herself why she was doing this, telling herself that it wasn't too late to turn and run, that she could escape, but her legs were already carrying her towards the altar, to where the minister stood, the marriage book open in his hands. Rays of sunlight slanting through the mullioned windows caught the diamonds glittering in her hair and her veil.

Rowland must have sensed her fear, for he smiled sideways at her and murmured, 'Take heart, Belle. The parson knows the difference between the last rites and a wedding ceremony.'

Smiling nervously up at him and taking reassurance from her grandmother, who was in the front pew where she should be, her heart began to lose the battle against terror—until her eyes focused on Lance. Dressed in a splendid suit of midnight blue and a pristine white cravat, he stepped into the aisle and waited for her to reach him. With his face partly shadowed, he looked so tall and powerful and dark—as dark as her future.

Belle was unable to quell the sudden ache that his grim expression aroused in her or the sorrow she felt when she remembered her girlhood dream of how she wanted her wedding day to be. How different this was. Her dream had been to go to her future husband with a heart bursting with love and joy. Instead there was only fear and dread and regret. But somehow she managed to keep her own expression cool and serene as she relinquished Rowland's arm and took her place beside Lance Bingham.

As the music soared, unaware of the moment when Belle had almost taken flight, Lance turned to look at her. To some degree his attempts to treat her impersonally and keep her at arm's length had helped, but on seeing the perfect vision walking slowly towards him, provocatively beautiful in her flowing ice-blue gown and gossamer veil, it was tantamount to being hit with a sledgehammer in a most vulnerable place, dispelling some of the gloom of his marriage ceremony from his heart.

It was with a feeling of intense pride that his intense blue gaze locked on to hers, and when she was in front of him, and before his features settled back into their grim lines of cynical indifference, briefly his eyes smiled down at her, and he said, 'You look extremely beautiful, Belle.'

The compliment was just what Belle needed to bolster her courage. Her heart swelled ready to burst as Rowland put her hand in Lance's, and she felt his long, strong fingers close firmly round her own in a reassuring grasp. If she had any remaining doubts about marrying this man, they were dispelled in that moment, and as they turned to the minister and she took her place by his side, she knew that with or without Lance's love, this was where she would remain for all time.

Everyone listened in breathless silence as the wedding ceremony was conducted. In muted, trembling tones, Belle replied to the questions the minister presented to her. The firm, deep voice of Lance echoed hauntingly in the stillness as he too made his responses, his voice deep and resonant echoing through the church, promising to love and cherish her, and endowing her with all his worldly goods. And then it was over and these two proud and beautiful people were pronounced man and wife.

'You may kiss the bride,' the minister said.

Lance turned and looked at her, his eyes gleaming with something that was so intense and so terrifying that Belle stiffened when he drew her towards him and his arms went round her, encircling her. Bending his head, he claimed her trembling lips in a long drawn-out kiss that brought a frown of disapproval to the minister's brow and a smile to the lips of all those present. Then he released her and took her arm. After signing the documents that made their union legal in the eyes of the law as well as God, with the sound of congratulations ringing in their ears, Lance led his bride down the aisle and out of the church.

Everyone was there to see Lance's shiny black carriage drive off, swaying gently along the road towards Harworth Hall. It was drawn by four prancing chestnut horses in magnificent silver harnesses. Two coachmen mounted in green velvet livery sat proudly erect in front.

Belle sank almost breathless with relief into the deep luxurious upholstery and looked down at the broad gold band which Lance had slid on to her slender finger—a bold statement, she thought, telling the whole world that she belonged to him.

When Rowland, in jovial mood, had leaned into the carriage and told him to go directly to Harworth, Lance had laughed, which went a long way to relaxing Belle. It was the first spark of humour she had seen from him in a long time. She cast a glance at her new husband as the carriage left the church and found his eyes assessing her. But then she caught the ironic flicker in his eyes and realised that perhaps nothing had changed. Trying to hide her disappointment, she turned away.

Seated beside her, Lance sensed her tension and her inner sadness, and realised, as if for the first time, just how difficult she must be finding this situation. This was her wedding day, the most important day in a girl's life. She was leaving everything that was familiar to her in order to face a new way of life at the side of a husband who, through his restrained manner and avoidance of her, he thought with a twinge of regret, must have given her the impression that he didn't want her.

Suddenly and without pausing to question the reason why, he wanted to make things easier for her, to show that he was willing to give their marriage a chance. Having a wife would

be a great benefit to him at Ryhill. And Belle was undeniably
lovely.

'I meant what I said in church, Belle. You look lovely,' he
uttered quietly, taking her hand and holding it in a firm clasp.
His tone held an odd note of pride, and perhaps awe, that
made her turn her head to him. With the dappled shade of
light playing across her creamy skin and wisps of hair escaping from their pins caressing her cheek, she was the most
beautiful woman Lance had ever laid eyes on. Whether due to
the gently curving bosom beneath the confines of her gown,
the satin softness of her skin, or the rosy blush that infused
her cheeks, brightening her eyes until they seemed to glow
with a brilliance of their own behind the thick, sooty lashes,
or the way her lips were softly parted, his attention was firmly
ensnared, such enticements being too much for any man to
ignore, much less one who had found himself hard pressed by
a lengthened abstinence and ever-goading passions.

Something in his chest tightened. When she lowered her
eyes he placed a gentle finger under her chin, compelling her
to meet his gaze.

'Kiss me, Belle.' His senses alive to the elusive perfumed
scent of her, and unable to resist the softness of her lips, he
drew her close. Wordlessly she offered him her lips. Her kiss
was tentative at first, as if she needed time to reconsider what
she was doing, but when his mouth opened over hers, as his
heat flowed into her she seemed to relax a little.

Taking her in his arms, covering her mouth with his own,
he kissed her long and deep. It was the first since they had
left London. Tonight was their night, when he would truly
make her his wife in every sense, and his blood stirred hotly.
Already he was mentally undressing and kissing her, caressing her with his hands and mouth until she was wild for him.

Having kissed her to near insensibility, he raised his head
and looked at her flushed face. 'Was that to your liking,
madam?'

'Mmm. It was so nice I wouldn't mind if you kissed me again.' She leaned forwards to steal another. Her husband readily accommodated her, this time making it far more sensual as his tongue slipped inwards to explore further. She moaned against him, and when he released her lips she pleaded for more.

'You're insatiable, my love, but I dare not continue lest I arrive at our wedding breakfast in a state of embarrassment.'

A shy but mischievous smile curved her lips. 'I've never kissed a man before in an open carriage. I feel almost wanton.'

'Kissing—or anything of an intimate nature—is not wantonness when it's between a couple who has been bound by marriage. It is an honest desire—and right now I want you with a craving that will not be appeased by a mere kiss.'

'Do you really want me, Lance?' she asked, a slightly anxious frown creasing her brow.

Now that he was no longer kissing her and he could think more clearly, Lance realised how much he did want her, that no power on earth would persuade him to cast her out of his life—and to reassure her, he kissed her again.

The wedding breakfast was quite splendid. The Dowager Countess of Harworth had spared no expense. When the guests had all arrived and made their way up the grand staircase, which was flanked by footmen standing stiffly at attention in blue-and-gold Ainsley livery, beneath a huge chandelier in the ballroom decked with summer flowers, Belle stood beside Lance while the butler, in a stentorian tone, announced each individual.

Belle was assisted into her chair at the table by her husband.

The meal was a splendid affair, and when the endless toasts offered for the bride and groom's health were over and the musicians struck up the first waltz, to the sound of hearty applause, blended with laughter, Lance led his bride on to the dance floor.

Relieved that he had lowered his guard at last and hoping it would continue, a sigh of relief slipped from Belle's lips as he swept her smoothly around the ballroom, continually turning in ever-widening circles until the faces of those who watched became an indistinct blur beyond his broad shoulders.

'How are you feeling now?' Lance enquired softly.

Belle laughed, evidencing not only her relief, but her pleasure at being able to dance for the first time with her husband.

'Better. I was worried about Grandmother.'

'I thought you might be—but she looks as if she's enjoying herself.'

'I'm sorry your mother couldn't make it back for the wedding. I look forward to meeting her.'

'She is impatient to meet you. My sister has been delivered of her baby—a daughter—and Mother is on her way home.' He looked at her upturned face, a teasing smile twitching at his lips. 'You dance divinely, wife. You are as light as thistledown in my arms.'

'I feel as if I'm floating on a cloud.'

A wicked, devilish grin stretched across Lance's lips. 'I hope that's the way you will feel when I make love to you—later.'

Before she could reply to his *risqué* remark, he had spun her round so that her feet almost left the floor. For Belle, nothing existed beyond her husband's encircling arms and the endless glitter of blue eyes that held hers captive. They spoke in muted tones—an intimate sharing of comments about the wedding. There was a warm, underlying excitement within Belle that Lance had kindled with his earlier kiss—a promise and a tingle of anticipation of that moment when she would be alone with him.

Lance was completely entranced with the soft eyes that

glowed with a shining lustre that radiated her happiness. Feeling immensely blessed to have found such devotion, and very much aware of her pliant body moving with his, as if their minds were joined in secret accord, he was impatient to whisk her away from the celebrations to Ryhill, for it was only there that they could be assured of adequate privacy.

Chapter Eight

It was close on midnight when they bade family and friends goodnight and left for Ryhill, half-an-hour's drive away. When they arrived, welcoming lights shone from the windows. Climbing out of the coach, before she knew what was happening, Lance swept Belle up into his arms and carried her laughing into the house, where he set her to her feet.

'Welcome to Ryhill,' he said, kissing her lips. 'Countess.'

She giggled, returning his kiss. 'How very grand it sounds. It's going to take some getting used to. I've only just got used to being addressed as Miss Isabelle.'

There was only Masters, the butler, to receive them. Having endured an agonising abstinence and wanting nothing to hinder his union with his wife, Lance told him to go to bed.

With a knowing smile Masters was happy to oblige.

Lance pulled his wife close. 'Would you like a drink—or would you like to see our bedroom?' he invited with a teasing smile.

Belle's eyes shone as they swept over her handsome husband, and her lips curved in a sensual smile as she looked into his lusting eyes. 'Only if you'll come with me.'

'You don't think I'd let you go without me, do you?' he answered her with a chuckle. 'And the way my mind's been working all day, it may be another week before I allow you to leave.'

He whisked her up the stairs to the master bedroom. Reluctant to release her, he kicked the door closed with his foot, glancing round quickly to make sure Belle's maid had done as he instructed and not waited up for her mistress. If there was undressing to be done he would do it himself.

With all his self-control, his breath came quickly and his heart beat high in his throat as he gathered her into his arms and grasped her tightly to him. 'Alone with you at last. I've wanted you for so long, hungered for you. For too long I've tried to avoid kissing you the way I've been yearning to for fear of where it would lead us. To put it bluntly, Belle, I'm almost starved for your kisses and all the other temptations I found myself facing whenever I was near you.'

Recalling the time he had made love to her and all the glorious things he had done to her, Belle grew heady with anticipation. Nothing he had done to her since had come equal to that exchange.

'Is that the reason why you've been avoiding me of late?'

'You noticed?'

'How could I not? It made me wonder if you would go through with the ceremony—that you might have had second thoughts and come to regret your decision to marry me after all.'

'I'm sorry if I gave you reason to think that. I did have reservations about our marriage—I told you that at the beginning—but now it is done I accept it.'

'Then you don't mean to avoid me any longer?'

'Just try to keep me away. I want our marriage to work, Belle, and I can see no reason why it shouldn't.'

His eyes looked down into hers and Belle saw he was sincere. Her lips curved in a gentle smile. 'Then what are you waiting for? Please, Lance—wait no longer.'

Looping her arms around his neck, she drew his head down to hers. His mouth eagerly sought hers and their bodies strained together hungrily. When they pulled apart, she kicked off her shoes and stepped back to slip out of her dress, tossing it over a chair. Raising her petticoat to reveal her long, sleek legs encased in silk stockings, held in place by white ribbons above her knees, she unfastened the ties. Suddenly she glanced at her husband. Had she issued an invitation to ogle the sights, he couldn't have been more eager to respond. With his shoulder leaning against one of the ornate posts of the huge bed, his expression was one of admiration. Already he had stored within his memory diverse views of her—this one he would install as the most tempting.

Ensnaring his gaze, Belle felt her lips curve in a smile. 'Didn't anyone ever tell you that it's rude to stare?' she teased, seeing where his gaze was fastened.

'I can't help it. The sight of you enslaves me. I've never seen so much perfection wrapped up in one woman.' When she bent over to remove her stockings, providing him with a generous view of her ripe, creamy breasts, he halted her. 'Leave them on.'

Making a pretence of being shocked, she giggled. 'Really, you have the strangest quirks, Lance Bingham.'

'You'll have a lifetime to become familiar with them, but I prefer to be about more serious pleasures now.'

'And what would they be?' she queried with her head tilted to one side and a provocative smile on her lips.

'I'll show you.' When she raised her arms to let down her hair, he relinquished his stance. 'Here, let me.'

His fingers freed her hair, which cascaded down her spine in a silken mass. His hungering eyes swept over her alluring form in a long, lingering caress. Then he was lifting her in his arms and carrying her towards the bed, where he stood her on her feet. They were both hit by a frenzy to undress completely—apart from Belle's stockings—and in naked splendour they caressed each other, Lance covering her body in greedy kisses, before tumbling her on to the bed.

Soon Lance's mouth was tracing over his wife's body, claiming a soft peak, his hand searching out the secret softness of her, and the fires of passion in Belle rose higher still, sweeping away her restraints until they blended with his in an erotic exchange that left them both heady with desire.

Lance's naked body covered hers and the probing of his maleness she willingly accepted. Then his narrow hips were passing over hers in long leisurely strokes. Deep within her, Belle could feel a heat overflowing her womanly ardour.

Luxuriating in the joy of being one with her, and consumed by her womanly warmth, Lance was thoroughly engorged with lust. A hot, pulsating flame quickened Belle's blood as his movements became more concentrated and increasingly forceful, igniting her fervour. Soon their passions were soaring out; Lance's control shattering and his own reservations shattering with it as he claimed her fully and filled her with the urgent desire he'd been keeping so tight in check since his first possession of her that moonlit night in the garden of Schofield House.

It was only when his shuddering release was over that he remembered why he had harboured any reservations at all. And by then, he couldn't find the will or the energy for regret. Their gasps were finally silenced, becoming soft, blissful sighs of contentment.

They lay in each other's arms, kissing, touching and whispering, Belle already luxuriating in her new wifely state. She existed in a warm glow. Never had she felt so happy or felt the way she felt now for another human being. But what did Lance feel for her? He wanted her body, that was clear—but desire and need were not love. Whatever interpretation she put on it, she was greedy to savour it all again. This time Lance made love to her in a most physical way, snatching her breath in a fierce ardour and forcing every pleasurable sensation that could be wrenched from her.

Everything outside that room had ceased to exist for her, for it was all here in her husband's encompassing arms. The intensifying hunger within her became almost insatiable, driving her to a kind of wildness that had her digging her nails into the flesh on his back. Then she caught her breath as pulsing waves of bliss washed over her. Feeling a feverish warmth filling her, she welcomed it, clasping her husband's tautly flexing body as he relaxed against her and rolled on to his side, taking her with him.

'The way you make love leaves my head in a whirl,' Belle murmured with a trembling sigh, resting her cheek on his furred chest.

His hand slid over her breast, causing her to catch her breath at the scintillating shock of pleasure he elicited as the tips of his finger passed over her nipple.

Lance was certain he had never experienced such exquisite fulfilment. He also knew he wouldn't have traded his freedom for what he had now. Belle was different from any other woman, a delightful creature in her innocence, and he could imagine that with a little more tuition from him, she would enslave his mind so completely that he'd willingly yield her anything.

'You're beautiful, my love,' he murmured huskily.

'I recall you telling me that the joining of our bodies in the ritual of making love would do wonders for relaxing me. How right you were. I feel as if I could float away. It's the same feeling I experienced when you made love to me before—only this time, as your wife and in your bed, it was so much better.'

'And your reputation is no longer in question. Now you are my wife, it will be more pleasurable,' he breathed as his hand slid down her smooth belly.

* * *

The gentle breeze stirred the curtains, the sun's rays illuminating the figures within the bed. Belle lay back on the pillows, wrapped in Lance's arms, her limbs entwined with his. Her eyes were closed, and a dreamy, contented smile curved her lips.

Lance was aroused from sleep by servants' voices outside the room. His movements roused Belle and she rolled closer, reaching out a hand to caress his lean, muscular ribs. Wanting nothing more than to remain in bed, but aware of the lateness of the hour, he swung his legs over the edge of the bed and sat up. Belle laughed happily and, springing up, embraced him from behind.

'What's this? Deserting your wife already?'

He smiled as he felt the softness of her breasts on his bare back, delighting in the feel of them. 'Absolutely not, my sweet,' he said, thrusting his arms into his robe. 'I shall go below and summon breakfast and instruct your maid to attend you.'

'Don't be long,' she told him, padding with unashamed nakedness across the carpet to her dressing room, where a large tub of scented water awaited her. 'Ooh, how lovely,' she gurgled happily, realising Daisy had let herself into the dressing room by another door so as not to disturb her mistress and her husband. 'I'll have a bath while you're gone.' She cast a playful, seductive look over her shoulder. If he could not declare his love for her, at least she could humour and tempt him. 'You can wash my back if you like.'

He grinned, tossing the robe aside, the temptation to join her at her toilet almost his undoing. 'Minx. You know how to tempt a man. Besides, it's large enough for the two of us. It would be a shame to waste the water.'

He took her in his arms, thighs and belly touching, feeling the thrust of her breasts against his chest.

'Let's get in the water,' she said, eager to get on with the process.

They soaped and lathered each other, teased and kissed. Belle was becoming more sure of herself now, sure as she had never been when she had climbed into bed with him last night, when it had been Lance who had dictated, who led the way. She had been a novice then, happy to follow, and because he was a good teacher, she had learned from it and now there was no need for him to guide, to provoke, to demand. But Lance continued to set his own pace, gathering her into his arms, wet and slippery, and then back to bed.

It was mid-morning the following day and Lance and Belle were in the drawing room, drinking coffee. Belle glanced to where Lance sat reading his newspaper. She couldn't believe that she was his wife. Wife. A glow warmed her at the thought. Perhaps now she would have the chance to prove to Lance that he hadn't made a dreadful mistake in marrying her. Perhaps their relationship would be different now that he had accepted their marriage.

Ever since he had decided to marry her, for most of that time he had existed in a state of smouldering anger over being forced to wed her. Letting her gaze wander to the window and the long curving drive beyond, she gave a wistful sigh. She was falling in love with him—or had fallen. It was the only reason she could think of for the excited quivering feeling that assailed her whenever she was in his presence. Happiness, joy, delight were welling in her, filling her because this handsome, vital man belonged to her, every glorious inch of him. She had been attracted to him from the start, to his strength, his passion. She was still considering this revelation and reflecting on the tenderness of Lance's lovemaking when she saw a landau was approaching the house.

Lance glanced up from his newspaper and looked through the window, recognising the equipage. 'Good Lord!'

'Who is it?' Belle asked when he discarded the newspaper and got to his feet.

'My mother.'

His announcement had Belle shooting out of her chair. She was sorry that Lance's mother had missed their wedding and she was looking forward to meeting her, but because of the past and not sure how she would be received, she did feel a certain amount of trepidation.

'Oh, dear. I wish I'd known she was going to call.' Her hand went to her hair. 'I must look a sight.'

Aware of her nervousness, Lance took her hand and gave it a reassuring squeeze. 'Don't be nervous. She won't eat you. And you look wonderful.'

'I feel terrified,' Belle confessed, without taking her eyes from the equipage in the drive, seeing a woman alight after a few moments. 'But what if she doesn't like me and resents me for snaring her son?'

'I'm sure she'll do nothing of the sort. Don't worry. She'll love you, you'll see.'

Unfortunately Belle did not share Lance's confidence.

When Lance's mother swept into the hall, they were both there to greet her. Lance left Belle's side to enfold the older woman in his arms, expressing his delight at seeing her.

'Mother, it's wonderful that you're back. I hope your journey was uneventful.'

'It was. I returned late yesterday. Naturally I was eager to meet my new daughter-in-law,' she said, looking past him to the nervous young woman, 'so I came straight over.'

Lance held his hand out to Belle, urging her forwards with a reassuring smile.

'Mother, may I present Belle—my wife. Belle, this is my mother.'

'I am very happy to make your acquaintance, ma'am.'

Elizabeth Bingham, with light blue eyes and grey-streaked dark hair, was reserved and considered Belle for a long, uncertain moment before she gave a quick, worried glance at her son. As if with decision, she sighed and took Belle's hands in her own.

'Welcome to Ryhill, Belle—and please call me Elizabeth. I'm happy to meet you and delighted to have you in the family. I can't tell you how sorry I am that I missed your wedding—but we have plenty of time to get to know each other and you can tell me all about it. How are you settling in at Ryhill? You're not finding it too daunting, I hope.'

'I must confess that it's not what I'm used to. Since coming to England I've lived with my grandmother so I have no experience about running a house—but given time and application, I shall soon learn.'

'I have every confidence in you, Belle, and I shall be glad to help in any way I can. The servants are extremely competent, so I am sure you'll soon get used to running such a large house. What a beautiful name you have.'

'Actually, my name is Isabelle, but everyone—except Grandmother, that is—calls me Belle,' Belle explained.

'I may call you Belle?'

'Of course you may. I would like that.' Belle was completely taken with the easy friendliness of this attractive woman and accepted the feeling as mutual as Elizabeth's slender fingers squeezed her own before releasing them.

Elizabeth studied the dark green eyes regarding her solemnly from beneath a heavy fringe of dark lashes, and finally managed a smile. 'I am well pleased that you and Lance are married. It's time he settled down. You must find living in the country so very different from London—and a big change from America, I am sure.'

'Very much so.'

'I can imagine your marriage to Lance has drawn much attention hereabouts; in fact, it all happened with such speed that I cannot believe it. One minute you are unattached, Lance, and the next you aren't and announce that you are to be married in just a few weeks. Everything happened so fast. I suspect there are a lot of disappointed young ladies hereabouts.' She smiled at Belle. 'Whenever he comes home he always sets all their hearts aflutter with dreams and aspirations of securing him for themselves.'

'Then they'll all be disappointed,' Lance said, smiling proudly at his wife of forty-eight hours. 'I am well satisfied with the wife I have. I want no other.'

'And I approve your choice. Belle is charming and I know we will become good friends.'

'Come,' Lance said, sliding his hand to the small of Belle's back, where it rested comfortably. 'Let's go into the drawing room, where we can have some tea while we catch up on everything. I'm eager to know all about Ireland and Sophie—and about my new niece.'

He was about to propel his wife towards the drawing room, only to be halted in his stride by his mother's next words, spoken sharply.

'Your niece? Your niece is doing nicely, Lance. Would that you could show the same interest in your daughter.'

For a moment a deathly hush fell upon the hall. The word *daughter* caught Belle's blurred attention. She stared with dazed shock at her mother-in-law. She wanted to ask her what she meant by that remark, but the grim expression on her face as she looked at her son made her wary.

'I take it you have told Belle about Charlotte, Lance? I sincerely hope so, because this is where she should be.'

'Charlotte?' Belle asked, bemused. Her heart contracted. Slowly she turned to look at her husband, so distracted by her own rampaging emotions that she never noticed the sudden hardening of his face or the way he faced his mother, as if he were bracing himself to meet a firing squad. 'Lance? What is this? Please tell me.'

For a man usually so mentally astute, Lance was too stunned to move.

'This is no place to discuss the matter. I think we should go into the drawing room,' Elizabeth said, going ahead of them into the room and closing the door when they were all inside. Before entering the house she had sat for a moment in the landau, gathering her courage for what she had come to do. She shrank from the pain she must confront, and the hostility she might encounter from her son. 'Lance has a daughter, Belle—a daughter he clearly forgot to tell you about.'

'I didn't forget,' Lance ground out—his face was white, taut with rage. 'If you don't mind, Mother, I would prefer not to have this discussion.'

'No, Lance, I don't suppose you would,' Elizabeth said, clearly determined to stand her ground. 'You never do. It is true to say that you seem to forget your daughter exists half the time. I'm sorry, but that's the way it is. Little Charlotte is so sweet and so exactly like you, more every day. She is your responsibility and of course she must come to you. She can't stay with me. It isn't right.'

From across the room, wildly Belle looked about her, her mind already realising what her heart couldn't bear to believe. She could not bring herself to go to him. Suddenly her knees went weak. Reaching out for the nearest chair, she sank into the seat. Her insides had gone cold with dread. She waited for Lance to tell her the child had nothing to do with him, but he didn't.

'Lance—is this true?' she asked when she could find her voice. 'Do you have a—a daughter?'

He looked at her, his face hard and cold. 'Yes, I do.'

No slap on the face could have hurt so much. A sudden weight fell on Belle's heart at what was happening. She was stunned, bewildered, and a thousand thoughts raced across her brain and crashed together in confusion. There was no room in her heart or her mind for anything but this vast disappointment, which had already become an aching pain.

'I'm so sorry, my dear,' Elizabeth said, feeling sympathy for this young woman who had married Lance in ignorance, and anger towards her son for withholding from her an important part of his life. 'I don't like doing this and I certainly did not intend distressing you, but you have a right to be told. While in Ireland Charlotte contracted a fever and was quite poorly. She had us all worried for a time. I couldn't bear it if anything should happen to her while she is in my care. So I made up my mind to return her to her father—where she belongs.'

'How old is Charlotte?' Belle asked, her throat so constricted she could hardly get the words out.

'Nine months,' Elizabeth provided.

In wretched disbelief Belle looked from her mother-in-law to Lance. 'Nine months? But—she is still a baby.' She swallowed convulsively. 'Lance—how could you do this—to your daughter—and to me? Is—is there something wrong with her?'

'Charlotte is a perfect child, Belle,' Elizabeth assured her. 'She is beautiful, warm and loving—and she needs her father.'

'And her mother?'

Lance's face twisted and darkened. 'Her mother—my wife—is dead,' he bit out. Pushing a hand, which had a curious tremble in it, through his thick hair, he took a step back, his face quite blank now. 'And now I would be obliged if we could speak of something else.'

'And I will not be so easily put off,' Belle was quick to retort, trying not to think of the woman—dear God, his wife— who had died such a short time ago, a woman who had borne him a child—a woman he must have loved and whom he still mourned. The thought was so immediate, so dreadful, that she didn't even want to think about it, for she could not bear it. She felt as if she had awakened from a glorious dream to a nightmare. 'Your mother is right. You should not have kept this from me. It was cruel and despicable. How did you think I would react when I found out—unless you didn't intend for me to find out and you planned to send the daughter you have so clearly abandoned to live somewhere in obscurity?'

Lowering her eyes, Belle smoothed the skirts of her gown with a hand that shook. Her dejection was caught by Lance. The muscles worked in his cheek as his jaw tightened and he turned and strode to the window. With his rigid back to them, his shoulders taut, he thrust his hands into his pockets.

Belle got up quickly. 'Please excuse me,' she said to Elizabeth, trying to keep her voice from trembling. 'I would like to be by myself for a while.'

Wishing she could find some words of comfort and support, but knowing there was nothing she could say just now that would help Belle, feeling that she must come to terms with all this on her own and that the questions would come later, Elizabeth gently touched her arm. 'Of course. I understand. Come to me when you want to talk.'

When Belle reached the door, Lance spun round. 'Belle— wait…'

She turned ferociously. 'Let it be, Lance. Enough. I have had enough for now. I don't think I can hear more.'

She went out and closed the door. She had learned many things since leaving her home in Charleston. Now she learned another, too. Anger was a great hardener, and it was this that helped her to walk across the hall and up the stairs to the room she shared with Lance.

Resting her back against the hard wood of the door, she looked at the bed, feeling a great urge to go to it and drag the covers off and rip them to shreds. Lance had not disputed the truth of what his mother had divulged, and offered no explanation. Belle wasn't physically hurt by this or wounded, yet inside she was bleeding.

Her cherished hopes were cold and dead, like a corpse, and could not be revived. She thought of Lance—her love—and all the feelings and emotions he had created were blighted and crushed, trust and confidence destroyed.

In her wretchedness she held herself tightly, her arms locked about her body. She had married Lance in the full knowledge that he didn't love her—and now she knew why. It explained so much. He had been married before. He'd had a wife who had been dead for just nine months. Deep in the recesses of her woman's heart, Belle had sensed there was something, and yet she had not recognised what it was. How could she?

That he had married her at all had made her happy. She believed he did care for her and that his fondness was growing into something deeper and stronger. Their loving in the privacy of their bed had delighted her, and it had seemed satisfying to her husband. She had been encouraged by it and believed they were putting down the roots of their marriage, when all the time he was a grieving widower who—she assumed for just then she could see no other explanation—must have loved his wife so much that he put the blame of her death on the birth of his child. What other explanation could there be for him to abandon her like that?

And what of his dead wife? Had he given to her what she wanted—his whole inner self a man gives to the one woman he loves? She, Belle, had given him her heart, though she supposed he was not aware of it. She had given him her trust—and that he had just broken. In fact, she had given him the sum and substance of herself, who had loved no man until him.

In the drawing room Elizabeth was about to leave, thinking it best to leave the newly married couple to talk, to sort out the whole sorry mess.

'Belle must be feeling quite wretched, Lance. Would you like me to go to her?'

He shook his head and turned to look at her. 'No—leave her. It's best that I go. We have to talk.'

Elizabeth went to him and placed a kiss on his cold cheek. 'Yes, you do. It is something you should have done before you married her. Don't hurt her further, Lance. She appears to be a strong and sensible young woman. She'll weather this—and I can only hope she will come to forgive your deception.'

When Lance entered the bedchamber it was to find Belle gathering toiletries and brushes from her dressing table.

'Going somewhere?'

Belle swung round at the scathing tone of her husband's voice. If she had expected him to fall on his knees in remorse for having deceived her, the moment she saw his face, as hard as a granite sculpture, it was obvious he would do no such thing. He didn't bother to come into the room, but instead remained in the doorway, his shoulder propped against the frame, his arms folded across his chest.

'I am moving to another room for the time being. I will get Daisy to move my clothes later.'

'You're what? Just like that?' he said in an awful, silky voice. Although Lance was willing to concede he had treated her badly, he had not expected anything like this, and nor was he going to allow her to deny him the physical side of their marriage. 'After two days of marriage, you want to move out of our marital bed?'

Belle took one look at the anger kindling in his glittering eyes and stopped what she was doing. Never had her heart felt so heavy. 'You must realise that this has come as a great shock to me. I need to be alone for a time—to think about what I am going to do.'

'And why do you think you have to do anything? You're staying here with me.'

The authority and the arrogance with which he spoke infuriated Belle. 'And you can go to hell, Lance Bingham. You cannot expect me to ignore your—indiscretion, to overlook what you have done and how it will affect me. I need to be alone for a time in order to think clearly.'

'You cannot separate yourself from me. You are my wife.'

'Then you should have shown me that courtesy,' she threw

back at him fiercely. 'Prior to our marriage you should have
told me you had been married before and that you had a child.
That you didn't was deceitful and despicable.'

'Have you come to hate me in so short a time?'

'I don't hate you, Lance, but I must be given time to think
through what I am going to do, how best to deal with this—
and ponder on what my feelings toward you are now. In the
meantime, with time to myself, I will then be able to determine my desires and hopes for the future without being unduly
swayed one way or the other.'

Lance's eyebrows rose in amazement, then dropped swiftly
and ferociously into a frown. Shrugging himself away from
the door, he moved further into the room. 'Stop this foolishness. I do not like your tone, Belle. There's no need for all this
melodrama.'

Belle moved forwards to confront him with her own rage.
'Melodrama? I am many things, but never dramatic. What
you like or dislike is of supreme indifference to me just now.
What were you thinking? You must have known I would find
out some time. You have a daughter,' she said forcefully. 'Did
you intend to hide her away from me? Did you really think
that I would not find out?'

'I have not hidden her away.' Lance's voice flared with what
could have been pain, but his face was black with anger. 'She
is with my mother. And there she will remain until I decide
what is to be done with her.'

'I think your mother might have something to say about
that. What's the matter, Lance? Don't you like children?'

'I do, as a matter of fact, and when we have children of our
own I will show you.'

'Children of our own?' she cried. 'Do you think I would
even consider having a child by you when you can't even bring
yourself to take care of the one you've already got—when
you can't bear to look at her?' She spun round only to have

Lance's hand clamp about her wrist and jerk her back to face him. 'Don't you dare manhandle me,' she warned.

Lance was confronted with a woman he didn't recognise—a coldly enraged, beautiful virago. Instead of apologising for his transgression, as he'd intended to do when his mother had left, he said, 'You're making too much of this. You are being totally irrational and absurd.'

Belle pulled her arm free with a wrenching tug that nearly dislocated her shoulder, then stepped back, well out of his reach, her chest rising and falling in fury as she mentally recoiled from the violence flashing in his eyes. 'You are a monster, and I am not being irrational or absurd so don't you dare say so. You have deceived me most cruelly, Lance. At this moment I am so angry that I cannot forgive you.'

'Why? For not telling you that I had a wife before you and that I have a daughter? Would it have made any difference to your decision to marry me?'

'I cannot answer that, but it would certainly have affected me.' She continued to face him, knowing it was quite hopeless, but she might as well say what she had to say. It could make matters no worse. 'What I don't understand is why she isn't here with her father—which is where she belongs.'

'She is being well looked after. She wants for nothing,' he stated coldly. 'I make sure of that.'

'Only her father. She has lost her mother. Are you so heartless you would deny her a father's love? To be without one parent is bad enough, but to be denied both because her father blames her for being the reason her mother died is the ultimate cruelty. Have you not thought how much you are failing her—and your first wife?'

The violent colour of his anger drained from his face, and his eyes glittered. 'What? What did you say?'

'That it would surely sadden your wife if she knew of your rejection of her child. Charlotte didn't ask to be born. At nine

months old the child has done nothing to deserve your condemnation.'

There was a deep and dreadful silence, a silence so menacing, so filled with the unwavering determination of the two
people involved. Lance took a step towards her, but Belle did
not flinch. Their eyes were locked together in awful combat.
Neither was about to retreat.

'You speak of things you know nothing about.' His face
was white and set with rage, his voice shaking with the violence of his emotion. 'How dare you speak of my first wife to
me—her name was Delphine and she died after giving birth
on the eve of Waterloo—of what her attitude might be, of
what she might be feeling? That is an outrage, one you have
no right to commit. Damn you, Belle, for saying it.'

'No, it is you who will be damned, Lance Bingham. You
and all the other men who take advantage and make a mockery of a woman's weakness—her vulnerable heart. Dear
God, what have I done that I must deserve this—that I must
endure…?'

'Nothing. You have done nothing at all. What I did was
before I met you and has nothing to do with us—with our
marriage. That is the reality of it, so you must accept it.'

'That's just the kind of arrogant remark I would expect
from someone who knows they have done wrong.' Belle held
herself erect and her words were as cold and cutting as a newly
polished and sharpened sword. 'I will not accept it since you
have a child that is going to play a big part in my life.'

'And I shall see to it that she has nothing to do with you.'

'We'll see about that. Now, since I can see no point in continuing with this conversation, I would be obliged if you would
leave this room while I finish collecting my things.'

He was startled. 'What?'

'Either you leave—or I will.'

'Don't be ridiculous.'

'At this moment I don't want anything to do with you. Your

attitude towards your own flesh and blood is unacceptable and disgusts me. I confess that I am not sure enough of my abilities as a mother, but I would care for Charlotte as if she were my own.'

Lance's face froze and his hard eyes locked on hers. 'Have a care, Belle. Do not cross me in this. You will not meddle in affairs that do not concern you. There is a line beyond which you must not go. You are almost at that line and you had best be careful you do not step over it.' He spun from her and walked towards the door.

'And Charlotte?'

He turned and looked back at her. His face was expressionless. His eyes were empty, a glacial blue emptiness that told her nothing of what he felt. 'Let's get this settled once and for all. I don't want her. She will stay at Bilton House with my mother,' he said, then, turning on his heel, his composure held tightly about him, he strode from the room.

Unable to move, Belle was unable to bear it. How could she? She turned her head away and stared, blinded and tormented, at the door through which her husband had just disappeared. Her throat ached and her eyes burned, but she would not cry. She held herself steady, resisting the urge to call him back, to let him take her in his arms, to hold her, and comfort her, and for her to soothe his agony with the outpouring of her own love, for this man whom she worshipped. But she could not.

Shortly afterwards she heard the sound of a horse's hooves on the gravel as Lance left to wherever it was he was going.

She didn't see him again that day. He hadn't returned by the time she retired to another room at the opposite end of the house to the one in which they had shared two wonderful nights making love until dawn. As she lay in the soft warmth of her solitary bed, aching for him, her heart felt sad. She had defied her husband—but at what price? She had seen him angry before, but his fury, his amazingly ominous objection to Charlotte being at Ryhill, was beyond anything she had imagined.

But she would stand firm on this. It was up to her to make him see that what he was doing was wrong. He was her husband for better or worse, and she wasn't going to run away at the first hurdle.

Two days, she thought with bitter cynicism, two days they had been married and already that first hurdle seemed a mile high, but it was not insurmountable. It was up to her to see this thing through. She was mistress of Ryhill, and if Lance still loved and mourned his first wife to the exclusion of his child, then she must be patient and wait for his wounds to heal, no matter how much she was hurting. In the meantime she saw it as her duty to bring Charlotte home.

The following morning Belle awoke late. Her head was aching, but she made herself go down to breakfast, to be informed when she enquired why Lance's place was not set that he'd eaten early before leaving the house. And so on the third morning of her marriage, Belle ate alone, having no idea where her husband was.

Bilton House was not as large as Ryhill nor as imposing, but surrounded by pleasant woodland and profusely flowering gardens, with a small lake where swans and moor hens floated aimlessly upon the tranquil surface, it was charming. When Belle's carriage drew up outside the door, Lance's mother came out to greet her. It was as if she had known she would come at that precise moment and was waiting. She kissed her daughter-in-law's cheek warmly and said how delighted she was by the visit.

'I think you know why I've come,' Belle said gravely.

Elizabeth smiled, walking with her to the door. 'To see Charlotte, I expect.'

'And to take her back with me to Ryhill—if you're in agreement, that is.'

'It is what I want—what I've wanted ever since the nurse turned up on my doorstep with Charlotte in her arms. I was beginning to despair of Lance ever wanting her.'

'He still doesn't—at least, not yet. But he will. He has to. If he could only try to accept Charlotte, she could be a source of comfort to him.'

Elizabeth paused in her stride and looked at her, her eyes dark with concern. 'Belle, I'm so dreadfully sorry if this has caused trouble between you and Lance. It is the last thing I want—and you so recently a bride.'

Belle returned her smile with a confidence that was not convincing to the older woman. 'Please don't worry. I'm sure things will turn out right. Lance is like a bear with a sore head just now, but this thing has to be faced and sorted out if we are to move on with our lives.'

'You're right. Now come inside and we'll have some tea. Then I'll take you to the nursery to meet your stepdaughter.'

They sat in a charming drawing room overlooking the gardens. Drinking tea and making polite small talk, Belle was relieved when Elizabeth suggested the two of them take a stroll in the garden. It wasn't until they were some distance from the house that she invited Belle to sit beside her on a bench beneath a trellised arch with trailing pink roses.

'I am glad for the opportunity to speak with you alone, Belle. I would like to speak to you on a matter other than Charlotte. I am not one for half-truths or evasion. Lance has told me how your betrothal came about, and I confess to being troubled about it at the time.'

An embarrassed flush mantled Belle's cheeks and she looked down at her hands. 'Yes, I'm sure you must have been.'

'I have to confess,' Elizabeth said tentatively, 'that because of what happened in the past between our two families, I can't pretend I wasn't shocked when he wrote and told me the two of you were to marry. I understand it was to salvage your reputation.'

'And my pride,' Belle added on a wry note.

'Lance's also. You have both been foolish. How did your grandmother react to what happened?'

'She was angry—and extremely disappointed in me. When I came to England, my social skills and knowledge about your ways were sadly lacking. Knowing very little of the kind of protocol that rules English society, she put so much effort into preparing me for the Season and had such high hopes for me.'

'The English Season, which is the time when young girls are introduced into society in the hope of securing a suitable husband, can be daunting at any time—but for a girl newly arrived from America, I'm sure it must have been terrifying. But please go on. How did your grandmother react to your behaviour?'

'When she learned of what I had done—and how Lance turned it to his advantage—considering my reputation to be more important than past indiscretions, and with the loss of a great deal of her pride, she insisted Lance did the honourable thing.'

'And she was right to do so. I would have done exactly the same.'

'Initially he didn't want to marry me—I now know it was probably because he was still mourning his first wife, Delphine. It was too soon. I can't blame him for not wanting to form any kind of relationship with another woman so quickly after losing his wife—never mind risk marrying one. To lose a wife on the eve of battle—to be thrown into the fray so to speak right away—I can't think how he's survived and stayed sane.'

'Lance is strong,' Elizabeth replied. 'He's one of the finest, strongest people I've known. I think he takes after his father in that. I realise that you were threatened with harsh consequences if he refused to marry you.'

'Yes,' Belle replied in a low voice, meeting the older woman's eyes directly. 'I compromised myself.'

'In a way, but from what I understand, Lance forced your hand when he took the diamonds.'

'Had I known that by rights they belonged to your family, I would have left well alone.'

'But you didn't.'

'No. Anyway, he did the honourable thing and agreed to marry me to save me from scandal, which would have ruined my reputation completely and devastated my grandmother.'

'I'm looking forward to meeting her—soon, I hope. It is my hope that we can put the whole sorry business of what happened so long ago behind us. But—you do care for Lance?' Elizabeth's concern that his business with Charlotte might have caused a rift in their relationship was evident in her voice.

'Yes,' Belle answered softly, in complete honesty. 'I care for him—very much.'

Elizabeth relaxed. She knew there was probably much more to the story than either Lance had cared to elaborate on or Belle was now revealing and that she hadn't been informed of the details. Nor did she think she needed to be. She knew her son was no saint—his hasty marriage to his first wife attested to that. And she really didn't care. She was just immensely relieved that Lance had married a woman of whom she approved and who cared deeply for her son.

'Well then, that's all right. I wouldn't worry about how you came together. I know my son, and he wouldn't let himself be forced into anything if he truly objected to it. Besides, you are underestimating your appeal. You're so lovely, my dear. Lance probably took one look at you and couldn't resist you.'

Belle smiled. 'Thank you for the compliment,' she said simply, with gratitude for being accepted so unquestioningly.

'He's already more than half in love with you.' When Belle stared at her with wide, questioning eyes, she smiled and patted her head. 'I saw the way he looked at you yesterday when I arrived at Ryhill. No man looks at a woman that way unless he's in love. I hope it works out for you both, Belle, I really do. Besides, I for one will be glad to put that wretched business of the diamonds behind us. I meant what I said. I look forward to meeting your grandmother—it cannot be soon enough.' She paused before saying carefully, 'Now, would you like me take you to see Charlotte?'

'Yes. I—am looking forward to seeing her.'

'She is quite adorable and has everyone eating out of the palm of her hand. Has Lance told you anything about his wife—Delphine?'

Belle shook her head. 'No.'

'Well, all I know is that their marriage was of short duration. That is what he told me. Apparently she was with him in Spain. When the fighting was over they parted. He had no idea she was carrying his child. It wasn't until the eve of Waterloo that he saw her again—she had just been delivered of Charlotte and wasn't expected to live. Lance did the right thing by her and married her.'

'Oh, dear.' Belle sighed deeply. 'He seems to make a habit of *doing the right thing* when it comes to women.'

Elizabeth laughed lightly. 'It does seem like that. I cannot speak for Delphine since I never met her, but where you are concerned, my dear, I really believe he has. Now come along,' she said, getting up and smoothing her skirts, 'I'll take you to the nursery.'

This was the moment Belle had worried about most, seeing Lance's child, his daughter, who would be a constant reminder of the woman he had married before her. Cool, steady, resolute, she tried to appear as though there was nothing out of the ordinary about the situation, though inside she was quaking.

She was aware of Elizabeth's eyes upon her as the nursemaid reached into the crib and lifted Lance's daughter out, holding her with infinite gentleness as she handed her to her grandmother. Elizabeth smiled tenderly at the pretty dark-haired bundle. Charlotte was awake and lifted her face from the hollow of her grandmother's neck and turned her head and peeped at Belle.

Belle's heart did a somersault. It was like looking at Lance. The same startling deep blue eyes and long black lashes. Her hair, a tumble of glossy ebony curls, lay in soft swirls about her small head. She even had her father's tiny cleft in her round chin. There could be no doubt that she was a Bingham and she was beautiful. Belle could not tear her gaze away from the child. She even had the same arrogant set to her baby jaw and the slight lift at the corners of her mouth that Lance had.

Belle was aware that Elizabeth was watching her closely. In spite of her determination to take her meeting of her husband's child in her stride, she felt her heart sink. Then she firmly pulled herself together. Charlotte was part of the legacy she'd inherited when she'd married Lance, so she'd better get used to it. Reaching out, she gently placed her finger in the little hand, smiling when Charlotte's tiny fingers curled round it firmly and she chortled happily.

'Are you all right?' Elizabeth asked, as if worried by her reaction. 'What are you thinking, Belle?'

She managed a courageous smile. 'I am thinking that I have a beautiful, adorable stepdaughter. I can see she favours her father. I confess I have been worried about this moment, and now I can't see why. You must be proud of her.'

'I am. Very proud—as I hope my son will be eventually.'

'You will miss her when she leaves.'

'I shall, but she won't be too far away for me to visit. Now, if you still want to take her with you, I'll instruct the nurse to make her ready.'

Chapter Nine

～～～⁂～～～

Belle's arrival at Ryhill with Charlotte and her nursemaid was expected. With great excitement servants were hovering in the hallway, longing to catch a glimpse of the master's child. The master himself had left the house after a hasty breakfast and had not yet returned, so he had no idea his offspring from his first marriage was about to take up residence in the nursery, which the mistress had ordered to be made ready for the young arrival.

The servants knew very little about the new Earl of Ryhill's private life, only that he was a military man and was the old Earl's nephew. They were aware that he had a child by his first wife, now deceased, living with his mother at Bilton House, so it was only natural she should come to Ryhill now the earl had a new wife.

The young nursemaid carried the bright-eyed, happy and gurgling child—who was delighted with all the attention she was receiving—up the stairs to the nursery. Two footmen emptied the carriage of all the paraphernalia that had accompanied the child from Bilton House.

Belle helped the nursemaid, who was thoroughly devoted

to her young charge, settle in. When Charlotte was washed and fed and put down for the night, Belle looked down at her stepdaughter and felt something permanent enter her heart. It was a warm, melting feeling that she supposed all mothers felt when they looked at their offspring. Yet this was not her child—but she was the closest thing to a mother Charlotte had. Whatever the future held, she vowed to get to know the child and to do her best by her. She really was beautiful, a fine child, healthy and robust, and she prayed Lance would come to love her.

When Lance returned later that night and Masters told him of the child's arrival, he was furious.

Belle heard his raised voice coming from the hall as soon as she left her room. After she smoothed the front of her skirt with slightly trembling hands, it was with a mixture of alarm and trepidation that she went downstairs to face the fireworks.

She found him in his study in the middle of pouring himself a drink. He had his back to her. He'd been riding in the rain and had removed his jacket, having flung it over the nearest chair. His white shirt was soaked, clinging wetly to his broad shoulders, and his brown riding boots were covered in mud.

Sensing her presence, he whirled round so violently that he sloshed brandy down his shirt front. He looked directly at his wife as she closed the door, and she felt the need to recoil from the expression in his eyes. They were hard, with nothing in them of the lively warmth, the good humour that had once lit up his face. They narrowed with what looked like venom and his mouth snarled in a cruel twist.

'So, you condescend to join your husband,' he uttered with a sarcastic bite. 'What you have done is heartless and arrogant. How dare you defy me? How dare you disregard my wishes and bring that child into this house to satisfy your own whim?

'It was not a whim and how dare *you* criticise me?'

'What's that supposed to mean?'

'I don't think I have to spell it out, Lance, do you? I am sorry if Charlotte's arrival upsets you, but she is here now so you had better get used to it.'

'You're sorry?' he mocked scathingly. 'Sorry for what? Defying me?'

'Yes, but not for bringing her here—to where she so rightly belongs.'

'I want an explanation from you—a reasonable explanation as to why you thought you had the right to go against my express wishes in the matter of *my* daughter.'

'Well, that's a start,' Belle bit back, thrusting her chin haughtily. 'At least you acknowledge you *have* a daughter.'

Lance's eyes had a terrible blankness in them and about his mouth was a thin white line of anger. He went to his wife, standing over her like a hawk over a rabbit, and Belle was aware that there was some dreadful destructive power in him which if released could destroy her. But she stood her ground, refusing to let him beat her on the matter of his daughter.

'You will take her back, do you hear me?'

'Take her back where?'

'To my mother.'

'Your mother, like me, is of the opinion that Charlotte is better off here—with her father.'

'Indeed, then we shall have to think of something—'

Belle cut through his words, trying to contain her mounting disgust. 'Dear Lord, Lance, your attitude to that child is inhuman. What kind of father are you? Have you never enquired about her—asked if she was healthy and whole? Are you really not interested at all? Charlotte is a baby—your baby—and this is her home.'

'I shall have her removed. There are ways and means.'

'Is that so?' Belle thrust her face closer to his. Her eyes had changed from their usual warm green to the cold spark of emeralds. There were spots of red on each cheek bone, and her mouth was as thinly drawn with determination as her husband's. She held her head high with defiance, and for an instant she saw a glimmer of something in Lance's eyes that, had she not known better, she might have called admiration. 'You should know that if she goes, I go, and there won't be a thing you can do about it.'

Lance stared at her in stupefied amazement as she spun round and stalked to the door. 'You? Don't be ridiculous. You are my wife. You are not going anywhere.'

Belle spun round, a savage, spitting she-cat in defence of herself and the child. She strode back to him, thrusting her face close to his. 'Try to stop me. I mean it, Lance. Your behaviour is totally unreasonable and quite unacceptable. If Charlotte goes, I go with her. I swear I will.'

'Your determination to defend my daughter is commendable, but Charlotte is not your responsibility. She is not your child.'

'No, she is yours,' she hissed. 'Accept it, Lance. That she is not of my flesh is quite irrelevant. I have made myself responsible for her since she is defenceless and she has no one else to speak for her.'

'Dear God, you will not do this. I will not allow it.'

'You will not allow? Ha! Your choice of words is disastrous, Lance Bingham. I am not a servant to be ordered about at will. I am your wife. I shall do whatever I please, and you shall not stop me.'

'Will I not? If you do not heed my warning—call it advice, if you like—you will get a taste of what I can do.' Lance's voice was coldly dangerous.

Belle was beyond caution. 'Advice? If I wanted advice,' she retorted, her eyes sparkling with jade fire, 'you would be the last person I would ask.'

His jaw tightened. 'My compliments,' he said curtly, and Belle watched his mercurial mood take an obvious, abrupt turn for the worse. 'You've learned very quickly what it takes to displease me.'

Fixing an artificial smile on her face, Belle said lightly, 'That wasn't too difficult. Before our marriage you found me strong-willed and direct. I even recall you saying how you admired those traits in a woman. Now you're complaining because I am those things. There is simply no pleasing you.'

To Belle's mortification, Lance didn't deny he found her strong-willed and direct.

'We can discuss how you can *please* me when you return to my bed.'

Outrage exploded in Belle's brain. 'How dare you say that?' she said, her colour rising with indignation. He expected her to resume physical relations as if nothing had happened. 'If you thought you'd married a complaisant, adoring female who would rush to do your bidding, you didn't get one.'

'I will.'

Belle tossed her head and turned. 'You're wrong, Lance Bingham,' she said and started for the door.

'Belle, you are my wife,' he informed her coldly.

She stopped and half-turned, her delicate brows arched in feigned surprise, her colour gloriously high. 'I am aware of that,' she replied, and with a calm defiance, she added, 'and much good it has done me so far.' Having thus informed him that she was beginning to regret her position as his wife, she turned and walked across the room, feeling his eyes boring holes into her back. Not until she put her hand on the handle of the door did his low, ominous voice break the silence.

'Belle.'

'Yes?' she said, looking back.

'Think very carefully before you make the mistake of defying my orders again. You'll regret it. I promise you.'

Despite the cold shiver of alarm his silken voice caused in her, Belle lifted her chin. 'Goodnight, Lance. I hope you find time to reconsider your attitude where Charlotte is concerned.'

At that moment the sound of a child crying in the upper part of the house could be heard. 'That is your daughter making her presence known. Perhaps she's as reluctant to be in her father's house as he is for her to be here.'

On that note she left him seething. Lance sank down into a chair, dark brows pulled together in a black frown. He would accomplish what he had set out to do, which was to make Belle understand the rules she would have to live by as his wife, and was certain he would succeed no matter how she fought against it. The very idea of being defied as she had defied him by bringing Charlotte to Ryhill, knowing how he felt, was unthinkable. Moreover his body's almost uncontrollable desire for her when he had faced her defiance, amazed him, and thoroughly displeased him, even though he realised her removal from his bed was partly the cause.

A reluctant smile replaced his dark frown. He realised Belle would never be a complaisant wife in her vibrant, feisty spirit, and with those stormy eyes flashing like angry sparks, her cheeks stained an angry pink, he would find ample compensation.

In an attempt to bring some kind of order into the house, over the days that followed Belle carried on as though the acrimony that existed between her and Lance did not exist, hoping that given time the tension would lessen. If the servants wondered at the manner in which the master and mistress treated one another it was not spoken of out loud, but they thought it odd for them to be at loggerheads after just two days of wedded bliss. There was no contact between them, no touching of hands as there had been at the beginning, no soft glances nor exchange of affection.

Charlotte was an easy, engaging child and everyone who came into contact with her was drawn under her spell—everyone, that is, but her father. Taking a genuine interest in the child, Belle spent a great deal of her time in the nursery, so that she and Charlotte could grow slowly used to one another. She would watch her crawl about the rug and sit before the fire with her on her lap, holding her carefully, liking the feel of the plump, sweet-smelling body against her own, her cheek resting on her ebony curls and listening to her baby talk. She sang soft lullabies to her to get her to sleep, and fully weaned, fed her custard and eggs and boiled milk, for the woman who had wet nursed her in the beginning had left to take up another position.

Determined not to keep her hidden away, on one occasion when Belle had carried her out into the garden, she saw Lance watching from the window of his study. She looked at him, hoping to see some sign of pleasure, of emotion, even senti-mentality, but there was nothing visible on his face. It was quite expressionless, and then he turned away.

A heaviness centred in Belle's chest whenever she con-sidered the days ahead. Instead of the tension easing, it only seemed to grow. She had driven Lance away, and this filled her with pain. But her own unfulfilled yearning for him was worse. She knew what it was like to be pleasured by a con-siderate and tender lover, and her discovery had marked her physically—a hot, restless longing that had her twisting and turning in her lonely bed night after night.

She wished they could share their thoughts and aspirations and truly talk together, instead of relying on the coldly con-strained words that usually passed for conversation between them. She wanted to reach out to him when they were together, to have him possess her. She did love him—so very much— why else would she be experiencing this painful yearning? She was finding it harder and harder to retreat into cool re-serve when she was near him, especially when memories of his kisses, his caresses and how it felt to wake in his arms, kept spinning around inside her mind.

But she could not bring herself to go to him. The only thing that could put things right was for her to take Charlotte back to his mother, and this she would not do.

Belle swept into the dining room, the skirt of her rose-pink gown swirling about her. Though she had been doubtful about the colour, Daisy had persuaded her to wear it, telling her the colour gave her a fragility and vulnerability her husband would find attractive. The neckline was scooped low and showed more of Belle's cleavage that she considered suitable for a quiet evening at home, but nevertheless she agreed to wear it, knowing that in his present state of mind, it would have no effect whatsoever on Lance Bingham.

And she was right. His deep blue eyes looked somewhere over her smooth, white shoulders as he handed her a pre-dinner glass of sherry, careful not to touch her hand.

She smiled at him. 'Thank you, Lance.'

He merely nodded curtly, his eyes still retaining their total uninterest, as though she were a stranger, so she was surprised when he said with cynicism, 'The colour becomes you—rose—but not without thorns, eh, Belle?'

'Please don't start, Lance. I hoped we could enjoy our meal together without arguing.'

'I have no intention of arguing tonight,' he said, sitting down and crossing his long legs. Reaching for a newspaper, he immersed himself in its contents, paying her no attention—it was as if she didn't exist.

With an ache in her heart, Belle looked at him admiringly. His athletic frame was resplendent in midnight-blue jacket and trousers, his shirt and neckcloth dazzling white. The flame from the candles turned his skin to amber and darkened his eyes to that of the night sky. His dark hair was still damp from his bath and curled vigorously in his nape. He was a vigorous man, and she thought of his smile, how his teeth would gleam in a bold smile.

Belle's young heart beat rapidly in her chest. No wonder she was so much in love with him.

'Have you made arrangements for us to go the picnic tomorrow, Lance?' she asked in attempt to break the uneasy tension that hung in the room.

Lance jerked his head up, lowering the newspaper. 'Picnic? What picnic?'

'At Sir John Bucklow's house. You can't have forgotten. It promises to be a lovely day. I'm looking forward to it.'

He raised the newspaper and continued to browse. 'That's too bad, because we aren't going.'

'Oh?' Belle said. 'That's a shame, for you will miss a splendid day out.'

Lance dropped the newspaper into his lap. 'I don't think you heard me, Belle. I said *we* weren't going.'

'I know. I heard you, but I have no intention of disappointing my grandmother and your mother. We have arranged to meet them there—to introduce them to each other.'

'Why?' he drawled with bitter irony. 'So we can play happy families?'

'It's about time, don't you think? I haven't seen my grandmother since our wedding, and I would like to see her. She has told me the Bucklows' picnics are most delightful and it promises to be a lovely day.'

Lance looked at her steadily. 'I am not going and I refuse to let you go alone.'

'Do you mind telling me why?'

'Because I'm in no mood for a picnic. When your grandmother and my mother meet, they can come here.'

'But it is arranged.'

'Then I will *unarrange* it. Is that clear enough?'

'Quite clear,' Belle told him. She was crushed, but when she looked at him and found him observing her pained reaction with cynical amusement, as hurt as she was, she became quietly angry and felt anything but meek or sad. So for no viable reason, Lance didn't intend to go the Bucklows' picnic, but she did. She knew she would be playing with fire and that she might anger him to the point where he would explode with rage, but she would continue to stoke the fire of his emotions—either fury or desire, for she was sure that one of them would eventually drive him from his stony silence.

When the food was brought in, seated across from Belle, after one mouthful, Lance put his fork down with a grimace of distaste.

'You don't like the salmon mousse,' Belle ventured to say calmly.

He shoved his plate away. 'Not tonight.'

'Would you like something else? I'm sure cook has something—some consommé, perhaps?'

'I do not want consommé.'

'Then—perhaps some—'

'Leave it, Belle,' he snapped. 'Why all the questions?'

'I was only trying to tempt you with something else.'

His furious gaze shot to hers. Tempt? she said. There was only one thing she could tempt him with and it wasn't his damned dinner. 'I'd rather you spared me the wifely concern.'

His sarcastic reply nettled her. His continued determination to punish her was beginning to get on her nerves, but it was pointless to attempt a discussion when he was in such a foul mood.

Lance suddenly threw his napkin on the table and stood up. 'I'm going out. Enjoy your meal.'

Alone, Belle put down her fork and sighed. She glanced around her at the beautiful room, at the candlelight gleaming on the tableware, shimmering on crystal glasses, and suddenly everything seemed so futile.

On the other side of the door Lance stood rigidly still, his hands clenching and unclenching as he tried to bring the onslaught of his fury under control. His breathing was harsh and ragged, his expression so incensed, so bleakly embittered by what Belle was doing to him. She was so damned lovely that it required all his self-control to be in the same room with her. Night after night he lay awake in his empty bed, trying to find an explanation for every unexplainable word or action on Belle's part.

Her determination to have her own way over the child, the way she had faced him in outrageous mutiny as she had re-proached him and defended Charlotte, had thrown him off balance; he had not expected her to react so strongly to him having been married before and producing a child from that marriage. And to have to sit across from her at the dinner table when she looked so unbearably beautiful, so young and vul-nerable despite the seductive allure of her gown, to smell the intoxicating scent of her so that he almost lost his resolve and dragged her into his arms, almost destroyed his sanity.

He didn't know how long he could stand this living ar-rangement. Perhaps if they weren't living under the same roof he could find some relief from his agony. His heart and mind understood the harsh reality that Belle would have nothing to do with him while ever he continued to have nothing to do with his daughter. But his body tormented him with the same insatiable desire for her he'd always felt.

Deciding to take up an invitation issued by a friend and close neighbour earlier to partake of a game of cards at his home with a group of others, he left the house. He would wel-come the diversion, and by dawn he would manage to drink himself into near oblivion.

On the morning of the picnic the sun caressed the land in a warm glow. Thinking she would be going with Lance in the carriage, Belle had arranged to meet her grandmother there mid-morning. Hoping Lance would have changed his mind and would go after all, Belle was deeply disappointed when he failed to put in an appearance. Having second thoughts about going in the carriage, she donned her riding habit and took one of the horses from the stable.

Belle had been gone half an hour when Lance arrived back at the house, having spent the night at his friend's house. The night had been a total disaster and he was not in the best of moods. No matter how much he'd drunk or how much he'd tried, he had been unable to concentrate on the game or the jovial masculine conversation of his friends. The annoying fact was that he'd been unable to dispel all thoughts of Belle from his mind.

He was beginning to think he had married a witch, a witch who had got under his skin like thorn with barbs. It was unbearable to have her there and it hurt like hell to pull her out. His mind kept wandering to the night before and how she had looked in that rose-coloured dress, with her charms displayed in fabulous wantonness. What the hell was she trying to do to him? His hands had ached to touch her, to feel her soft skin next to his, and his desire had been almost beyond bearing. Desire and lust. He told himself that that was what he felt for Belle—desire and lust—but deep down inside him he knew it was more than that, much more.

She had been disappointed when he'd told her he had no intention of taking her to the picnic, as if he were doing it to torture her—which made him ask why he had done it. Was it to hurt her, to spoil her pleasure? Hell, he had no rational reason for not going and it was inconsiderate on his part to ruin his mother's and Belle's grandmother's plans to become acquainted at the picnic.

Without more ado he bathed and dressed and went in search of his wife, but failed to locate her. Being told by Masters that she had already left for the picnic, Lance absorbed this with stunned disbelief. Turning on his heel, his face glacial, he headed in the direction of the stables.

* * *

Belle arrived early at the Bucklows' residence. Carriages, curricles and horses were scattered in the copse where the picnic was to be held, with men and women dressed in their finest clothes, the women parading about holding brightly coloured parasols. Some of the guests were on horseback, ready for the start of the ride across country before the picnic commenced.

Seeing her grandmother already ensconced beneath a large parasol, Belle left her horse tethered to a post and went to sit with her. Not having seen her since the wedding, she was relieved to find her sitting alone. There were things she had to tell her that would both upset and shock her, but she had to be told before Lance's mother arrived.

Belle smiled and kissed her grandmother and they exchanged pleasantries and discussed the wedding, but the troubled look in her granddaughter's eyes did not deceive the dowager countess. Something was wrong, very wrong, that was obvious.

'You look troubled, Isabelle. Is something worrying you? You are happy at Ryhill, and your husband is treating you well, I hope?'

Belle sighed. 'There is something you should know, Grandmother. Something has happened—something that Lance should have made known to me before I agreed to marry him.'

The smile on the dowager's face faded when she saw the unhappiness in her granddaughter's eyes. Her mouth went dry and her heart began to beat in heavy, terrifying dread as she prepared herself for the worst. 'Tell me.'

It didn't take Belle long to recount everything that had occurred since her marriage to Lance. She spoke calmly, telling her of how Lance had been a widower when they had married, how she had fetched Charlotte from Bilton House and that the child was now living at Ryhill, where she belonged.

The dowager was not at all pleased by this latest crisis. 'I am shocked—deeply so. Your husband should not have kept a matter of such importance from you. You should have been told. Of course you are angry—justifiably so. But how has all this affected your relationship? Are you…?'

'Estranged?' Belle smiled and shook her head. 'No. Things are strained between us, but I am confident that everything will be resolved. Lance is suffering very badly. He cannot bring himself to accept his child. It seems grossly unfair that he should blame Charlotte for her mother's death, but he is battling with himself to accept her. I am sure of it. He no longer mentions her going back to his mother, so I am hopeful that it won't be long.'

'For your sake I sincerely hope you are right. The scandal that brought the two of you together will be as nothing compared to this. You have had an immense shock, a terrible disappointment, but you are an Ainsley and will bear it well. If you had known any of this before you agreed to be his wife, would it have made any difference to your decision?'

'No, I don't think it would. Lance is a good man, a fine man…' She fell silent, unable to say the words she wanted to say. But her grandmother's astute mind had already picked up on what she had been about to say.

'And you love him.'

Belle nodded, meeting her gaze calmly. 'Yes. I do. I love him very much, and I will do all I can to help him get through this.'

'Then I can only hope he is deserving of your love.'

When her grandmother stood up to acknowledge an acquaintance, Belle's attention became distracted when she saw the daunting figure of her husband astride his horse in conversation with a group of gentlemen across the copse. Jolts of shock and panic shot through her. His eyes were levelled on her like a pair of duelling pistols, impaling her on his gaze, leaving her in no doubt that he intended to seek her out at the first opportunity and berate her most severely for defying him again.

But, strangely, she was encouraged by his arrival, encouraged because on being informed that she had left for the picnic, he had cared enough to come and look for her. Belle slanted a long, considering look at him as he sat his strong, well-muscled hunter. Attired in a dark green coat, gleaming brown-leather riding boots and a pair of buckskin riding breeches that fit him to perfection, in her opinion he was by far the most attractive man present.

She watched him as he talked and joked with lazy good humour with those in his group. He looked completely relaxed as he dismounted some distance away from her. His horse shied slightly. As if wishing to restrain it, he ran his hand down the sleek neck, showing that the beast belonged to him and that he knew how to make it obey. Looking in her direction, he began to lead his horse to where she stood.

Unfortunately, he was too far away to reach her before there was a blast on a trumpet heralding the start of the ride. Beneath Lance's glower, Sir John Buckley, who had eyes for no one but Belle, rushed forwards. He bent and clasped his hand to receive her dainty foot, then raised her up. After seating herself and placing a knee about the pommel, taking the reins in a practised grip and completely avoiding looking in Lance's direction, Belle laughed and urged her mount into an easy canter across the fields with the rest of the riding party.

To be so ignored, angered beyond bearing, leaping up astride his own horse, Lance sent the huge black stallion thundering after her, his huge hooves sending clods of earth flying. A race ensued and Belle, with light-hearted abandon, followed the others through the trees and along winding paths, her mare holding her own until they reached open fields and she could stretch her legs to their advantage. They galloped on, Belle urging her mount over any obstacle in her path with a fearless abandon that had Lance filled with admiration one minute and furious that she could be so reckless the next.

When the pace became less hectic and the exhilarated riders slowed their mounts to a sedate walk back to the copse. Lance rode towards Belle, but, to his fury, the overzealous John Buckley was there before him and chatting to her amiably.

Belle was happy to converse with the young man about the pleasant countryside, when a sudden awareness swept over her. One moment she was thoroughly occupied with learning about the different landmarks, the next she was oblivious to everything but her heart gathering speed and the certain, inexplicable realisation that Lance was close at hand.

The perception was quickly confirmed, when his cold voice said, 'If you don't mind, Buckley, I would like a word with my wife.' His eyes raked them both, considering each of them, increasing Sir John's discomfiture by no small degree.

Even though there had been no slightest hint of impropriety, Sir John stiffened apprehensively and stammered, 'I—I beg your pardon, Bingham, b-but Lady Bingham expressed an interest in her surroundings. I was just…'

'Then I shall be happy to familiarise her with them myself.'

Sir John fell back, and, after excusing himself, rode away.

One quick look at Lance's face convinced Belle that he was absolutely furious with her. Not only were his eyes glinting like shards of ice, but the muscles in his cheeks were tensing to a degree that she had never seen before.

'Your skill is exceeded only by your common sense, Belle,' he reproached severely. 'Did you have to take those jumps? You could have broken your neck.'

'Really, Lance, there's no need to get all hot and bothered about a few measly hedges and fences. I've ridden harder courses than that and jumped obstacles twice as high. And you should not have spoken to Sir John like that—making him think you were jealous...'

Lance squinted in the sun's bright glare. 'Damn it, Belle, I *am* jealous.'

His simple acknowledgement confused Belle so completely that for a moment she could find nothing to say. To feel jealousy one had to care. As usual, his tall, hard body radiated strength and vitality, but his dark blue eyes held a dangerous glitter. A winsome smile touched her lips. 'Why, Lance, you really are quite terrifying when you're angry—and jealous.'

'I'm jealous of any man who claims even a moment of your time when that moment could be spent with me,' he snapped unreasonably, his thigh brushing hers as their horses bumped together. The unexpected contact made him acutely conscious of the celibate life he had led since she had deserted his bed. He was hungry for her and could hardly restrain himself from reaching out and dragging her from her horse into his arms and finding the softest grass on which to lay her. 'Was it too much for you to wait and ride with me? It was my intent. Or have you come to regret our marriage and want rid of me?' The fact that she might, cut through his heart like a knife.

Belle gasped, astounded that he should even think such a thing, let alone voice it. 'Be assured that despite everything that has happened lately, I have not. Nothing could be further from my mind. I was merely enjoying myself and couldn't resist riding off. I couldn't help myself.'

'Just like you couldn't help yourself when you defied me yet again and came here when I expressly told you the picnic was off. Your flagrant disobedience in coming here without me deserves retaliation.'

Belle looked at him with considerable amusement. 'Retaliation? Goodness! How interesting. How will you do that? Will you beat me—lock me in my room and starve me? What?'

Unmoved by her humorous account of the punishments he might mete out, Lance scowled darkly. 'Don't be ridiculous. I don't know what is going on in your mind, Belle, but I cannot imagine giving you up. Indeed, the very idea of you being pursued by another man rankles sorely.'

'That is not what I want either, Lance,' she answered softly, truthfully, in an attempt to placate his ire. What he said confused her, for it was in complete variance to his behaviour of late. Unhooking her leg from the pommel, she slipped off her mount with an easy grace.

'Of late you have been avoiding me as if I carried some contagious disease,' he growled, also dismounting, and cursing the lack of privacy they had. 'Indeed, my dear wife, if I did not know differently I would say you protect your virtue more adroitly than any chastity belt ever could. I am both puzzled and concerned at the way you are behaving.'

'How am I behaving?'

'You are cool and unresponsive.'

He towered over her, his overpowering physical presence so close that Belle felt dizzy. An ache lodged in her chest. His accusations were true. But how else did he expect her to behave? Her grandmother had taught her to be a lady, to exhibit restraint and proper decorum, even in the most trying circumstances, and her upbringing made it impossible to be other than cool when she was upset. Bleakly she glanced up at him. She truly was deeply in love with him. Why else would she be experiencing this painful yearning? She was finding it harder and harder to retreat into cool reserve when she was near him.

'Do you not agree that I have justifiable reason to be cool and unresponsive?'

'Absolutely not.'

She could not bring herself to melt towards him, not when he had made no move to approach his daughter and only seemed to want her, his wife, for the physical pleasure her body could bring. Not when he would satisfy only her wanton need and not the ache in her heart. Yet she felt a strange, satisfying contentment that her nearness could affect him even in the company of so many.

'If we are not together as much as you would like us to be and it upsets you, Lance, then I apologise. Perhaps if you were at home more—with your family'

'Stop it, Belle. I know what you're saying and nothing is changed.'

'I'm sorry.'

Lance wasn't willing to be denied. Taking her arm, he drew her into the shade of a large beech tree, out of sight of prying eyes.

'I'm sorry if I've made you angry,' she said. 'I didn't mean to.'

'You did, and it matters to me. A lot, in fact! I recall you saying that there was nothing you wanted more than to be married to me. You sure as hell have a funny way of showing it.'

Belle was overwhelmed by his sarcasm. 'You are foolish if you imagine that because I have withheld myself from you, that I want no part of you. If you do, then you are both blind and witless,' she said quietly.

He scowled at her darkly. 'Am I?'

'Yes.'

Placing a finger lightly under her chin, he tipped her face up to his, his anger of a moment earlier dissolving when he looked into the depths of her eyes and saw pain. 'I'm sorry, Belle. We haven't got off to a very good start, have we?'

'We could start again with you telling me about Delphine, and why you married me when you were still mourning her loss.'

Pain clouded his eyes. 'I could, but it won't change anything.'

'You mean it won't change how you feel about your daughter.'

He nodded.

When Belle saw the taut line of his jaw and how his expression had hardened slightly, her mouth went dry and her heart began to beat in heavy, terrifying dread as she sensed that again he had withdrawn from her. 'I know you are a very private person, but I am your wife. If you cannot open up to me, even if it is just a little bit, then it bodes ill for the future.'

'You are right. You should know about Delphine—and why I married you. When your grandmother suggested we should wed, I was repulsed by the very idea of having my life laid out and being forced to commit to something I had not thought of myself. Yet much as I wanted to rebel against it, I found myself wanting you.' His eyes suddenly twinkled with amusement. 'Besides, your grandmother was not above forcing an appropriate response in a wedding ceremony by surreptitiously holding a gun directed towards my head,' he said, chuckling softly, forcing a smile to Belle's lips at the vision of this tall, broad-shouldered man standing in wide-eyed alarm before her much smaller grandmother.

Belle's heart soared and his confession brought a smile to her lips, but the grim expression that suddenly appeared on his face gave her a sense of unease and made her wary.

'I also wanted you to be quite sure that marrying me was what you wanted. Marriage is a great step. I realised how fast things were happening, that you'd scarcely had time to draw breath since that night at Carlton House.'

'It was my entire fault, despite my grandmother blaming you, for what happened. It was down to me. I stole into your house, into your bedchamber. It was unfortunate that you had half the *ton* dining with you that night and to witness my indiscretion.'

Lance looked at her and his expression softened as his conscience tore at him. 'The blame was all mine. If I hadn't taken that damn necklace in the first place you wouldn't have been driven to do what you did. I had no reservations about making you my wife. There was nothing I desired more than that. But you might not have been so enthusiastic about having me for a husband if I had told you about Delphine—that I'd been married before and had a child.'

'But why should it mean anything? Plenty of people marry twice. There is no shame in that. Your wife was dead—in the past. She couldn't pose a threat now. Could she? When, Lance? When did the two of you marry?'

'On the eve of Waterloo. Shortly after Charlotte was born.'

'You were only recently a widower. That much I have learned. I don't wonder you were against marrying again so soon after Delphine. Did—did you love her very much?'

He turned a glacial stare upon her. 'Only a woman would ask such a question.'

'A wife would want to know if her husband's dead wife was still a threat,' Belle replied coolly. The harshness of his voice told her that whatever feelings he'd had for Delphine had left scars, as yet unhealed. She had revived painful memories for him and she regretted her curiosity.

His voice was mocking when he eventually spoke. 'Aren't you going to ask me who she was, and how long we had known each other? Women always want to know everything.'

'If you want to tell me, you will.' She turned her head and looked at him. 'You spent many years as a soldier in Spain. I already know that. You must have known many women on your travels. I don't mean to pry into your relationship with Delphine.'

Lance was drawn by the sincerity in Belle's gaze. He felt his resistance waver. 'In truth, I don't know what I felt for Delphine. It was—complicated.'

'Was she very beautiful?'

'In an exotic kind of way. She was an actress. I met her in London at the theatre where she worked. She was happy and vivacious. We got together and when I went to Spain with the army she followed me. I knew nothing would come of our relationship. She understood that—but she always lived in hope. I was in Paris with the conquering army when I sent her away, believing I would never see her again. She didn't complain or try to persuade me to let her stay. She just accepted it—which was her way.' His voice hardened. 'It wasn't until the eve of the battle at Waterloo—when she was on her deathbed, having given birth to my child—that we were reunited. She knew she wouldn't survive the birth and came to Belgium to find me—to ask me to look after the child. There was a priest. We were man and wife for no longer than ten minutes.'

'You didn't know about the child?'

For a long moment his gaze held hers with penetrating intensity. 'Had I known, I would never have sent her away. Had I not sent her from me, she would have had the care she needed and she would never have died.'

'And for that you blame yourself—and Charlotte.' The intensity of his stare was so profound that Belle thought he was about to admit what she had said, then he turned his head away.

'Damn you, Belle. Too often for my peace of mind you get beneath my guard, under my skin. I shall have to keep a tighter rein on my tongue in future.'

'I don't mean to. I'm sorry. No more questions.' And there wouldn't be. Belle had her answer. By not replying to her question he had given her the answer. He had sent Delphine away from him. He would not have done that had he loved her. The Lance Bingham she knew wouldn't have allowed anything to stand in his way. Clearly he blamed himself for her death—and Charlotte was a constant reminder that he had failed Delphine. That was why he couldn't bear to look at her.

'Thank you for telling me about Delphine, and I promise I will try not to be too hard on you in future,' she said, as they got to their feet. The look she gave him accompanied by a teasing smile hardly portrayed the emotions she was struggling with. Every time they were together she was aware of a potent sense of longing inside her. It was a desire so strong that she wanted to cry because she had made it her endeavour to detach her heart from him until he could accept that Charlotte was his daughter.

At that moment her horse, which had wandered off to nibble a tuft of long grass, disturbed a brightly coloured cock pheasant, causing it to fly up in indignant alarm. Belle jumped and immediately Lance's hands came to steady her.

'Oh, the bird startled me,' she breathed, knowing her tension came far more from Lance's gentle grip on her arms than from the bird's quick flight. He seemed to be aware of the intimacy of the moment as well, for something flickered in his eyes and his gaze dropped to her mouth. He was close. So close that she could smell the clean, fresh scent of his cologne. So close she wondered with a sudden thudding of her heart if he meant to kiss her. But disappointingly he released her.

'I think it is time we sought out your grandmother. My mother will have arrived and will be wondering where we've got to.'

Knowing how difficult it was for her grandmother to receive a family she had distanced herself from for many years had troubled Belle from the start, but now she saw there was no need when she saw her chatting amiably to Lance's mother beneath the shade of the parasol. Such was Elizabeth Bingham's kindness and compassion, that when she had taken the older woman's hands in her own and smiled as she assured her how delighted she was to meet her at last, skilfully dispatching the past with a graciousness that was irresistible, after fifty years the ice was broken.

'I see the two of you have met,' Lance said, greeting his mother with a light peck on the cheek.

Elizabeth smiled at them both. 'It's good to become acquainted at last.' She turned to Belle, putting a hand on her arm. 'I am so ashamed of myself, my dear, for speaking out so soon about Charlotte,' she said, having made up her mind to speak openly about her granddaughter in front of Lance.

He must be made to realise the child was a part of his life and accept it. 'How has she settled in at Ryhill?'

'Very well,' Belle answered. 'She is an adorable child and so engaging. Already she has everyone eating out of the palm of her hand.' Everyone except the one person the child should be closest to, she thought sadly, looking at her husband's face, which was quite expressionless. He did not show even the slightest interest in the conversation about his daughter, but Belle now knew that was not out of coldness. It was out of fear, fear that if he stopped blaming Charlotte for Delphine's death, the full force of that blame would be laid on him.

Chapter Ten

Finding himself on the same landing as the nursery and not quite knowing how he had come to be there, after pausing for an indecisive moment outside, hesitantly Lance pushed open the door, unprepared for the scene his eyes beheld.

The nursery was filled with bright sunshine pouring through diaphanous white curtains. It was a warm, balmy day. Some of the windows had been opened and curtains gently stirred in the slight breeze. The silence of the house weighed heavy. Pictures of flowers and birds and fairies hung on the floral-papered walls, and shelves crammed with books and baskets of toys were everywhere. A clockwork rabbit along with a big brown teddy bear sporting a shining red bow round its neck had been left on the bright blue carpet, and an assortment of dolls were propped up in the window bottom. There was a colourful doll's house in one corner and a child-size table and four chairs in the other, and set at right angles to the hearth, two comfortable easy chairs. The previous occupant of the nursery must have been female, he realised, and as Charlotte developed she would get much pleasure from these toys. For a moment he was distracted from his purpose by the homely tranquillity that protected the child's young life.

The room where the nursemaid slept was through a door adjoining the nursery. The door was slightly open so the nursemaid would hear her charge when she woke from her nap.

It was to the crib in which the child slept that Lance directed his gaze. She was lying on her back, her hands on either side of her face, her chubby palms open. She had kicked away the covers so her baby legs were bare. Not wishing to alert the nursemaid of his presence and careful not to wake the child, curious to get a closer look, he edged closer to the crib and looked down.

He was totally unprepared for the feelings and the emotions that almost overwhelmed him. As memories of her birth assailed him, remembering how he had held her in his arms shortly after her birth, and the promise he had made to Delphine that he would take care of her, he gulped at the air, trying to drag it into his tortured lungs, fighting for breath, for control. He had failed Delphine miserably. How could he have ordered this child out of his life, abandoned her to whoever was prepared to take her?

Not having seen her since her that night, he had no particular feelings for her, beyond holding her—in part with himself—responsible for Delphine's death. The servants were forever singing her praises, telling him how delightful she was, and on occasion he had seen her with Belle or the nursemaid and watched her crawl about the lawn and heard her baby laughter and sometimes heard her cry. From such a distance she had made no impression on him, but here, alone with his daughter for the first time, he accepted that she was his responsibility and his heart was stirred with a sense of pride in her infant beauty.

The fan of her dark lashes shadowed her plump, rosy cheeks. Her rosebud lips were soft and pink and slightly open. Her head was covered with a mass of glossy ebony curls, and her eyes—he couldn't see her eyes. What colour were they? he wondered. Did she have his blue eyes or Delphine's brown? Suddenly he was overcome with shame and remorse and a terrible guilt ripped into his heart. This child was flesh of his flesh, and yet he did not know the colour of her eyes.

He thought of how he had berated Belle—Belle glowing and strong, protective and loyal, with a will of burnished steel as she had stood up to him. He had ordered her to take the child away—anywhere, as long as she was not within the vicinity of his sight. In her compassion and understanding, defiant and brave and with blazing eyes she had defied him. She had subjected him to the most massive dose of guilt, coercion and emotional blackmail that he had ever seen anyone hand out.

Fiercely and strongly she had been challengingly ready to defend his child, throwing his scorn back in his face.

In the headlong strength of her mind and body, in the sweet kernel of her heart, now he could see her clearly he knew that he loved her. She had succeeded in breaking down all his defences and he could not bear to lose her. Her smile warmed his heart, her touch heated his blood. The unpredictable young woman had the power to enchant him, to amuse and infuriate him as no other woman had ever been able to. He wanted to have her by his side—and in his bed, to feast his eyes on her and hold her, and to know the exquisite sensation of her slender, voluptuous body curved against his. She stirred his heart which he had thought to be dead, and she stirred his blood to a passion that given a chance would be everlasting.

Reaching into the crib, he touched one of the soft cheeks with the tip of his finger. The child stretched her tiny body and yawned. Something stirred in Lance, growing quite dramatically into an emotion he did not at first recognise but which, when he'd studied it, he was certain he would find gratifying. And then her eyelids fluttered and opened a little in sleep before closing once more, not yet ready to wake. But the man responsible for the brief disturbance in his daughter smiled to himself, a satisfying, jubilant smile that warmed his heart.

Charlotte's eyes were blue, just like his own.

Lance was unaware that his wife, coming to check on her stepdaughter, had paused in the doorway. Belle saw Lance leaning over the crib and her first reaction was one of alarm, until she saw his face. Her breath caught in her throat and hope stirred. There was a softening to his features as he looked at his child. Was this the awakening of a father's love for his child, or a long-delayed sense of responsibility? Was he suffering guilt at the way he had kept the child away from him since birth?

Not wanting to disturb this precious moment, without making a sound Belle stepped out of sight.

Later, when Charlotte had woken from her afternoon nap, with the little girl propped up and taking note of everything she saw, Belle wheeled her along the garden paths in the baby carriage, which had wheels and a handle to steer it. She took her to the paddock behind the stables to see her husband's horses. Charlotte, wide eyed and wondering, began to rock excitedly in her carriage as one of the horses craned its neck over the fence to take one of the sugar lumps Belle always carried in her pocket as treats.

When Charlotte squealed with delight and held up her arms to be lifted out of the carriage, Belle picked her up and settled her quite naturally on her hip, the well-fleshed legs straddling her waist. The horse nudged its head against them and together they stroked its nose. Charlotte was completely unafraid of the huge beast, as clumsily her little hand patted the patient horse, her bright eyes like violets in her laughing face.

Coming round a corner of the stable block, Lance saw them and paused to watch, mesmerised by the lovely picture they made. Belle and the child made a delightful scene and the impact it had on him rooted him to the spot. Their laughter was infectious and brought a smile to his lips, and he felt himself drawn towards them, to his lovely young wife and the enchanting child she was bringing, by her own efforts, to his notice.

Moving soundlessly towards them, he listened to Belle's words as she talked to the child, telling her how one day her daddy would buy her a beautiful white pony of her very own to ride, of how she would gallop over the fields as free as a bird.

It was the child that became aware of him first. Her head spun round and she looked at him, her little face aglow with such happiness that Lance's heart turned over. Aware that Charlotte's attention was directed elsewhere, Belle turned to face her husband.

'Lance! You startled me.'

Lance's gaze went to the child. Not knowing who he was, she was shy of him and hid her face in Belle's neck, but her curiosity getting the better of her, slowly she twisted her neck round so that she could look at him. Lance saw a small dark head wearing a white frilled bonnet and two bright blue eyes looking at him. A small hand with plump and questing fingers reached out to the bright buttons on his jacket and the blue eyes smiled. They were his eyes, he saw, so blue as to be almost violet, and two tiny teeth like pearls were revealed between parted pink lips.

Belle stood and watched, not saying a word, as father and daughter looked at each other properly for the first time. Her heart was in her mouth, fearing and expecting Lance to walk away.

The small bud of feeling Lance had experienced in the nursery when he'd looked down at his daughter's sleeping face, moved somewhere inside him and began to grow. He smiled back at his child and put out his hand to her. Instantly his finger was gripped by her tiny hand. Lance felt it, and it was as though a steel band had wrapped itself round his heart and would never let go.

'She is lovely, Lance, is she not?' Belle murmured, deeply moved by this moment.

'Yes—yes,' he answered hoarsely, 'she is', and then a shutter came down on his face and he turned away sharply, disengaging his finger from Charlotte's grip. 'Excuse me. I have things to do.'

Belle watching him stride away, his shoulders stiff, his head erect, but she was satisfied. The ice was broken.

After settling Charlotte in her crib for the night, Belle went to her rooms, meeting Daisy on her way out. With a bundle of Belle's clothes in her arms to take downstairs to be ironed, she paused and pointed to a slender vase on her dressing table, which held a single pink rose.

In bewilderment, Belle moved towards it, eyeing the rose with suspicion. 'What's this, Daisy?

'It looks very much like a rose to me.'

'But—where has it come from?'

'Your husband brought it before he went out.'

'Oh—I wonder why.'

'Looks like he's trying to make amends to me.' Daisy knew how things stood between her mistress and her husband, and was as impatient for matters to be resolved as her mistress. 'Surely you do not doubt his feelings now?'

Alone, Belle fingered delicate petals of the rose, wondering what could have prompted Lance to give it to her. And then she remembered the night she had worn her rose gown and the comment he had made, telling her the colour suited her, but reminding her that the thorns of the rose were like her and had pierced deep beneath his skin.

So what did this mean? What was he trying to tell her? She was given the answer when she removed the rose from the glass vase and saw it was without thorns. She smiled. It was his way of telling her that the barbs had been pulled from his flesh and that he accepted responsibility for Charlotte, that he no longer blamed her for Delphine's death, and that he no longer wanted to send her away. In doing so, was he also making a genuine confession of his love for her, Belle? she wondered. But, no, surely she had misread the sign, for it did not make sense. He had certainly not loved her in the beginning, so why should he love her now? No, it was not possible, for she knew the foolishness of that far-fetched idea.

Tears started to her eyes and blurred her vision, but she blinked them away, refusing to cry. It would be enough for her that he learned to love his daughter, but deep down inside her she hoped and prayed fervently that he would have a little love left over for his wife.

Suddenly a keen awareness swept over her, causing her to place the rose back in the vase. Then she turned and saw a tall, broad-shouldered form advancing towards her from the doorway. She blinked, wiping desperately at her tears. Then she saw her husband's smiling face and his arms extended toward her, and all of heaven opened up to her. In an instant she was flying across the carpet into his embrace and being lifted off her feet. She wrapped her arms tightly round his neck, laughing and crying like a crazy woman as he covered her face with kisses before his mouth snared hers in a wild, ravenous kiss.

When his lips released hers after what seemed like an eternity, Lance held her close to his chest. 'I've missed you so much,' he whispered, brushing his lips across her brow. 'You'll never know how much.'

'I do, because I've missed you also. Do you hate me for what I almost did to us?'

'Hate you?' Lance was incredulous. 'Good Lord, woman, how could I possibly hate you when I'm sure the sun rises and sets with you? Can't you understand by now how much I love you?'

Pulling herself away from his chest, but remaining within the circle of his arms, Belle searched his handsome face. 'Are you sure it's not your lusting instincts?'

His hands pulled her back to him. 'If it were, my love, I would have been able to find appeasement with any woman, but I wanted no one but you. One way or another you've held my mind ensnared from that moment I saw you at Carlton House.'

Belle traced her finger down the front of his shirt. 'Then I must tell you that I've been in love with you ever since you agreed to marry me.'

His dark eyebrows lifted in a small shrug. 'I always hoped that, but you led me to believe otherwise when you stood against me and tried to send me packing when I came to rescue you at the Schofields' ball.'

'And I thought you'd hate me for making you feel obligated to doing the gentlemanly thing.' She looked up at him, searching his face. 'I thought you had gone out.'

'I did,' he said, cupping her face with hands, 'but I came back. I wanted to be with my wife—and child.'

'Oh, Lance. And the rose? Does this mean you no longer want to send Charlotte away?'

'Yes, my darling, that is exactly what it means,' he said, taking her hand and pulling her down on to the bed beside him. Belle saw his regret, heard it in his voice when he again looked at her and said, 'I have been a fool. I should have realised my responsibilities a long time ago and honoured the pledge I made to Delphine.' His voice was harsh with self-recrimination. 'I promised her I would support her in a manner suitable to her upbringing. I gave my word and I broke it.'

'You are too hard on yourself. I don't see it like that. You made provision for her. You made sure she was taken care of by sending her to your mother, where she received the very best of care. Where she was loved.'

'But how could I have blamed Charlotte for Delphine's

death? I'm not proud of myself,' he admitted. 'Fear had something to do with it—fear of recognising that her death was down to me entirely. I lived in daily dread of the day when I would have to look on Charlotte's face—when I would have to confront what I had done, because she was the living proof of it. It was the most despicable thing I could have done.'

Lance looked at Belle, waiting for her to comment, and when she didn't, he said, 'It would mean a great deal to me, and to our future together, if you could find it in your heart to forgive me.'

'I have nothing to forgive you for. That you realise it now is a good thing, Lance. Now you can honour the promise you made to Delphine and get to know Charlotte. She is a baby still. You have only a little time to make up—and I know you will make a wonderful father.'

'Nevertheless, it was wrong of me to cast her off like I did.'

'You didn't know Delphine was with child. I'm sorry to say this, but she was equally to blame. She should have told you—or contacted you in some way when she realised she was pregnant.' Belle sighed, placing her head on his shoulder. 'The fates played against you, Lance, and there is no turning back the clock to right the wrong. It is the future that counts—a future that includes Charlotte.'

Placing his arms around her, he drew her close, kissing her cheek. 'I don't deserve you, Isabelle Bingham. When I consider the way I treated you in London, when your grandmother insisted I did the honourable thing and marry you, when I finally agreed to it, you were already half-convinced my proposal was made out of pity and regret. You didn't like me very well as it was, and you didn't particularly trust me, either,' he reminded her, 'and I knew you found it extremely difficult to forgive me for hurting you, and for shaming you. I never imagined, though, the extent you would actually go to to retaliate against me by leaving my bed in defence of my daughter.'

Lance saw the pain in her eyes, and despite his belief that all this had to be said, it took an almost physical effort not to ease her hurt with his hands and his mouth.

'It wasn't retaliation, Lance, please do not think that. It's just that I knew you were a fair man and that something about Delphine's death had hurt you very badly. Your reticence to your daughter almost broke my heart. That you reacted the way you did to my trying to bring about a reconciliation between you and Charlotte was unfortunate, but I did what I thought was for the best.'

That she didn't blame him or argue made Lance realise that Belle might be very young and inexperienced, but she was also very wise.

In the flickering candlelight Lance and Belle lay together and made love with a fierceness, unable to control the tormenting demands of their bodies, as if to make up for the time they had lost from being apart. Belle's sighs were soft and seductive as she stretched out alongside this man she adored. Not only had she a husband but a lover. His irrepressible carnality enthralled her.

Blue eyes were now dark eyes, passionate eyes, burning eyes, gazing down into hers. Here they were again, doing the most wonderful things, lovely things, and a shivering ecstasy pierced her entire body, sending streaks of pleasure curling through her. One kiss led to another and soon Lance's virile body blended with that of his wife's in an erotic exchange that left them both heady with desire.

The sharp spasm was so insistently physical. Suddenly Belle felt a burst of the wildest wantonness in her body and such urgency that she did not recognise herself, so foreign was it to her, so alien, that she lost all sense of decorum as he drove her into sweet oblivion.

Lance pulled her with him on to his side, his breathing still laboured as he kissed her forehead and moved her rumpled hair off her face. 'How do you feel now?' he asked softly.

She sighed, nestling closer to him, their bodies as sleek and wet and lithe as the fish in the lake. Her long curling lashes fluttered up, her eyes still dark with passion. 'Like a wife,' she murmured. 'Like your wife.'

His expression was tender as he gently kissed her lips. 'You are, my love, without doubt.' He groaned as she writhed against him. 'Do you know how erotic you are,' he murmured, running his fingers down her spine to the swell of her buttocks with such delicate tracery, such tenderness, that Belle scarcely knew her own body as they started again, another shuddering tournament of making love.

Belle had come to the realisation that she had never been happier in her life. She was married to the most wonderful man whom she adored, and with each passing hour their love for each other deepened. They enjoyed being secluded and made much of those interludes in the privacy of their home.

Charlotte was a constant delight to them and they could frequently be found in the nursery happily watching her crawling on the rug. Lance, now a besotted father, was quite enthralled by her noisy antics and couldn't believe his reluctance to have anything to do with her. He looked at Belle, unable to believe how much he loved her, and how much he owed to her for bringing it about.

'You do not object to a ready-made family, Belle?'

Her cheeks dimpled impishly. 'On the contrary. I mean to add to it just as soon as I can,' she said softly. 'Charlotte is a darling child and I love her as if she were my own.'

Drawing his daughter into the crook of his arm, where she settled down willingly since this was where she most liked to be, Lance placed a finger under Belle's chin, turning her face towards his. He searched her eyes for a moment, then shook his head. 'You are quite remarkable, do you know that?'

Belle wasn't certain, but she thought it might be a compliment. It flustered her to have him looking at her so, as if she had accomplished some great deed rather than spoke well of his child, and his simple words flustered her more.

'Thank you,' he said, his husky voice warming her as she gazed into his eyes. After the night he had just spent with her, Lance was certain he had never experienced such fulfilment. He also knew he wouldn't have traded his freedom for his darling wife, his mate for life.

Belle felt herself being drawn into his gaze, into the vital rugged aura of him. Being so close to him was having a strange effect on her senses. She was too aware of him—of his power and his strength. She couldn't mistake the approval in the tender smile he gave her. It was reward enough, she decided, for her efforts to accept and love his daughter.

* * * * *

Fugitive Countess

ANNE HERRIES

Prologue

France 1520

'This is a fine spectacle, Father. Thank you for bringing me today.'

'It was His Majesty's wish that you accompany us, Anton.' Andrew, Marquis of Malchester and Earl of Gifford, smiled. 'But you speak truly. It is a day that people will remember for ever, and you will be proud to tell your grandchildren that you were here.'

Anton's smoky grey eyes travelled round the glittering gathering, hungrily absorbing the scene. His father had no need to remind him of the importance of the occasion, for he was well aware that this was a special day in history. He and his father were amongst those fortunate enough to accompany King Henry VIII of England to France. Here on this field the nobles of both King Henry and King Francis I of France had gathered, to witness the meeting of the two kings. It looked like a field of gold, the richness of the gowns and jewels worn by the wealthy men of two countries beyond anything anyone had ever seen. It was, Anton thought, as if the two monarchs wished to outshine each other.

At just seventeen, Anton was already a man of some stature: broad-shouldered and long in the leg, his dark hair cut so that it turned under and just brushed the gold lace ruff he wore about his throat. His jerkin of black velvet was slashed through with gold, and he wore tight-fitting hose of cloth of gold with soft leather boots that came halfway up his calf and boasted tassels of pure gold. His flat cap was black, but in honour of the occasion it had a feather fastened with a huge emerald and gold pin. Across his body was a sash of gold sewn with precious jewels; his sword was encased in a scabbard of leather set with semi-precious stones. He looked what he was: the son of an extremely wealthy man, and his position in the King's train showed that His Majesty held him in some esteem.

Anton took his place in the world for granted, sitting astride his horse proudly as he relished the glittering scene. More and more nobles were entering the field, some of them riding carelessly, their horses jostling for position as they tried to get closer to where the two kings had come together to exchange greetings and promises of friendship. Anton was feeling excited, for his father had told him that King Henry had spoken of giving him a more prestigious position at court. Despite his father's wealth, Anton knew that he was expected to make his own way in the world. He would one day inherit a fortune, but it had always been clear to him that he must win honour and fame for himself.

It was so exciting to be a part of this momentous occasion. Anton did not wish to miss anything, his gaze travelling constantly from one face to another, unwilling to miss a moment. Young and strong, he had proven himself on the training ground and now longed for adventure.

He suddenly noticed a fracas going on to his left, and realized that some of the proud nobles were not satisfied with their position. An English noble he recognized and a French lord he had never seen before were trying to edge each other out, their horses jostling and shying. One of the horses close by was snorting, clearly nervous of the crowd. As Anton watched, it reared up and started to kick out at the nearest horse, which made that beast snort and shy sideways, in turn causing some of the others to panic. It was obvious that some of the horses were on the verge of mad flight. One fine chestnut mare reared up and dislodged her rider.

As the rider screamed and went tumbling, Anton leapt from his own horse and rushed towards the lady, scooping her up out of the way of flailing hooves. The nobles were starting to bring their horses under control once more as Anton pushed his way through the crush, carrying his precious burden to a place where pavilions of rich cloth had been set up apart from the crowd. The lady had been frightened, and clung to him as he carried her to safety, but he thought she was not seriously harmed.

'Are you hurt, little mistress?' he asked as he set her down, for he thought her not more than thirteen or so, and little more than a child. Her breasts were mere buds beneath the silk gown that clung to her slender form. Her hair carried a hint of red in the gold, and her eyes were more green than blue. He thought that she was fair, and would be beautiful one day, and he was angry that she might have been seriously harmed. 'The fool who caused your horse to rear like that should be flogged for his life.'

'Oh, no…please…' The girl blushed delicately. She spoke English well, but with an accent that told of her French birth. 'I would not have a fuss made, sir. My father would be angry. He wanted me to ride pillion behind my groom, but I insisted that I could manage my horse. I did not expect such a crush.'

'I dare say no harm has been done.' Anton smiled at her, for she was both pretty and sweet, her face that of an innocent angel. He glanced round. 'Someone has rescued our horses, it seems…' He saw his squire leading his mount, and a French vassal was bringing the spirited chestnut that had thrown her.

She touched his arm to reclaim his attention. 'Will you tell me your name, sir? I am the lady Marietta Villiers…'

'I am honoured.' Anton bowed gracefully. 'Anton of Gifford—son of the Marquis of Malchester and Earl of Gifford.'

'Thank you for my life, Anton of Gifford.' Marietta reached up and kissed his cheek. There was a faint flush in her cheeks, but her eyes were as bright and clear as the summer sky. 'I shall honour your memory for as long as I live. I must go, for my groom comes and my father will be anxious…'

'It was nothing…' Anton said. He hesitated, wanting to ask more—who her father was, where she came from—but he knew that he too was looked for. He must return to the King's train, for he might be summoned to do His Majesty some service. The girl had had a fright, but she had borne it well and she was not alone. She was but a child, and they were not likely to meet again. He must forget her and remember his duty to the king.

He relinquished her to the care of her groom and made his way back to where his father waited. The Marquis had noticed his act of gallantry and nodded, a look of approval in his eyes. It was no more than he would expect of his son.

'That was well done of you, Anton. I dare say it did not go unnoticed by others. As you know, we are to accompany His Majesty to the court of Charles of Spain. Charles has recently been appointed the new Holy Roman Emperor and Henry must pay his respects.'

'Yes, Father. I am happy to be a part of His Majesty's train.'

'I think you will find that Henry thinks much of you, Anton. It may be that you will be given a position of more importance than you imagine…'

Anton felt a surge of excitement. He was not sure what his father meant, but the future held a golden promise. He was strong, ambitious, and impatient for the good things life had to offer. All thought of the young French girl was forgotten as he watched the moment when the two kings greeted each other. It was good to be young and on the verge of something wonderful.

Later he would remember the girl he had rescued and smile, tucking the memory away deep in the back of his mind, but for now history was in the making!

Marietta looked at the man who stood beside her father, to the right of the French King. It was due to the Comte that they had been invited to this glittering affair, and she must be grateful for the privilege. The Comte was not ugly, for his years sat well on him, and though of a heavier build than she found attractive, he seemed strong and noble. Her father, brought to the verge of ruin by foolish investments, had given her to this knight in return for the right to live in peace on his own lands. She was fifteen years of age and it was time for her to be wed. The Comte de Montcrief would make her a good husband, for she knew him to be a kind and generous man.

However, his smile did not make her heart beat faster—the way the young English knight's had when he'd held her close to his chest. He was so bold, so strong and so handsome! She had felt so safe in his arms! More than that, she had felt a warm melting inside her, like liquid honey that curled through her body, arousing sensations she had not known existed.

Anton of Gifford—the son of the Marquis of Malchester!

Marietta knew that she would never forget the man who had rescued her from what might have been painful injury or even death. Something in her had responded to him as he'd looked down at her with those serious grey eyes. In those brief moments she had experienced the strangest feeling—as though she had met her destiny. She had kissed him impulsively, but wished that he had kissed her back—on the mouth. Instinctively she wanted so much more that in her innocence she did not understand.

She was so immodest! It was as well that neither her father nor the Comte could read her mind. Her thoughts were wild and romantic—the foolish dreams of a young girl. She had listened to the storyteller and his fables of courtly knights too often! The reality was that she must marry a man she did not love or see her father dispossessed of all he owned and both of them turned out to beg for their living.

Marietta might instead have chosen life as a nun, but she doubted she would be taken without a dowry, which her father was unable to give her. Perhaps if she had felt a true vocation she might have chosen that life rather than marry the Comte, but her father would still have been faced with poverty. By agreeing to marry the Comte de Montcrief she had ensured that her beloved father would end his days in his own bed.

She must think of the good she had done, Marietta decided. Her future was not what she would have wished, but she must do her duty. She would be a good wife to the Comte and bear his children—and she would try to forget that *once* a young man had made her long for so much more…

Chapter One

France 1525

'Marietta.' Comte de Montcrief greeted his wife with a smile as she entered his chamber, carrying a pewter cup and a small flask containing a dark liquid. She grew more beautiful with every day, her red-gold hair like threads of silken sunbeams and her eyes more brilliant than any jewel. 'You never fail to bring my medicine when I need it. I do not know how I should have managed without you this past winter. I am sure that without your nursing, my dear wife, I should have died.'

'I know this eases the tightness in your chest far better than the mixture the apothecary sent you, my lord. I believe the fluid on your chest is easing, is it not?'

'Yes. I grow stronger every day, thanks to you, my love. I was blessed when your father gave you to me, Marietta.'

'I have been blessed in giving you a son,' Marietta replied. 'I failed twice, and thought it was God's will that we should not have a child—but our little Charles flourishes. He has passed his first year, and as you know too well 'tis the first few months that are so dangerous for vulnerable babes.'

'You have given me a fine heir, but I hope he will not inherit too soon…' The Comte frowned. 'It worried me when I was ill, for though I know you are both brave and wise, it would be hard for you to hold the castle against the barons who might seek to take it. The nobles are a greedy rabble, Marietta. If I should die before our son reaches his maturity I have left the care of him and my estate to you, to hold for our son until he is old enough to take it—but I would urge you to choose a husband as soon as you may decently marry. I have no doubt that you will have many offers, but choose wisely. You must take a man with fortune enough that he will not covet our son's inheritance—and one who will treat you well.'

'Please, my lord, do not speak of such things to me,' Marietta begged. 'I am not sure that I would wish for another husband. You have been good to me, and to my late father.'

'Your poor father suffered greatly towards the end, and I was pleased that you should nurse him here in our home. I would do anything to please you. I am too old for you, Marietta. I offered for you when your father told me of his need—but I think I have not been fair to you. You should have had a fine young husband to bed you and give you many sons. It lies heavy on my conscience that I took your youth and squandered it when you might have had so much more.'

'Hush, my lord.' Marietta held the cup out to him. 'Drink this and ease yourself. You have been a kind husband, and many are not. I am content with my life, especially since we have our son.'

The Comte smiled indulgently. 'You have been a good wife. I shall buy you a present. What would you like?'

He took her hand and she felt the press of the heavy gold ring he wore on the middle finger of his left hand. It had a huge cabochon ruby and was very fine.

'I ask for nothing but your affection, my lord—but if you will give me something, let it be a lyre. The one I have has cracked and is no longer sweet in tone.'

'You shall have the finest that can be bought,' the Comte

said, and kissed her cheek. 'And perhaps a ring for your finger too. Now, go about your business, Marietta. I would sleep.'

Marietta sighed as she made her way to her solar in the south-facing turret of the castle. When she had married her husband he had given her all the rooms in this tower, so that her ladies might be there to serve her. She had a bedchamber, a chamber where she could sit with her ladies and sew, and there was another chamber where her clothes were kept and her ladies slept on pallets that were stowed away during the day.

Montcrief seldom disturbed her these days. He had always been considerate. Marietta believed that if she had given him a son the first time she had conceived he would not have troubled her again. She knew now that he felt he had wronged her by taking her to wife. The difference in their ages had shown more as the years passed; he was too old for her, and his health had deteriorated suddenly after a fall from his horse. They had been fortunate that she had managed to produce a healthy heir. Her son, to the joy of both his parents, thrived.

Marietta had long since ceased to regret her marriage. She enjoyed being the chatelaine of a fine castle and ran her home with ease. Her child had brought her great joy and made her sewing a pleasure, for she liked to see the boy dressed in fine gowns and spent hours at her embroidery.

Yet Montcrief *was* too old, and although Marietta loved him it was more the love she would give to a dear uncle or friend. However, she had never thought of betraying him… except for once or twice at the start, when the picture of a handsome Englishman had popped into her head as she lay beside her husband.

It was nearly five years since the day she had almost been trampled beneath the hooves of that horse. Marietta sometimes wondered where Anton of Gifford was, and what he had done in all those years. She imagined him living on a fine estate in England. She knew that the countryside was beautiful there for her mother had told her. Baron Villiers had married an English lady of great beauty but little fortune.

Jane, Lady Villiers, had been a sweet lady, and had taught her daughter much before she died.

Marietta knew that a distant cousin of her father's had married an English gentleman. Claire Melford had sent a letter when she had learned of Marietta's marriage, and Marietta had written to her a few times over the years. Claire had asked if they would visit, but Montcrief was always too busy. He went often to the French court. At the start he had taken Marietta with him, but when she'd had her first miscarriage she had asked that she be allowed to stay at home. Now that she had her son, she might accompany her husband next time he went.

She entered her chamber, glancing at the child who lay sleeping in his crib. Charles was resting well, his chubby face flushed and glowing with health. He had recently been weaned and no longer needed the wet nurse's milk. Bending down to kiss his brow, Marietta thought that she must count her blessings. She had thought that her life was finished when she came here as a bride, but she had made the best of it and was happy enough. Only now and then did she allow herself to think of the young man who had saved her life. For one moment she had glimpsed how sweet life might be, but that was mere fancy, a romantic notion that she had put away as she became a woman and her girlish dreams faded.

Anton bent to lay a single yellow rose on Isabella's grave. She had been buried with her unborn child these six months gone. Not one day had passed in all these months when Anton had failed to blame himself for his wife's death. It was because of him that she lay beneath the earth, her young life extinguished.

'Forgive me!' he cried. 'Sweet lady, forgive me, I beg you!'

Tears ran down his cheeks for the guilt was strong. If he had not flown at her in a jealous rage that last day would she have gone walking and fallen, striking her head against a stone at the foot of steep steps? She had died instantly, and her unborn child with her, for her body had not been found until it was too late and the physicians could save neither her nor the son she'd carried.

When they married, Anton had believed himself to be passionately in love with his wife. However, something had changed between them after the birth of their first child. From the start Isabella had shown little response to his lovemaking. He had thought it was simply her innocence, but after their daughter was born she had complained of headaches, begging to be left to sleep alone. The realisation that his wife did not love or want him had been hard to accept at first. But gradually he'd discovered that he no longer felt anything for her, and understood that the marriage had been a mistake. Divorce had been impossible, for Isabella had been a Catholic and Anton's strong sense of duty, both to his wife and his daughter, had driven him to make the most of what he had.

For months he had done his best to please Isabella, and then one night she had come to him in his bed and asked him to love her. He had responded with warmth and pleasure, believing and hoping that they could begin to build something worthwhile that would give them both a measure of happiness. When she had told him she was with child once more Anton had been delighted. He loved his daughter, and hoped for a son, but a little over a month before Isabella's death he was told something in an unsigned letter that made him suspect she had betrayed him with another man. He had carried the nagging doubt inside him for weeks, reluctant to believe that the tale was true.

It must be a lie! Surely it could not be true? His mind had twisted and turned, seeking a way out of his torment, remembering and analysing. His wife had suffered so much during her months of childbearing, always complaining of sickness or discomfort, hardly able to bear the touch of his hand on hers.

The uncertainty had tormented him beyond bearing. In the end he had asked Isabella if the child she carried was his. The look on her face had been such that he had felt as if she had struck a knife to his heart.

'You can ask that of me?' she said, in a voice that was so faint he could scarce hear it. 'You think I would betray you—betray my honour?'

Anton seized her wrist so fiercely that she cried out. 'Tell me, is this story true or a lie?'

'Believe what you will,' Isabella said, her face proud. 'Unhand me, sir. You hurt me. Remember the child I bear, for he is yours…'

'Isabella…' Anton cried as she walked away, her gown making a swishing sound on the marble floors of their Spanish palace. 'Forgive me. It was told to me and I could not forget…'

Isabella did not look back. The next time Anton saw her, she was lying at the foot of some stone steps leading to the sunken gardens, her neck broken.

Anton had wept over her dead body, but it was too late. He was the murderer of his wife and child! Yet he could make amends—must make amends for the wrong he had done his wife.

In his agony over Isabella's death he had neglected Madeline, his beautiful daughter, who was now almost eighteen months old. He had loved her from the moment of her birth, but for months he had scarcely seen her, leaving her to the care of her nurse Lily—an Englishwoman who had come to them after the death of her Spanish husband.

Anton's expression was bleak as he straightened from kneeling by the grave. He could not bring Isabella back, but he would devote himself to the care of her daughter.

He was tired of living in this country, though he was well liked at court and he spoke the language fluently. Isabella had helped him, laughing at his clumsy pronunciation at the start. Because of her he had done well in his position as the eyes and ears of England's king, but now he wanted to return home. To stay here with his memories would make his life unbearable. Here in the home he had shared with Isabella he would be for ever haunted, seeing his dead wife's face at every turn, her dark eyes accusing—always accusing.

He would return to England and make a new life for himself. Isabella had brought him a small fortune in jewels and gold when they married. Combined with the fortune he had won for himself, he could buy a large estate and build a house. Perhaps in time he might find a woman willing to share his life and give him an heir. He could never offer a woman love, for his heart had died with Isabella, but his wealth might be sufficient for some. It would not happen yet. His wounds were too raw to think of marriage. Until his home was built and a mother for Madeline was found he would give the child into his mother's care.

All Anton wanted for now was peace. Perhaps in England he would be able to sleep…

'You will come with me to the tourney?' Montcrief looked pleased as Marietta inclined her head. 'You will do me the honour, wife? You are even more beautiful than when we married. I shall be glad to have your company.'

'You know it gives me great joy to ride—and now that you are well again we shall go out together more.'

'We shall go riding tomorrow,' he promised her. His steward approached, bearing a letter on a salver. 'Excuse me…' He broke the wax seal and frowned as he read what it contained. 'In God's name, what does *he* want here?'

'Is something wrong, husband?'

'Rouen asks if he may visit with us.' The Comte looked annoyed. 'I have told you that he is the bastard my mistress bore me when I was young? She was a woman of Rouen, and he takes her name instead of mine.'

'Yes, my lord.' Marietta's gaze was steady as she met his look. 'I have heard it said that had I not given you a son you might have left your estate to the Bastard of Rouen—is that so?'

'It was in my mind. I have told you that it needs a strong man to hold the castle and lands. Rouen is a good soldier—but coarse like his mother, and baseborn. He would not learn from books when he was young and thought only of fighting. Our son will learn to be noble of mind as well as birth. I want you to make sure of it if something should happen to me.'

'You are well again, husband,' Marietta said. 'You will live long enough to teach Charles these things yourself.'

'I intend to live to see him grown if I can,' Montcrief agreed. 'But I wish you to be aware of these things just in case. Life is never certain, my love. A man may die in many ways.'

'That is true, for many die of poverty and sickness. I tend those I can at Montcrief, taking them cures and food—but the poor are everywhere.'

Montcrief nodded, but she could see his mind was elsewhere. 'I suppose I must allow the visit. I do not wish for it, Marietta. He is a surly brute, and I do not quite trust him, but it is sometimes better to keep your enemy close.'

'You think of Rouen as your enemy?' Marietta was startled, for she had imagined that there was some affection between the two. Why else would Montcrief acknowledge him as his bastard?

'Perhaps I chose the wrong word. At one time I was proud of the boy, but as he grew he became surly and wild, fell into bad company. I would have been loath to see him the master here, though had we not been blessed it might have come to that…' Montcrief looked thoughtful. 'He has learned to expect something of me. I dare say I must make him a gift, though not lands—but money. Yes, I may offer him five hundred silver talents. We may see him at the tourney. Perhaps the deal may be struck there.'

'Five hundred silver talents is a great deal of money, my lord.'

'You are right—but 'tis a fraction of my fortune. Our son

will inherit much more when I die, Marietta, and you will have your portion. You do not begrudge Rouen the peace offering?'

'No, my lord. I would never seek to influence your judgement in such matters. You must do as you wish.'

'Well, I think it best. I do not wish him to feel resentment against Charles. With his own small fortune he may buy land, if he wishes, or seek out a trade.'

Marietta smiled and left him to his thoughts, for they both had many duties.

'We should stop for a while,' Lily Salacosa told her master. 'Madeline suffers from a fever. I do not think it serious, but constant travelling is making her tired and fractious. Could we not rest at the next inn for a day or two?'

Anton looked at the babe she held in her arms with concern. His daughter's face was flushed, and when he touched her face she felt too warm.

'Yes, we shall rest, mistress,' he told her. 'I sent ahead to take rooms at an inn near Rouen. We shall break our journey there. If Madeline continues to be unwell you must summon a physician to her.'

'I think it merely teething, my lord, but she will recover sooner with a few days of rest.'

Anton smiled and bent to kiss his daughter's forehead. She would be as beautiful as her mother one day—a fair, pale goddess who would set the hearts of her suitors racing. Anton knew that he had not been Isabella's only suitor. She had seemed pleased to wed him, and happy in their marriage at first, but had she hidden her true feelings from him?

Anton squashed the thought. That way lay madness! His wife was gone and he would never know the truth. He must think only of the future and his beloved daughter.

A poster nailed to a tree caught his eye. A group of men were clustered about it excitedly, chattering and laughing. He called out to them in French, asking what was going on.

''Tis the day of the tourney,' one of the men responded. 'The winner of the games may win a silver arrow and all may enter. Only a man skilled in wrestling, throwing and archery can win. Men come from far and wide to enter.'

Anton nodded. As a youth he had often entered such tournaments, and the idea appealed to him. Since he must tarry a few days for the sake of his daughter, why should he not take a little time to amuse himself?

The day of the tourney had arrived. Marietta dressed in a gown of rich dark blue embroidered with silver beads and braiding, her long hair covered by a hood of matching cloth laced through with silver.

She felt proud to be riding by her husband's side as they approached the field outside the city of Rouen, where the great fair was held every year. Nobles and freemen from all corners of the land would journey here, for the contest was a rich one. The young men entered contests of running, throwing a spear, shooting arrows at a barrel and wrestling. For the past weeks posters had been placed about the countryside, inviting all the young men to enter, and they would come from all over France. To win the silver arrow a man must be the winner of all four events. If the arrow was not won small prizes were given to the individual winners.

Marietta took her place in one of the most prominent seats, smiling as she looked about at the happy faces of the populace. The people were of good cheer, and they waved, calling out greetings to the nobles they knew or served as they arrived.

A fanfare of trumpets announced the arrival of the contestants and some twenty men rode into the arena; these were the nobles who had entered the tourney and would give the spectators a magnificent show. The battles were merely to show skill and strength, and there would be no fights to the death, as there had been in years gone by. Behind the nobles came the freemen, sons of noblemen and burghers, who were to enter the contest for the silver arrow.

For the first hour Marietta watched the nobles tilting with their fearsome lances, trying to unseat one another. Some of them went on to fight with heavy broadswords until one or the other asked for quarter. She applauded the winners when they came to take their bows. One knight vanquished all five of his opponents and was given a fine dagger with a jewelled hilt as his prize.

After the show of valour by the nobles there was a display of tumbling and dancing bears. Then the trumpets announced the contest for the silver arrow was about to begin.

The men were announced one by one. The Bastard of Rouen was the tenth man to present himself, and the cheers for him were deafening for he had won this prize twice before and it was obvious the people considered him their champion. He was a tall man, thickset, with a reddish beard and a scar at his temple.

He came to bow before the watching nobles, bowing his head to his father and to Marietta. She had an uneasy feeling, a trickle of ice sliding down her spine as she felt his gaze on her. Lifting her head proudly, she gave him a cool smile and saw a flicker of anger in his eyes.

The next man to present himself gave his name simply as Anton. He too was a tall man, strong with dark hair and grey eyes—and Marietta tingled as she knew him. He was Anton of Gifford, the son of the Marquis of Malchester: the man who had saved her on the Field of the Cloth of Gold. He was as she remembered, and yet he was so different. He looked older, stronger—his eyes cold and unsmiling as they moved over the assembled nobles and their ladies. He gave no sign of recognition, and she felt a little pang of disappointment as she realised that he did not know her.

She held back the rush of tears that suddenly threatened. How foolish of her to imagine that he might know her! Why should he? Too many years had passed, and she had changed. Something in her had known him instantly, despite the changes to his appearance, but he felt nothing.

She sat back, struggling to control her disappointment. Even if he had remembered her it could make no difference. She was married and had borne her husband a child. Nothing had changed, but her insides churned with emotions she could not control. That day had been enshrined in her memory as something magical, helping her through the worst days, helping her to do what she must.

The contest had begun. The men were lined up for the race, which started from a line in front of the dais and continued over the surrounding countryside, ending back at the same spot. Once the men had left the field on the start of their gruelling race, the nobles and their ladies were served with food and wine.

Marietta ate little. It was foolish, but much of her pleasure in the day had disappeared when she had looked into a pair of cold grey eyes and seen no flicker of recognition. In her dreams, which she had treasured, when they met again Anton of Gifford had smiled and told her that she had remained in his heart and mind all these years—but such dreams were foolish!

A cheer went up when the runners returned. She saw that two of them had far outpaced the others: neck and neck, they raced to the dais and arrived at precisely the same moment. Wild cheering for the Bastard of Rouen broke out as the crowd chanted his name.

The master of ceremonies held up his hand and the crowd quietened.

'For the first event we have two winners, for they could not be parted. It is the first time this has happened and each has one talent to take forward.'

Some cheered wildly, others grumbled, for they had wanted the Bastard to win. However, the second contest was announced and the spear-throwing began. Each man had three throws. The first to throw was the Bastard, and his spear reached to the second marker. Another contestant stepped forward, his spear flying through the air to within a fraction of the Bastard's. Three other men threw, but could not reach the second marker. Then Anton stepped forward. His arm went back and the spear flew through the air, almost reaching the third marker.

The Bastard stepped forward to throw again. His spear landed a fraction behind Anton's; the next contestants could not reach even the second marker. Anton threw again, but this time he did not reach his first try.

People were calling out, cheering wildly as the Bastard stepped forward. He drew back his arm, putting all his effort into the final throw, and his spear went past Anton's first marker by no more than a handspan. A huge cheer greeted his efforts, especially when none of the others could come near. Then silence fell as Anton stepped up. He drew back his arm and threw for the final time. The spear flew through the air and finished level with the Bastard's.

There was a buzz of excitement as the crowd waited to hear who would be announced the winner. The master of ceremonies stood up, holding his hand up for silence.

'On the third throw they are equal,' he said. 'But Anton threw further with his first spear. He is therefore the winner.'

Marietta was watching the Bastard's face. He looked furious, for it meant that he could not now win the silver arrow. Only Anton could win this coveted prize, if he gained both the archery contest and the wrestling crown.

The archery came next. People were murmuring with excitement, for though some stayed loyal to their champion, others were willing the stranger on. It was known that archery was the Bastard's weakest skill, and they wondered if Anton could win yet again. He could and did, easily.

Last came the wrestling. No one had ever beaten the Bastard of Rouen at wrestling. A hush fell over the crowd as the master of ceremonies stood up.

'It has been decided that the contest shall be settled by three bouts between the Bastard of Rouen and Anton…'

Marietta gasped as she heard the announcement. Her gaze

flew to the Bastard's face. She saw the gleam of satisfaction in his eyes and knew that he was confident of winning this contest. She sat back, feeling that she could not bear to watch, for she did not wish to see Anton humbled. He was such a worthy champion, and she guessed that the Bastard meant to humble Anton if he could.

As the contest began, Marietta closed her eyes. She was sure that the Bastard would do his best to cripple or injure his opponent. Once she had seen a man suffer a broken arm, and she could not bear to see Anton hurt in this way. She was so tense that she thought she might faint.

Hearing the gasp of astonishment and a new buzz of excitement, Marietta opened her eyes to see that Anton had taken the first fall. Her gaze fell on the Bastard. She was shocked by the look of hatred in the man's narrow-set eyes. He looked as if he would like to murder Anton!

Her heart beating wildly, Marietta sat forward to watch. The Bastard had never been beaten in this contest. Surely Anton could not best him again? She turned her nails into her hands as the two men came to grips. The Bastard was so strong, and he seemed to have Anton in his grip. He must win this time!

It happened so quickly that Marietta scarcely realised what had occurred. One moment the Bastard seemed to have Anton in an unbreakable hold, the next he was lying face down in the dirt, his arm twisted behind him and unable to move.

Wild cheers broke from the watching crowd. The nobles were on their feet applauding, the ladies threw scarves and flowers to the champion. A hush fell as the master of ceremonies stood up and announced Anton as the winner of the silver arrow.

Marietta's husband stood up. It was his privilege to present the prize to the winner. She was shocked when he turned to her, presenting the silken cushion with the arrow.

'Take it, Marietta,' he said, and smiled. 'Today my wife will present the winner with his trophy.'

Marietta hesitated, then picked up the arrow and went down the steps to where Anton was standing. She smiled as he made her an elegant bow, and a thrill went through her as she saw the gleam of triumph in his eyes. He might not recall the day he had saved her life, but he had been her champion since that time and she was delighted that he had won this prize.

'You were a worthy winner, sir,' she said. 'I am proud to give you the silver arrow.'

'I thank you, my lady,' Anton said, inclining his head. For a moment his gaze intensified as he looked at her, but no flicker of recognition showed in his eyes. 'I am honoured.' He turned and showed the arrow to the crowd, bowing as they cheered him.

Marietta turned to leave. She put her foot on the first step leading back to the benches where she had sat with her ladies, and then suddenly a dog came rushing towards her from no-where. It was a huge fierce hound with a brindle coat, and his mouth was drawn back in a snarl. A scream left her lips as the hound sprang at her for no reason, sending her to the ground. Putting up her arms to protect herself, she felt its teeth graze her flesh, and then someone was there, pulling the hound away from her, whipping it with the flat of his sword. The sound of its howling as it fled from the angry avenger was terrible.

'Lady, are you hurt?'

Half fainting, blood trickling from the wound to her arm, Marietta felt herself lifted in strong arms. She was being carried away from the scene. Dimly aware that it was the champion of the day who had saved her from the dog, she tried to thank him.

'I need no thanks, lady,' he said as he strode towards a tent. 'That beast should be destroyed. I believe it was meant to attack me, not you.'

Marietta was feeling too faint to enquire more as she was set down on a pile of soft cloaks and silks in a tent she realised must be the one the knights used to change into their armour. The man she believed to be Anton of Gifford knelt at her side. He took her arm and examined it, his fingers firm and gentle.

'The beast merely grazed the skin,' he said, and poured water from a flask onto a linen cloth, bathing her arm and wiping away the blood. 'It will hurt for a day or so but there is no real harm done.'

'Thank you. You saved my life.' Marietta was beginning to revive. She wanted to confirm if he were indeed the young man who had saved her life once before, but before she could say anything more the tent flap was lifted and her husband entered together with the Bastard of Rouen.

'Marietta, are you harmed?' the Comte asked anxiously.

'This knight acted promptly and drove off the beast,' Marietta told him. 'I was faint for a while, but I am feeling much better thanks to my brave rescuer. He has bathed the wound and I believe I have taken no harm.'

'The brute should be put to death,' her husband said, and glanced at the Bastard. 'It belongs to Rouen. I have told him he must get rid of it after what it did to you.'

''Tis a hunting dog and knows no better,' the Bastard muttered. Marietta saw him glance resentfully at the knight who had bested him, and felt an icy shiver down her spine. He would not forget this day!

Marietta stood up. She was still trembling, but felt better. 'I am well enough to leave now, husband.'

'If you are sure we shall leave at once.' Comte de Montcrief turned to Anton. 'You have my gratitude, sir. I hope that you will allow me to repay you in some way?'

'I did only what any knight of honour would do, sir. I am glad to have been of service and need no repayment.'

'Then I offer you friendship. If I may be of service to you, you have only to ask.' The Comte offered his hand and they clasped hands. He turned back to Marietta. 'Come, my dearest, take my arm. You must tell me if you feel faint and I shall help you.'

Marietta took his arm. At the door, she turned back and smiled at the knight who had saved her for the second time.

'Thank you, sir. I shall not forget...'

He inclined his head to her but made no answer.

Anton felt a deep satisfaction as he walked away from the field. To become the champion and save a beautiful woman from a savage dog in one day was an achievement that sat well with him.

It was mere chance that he had entered the contest at all. He had told his men to wait for him at the inn, to guard his daughter and her nurse, but it was really because he'd wished to enter the contest incognito. He had been in no mood for the knightly display of skill. Had he wielded a weapon of war, he might in his present mood have struck too hard and killed his opponent.

When he'd seen the notice announcing the contest for the silver arrow he had been intrigued and amused, intending at first to be a spectator. Then he'd seen men lining up to enter the contest and something had driven him to sign his name. As a young man he had loved sport, and he had been the champion of many a fair. He had entered on a whim, unsure that he would excel in all the contests, but the years of training and exercise in the Spanish sunshine had kept him strong.

In the first race he had suddenly felt alive in a way that he had not since Isabella's death. The black shadows had fallen away from him as he'd sped over the course. He had run for himself alone, and he had been surprised to discover that he had been one of the winners. The feeling had exhilarated him, giving him such pleasure that he had thrown himself into the rest of the contest with gusto.

He was laughing inside, because he had never thought to win the prize and was still surprised that he had thrown the great bear of a man who called himself the Bastard of Rouen.

Anton knew that in winning the wrestling so easily he had

made himself an enemy. He shrugged. What did it matter? He would be in England within a couple of days and it was unlikely he would see the man again.

A frown creased his brow as he thought about the young woman who had presented him with the silver arrow. What was her name—the Comtesse de Montcrief? He had taken little notice of her until the dog attacked her, but when he had carried her to the tent to tend her wounds he had been tantalised by the scent of her hair, which had wafted towards him. He had felt as if he should know her.

Had they met before? Anton could not think it. It was years since he had been in France and that for but a brief time…

Surely not? A vague picture came into his mind. There had been a child…a young girl he had rescued from beneath the flailing hooves of her horse.

Anton could not be certain that the beautiful woman he had helped today was the young girl he had rescued from the hooves of a terrified horse all those years ago. It was unlikely that fate should bring them together twice in similar circumstances. He struggled to bring the earlier memory to mind but the child's face was unclear; she had been forgotten in all that came after.

Anton was fairly certain that the dog had been ordered to attack. He was the most likely intended victim, because he had humbled Rouen in a sport in which he believed himself invincible. Surely he would have no reason to want to harm the wife of the Comte de Montcrief? He frowned as he wondered if he ought to have told the Comte of his suspicions.

Why did it matter? The woman's husband was responsible for her protection. She was the wife of a powerful man, and could mean nothing to Anton. Besides, he had no wish to marry yet. When he did it would be to a deserving widow, an older lady, someone gentle and kind who would love his motherless daughter. The suspicion that Isabella had betrayed him with another man, and that the child she had carried with her to the grave had not been his, was like a bitter taste in his mouth. She had seemed so innocent and lovely when he wed her; how could he ever trust again?

'I have written to the Bastard,' the Comte told Marietta the next day when he came to her as she sat sewing in her solar. 'He disappeared after the contest and I fear he was displeased that the prize went to another. I believe I must make my offer soon. I would not have him my enemy.'

'I did not like the way he looked at me,' Marietta said. 'I believe he resents me. It is very strange that his dog should attack me.'

'The brute was out of control and has been dealt with. Rouen resents the truth, which is that you have given me a legitimate son.' The Comte sighed. 'I was wrong to let him believe that he would succeed me here. I should never have recognised him—but my first wife could not bear a living child and I thought I might never have an heir.'

'Then you must make your peace with him, husband.'

'Yes, I must.' The Comte smiled at her. 'You were much admired yesterday, my love. I think that we should give a feast for our neighbours soon—perhaps after the Bastard has visited us.'

'Yes, we should...'

Marietta held her sigh inside until her husband left her. It was ridiculous to feel so unhappy. Nothing had changed just because she had seen a man she had never thought to see again.

Anton of Gifford. The years had been kind to him, for he had grown stronger and more handsome. Watching him as he won the silver arrow had made her realise all that she had lost, but had the incident with the dog not happened she would probably have found it easy to forget. The memory of him driving off the brute and tending her arm was something that would live with her for a long time. It seemed that it was her destiny to be rescued by Anton of Gifford, for she was certain in her own mind that it was he.

She shook her head. It was useless to repine. She had never had a chance of being the wife of the man she admired. She knew nothing of him other than that he was bold and strong. He might be a rogue! He had certainly not declared his true title when he entered the contest. Marietta must never think of him again. She must be satisfied with what she had, and, indeed, most of the time she was content.

It was just that she could not help wondering where Anton was now and what he was doing…

'I am glad to be home, Father,' Anton said as his father came down the stairs to greet him in the large hall of their home. 'I have done all His Majesty bade me, but Spain no longer hath anything to hold me. I believe I shall do better in England.'

'I am glad to see you home,' the Marquis said, and his expression was grave. 'I was sorry for your loss, my son. To lose a wife and child so young was a great tragedy.'

'Isabella was not truly well the whole time she was carrying the babe. Her death was an accident. The physician thought that she had turned dizzy and fell down the steps leading to the sunken garden. I have grieved for her and now I have come home to begin a new life here in England. God saw fit to give us a beautiful daughter and I shall make a new life for her.' The new lightness of mood after the contest had stayed with him and he had begun to make plans for the future. It was time to move on—to try and put the bitterness and his doubts behind him. 'I am come to beg my mother if she will care for Madeline until I can provide a home worthy of Isabella's daughter.'

'You have come back to your family.' His father was nodding and smiling. 'I am glad of it, for I thought at one time that you might never return. You need not ask, my son. Both you and the child are welcome here until you are ready to move on.'

'Thank you. I was sure it would be so. How is all my family, Father? Your steward told me that Mother has not been well?'

'Catherine had a nasty chill that settled on her chest. It has pulled her down and I have been anxious for her sake. She is on the mend now and will be pleased to see you.'

'I shall visit her at once.'

'Stay and talk with me for a moment longer. Your sister is with her. Her women usually tend her at about this hour.' The Marquis was thoughtful. 'Your coming is opportune, Anton. Sarah has been with us for the birth of her child. Now that she is well, and the boy thrives, Lord Sheldon has asked that she join him at court. I would prefer not to escort her there, for I do not wish to leave your mother until I am certain she is truly recovered.'

Anton was silent for a moment. He had hoped to have some time with his family before visiting the court. It was possible that the King would have some task for him once he presented himself, and Anton was not sure that he wished to serve at court. He believed that he might prefer life as a country gentleman. However, his father had asked a favour of him and he would be churlish to refuse.

'Of course,' he said. 'I shall be pleased to escort my sister to the court.'

'I would not press you to wed again,' his father said. 'But I hope that in time you will find a lady who can make you happy, Anton. It might be that you'll meet someone at court.'

'I thought a kind, gentle lady—perhaps a country woman who would love and care for my daughter...'

'Such a marriage would bring you comfort, but I am not certain it would bring happiness, my son.'

Anton made no answer. It was too difficult to explain the hurt and anger that lived inside him. He had decided that he would not look for love or passion in his next wife. However, as he left his father and went to find his mother and sister, the picture of a woman's face was in his mind: a beautiful woman who had smiled as she gave him a silver arrow—a woman who had felt so good in his arms as he carried her to his tent.

Chapter Two

Marietta felt the man's hot gaze on her and her skin crawled. She had disliked her husband's bastard the first moment she laid eyes on him, and his behaviour at the tourney had not endeared him to her. There was something menacing in the way he looked at her. She felt as if he stripped her naked with his eyes, exposing her flesh to his lust. For Montcrief's sake she had greeted him politely, but all evening she had longed for the moment she could leave the feasting and return to her chamber. At last the time had come, for the hour was late.

'I shall retire now, my lord,' she said softly, leaning towards her husband to whisper in his ear.

'Yes, do so, Marietta. Some of the men grow lewd and coarse. I do not wish you to be exposed to such behaviour. Go to your chamber now and lock the door. Do not expect a visit this night for I have business that will not keep.' He smiled and touched her hand.

Marietta nodded. She knew that he meant to get Rouen to sign the paper he had had prepared and be done with it that night.

'I wish you goodnight, my lord. May you sleep peacefully.'

'Send some of your mixture to my chamber, my love. My chest feels tight this evening. I do not wish to be ill again.'

'My woman shall bring it to your chamber. It will be there when you retire.'

Montcrief inclined his head, smiled at her and waved his hand. Marietta beckoned to her ladies. The three of them exited the hall together, leaving the men to their drink and their jesting. Beyond the lights of the hall there were shadowed passages and dark corners, the chill of the stone walls striking even the most hardy.

In her bedchamber, Marietta went to her cabinet, unlocked the door and took out a small bottle.

'When you have helped me to disrobe, take this to my lord's chamber and place it on the table by the window. He will see it there and know what it is when he retires.'

'Yes, my lady.'

Jeanne took the bottle and stood it down while she helped Marietta to remove her rich tunic and gown of green cloth.

'I can manage now,' she told her ladies. 'Go to your beds— but do not forget the medicine for my lord, Jeanne.'

When her ladies had gone, Marietta went into the small alcove where the child's cot was placed. Charles was fast asleep. She smiled, resisting the temptation to touch his cheek lest she wake him. Feeling glad to be alone at last, Marietta sought her bed and was soon asleep.

It was barely light when the noise of shouting and lamenting woke her. She sat up as the door of her bedchamber was opened and Jeanne came rushing in, looking strange…almost frightened.

'What is it?' she asked. 'What is all that shouting and wailing?'

'I bring terrible news, my lady,' Jeanne said. 'I do not know how to tell you—your husband is dead. His steward found him lying on the floor of his chamber…'

'My lord is dead?' Marietta gave a cry of alarm and jumped out of bed. She was reaching for her robe as her other women entered the room. 'How did he die? Was it a seizure?' She crossed herself. 'God save his soul.' Tears stung her eyes, for her husband had been good to her despite the differences in their ages.

'He was bleeding from the mouth,' Louise said, and looked awkward. 'Some are saying it must have been poison...'

'Poison? Who would poison my lord?' Marietta looked at Jeanne's face and saw the guilt. 'You do not think that the medicine I sent Montcrief last night would harm him?'

'Of course it would not,' Rosalind said staunchly. 'You use only herbs that do good, my lady. Your cures saved him last winter, for without them he would have died.'

'But some say it...' Jeanne turned red as the other serving women looked at her. 'I do not say it, my lady. You know that I am loyal to you—but Lord Montcrief's steward questioned me. He saw me leaving the master's chamber last night and asked me what I did there. I told him I took the master's medicine to him. The look in his eyes frightened me, my lady: it was a crafty, malicious look. I do not think he likes you.'

'You are right, he does not. Drogbar thinks that I whispered against him to my husband and caused him to lose face. It is true that I suggested we might be served faster at table if the kitchens were brought closer to the great hall, for the food was always cold when I first came here. Montcrief ordered it changed and laughed at Drogbar for not thinking of it sooner. I think the man has not forgiven me.'

'He hates you,' Jeanne said, and shivered. 'He is a powerful man, my lady. He would not dare to speak against you while the master lived, but now...'

'No one will dare speak against her. She is the mother of the new lord of this manor,' Rosalind said. 'Do not forget that she bore the master a fine son.'

'There are those who wonder how it was possible, for the lord was too old to father a child; they hint at the black arts—' Jeanne broke off as all eyes turned on her. 'Forgive me, lady—but it is whispered of you, here at the castle and in the village.'

Marietta's gaze narrowed. 'I have never heard these tales. I have always tried to help people. Why should they say wrong of me?'

'They whisper you are a witch...' Jeanne crossed herself. 'Forgive me! I know that you help people, but there are some who whisper that you could not have saved the master's life had you not bartered with the Devil himself.'

'Be quiet, you foolish woman!' Rosalind said, and her eyes flashed with anger. She had come to Montcrief with Marietta, and known her since they were both children. 'My lady is not a witch. Those who speak so foully abuse her good nature. She has shown you nothing but kindness, Jeanne—nor you Louise.'

'I would not spread such tales,' Louise said indignantly. 'I know my lady is a sweet angel.'

Jeanne looked at Rosalind, and then at her mistress. She fell to her knees before Marietta. 'Forgive me, my lady. I do not believe the tales, but I thought you should know what is being whispered.'

Marietta's face was pale. Inside, she was grieving for her husband, and all this talk of witchcraft was too foolish to be borne.

'Enough of this nonsense!' she said. 'I must go to my husband at once.'

'My lady...is that wise?' Jeanne asked.

Marietta ignored her. She swept out of the chamber and ran down the stairs of her tower. Going through a narrow passageway, she entered the Great Hall and ran across it to the private chambers that belonged to Comte de Montcrief.

As she tried to enter the steward blocked her path, his eyes staring at her with hatred, dark and malicious. 'None may enter here.'

'Stand aside, sirrah,' Marietta commanded. 'How dare you deny me entrance to my husband's chamber?'

'It was the new lord's orders that none should enter.'

'My son is the new lord Montcrief—and I am custodian of his manor until he reaches maturity.' Marietta's eyes flashed at him. 'Stand aside or I shall have you flogged for your impudence.'

'Do as the lady says,' a voice said from behind her, and Marietta whirled round to look into the face of the Bastard of Rouen. The sneer of triumph on his thick lips sent a chill through her. 'I did not tell you to deny my father's wife the right to pay her last respects. You may go in, lady.'

'By what right do you assume command here? My husband gave me the custodial rights until my son is sixteen. I know his will is lodged at court and once it is read everyone will know that my claim is just.'

'I would not dream of interfering with your ordering of the household and your son, lady.' The Bastard inclined his head to her. He was a handsome man, in a coarse, rough way, his eyes a chilling blue. 'However, I believe you will find that the men follow me. How can you hold this land for your son, lady? It needs a strong man—as you would soon discover if I rode away and deserted you.' He moved closer, towering over her. She could smell an overpowering perfume that hid the smell of dried-on sweat. 'Do not fear, lady. I intend to stay here and protect you and your sweet son, as my father would have wished.'

His mocking smile infuriated her. How dared he take command here? Marietta was tempted to throw the truth in the Bastard's face. She knew that her husband had tried to prevent this very situation, but something had gone wrong. Montcrief had died suddenly and the Bastard had seized his chance. For the moment Marietta was powerless. Instinct told her that it would be foolish to antagonise this man.

'I thank you for your kind thought for me and my son,' she said proudly. 'For the moment I shall accept your protection.'

'You are gracious, my lady.' His eyes gleamed with anger as he bowed his head to her.

Marietta went into her husband's chamber. One of the men who had served the lord was washing his face, but he bowed his head respectfully and drew back. It was obvious that he intended to leave, but she held out a hand to stay him.

'Tell me, please, how my lord looked before you washed him?'

'There was blood on his mouth. It had run from the side—a mere trickle, my lady.'

'And his expression? Were his eyes open or closed?'

'Open, my lady. I closed them and put the silver coins there to protect him on his journey across the Styx. If he goes prepared he may pay the boatman.'

'You believe in such things, Jolyn?'

'Yes, my lady.' He crossed himself and glanced over his shoulder. 'I know there are many things that we cannot understand. Some speak of the Devil and evil, but these powers may be used for good. I know that my lord spoke often how much better he felt after you gave him medicine, my lady.'

'Thank you,' Marietta said. 'You may leave me with my lord, but return soon to finish what you have begun.'

Jolyn bowed his head and left the room. Marietta bent over her husband and kissed his brow.

'Forgive me that I was not here when you needed me, my lord,' she said, and the tears wet her cheeks. 'I have been fortunate and I shall miss you.'

She bent her head as the tears trickled down her cheeks. Montcrief had treated her kindly and he had protected her. Now she was a woman alone and at the mercy of others. The Bastard of Rouen had taken command here and for the moment there was nothing she could do—except protect her child and wait. If she could get word to the French court perhaps the King would help her, but would she still be alive or would she be the next to die—and her son with her?

* * *

'We are pleased to see you at court.' King Henry VIII of England stood up to offer his hand to Anton. He clasped him by the shoulder. 'We were sad to learn of your loss, sir—but welcome you home. You have served us well.'

Anton bowed gracefully. Clad in black from head to toe, with only a fringe of silver to his sash, he was a distinguished man who turned heads as he walked through the court.

'I am honoured to be received privately, Sire. You show me great favour. It is good to be home again.'

Henry studied him in silence for a moment, then, 'You have brought the Lady Sarah to her husband, for which I am sure he expressed his thanks, but what is your intention now, sir?'

'I believe I shall buy land and build my house. In time I may marry again, and I hope to have several sons. My father has but the one son, and if I fail the name dies with me…'

The King looked at him oddly, a glint of displeasure in his eyes. 'It is the hope of all men to have sons, sir. The Queen hath given me a daughter but as yet I have no living son.' He crossed the room to look down at the courtyard garden below. Through the opened window floated the sound of ladies laughing. The King raised his hand and called out. 'Tell me, my lady Anne—is it warm today?'

Anton did not hear the lady's reply, but when the King turned back to him the look of displeasure had gone from his face.

'The Lady Anne Boleyn is walking with some ladies. I think we should go down and join them, sir. The getting of sons is an ambition I share with you. Choose your wife carefully, my friend. Divorce is no easy thing, especially if you be a king.'

'I imagine it must be difficult, for many in the church would be against it…' Anton knew he must tread carefully, because he had heard the stories and knew of the rumour that the King was seeking a divorce from Queen Katherine so that he might marry Anne Boleyn.

'And you—what is your opinion?'

'I think no man should stand above the King, Sire.'

'You have learned your trade well,' Henry said and smiled. 'I see you are a true diplomat. Tell me, Anton of Gifford—will you do your King a further service?'

Anton bowed his head. It was as he had feared, but he knew he could not refuse. He had become wealthy, and he had learned much from his position at the court of the Holy Roman Emperor—and he had this king to thank.

'Of course, Sire. You have only to ask.'

'It will mean a short journey to France—but we shall talk of this another day...' Henry smiled. 'It is too pleasant to talk of politics. We must find a way of amusing the ladies— perhaps a game of tennis might please them. Tell me, do you play—are you a good sportsman? Shall we match ourselves for the ladies' pleasure?'

'I have some skill,' Anton replied, smiling inwardly as he recalled the day he had won the coveted silver arrow—and the woman who had presented him with his prize. It was odd, but she had been much in his thoughts of late. He was angry with himself for letting her take root in his mind. Isabella's loss was still a cause of raw grief and he needed to atone for her death! 'Why not, Sire? I may be able to give Your Majesty a little sport...'

'You are sent for, lady,' Jeanne said, her cheeks hot as she avoided looking at her mistress. 'The lord asks that you join him at table this evening.'

'I am in mourning for my husband,' Marietta said. 'Please tell the Bastard of Rouen that I shall not come down this evening.'

'It is forbidden to call him by that name. He is lord of Montcrief now,' Jeanne said, and her eyes were wide with fear. 'He told me that if you did not come he would send men to fetch you.'

'He has threatened you?'

'It was I who took the medicine to the Comte's chamber the night he died. The new lord says that if I do not obey him he will charge me with the Comte's murder.'

'Does he dare to suggest that my husband was murdered?' Marietta's gaze narrowed as the woman hung her head. 'And who is supposed to have put the poison into the medication—you or me?'

'I swear I did nothing wrong!'

'I have accused you of nothing. There was naught to harm my husband in the cure I sent him—but it may have been contaminated later.'

'Will you come, lady? I fear the lord's wrath if you do not. He says I shall be beaten if you do not obey him.'

'Very well. For your sake I shall come.' Marietta waved her away. 'Leave me. I must prepare myself.'

She turned to Rosalind as the door closed behind the other woman. 'Now I am bidden to table because he desires it. Where will it stop?'

'I have seen his eyes on you, my lady. He wants everything that belonged to his father. He wants more than your obedience—and I fear he will take it whether you will it or no.'

'You think he will force himself on me?'

'I think he intends to marry you, my lady. Sandro heard him say as much to Drogbar. It is the only way he can claim your husband's lands legally. At the moment he holds them by force—but if the King sends a force against him he must surrender.'

'You sent my message to the King?'

'It was done at once, my lady, and in secret. The messenger has not yet returned with a reply.'

'The Bastard needs me and my son for the moment, which is why we are still alive,' Marietta said. 'But if my son should have an accident…should die in his sleep…'

'The Bastard of Rouen would be accepted as the new Comte de Montcrief. He has his father's blood; the master accepted him—would have left the manor to him had you not given him a child.'

'Then if my son were dead he would have all that he craves.' Marietta looked at her, her fear plainly writ on her face. 'I must take the boy to safety, Rosalind.'

'Where will you go, my lady?'

'I do not know…' There was no one in France to help her! For a moment she thought of the man who had once saved her life—the man to whom she had presented the silver arrow. If only he were here! Her instinct told her that he would protect any lady in need. Yet what right had she to ask for his help? Who could she turn to in her need?

Marietta paced the floor, her eye falling on a scarf that had been sent her as a Christmas gift the previous year. 'I shall go to my father's second cousin in England! Lady Claire Melford has asked me to visit so many times. She will help me, and perhaps her husband might intercede with the English King to help me regain my son's birthright.'

'If you run away they may say that you murdered the Comte by witchcraft and were afraid of the consequences.'

'If I stay I may be forced to marry the man I believe truly committed that foul act…'

'My lady…' Rosalind stared at her in horror. 'You think the Bastard murdered his father? If that is true…'

'He will stop at nothing to gain what he wants.' Marietta lifted her head, her face proud. 'I must go down, for he will send an escort to force me if I do not—and I would not have Jeanne beaten, though she thinks me a witch.'

'She cannot!'

'I am certain she believes it. The Bastard has her in the palm of his hand. I do not trust her, Rosalind.'

'You can trust Sandro and me. I swear that we will serve you. We would both give our lives for you and the baby, my lady.'

'Thank you,' Marietta said. 'I believe we must leave as soon as we can arrange it. We shall not be able to take much, but I have some jewels and a little gold that my husband had hidden in his room.'

'If we can get to England you will be safe.'

'I pray that it will be so,' Marietta said. 'Now I must go, before I am taken to the hall by force…'

She walked from the chamber, her head high. Rosalind was not the only one who had seen the look in the Bastard's eyes. His lust was hot and it was the only reason he had not already given her up as a witch. He wanted her. If he could have her as his wife his claim to the manor would be much stronger, and once he had tired of her he would dispose of her as he had her husband. Marietta knew that her life, and that of her son, hung in the balance. She must escape before morning or it might be too late.

Anton reined in as he approached the Castle of Montcrief. King Henry had sent him to the Comte with a message, which he believed was of some importance. A return to France was not something he had wished for, but when he had learned what the King desired he had not felt able to refuse him. And at the castle of Montcrief he was bound to see the lady he had rescued from that brute of a dog.

He was aware of a flicker of something that might have been anticipation. Perhaps during this visit he might learn if the lady who had presented him with the silver arrow was truly the child he had rescued that day on the Field of the Cloth of Gold. She had been much in his mind of late, though he was not certain why. When the King had asked his favour it had seemed as if Destiny had spoken.

He sat his horse, looking at the castle for some minutes before giving the order to move on. His instincts were telling him that all was not as it should be. He could see that the draw-bridge was down and the flag was flying at half-mast. Men were on the battlements, but he was not challenged as he and the ten men-at-arms he had brought with him clattered over the bridge into the inner bailey. Anton was clad in armour, his head covered with a helmet. His standard bearer was carrying his own pennant and another that bore the arms of the Tudors, showing that he was an envoy from the English court.

'If anyone questions your mission, tell them merely that I have sent greetings to an old friend,' the King had instructed before Anton left the English court. 'You must deliver my letter into the hands of Comte de Montcrief himself. If for any reason he is not there, you will return it safely to me. The letter is writ in code, but if any other should decipher it, it might cause further trouble between England and her enemies.'

'I shall do as Your Majesty asks.' Anton had bowed his head. 'I shall present my credentials and keep your letter close to my heart until I meet the gentleman himself.'

Now, looking about him, Anton wondered at the lack of order. Where were the men-at-arms training? Where was the steward who should have been told of his coming and been here to meet him? Where were the villagers bringing carts of food and supplies? Instead of order, there was an air of neglect about the place, as if the servants did not care to obey their master. It was not what he would have expected of the powerful lord he had seen at the tourney.

The castle looked almost deserted, apart from a few house-carls in the courtyard. He summoned one to him and the man came hurriedly.

'Forgive us, your honour,' he said, cringing as if he expected a blow. 'The steward is with the lord and everyone else is out searching for *her*...'

'Searching for whom?'

'The witch of Montcrief. She that murdered her gentle husband by foul witchcraft.'

Anton frowned as he remembered the beautiful lady who had given him his prize and a chill ran down his spine. 'Do you speak of the Comte's wife? By what right do you call her a witch?'

'You! To the kitchens, or I'll have you flogged until the skin falls from your back!'

A man had come striding into the courtyard. The Bastard of Rouen! Anton knew him instantly and was immediately suspicious. What had happened here? How came such a brute to be the master of Montcrief's castle? The house-carl had run away as fast as his legs would take him, looking as if the Devil himself were after him. It might be best not to let the Bastard realise that he was speaking to the man who had bested him at the tourney. Anton knew that he looked different in his armour and could only hope he was not recognised.

'Sir, I have come to bring the Comte de Montcrief greetings from Henry Tudor, King of England.'

'Your messenger arrived an hour since,' the Bastard replied, eyes narrowed, calculating. Anton had brought ten of his men into the bailey with him, but more were camped outside, waiting his return. 'You are welcome to stay here with your men, my lord—but I fear your journey has been wasted unless you carry a message you may pass to me? I am the master here now.'

'The message is in my head. It is merely that Henry wishes to congratulate the Comte on having a fine heir—and to assure him of friendship should he visit England.'

'My father died some five days ago. He was killed by witchcraft and poison—and the culprit was his wife. She has stolen her husband's son and fled, taking gold and jewels with her. Most of my men are out, searching the countryside for her and the servants who assisted her flight. They will suffer the same fate as their evil mistress when they are caught.'

'Witchcraft is a wicked crime,' Anton said, resisting the urge to wipe that look of satisfaction from the other's face. 'Has the witch been proved?'

'She escaped before she could be put to the test. I was at first deceived in her, for she pretends to be modest and God-fearing. However, her flight is proof enough. She had heard the rumours that she was to be accused of her husband's murder and fled in the night before she could be apprehended.'

'I see that you have much to occupy you,' Anton said. His

instincts told him that this man was not to be trusted. He did not like him, and caution told him that it would be wiser not to take his hospitality. His men would prefer to rest under the stars rather than be murdered as they slept. 'I am sorry for your trouble, and I shall move on rather than cause you more bother.'

He remounted and signalled to his men to follow him from the castle. Anton was aware of a prickling sensation at the nape of his neck. Something was wrong here. He could not tell how much truth there was in the tale of the lady murdering her husband, but he could not believe that she was a witch. Many women were hanged or burned to death as witches, because they had failed the barbaric acts that put them to the test and proved their guilt. The thought of such vile cruelty left a bitter taste in his mouth. He shuddered as he pictured the woman he had seen at the tourney being tortured and then burned in the flames.

He could do nothing to help her. Nor should he if she were truly the murderer of her husband. Yet he could not believe it of the woman he had seen at the tourney. Something was wrong here!

His mission was at an end. Instead of staying here overnight he would turn north towards the home of Lord de Montfort. It would mean one night more upon the road, but his aunt Anne's husband would welcome him and he would deliver a message to their son Sebastien. King Henry had charged him to invite his cousin to visit the English court.

Anton frowned as he gave the order to move north. He would be glad to put a few leagues between him and the upstart who claimed that he was the new lord of Montcrief. There had been a look of slyness about the man that made him wonder just what was behind his invitation to stay the night. Anton had no doubt that he and his men would have been killed as they slept, perchance to be robbed for their armour and possessions. He was glad to leave, and could not help but think of the woman who had been forced to flee her home.

He remembered how beautiful she had looked that day at the tourney. The wife of a powerful noble, she had had everything she could want—and now she was a fugitive in fear of her life.

Marietta screamed as she saw the small party of men riding towards them fast. She knew the pennant well. These were the Bastard of Rouen's men and they would catch her and take her back with them. She had brought her fate on herself by defying the Bastard, but her son was innocent.

'Take Charles and run that way,' she said to Rosalind. 'I shall go this—perhaps if they come after me, you and Charles may get away...'

'I cannot leave you, my lady.'

'Go! I command it!' Marietta cried. 'I charge you to take care of my son. He must live even if I die...'

She gave her woman a little push, but then she saw it was too late. A larger party of men were coming towards them from the opposite direction. They were caught between them and there was no escape. She screamed despairingly and began to run towards the woods. Perhaps if she could reach them she might escape for long enough to hide her child. Even if she died, Charles must live...

The sound of yelling and screaming made her glance back over her shoulder. She was stunned as she saw that the larger group of men seemed to be attacking the Bastard's soldiers. What was happening? Who were the strangers, and why were they fighting the rogues that would have taken her prisoner?

Instead of fleeing into the woods to hide, as she had planned, she stood, her heart beating frantically as she watched the fight.

After a short skirmish, the men she feared had turned tail and were running for their lives. Marietta stood still as one of the strangers rode up to her; her heart was pounding and she wondered if her last moment had come. She pulled her shawl over her head, trying to hide her face. She was frightened. Did these men know who she was—had they saved her because they wished to sell her to the Bastard for gold?

'You are safe now, mistress,' the knight said, and raised his visor, revealing his face. Marietta's heart stopped as she knew him. For a moment relief flooded through her. It was Anton of Gifford—but would he remember her? Surely he must after that day at the tourney! Would he believe her innocent if she told him her story? She pulled her shawl tighter around her face, hoping that he would not recall that she had given him the silver arrow or the incident with the savage dog. 'Come, I shall take you up with me.'

'No...' Marietta hung back. She hugged the child to her. She was nervous, because she did not know how he would react if he knew who she was and the crimes of which she stood accused. 'Please, allow me to go on my way.'

'If you do not come with us those villains may return. Where are you travelling to, mistress?' her rescuer asked. His eyes were narrowed and intent as he gazed down at her. 'We go north, to the estate of my uncle Lord de Montfort. Then we will travel back to England.'

'I was on my way to England myself,' Marietta told him. 'I need to reach the coast by nightfall.'

'Then we shall take you some part of your way. I am Anton of Gifford, mistress. I shall take you to safety, and then we shall discuss what you should do in the future...'

Had he recognised her? Did he know that she had been forced to flee her home? Marietta trembled inwardly. So far he had been kind, but what would he do if he knew that she had been accused of witchcraft and murder? It would be best if they parted before he discovered the truth.

'You saved our lives, but if you set us down when we have put some distance between us and those rogues we shall do well enough.'

'Will you not tell me your name, mistress?'

Marietta hesitated. 'It is Marie—Marie de Villiers.'

She saw a flicker of something in his eyes. Had he remembered her? Would he denounce her as a wicked murderess?

'Come then, Mistress Villiers,' he said, and offered his hand. 'We waste time and night falls…'

Marietta stood still as he dismounted and lifted her to the saddle, remounting so swiftly that she almost fell as the great horse moved forward. She had slipped the babe inside the shawl she had wrapped around her head and body, leaving her hands free so that she could hold on to the knight's cloak. The knights were regrouping after routing the Bastard's rogues. She saw that one of them, a man with a fearful scar on his face, had taken Rosalind up behind him, and Sandro was riding the pony they had brought with them, their few possessions strapped to his back. It seemed that she had no choice but to go with them.

Sitting behind Anton of Gifford, Marietta was aware of mixed emotions. How long had she dreamed of meeting this man again? Yet now it had happened she had the shadow of murder hanging over her.

Anton called a halt as the gates and wall that bounded the estate of Lord Simon de Montfort came into view. He dismounted and signalled to his men to do the same. He had brought the man and two women this far, and he believed they must now be safe enough to continue their journey. He assisted the woman he had taken pillion to the ground and gazed down at her. He had known her the moment he looked into her face. She was the woman who had given him the silver arrow at the tourney—the wife of the late Comte de Montcrief, the woman whose perfume had haunted his senses since he held her in his arms. So why had she given him a false name? Did she think that he would betray her to the Bastard of Rouen? Did she even remember giving him the silver arrow?

The questions chased each other through his mind as he considered what he should do now. She had asked to be allowed to go on alone, but if he abandoned her she and her servants would be recaptured within days.

Deciding not to press her for the truth, or reveal that he knew she had lied about her identity, he told her, 'My aunt will give us shelter for the night. You are safe now, lady.'

'I thank you for your kindness, but we travel to the coast for we mean to take ship for England. I should not wish to trouble your aunt…'

'It will be no trouble. You are weary and can go no further this night, Mistress Villiers. Rest here and I shall escort you to the coast in the morning. You will be safer with us.'

'No, no, sir. We should go on…' Marietta hung her head, seeming afraid. Did she think that he would denounce her as a witch? 'I think we should not put you to more trouble, sir. Just allow us to leave and we shall delay you no more.'

Anton looked down at her. She was pale, and she looked exhausted. He felt something stir inside him. This woman could not be guilty of murder! As for the charge of witchcraft—he had no patience with such nonsense.

'You will stay here this night,' he said. 'My aunt will give you a room where you may rest and tomorrow we shall go on board my ship.'

'No. I must go…' Marietta tried to pull away from him, but gave a little cry and stumbled. Anton saw that she was faint from hunger or exhaustion, and caught her in his arms before she fell.

When Marietta came to herself once more she was in a small chamber that might belong to a servant of some importance. It was clean, and the sweet-smelling sheets on the bed were fresh, though of a coarse cloth that felt hard to someone who had been used to the finest of linen and silk. She moaned slightly and someone came to her, bending over to apply a cool cloth to her head.

'You fainted, mistress,' Rosalind told her. 'It has all been too much for you—and you have not eaten properly for two days. Lady de Montfort has sent you soup and bread. Will you not eat a little?'

Marietta sat up. Her head was aching, but she could smell the beef broth and it was good. She was suddenly aware of a ravenous hunger.

'My son, Charles—where is he?'

'Lady de Montfort took him. She says that she will feed and care for him until you are better. She likes children, and she has but one son who is full grown.'

'Has she asked questions?'

Rosalind brought the soup and bread on a board, placing it over Marietta's knees. 'I think the lord told her something. She has been nothing but kind, my lady.'

'You must not call me that,' Marietta warned. 'Marie or Mistress Villiers will do.'

'I do not like to address you so,' Rosalind objected. 'But if you wish it I shall try.' She hesitated, then, 'The lord seems fair-minded—could you not tell him your story?'

'No! We do not know him,' Marietta said. 'How can I trust a stranger? He might believe that I am a witch and that I murdered my husband.'

'Surely he would listen if you told him the truth?'

'I dare not risk it. We must leave here tonight and make for the coast ourselves.'

'Is that wise, mistress? Even if we reach the coast safely, we may not be able to find a ship to take us to England. If word hath reached the coast they may be looking for us...'

Marietta sipped the soup and found it good. She ate a mouthful of bread and then some more soup, looking at her serving woman thoughtfully. Perhaps Rosalind was right. Perhaps it would be better if they stayed with the men who had rescued them until they could find safe passage to England.

Anton of Gifford was brave and honourable. He had saved her twice before. Surely he would do nothing to harm her? Yet if he thought her a murderess he might feel it his duty to give her up. She had no choice but to accept his help, but she would not reveal herself to him just yet.

'You speak wisely. I thought to flee, but that would merely arouse suspicion. We shall accept the lord's escort until we are safely able to get to England.' She crossed herself. 'I pray that neither he nor his men guess who I am…'

Anton opened the door of the guest chamber with caution. He did not wish to wake either the woman who called herself Marie de Villiers or the maid who slept by her side, yet he had been unable to rest without seeing for himself that she was well and safe.

He approached the bed softly, his bare feet making no noise on the stone flags. Gazing down at her face as she slept, he felt his heart contract with an odd pain. How beautiful she was! She looked innocent as she slept, murmuring something that was indistinguishable, one hand beneath her cheek. How could a woman like this be guilty of murder?

He felt a wave of anger sweep through him as he thought of how cruelly she had been treated by the Bastard of Rouen. The man was a rogue, and Anton suspected that he had begun this tale to rid himself of his father's wife and gain all Montcrief's wealth for himself.

If that were true the woman had been cheated of her rights. Yet how could he be certain that his instincts were true? He had believed Isabella as innocent as she was lovely, but she had turned from him to another. Was it wise to trust any woman?

Even if she were innocent, it would be better to deliver her safely to her chosen destination and forget her. Isabella had taught Anton a hard lesson. He had thought he loved her, but her coldness, her petulance and her betrayal had made him realise their marriage was a mistake. He still felt the guilt of her death heavy on his conscience, for even if she had taken another man as her lover she had not deserved to die. He hoped that he would have been man enough to release her and let her find happiness if she had confessed the truth to him. Yes, he had raged at her, but in the end he believed that he would have done what was right.

When the time was right he would marry again, but he would take great care in his choice of a wife. A woman such as the Widow Montcrief was beautiful, but if he were foolish enough to let himself be caught she would wind her fingers about his heart and eventually destroy him.

Turning away, Anton closed the door softly behind him. He did not know why this woman had touched something inside him, but he would not allow her to take root in his heart.

Chapter Three

'Who are they?' Anne de Montfort asked of her sister's son later that night. 'I think that the mother of this delightful child is a lady, despite her clothes. I saw her face as we put her to bed and her features are too delicate to be those of a peasant.'

'She says that her name is Marie de Villiers.' Anton thought carefully. He considered that it would be best to tell no one that he knew the lady to be the widow of Comte de Montcrief. 'In truth I do not know who she is, Aunt. I rescued her from rogues upon the road and that is all I can tell you. I dare say she would have gone on her way had she not been overcome by faintness. She says that she wishes to travel to England— and since I have a ship waiting...'

'You intend to take her there.' Anne smiled. 'I think my sister is blessed in her son, Anton. I love Sebastien dearly, but he tends to be wild and reckless. Mayhap he has been spoiled because he was our only child. You have such fine manners and it is a pleasure to have your company.'

Anton murmured something about her son being young as yet. He was vaguely troubled in his mind concerning the lady he had brought to her house. If the lady were indeed the

Comte's widow, as he firmly believed, she might be guilty of her husband's murder, though he had instantly acquitted her of witchcraft. He knew that some of his men would certainly look at her askance if they suspected anything of the kind. Fortunately, he believed that none of them had been present at the tourney where he had taken the silver arrow from her hand and then rescued her from a savage brute of a dog.

He frowned, because the idea that she might actually have killed her husband left a bad taste in his mouth. He knew that women could be faithless. Had he not been given ample proof? Isabella had been lovely and seemed innocent but she had destroyed his faith in women. This French woman was beautiful, but was she also a wicked murderess? No, surely not!

He decided that he would deliver her safely to England, but after that he would leave her to make her own way.

'It has been good to see you,' Anne told him, and kissed his cheek. 'One day you must bring your daughter to visit me.'

'Yes, I shall—one day.'

Anne wondered at the odd look in his eyes. She supposed that the sad, sometimes desperate look she had seen there at times must come from the grief he felt at the loss of his wife— but what else had made Anton so serious?

Marietta glanced back at the château as they rode away. Lady Anne had spoken kindly to Rosalind before they left, giving her food for the journey. Rosalind had been taken up behind the knight with the scar on his face. She knew that his name was Miguel Sanchez, and he had told Rosalind that he was a friend of Anton of Gifford's. As yet she had not spoken to him herself, but she had noticed him staring at her and something in his look had made her nervous. Did he know who she was? Would he betray her?

Marietta was riding just ahead of Anton of Gifford. Dressed in his black armour, with a visor over his face, he seemed a fearsome warrior, and his grip on her wrist when he had refused to let her go on her way alone had been strong.

She had been well treated at the home of Lord and Lady de Montfort, and she was feeling better for the rest and good food, though she had seen nothing more of her rescuer until this morning.

She had been surprised when the horse had been brought out for her to ride, because it was a fine specimen and the kind of mount only a lady would ride. She feared that the man who had rescued her was aware that she was not who she pretended to be—but did he know her real name? Had he remembered her from the tourney at last?

'Why am I to ride a horse like this?' she had asked as he had offered to help her mount.

'It is fitting that you should, lady,' he said softly. 'Come, there is nothing to fear. Believe me, I mean you no harm.'

'I believe you, sir,' she said, and took his hand, allowing him to help her up into the saddle. She gazed down at him, wishing that his visor were up so that she might see his face. 'You are generous and I thank you for everything you have done for us.'

'It was little enough.' The knight's eyes gleamed behind the visor that masked his face. 'We shall soon be on board my ship, and within a few hours you will be in England.'

'Thank you...'

Marietta's stomach tightened with nerves. This knight had such a strange effect on her. His touch made her tingle, and she was apprehensive of what he would say if he ever discovered that she had been accused of witchcraft, and yet instinctively she wanted to trust him. If only she dared tell him the truth and throw herself on his mercy!

Anton chose to ride just behind Marie de Villiers, as she called herself. He could watch her and stop her if she tried to ride off alone—or protect her if another attempt were made to snatch her. He had seen the puzzled look in her eyes earlier, and knew that she was wondering about him. Was she afraid that he would betray her to her enemy? Was she worried that he'd heard the rumours about the death of her husband?

Anton had dismissed the idea of witchcraft instantly. He was aware that many believed in the power of evil, and feared it, but he was inclined to think that evil lived in the minds of men who practised it. He would sooner believe the Bastard of Rouen capable of murder than this gentle lady.

Some would no doubt say that she had cast her spell over him. Even his friend Miguel might turn against her if he knew that she was accused of witchcraft. If he were to deliver her safely to her destination Anton would need to be careful. It would be better to plead ignorance than admit that he knew her. Once they were in England she should be safe from the man who wanted her dead.

Anton had no doubt that the Bastard of Rouen had seen his chance to take what rightfully belonged to the Comte's legitimate son. It would not be the first time it had happened and would not be the last. The Comte's widow might be able to prove her innocence and try to take back her husband's estate once she reached England—but could she hold it? The Bastard of Rouen was not the only man who might try to take it by force. A woman alone was not safe in turbulent times, and the barons of France were fiercely independent and jealous of their privilege—hungry for power and wealth, they would see his widow as a prize to be taken.

The Comte had neglected his duty. He ought to have set men in place who would protect their mistress to the death—but perhaps he had. They might already be dead or imprisoned...

Anton frowned. It was not his place to enquire. He had a duty to return the King's letter and tell him what had happened at the Castle of Montcrief. Once the lady was safe in England he should forget her. A wry smile touched his mouth, for it was easy to make the decision but not as easy to carry it through.

* * *

Marietta stood on board the ship and watched the shores of France slip away into the mist. She felt strange, as if she had said farewell to everything dear and familiar to her. It was doubtful that she would return to France—unless she could find someone who would intercede with the King for her?

'You should go below, lady.'

Marietta turned as Anton of Gifford came up to her. 'I wanted to watch until the land was gone, sir. I am not sure that I shall ever return to France.'

'You do not know that, lady. Things may change in the future.'

'They cannot change for me. I do not mind for myself, but I would have justice for my son.'

'Indeed? In what way?'

'It does not matter.' Marietta turned away. She did not dare to trust him, for even in England a witch could be hunted and condemned to death. 'You said that I should go below. I shall do as you ask, for I would not wish to be in the way…'

'It was for your own sake that I advised it,' Anton said. 'The captain tells me that there may be a storm.'

'I see…' Marietta inclined her head. 'Excuse me, I must make sure that Rosalind and my son are safe. I speak a little English, but my…friends have none.'

'How is it that you understand the English language so well, mistress?'

'My mother was an Englishwoman. I learned to speak the language at her knee. Excuse me, I must go below.'

She did not look back as she walked away and started to descend the ladder leading to the cabins on the next deck, but she was aware that he was watching her.

Anton had discarded his heavy armour as soon as the swell became too great. If the storm should become too fierce and the ship sink, neither he nor his men would stand a chance wearing their armour. Accordingly, they had all removed it, and were wearing only their short jerkins and tight-fitting hose, with shoes that could be kicked off in an instant.

Anton was an experienced sailor. During his time as an ambassador at the court of the Holy Roman Emperor he had often travelled between Spain, France and Italy. He had gone back on deck when the storm struck, to see if he could be of help, and also because he knew it was easier to ride the heavy swell on deck rather than lying on a bunk in his cabin.

He was watching a particularly large wave coming towards them when someone touched his arm, and he turned to look into the face of the groom Sandro.

'How may I help you?'

'Forgive me, my lord, but my lady is very ill. We have nothing to give her, and we wondered if you had a little wine to settle her stomach?'

'I have something better than wine, though 'tis best given *in* wine. I shall go to my cabin now and fetch it for her.'

'Thank you, my lord…' Sandro looked a bit green in the face, and suddenly dashed to the side of the ship, retching over the side. Anton smiled grimly. At least the man had the sense not to vomit into the wind!

He left the man staggering back to safety and went down to his cabin. It took him only a moment or so to find the powder given him by a Spanish doctor who was part Arab, and another to mix it into a cup of wine. He hung onto a wooden beam as the ship lurched, protecting the cup and managing to keep it upright.

The ship righted itself as Anton made his way to the cabin next door and knocked. Rosalind, who looked little better than Sandro had a few moments earlier, opened it.

'I have brought this for your lady,' Anton said. 'You look ill yourself, mistress. Go up on deck for a moment and get some air. It may ease you.'

'I cannot leave my…' Rosalind gasped and rushed for the chamber pot, vomiting into it. 'Forgive me, my lady…'

Anton went towards the bed. He saw the woman lying

on the bed, her hair in disarray about her on the pillow. She
had her eyes closed and she was moaning, clearly in great
distress.

'Come, lady, you must drink this,' Anton said. He perched
on the edge of her cot, slipping an arm beneath her shoulders
to lift her. Marietta's eyes flickered open. A little sigh escaped
her, but she parted her lips, swallowing obediently. 'Drink it
all. In a little time you will feel much better. I never travel
without this cure. I am seldom ill these days, though I have
suffered in the past.'

'Thank you…' Marietta lay back, a tear slipping from the
corner of her right eye. 'You are so kind…'

Anton stroked back the damp hair on her forehead. How did
she manage to look so lovely even while she was ill? Seeing
her like this moved him, arousing strong emotions; he felt
protective, wanting to ease her.

'Do not try to talk. I shall go to prepare a cup for your serving woman and return in a moment or so…'

Marietta made no answer. Anton returned to his cabin and
made up more of the mixture. He took the mixture back to
Rosalind, who gulped it down gratefully.

'Go on deck for a while,' Anton advised. 'The mixture will
work in a short time and the air will refresh you.'

'My lady…' Rosalind glanced at the bed where Marietta
lay.

'Is safe with me. I give you my word of honour as a knight
and nobleman of England.'

'God bless you, sir!' Rosalind said, and stumbled through
the door, clearly still feeling groggy.

Anton went to stand at the foot of the bed and gazed down
at the woman who lay there. Her red-gold hair was spread on
the pillows and she looked beautiful, desirable, despite her
distress. The colour was returning to her cheeks. He smiled,
because he saw that her hands had unfurled and she was no
longer moaning. The mixture had begun to work its magic—
though it was no magic but just a simple cure that the phy-

sician had learned from his brethren. The Arabs had many cures that would be thought witchcraft by some.

This lovely woman could not be a murderess! Anton swallowed hard as he gazed down at her face, feeling something move about his heart, as if a shadow that had lain there had shifted and eased. How could anyone accuse her of such evil? She had the look of an innocent angel. He thought her one of the most beautiful women he had ever seen—and he felt the first stirring of forgotten desires deep in his loins. He moved towards her, driven by the need to touch her. The strength of the feelings she aroused shocked him. Even when he had courted Isabella he had never experienced such an overwhelming desire to touch and hold as he felt now. Bending over the Frenchwoman, he smoothed her damp hair back from her forehead. Her eyelids flickered and she looked up at him.

'Are you feeling better, Mistress Villiers?'

'A little…yes. I am better than I was. Thank you…Anton of Gifford. Why are you so kind to me?'

'I am at your service, lady. Do not fear me. I shall not betray you. Your secret is safe with me. I know you are not a witch, for I do not believe in such tales, and I cannot think you guilty of murder.'

'You knew me from the first?'

'You are the late Comte's wife. Of course I remembered you from the day of the contest, when you gave me the silver arrow and that dog attacked you.'

'You must believe that I didn't murder my husband. I cared for him deeply, despite the difference in our age. I am innocent of the charge against me…' Marietta said, and sighed. Her eyelids flickered. 'I am so very tired.'

'Sleep in peace, lady,' Anton said softly. He knew that she was hardly aware of what she had told him, for her mind was confused by sickness. Bending his head, he placed a gentle kiss on her brow. 'No one shall hear your secret from me. You are safe now.'

'Thank you, Anton,' Marietta said, gave a faint sigh and fell asleep.

Anton stood for a while, watching as she slept. She had sworn that she was innocent of any crime and he wanted to believe her. He did believe her! He might be a fool to accept her word, and yet his instincts had told him from the first that she could not be guilty of murder.

Would she tell him everything once she was well again?

Her plight touched his heart—a woman and child alone save for her servants. What would become of the young Comte now? He was but a child, and had lost both his father and his birthright. At least his daughter, Madeline, had her father and a loving family, but who did the young Comte have to protect him?

The thought occurred to him that he could stand as both the young Comte's and his mother's protector. If he championed her cause something could be done to put right the wrong that had been done mother and son.

Anton shook his head. To become too involved in this woman's story might be foolish. Perhaps it was best if they parted without speaking of the truth. He had brought her to safety, but when they reached England he would let her go on alone.

'Where are you headed?' Anton asked as the horses were brought. Foolish as it might be, he had discovered that he was reluctant to abandon her to her fate. A slight detour on his part would be no trouble. 'I must go to London soon, but if it is on my way I could escort you to your destination.'

'I go to stay with a distant cousin.' Marietta fumbled with the strings of her purse. 'I have her letter here. Lady Claire Melford. She is the wife of…'

'Sir Harry Melford. He is my uncle, and has lately been made the Earl of Rundle for services to the King.' Anton frowned. 'How come you to know the lady Claire?'

'Her father was cousin to my father,' Marietta said. 'She

has written many times, inviting me to stay, but…my husband was too busy to accompany me and I would not desert him.' Her eyes were on his face. 'How strange that we should have family ties and not know it.'

'Fate, perhaps?'

'Yes, perhaps.'

'What makes you think Lady Claire will receive you?' Anton's eyes narrowed. 'Will you tell her the truth? Will you tell her that you were accused of murdering your husband by witchcraft?'

'My husband did not die by my wish nor at my hand,' Marietta said. Her cheeks were pale and she would not look at him. 'I was falsely accused because Rouen wanted me to take him as my husband and I would not. He threatened me, tried to force me to wed him, so I ran away…and then he accused me of murder and witchcraft.'

'I suspected as much. The Bastard of Rouen is a rogue— but had you no one to protect you?'

'My husband was trying to protect both his son and me,' Marietta said. 'He required his bastard to sign a paper renouncing all rights to his fortune in return for money.'

'But he died before it was accomplished. Does that not seem suspicious to you?'

'I believe he may have killed my husband, but I could not prove it. People believe the tales that I am a witch, perhaps because I have some skill in healing.'

'Yes, I know that women healers are sometimes suspected of using the black arts—but you do not dabble in such things?'

'Never!'

'I thought not. I do not believe in such powers but many do—and it can be dangerous for women.'

'I know…' Marietta looked uncertain. 'I mean to tell Lady Claire—but perhaps she will not wish to see me…'

Anton hesitated, then, 'May I see Lady Claire's letter inviting you to stay?'

Marietta felt inside her purse and took out a sheet of vellum, handing it to him. Anton read the letter and saw that it was addressed and written in fond terms that would indicate a liking on the part of his uncle's wife. It was clear that Lady Claire liked and approved of the Comtesse.

'I believe you should give Lady Claire a chance to hear your story,' Anton said. 'It will not trouble me to see you safely there, lady—if you should wish for my escort?'

She seemed to hesitate, then lifted her clear eyes to meet his. 'You have done so much for me already, sir. I cannot repay you, but if you would be so good as to see me to my kinswoman's house I should be grateful.'

'Then we shall accompany you, lady.' Anton inclined his head.

It was foolish to feel pleased that she had accepted his help. Their lives must soon turn in different directions, for he was certain the King would have more work for him and she was not for him—yet there was something that drew his eyes to her again and again as they rode. She was beautiful, but he had met others as lovely. There was pride in her, but something more...something that tugged at the secret core inside him.

His lips settled into a thin line. It would be wrong for him to think of love and marriage with a woman like this, because his stupid jealousy had caused his first wife's death. Even if Isabella had betrayed him, she had not earned her cruel fate. He did not deserve to find love again and he would not look for it.

He would deliver Mistress Villiers to her kinswoman and then forget her. It would be better for both of them so.

Marietta was aware that Anton looked at her often. What was he thinking? Did he suspect her of murdering her husband?

He had been so gentle when he gave her the medicine that had eased her sickness. For a moment as he had stroked her forehead and comforted her it had been almost as she had seen it in her dreams—when he held her and kissed her and vowed to love her. Her dreams of romantic love had sustained her as she cared for and nursed a husband who was more suited to be her father, but they were all foolishness. She had known marriage, and a kind of love, but the feelings she longed to experience were merely the imagination of a lonely girl.

Marietta fought down the wave of longing and regret. If only she hadn't been obliged to marry the Comte. She had accepted her fate, and been a good wife to him, but now she was alone, with only a few jewels to help her make her way in the world. Having always been loved and indulged, she was not sure how she could make a living—unless perhaps she could take on some sewing? Her embroidery had often been praised, but would it be good enough to earn enough food to keep her child and her servants alive?

Her thoughts were heavy, sometimes dark and fearful as they rode through countryside that seemed very different from that she had known all her life. England was beautiful in its own way, but it was not France—it was not her home. Her knowledge of the language was not as strong as it ought to be if she were to live here, and not everyone would speak French as well as Anton of Gifford. Her servants would find it even more difficult to adapt, for they knew hardly a word of English.

'You have looked pensive all morning, lady,' Anton said when they stopped for refreshment. She was sitting on a fallen tree, her child in her arms, a picture so enchanting that his heart caught. 'Does something trouble you? The boy is not ill?'

'No, Charles seems to thrive. I believe he is enjoying the adventure.'

Anton knelt down, looking at the boy's face. His eyes were wide and enquiring, and, as he saw that he was the centre of attention, he chortled with glee and leaned forward to touch Anton's hand. Caught by this unexpected gesture, Anton reached out and lifted him, then swung him high above his head, holding him safely so that Charles shouted and laughed, clearly enjoying the encounter.

'You are good with children,' Marietta said, and smiled as Anton returned the child to her arms. 'His father played with him that way sometimes.'

'He will miss his father, I think.'

'Yes. We shall both miss the Comte...'

'Is that why you are sad? Because your husband is dead?'

'I grieved for his death because it was cruel and wrong, but I am not sad because of it...'

'Then why?' Anton's eyes quizzed her.

'It is just that everything is new and strange here,' Marietta said. 'I dare say the countryside will seem more familiar as time passes.' She did not say that she feared for what her future must be without a husband to care for her and her son.

'Yes, it must seem different,' Anton agreed, and looked thoughtful. 'But we shall soon be with Lady Claire, and then you may feel more comfortable. You will be able to care properly for your son there.'

'He is very precious to me.'

Anton nodded. 'I can see that, *madame*. I have a daughter, perhaps a few months older. I think much of providing a good home for her future, for she is all I have left now.'

'Your wife died?'

'Yes. It seems that we have something in common—a shared loss. You must cleave to your son and find happiness in him, lady.'

'Yes, I shall.' A delicate blush touched her cheeks. He had been married and widowed! How foolish all her dreams had been! He had never thought of her after that day on the Field of the Cloth of Gold. 'If I can stay with Lady Claire for a few weeks I may find some way to earn my living.'

'I am sure the Countess has room for one more lady in her household.'

'I am good with my needle.'

'Then I am sure she will be happy to have you as one of her ladies.'

'Yes, perhaps…'

Marietta was thoughtful as they remounted and started on their way once more. Seeing Anton with her son had shown her another side to him. He had a daughter he loved and he had once had a wife. Perhaps the reason he sometimes looked so stern was that he was grieving hard for his wife.

She tried not to think of what might have been. Her future was in the balance, for she could not know how she would be received when they reached the home of her kinswoman.

Marietta was sitting in the inn parlour nursing her son when Anton entered. Charles had been crying and his face was flushed. She thought that he might have a tooth coming through, and she ran her finger over his gums, rubbing on a little of the mixture she used when he suffered this way.

'What ails the boy?' Anton asked, frowning.

'I believe he has a tooth coming,' Marietta replied without looking up. 'He cried when I gave him his milk this morning, and he is not usually fretful.'

Anton picked up the little pot she had been using and held it so that he could smell the substance inside. 'This smells like honey?'

'It is a mixture of many things, but I sweeten it with honey so that he does not refuse it.'

Anton nodded, his eyes going to her face as she nursed the boy.

'You look tired. Where is Rosalind?'

'She is rinsing some cloths for the boy. I cannot expect her to care for him all the time. He kept us both awake last night.'

'Give him to me,' Anton said, and took the child into his arms. As if by magic Charles's cries stopped, and he lay looking up at Anton, eyes wide with wonder.

'He feels safe with you,' Marietta said, and smiled.

She could see that he was accustomed to handling a child and wondered at it, for it was unusual in a knight of his standing.

'My husband loved the boy but he seldom had time for him. Though when he did make the time Charles loved it.'

'A father should always have time for his son.' Anton handed the boy back to her. 'We could rest here for today if you wish? If the travelling is too much for you or the child it would add but one day to our journey.'

'I thank you, but I am sure you have more important business, sir. Charles will come to no harm if we continue our journey.'

'Yes, perhaps it is best, for once we are at your kinswoman's house you will be able to rest and see your child properly cared for.'

'Thank you…' Marietta felt a pang of regret. It might have been nice to take the journey more slowly, because it would have given her time to get to know Anton of Gifford—yet perhaps it was for the best after all. 'You have been kind, sir.'

'I did what any honourable knight would do when finding a lady in distress,' he said, and then turned on his heel and walked away.

He was a man of many moods! Marietta held the sigh inside. It would only bring her heartache if she began to like Anton of Gifford too much…

'Marietta, dearest!'

Claire embraced her, the delight in her face evidence that she was thrilled that her kinswoman had come at last. 'I am so happy that you have come to visit me. When I wrote I thought you might be too busy to leave your home, for I dare say there are many duties to keep you there?'

'Once I had many duties, but no longer…' Marietta saw the questions in her cousin's eyes. Her heart ached, for she could not tell if she would be welcome once she had confessed the truth. 'I would tell you privately.'

'Of course. I have many questions, but they can wait. You have travelled a long way and must be tired. When Anton's messenger told us you were coming I prepared a chamber for you. I shall take you up, my love, and you may rest and take a little food and wine before you join us.'

'You are very kind, Countess.'

'No, my dear. You must call me Claire. I insist on it.'

Marietta smiled, allowing the Countess to lead the way up the wide staircase to the gallery above. A servant sprang to open a door and they went into a room of fair proportions. At once Marietta saw that this was to serve her as a bedchamber, but also as somewhere she could sit alone with her embroidery if she wished to be quiet. She knew instantly that it was one of the best chambers and her guilt was heavy.

'I shall leave you to rest, my love. We shall talk later.'

'It is best that I tell you now,' Marietta said. 'I would not wish to deceive you.'

'You look so serious. Tell me, then, since it concerns you.'

'Sir Anton saved my life. I was being pursued by men who meant to force me to stand trial as a witch. I should have been condemned on the word of a man who has stolen my husband's estate from my son—and I believe may have murdered the Comte. He accuses me of killing my husband by witchcraft or poison, but I swear to you that I am innocent. I did not kill my husband and I am not a witch.'

'Of course you are not! I know well that you nursed your husband through his illness last winter. What a wicked man, to steal what belongs to you and your son. If he killed his father he is evil beyond words.'

'I believe that my husband died of poison. I sent medicine for his chest that night, but he had taken it many times before. I can only believe that something was added to the mixture—something that caused his death.'

'Oh, the wickedness of it! And then to accuse you of the crime to cover his own! He should be punished for what he has done, Marietta.'

'I wish I thought it could be done. I was forced to leave under cover of darkness, which must make me appear guilty in the eyes of many. I swear I have never used what skill I have for anything but good—but there are many who condemn me.'

'It was unfortunate that you were forced to flee, but had you not left you might be dead—and your son.'

'I have no doubt that Rouen would kill Charles if he had the chance. I did not know what to do for the best. All I could think of was to escape and bring my son here...' Marietta faltered. 'I do not know if you wish me to remain now that you know...'

'Of course you must stay, for as long as it suits you,' Claire said. 'My husband would say the same if he were here. He has been called to court, as he frequently is. His Majesty often has some small service that Harry must perform for him, but we have been well rewarded for it so I do not complain.'

'I am good with my needle. If I may serve you as a seamstress...'

'Nonsense! You are my dear cousin, and shall be treated as my equal—as you are. We must see what can be done to restore your son's birthright.'

'Would your husband speak to King Henry for me?'

'The best person would be Anton, for he is much in favour at court.' Claire saw her expression. 'Have you not told him—asked for his help?'

'He knows the truth, but I did not think to ask him to intercede with the King for I did not know it was possible for him to do so.'

'I do not know Anton well,' Claire said, 'for he has been away some years, but as a boy he seemed honourable and kind. He may still be in the hall downstairs. Why do you not go down and speak to him before he leaves?'

Marietta had moved to the narrow window to glance out at the view. She watched the party of horsemen riding away, Anton at their head. He did not turn back to look for her.

'It is already too late,' she said, feeling a wave of loss and regret. He had gone without saying goodbye to her. She had been foolish to imagine that he might care what became of her. 'He has been kind to me. I suppose he might have helped me had I asked him.'

'Well, all is not lost,' Claire told her. 'I shall send a letter to my husband asking him to visit us, though it may be some weeks before he is able to come home. I know it is distressing for you, but you are safe with me, my dearest. You and your son will have a home with me, and all that is possible will be done to restore at least a part of what you have lost.'

'For myself, I do not mind. I never wished to be a comtesse, or the wife of a rich man, but my son has been cheated of his rights and that hurts me for his sake.'

'I should feel the same,' Claire said, and kissed her cheek. 'My daughter Annabel has been betrothed to a young man some months, and we are to see her married within the year. Once Harry is home the arrangements will be made. I shall leave you to rest for a while, my love. Come down when you are ready and meet her...'

Marietta thanked her. She sat down on the edge of the large bed, which sank beneath her. It had a goose feather mattress, and would be more comfortable than the beds she had slept in as they journeyed here, for the guesthouses at the various monasteries and inns were not given to such luxury.

She felt like weeping. Whether because Claire had been so kind, or whether because she had the odd feeling of having lost something, she did not know. It was unlikely that she would see Anton of Gifford for a long time, if ever. Why should he bother about a woman he hardly knew?

Perhaps she ought to have enlisted his help with the English King—but it was too late now.

Anton had watched as his uncle's wife greeted her visitor with pleasure. It was obvious that she was welcome here, which meant that he could leave with an easy heart. Had the

Comtesse de Montcrief been turned away, he would have felt it incumbent upon him to extend his protection. Now he could simply ride away and forget her.

Anton had done his duty. He must think now of the future. The King might ask further favours of him, but for the moment his daughter was safe with Anton's mother. When he had time to return for her, he would look for that sensible woman who would be a good mother for his child and ask nothing more than his name and wealth. It would be wrong to think of finding love again.

He hoped that the King would release him so that he could return to the child he loved and begin to make a new life for them both. He would think no more of the beautiful woman he had left with Claire Melford.

Yet the memory of her scent, and her laughter when he had watched her playing with her son, remained in his mind, like a haunting melody that he could not forget. Was he a fool to cut her from his life? He needed a wife—why should that wife not be Marietta?

No! He crushed the thought ruthlessly. He had learned that beautiful women were faithless. He would be a fool to give his heart to a woman like the Comtesse de Montcrief.

'You say Montcrief was murdered?' King Henry frowned. He took the letter, broke the seal, glanced at it and tossed it into the fire, watching as the parchment curled, turned brown and then crumbled into ash. 'You did well to bring this back to me, Gifford. This man who has taken command at the castle— what is his name again?'

'They call him the Bastard of Rouen, Sire. He has men to follow him, and I believe he is popular with the rabble.'

'What makes you think that?'

Anton explained about the tourney and the way the crowd had reacted, cheering the Bastard until the last, when they transferred their support to him.

'Did he not recognise you as the winner of the contest?'

'Not immediately,' Anton said. 'I was not wearing armour that day—but he may have on reflection, for we were later attacked by rogues I suspect to be his men. I believe he must hate me, for he felt humiliated that day.'

Henry nodded, his gaze narrowed. 'The widow—what do you know of her?'

'Very little, Sire.' It was not quite the truth, but Anton was wary of telling the King too much at this stage. He still felt protective towards Marietta, though he had determined to put her out of his mind.

Henry looked thoughtful. 'If she has been unlawfully dispossessed of her husband's estate something should be done. My brother of France might take a dim view, but I think some show of power should be made. When a bastard can take what rightfully belongs to Montcrief's son the law is slighted. As for the widow, it depends whether she be guilty of murder or innocent.'

'Your Majesty speaks truly.'

'My father curbed the power of the barons here. It would do my brother of France no harm to copy his example.' Henry glanced out of the window and smiled. 'I must go down and walk with Mistress Boleyn. I shall think on this, Anton. When I have decided I shall speak to you again.'

'Yes, Sire.'

'We must set up a contest. I love to wrestle, and you sound a worthy competitor. I would like to see your silver arrow...'

'I do not have it with me, Sire. Perhaps another time?'

King Hal nodded, a gleam of anticipation in his eyes. 'Come—we must not keep the ladies waiting...'

Anton could only acquiesce. He was impatient to return to his mother and enquire after Madeline, but for the moment he had no choice but to obey the King.

Marietta walked in the gardens near the house. She had been a guest here for three weeks now, and was becoming familiar with her surroundings. At first she had felt uncomfortable, but Claire and her daughter Annabel had been so kind that she had almost lost her fear of intruding in their family circle. It was not and never could be like her own home, but she would do her best to repay the kindness she was receiving and hope that one day she might have her own house again.

A sigh left her lips, because she could not see how that would ever happen. With a cloud of suspicion and disgrace hanging over her, it was unlikely that she would have many suitors. As the widow of Comte de Montcrief with her reputation intact she would have had barons queuing up to offer for her, but as a woman alone with little fortune she had small chance of finding happiness.

Perhaps she ought to have asked Anton for help. Had she done so, he might have interceded for her with the English King.

Marietta glanced round as she heard a twig snap somewhere in the shrubbery. She had been sitting on a wooden bench lost in thought for nearly an hour. Claire would be wondering where she was.

Getting to her feet, she saw one of the bushes move slightly and a chill ran down her spine. Was someone there? Was that person watching her?

'Is someone there? What do you want?'

Silence. Marietta debated whether to investigate, but then she heard a voice call to her and saw Claire at the window, beckoning her to come inside.

Marietta walked towards the house. She told herself that she had been jumping at shadows. Why should anyone be watching her? She knew hardly anyone in England. It was foolish to worry. The Bastard of Rouen had all that he needed. Why should he come looking for her here?

She was safe in her kinswoman's house. And if sometimes she wished for more to occupy her time, she must accept that she was a guest here. In time she would find a way of repaying her hostess's generosity. Thinking on it would surely distract her, too, from her thoughts and feelings for Anton of Gifford.

Chapter Four

'We have made our decision concerning Montcrief's widow,' King Henry said. 'Bring her here to us, Anton. We would hear the lady's story, and if we believe her innocent we shall use our influence with our brother of France. Her lands and all that has been lost shall be recovered if it be possible.'

'I believe her innocent, though she was hunted for a witch, and would almost certainly have been burned had she been taken…'

'I have no doubt the Bastard will kill her if he can. All the more reason for you to bring her to court. If she be innocent she needs our help.' He held out his hand. A fine ring of heavy gold set with a deep red cabochon ruby adorned his little finger. 'Find also the twin to this, if you can, and bring it to me. Montcrief had it and wore it always. If his widow took his jewels she may have it—if not it may be at Montcrief. I would have it if 'tis found.'

'Yes, Sire. I will ask if she has such a ring.'

'Go, then. Bring the lady to court.'

'As you wish.'

Anton bowed deeply and left the presence chamber. His mind was in turmoil. What was he to do now? Should he return to the home of his uncle and warn Marietta? King Henry was a fair man—but supposing he did not believe her story? The punishment in England for witchcraft was hanging; her body would be taken down after she was dead and burned so that she could not return to it—a cruel fate for one so fair.

Superstitious nonsense! Anton instantly dismissed the charge of witchcraft, but that of murder was not so easy to dismiss. Anton believed her innocent, but others might find against her and she could be hanged or beheaded.... No! It would be a crime to see her head parted from her body.

There must be some way of proving her innocence! Anton was frowning as he went out to the courtyard. He mounted his horse, signalling to his men to follow.

When Anton had left Marietta at his uncle's house he had meant to forget her. She was beautiful, and she inflamed his senses, but to fall in love with a woman like the Countess of Montcrief might bring heartache and regret. Yet the sense of duty was ingrained in him: he could not disobey the King. He could take Marietta away, where she was not known, but would she ever be safe unless her innocence was proven? To run away again would seem to prove her guilt. There was nothing Anton could do but take her to the King and plead her cause.

Marietta stared out of the window. The sun was warm that day, and she was tempted to go out for a walk, but of late she had had an uneasy feeling that she was being watched. She had said nothing to Claire or Annabel, because she did not wish to worry them. Had the Earl been at home she would have told him that she was afraid the Bastard of Rouen's men had found her, but he was away on some business for his estate.

Yet perhaps she was imagining things. She only knew that she was reluctant to walk alone.

Hearing a knock at her door, she called out that whoever it was might enter, and smiled as Claire's daughter came in.

'Annabel,' she said. 'I was just about to ask if you would care to walk in the gardens with me?'

'I should enjoy that,' Annabel said, and blushed delicately. 'My betrothed is here, Marietta. John would be happy to meet you—and to stroll with us.'

'Oh, I have looked forward to meeting him,' Marietta said. 'Will the wedding be soon now?'

'My father has sent word that he will be home in a few days. We shall make the arrangements then.'

'I am sure you are impatient for the day,' Marietta said, and picked up her cloak. 'Shall we go down?'

'We have been followed since we left the court,' Anton told his men. 'I do not know whether they merely mean to pursue us—or to attack once the light fades.'

'We should plan a little surprise for them rather than wait,' Miguel suggested. 'I noticed them an hour since, and I think some of us should gradually split off and wait for them to pass. When you give the signal we shall come on them from behind.'

'I agree,' Anton said. 'We shall come to the forest in a few minutes. Take your chance to slip away one at a time, and then meet up after they have passed. When we reach the clearing we saw as we came this way a month ago I shall turn and face them, and you will lead the charge from the back. We shall see then what they intend...'

There was a murmur of agreement, the men looking at one another, pairing up as they decided to slip away. It was dangerous to travel at any time, for there were bands of beggars and rogues that would attack the unwary, but this was different. They had been followed for hours, and they knew it might mean a fight to the death.

Marietta was at the top of the stairs when she heard a commotion in the hall below. Several people had entered and the voices were all male.

'We were attacked on our way here.' Anton's voice carried to her, and his voice sent shivers down to her toes. 'We drove them off, but it was a bloody fight and one of my men was killed—two more are injured.'

'You were attacked?' The voice belonged to the Earl, who had arrived home the previous day. 'Damn the rogues! Have you any idea who they were—not simply beggars or itinerants if they managed to kill one of your men, Anton?'

'Neither vagrants nor thieves, I think,' Anton said in a cold, angry tone. 'I think I know who sent them, for during the fight I was warned that I should die if I continued to protect her.'

'Protect whom?' Harry sounded puzzled. 'Surely not the lady you brought to us? Who could wish to harm such a lovely creature? Claire adores her.'

'Has Claire told you why she left her home? Perhaps you should know that she was accused of...'

Listening, Marietta felt ice spread all over her. She would have gone down to see if she could help with the injured men, but there were servants enough. The anger in Anton's voice had shocked her. Why had he returned here? Had he come here to take her to court—was she to be tried for witchcraft and murder?

Filled with dread, she fled up to her chamber, locking the door behind her. She was trembling all over, her face hot, her eyes stinging with tears. Anton had sounded as if he hated her. She sensed that he was blaming her because of the attack that had left one of his men dead and others injured.

Marietta felt an overwhelming desire to weep. She brought bad luck to anyone she cared for. Her husband was dead, and now Anton had been attacked and threatened. If she stayed here she might cause trouble for her kind hostess—but where else could she go?

Claire would not hear of her leaving. They had grown fond of one another, and Marietta felt miserable at the thought that she might be forced to leave. Hot tears built behind her eyes but she would not let them spill. She raised her head. Whatever the future held, she must bear it.

Her first rush of emotion conquered, she knew that she must go downstairs and see if she could be of help. She had some skill in the stillroom and with healing. Anton might hate her, but she must remain calm and hide the pain his anger caused her.

Anton was in the hall speaking with Claire when Marietta went down to enquire if she might do anything to help. She was wearing a gown of pale blue cloth, her hair dressed back from her face and secured with combs, and amethyst earrings suspended from her lobes. His eyes dwelled on her for a moment, narrowing, it seemed to her, in deep suspicion.

'You look well, lady,' he said, inclining his head, a flicker of approval in his eyes. 'Better than when I saw you last.'

'Marietta, my love,' Claire said, smiling at her. 'We are tending the wounded and there is nothing for you to do—but you may talk to Anton. I believe you have something to say to him…'

As Claire walked away, the train of her dress brushing over the marble floor, Marietta found Anton's eyes on her once more.

'You wished to speak to me?'

Her stomach clenched with fear. When he looked at her so sternly she was afraid of his hatred and his anger, and the hurt struck deep into her heart. Dreams died hard, and she had cherished hers for so long, but the man of her dreams was a gallant youth and this stony-eyed man was someone different.

'Claire thought that I should have asked you to intercede for me with His Majesty.' She swallowed back the foolish tears. 'I ask nothing for myself—but for my son…'

'You ask me to plead for you?'

'Yes…' Marietta's breath was expelled nervously as his gaze narrowed, becoming harsher. He looked at her so coldly that she trembled inside. 'I know it is a great deal to ask of you, but Claire thought you the best person because of your position with the King.'

'You have told me you are innocent, and I believe you, but I cannot promise that the King will find in your favour. He has commanded me to bring you to him and I must obey. What would you have me say to him on your behalf?'

'I am guilty of neither witchcraft nor murder. It is true that I sent medicine to my husband that night, but it was the same that had eased him many times. He asked me for it in front of everyone. One of my ladies took it to his chamber, but Jeanne would not have dared to tamper with it. Yet I believe someone did, for I am sure that he was poisoned.'

'Who added the poison—the Bastard?' His eyes seemed to burn into her. 'Did he have opportunity or reason?'

'Perhaps. My husband intended that he should sign a paper relinquishing all right to the name and estate. Montcrief thought it the best way to protect our son, because his own health was uncertain and he feared for the future. Perhaps it made Rouen angry and he killed my husband rather than sign away what he believed his. I do not know.'

Anton looked at her thoughtfully. 'Rouen accused you and you accuse him. Where is the proof?'

'I have none.' Marietta raised her clear eyes to meet his. 'If you or others think me guilty I cannot prove otherwise—but I would never murder anyone. I sought to be a good wife and mother. I have made cures to help people but I do not use witchcraft. If these things are crimes, I am guilty.'

Anton met her unflinching stare. 'The rogues that attacked me said I would die if I harboured the Witch of Montcrief. I believe you innocent, lady—but His Majesty has commanded me to take you to him.'

Marietta looked at him apprehensively. 'Supposing the King does not believe me?' An icy shiver ran through her. 'What will happen to me?'

'I shall plead your case. I think it likely the Bastard killed your husband for his wealth—but the King is the law. If he finds against you there is little I can do.' Anton reached out to touch her hand. 'I would take you away to safety, but unless your innocence is proven you could be accused wherever you go. You would never truly be safe.'

Marietta inclined her head. Tears burned behind her eyes but she refused to weep or beg for mercy. 'I do not mind so much what happens to me, but I fear for my son.'

'Your son shall remain here. If you are cleared of blame I shall bring you back to him—if not I swear on all I hold sacred that he shall be cared for. I know that Lady Claire would care for him, but if you wish it I will take him into my household and he may grow up with my own children.' His words were generous, but to Marietta his manner seemed remote, as if he were deliberately keeping her at a distance.

'Thank you…' Marietta's throat felt tight. She gave no sign of the fear or the hurt his coldness aroused in her. 'I know that Claire would care for my son, but he should be the Comte de Montcrief. You might be able to help him regain what has been stolen from him. If I die will you do what you can to restore him to his rightful inheritance?'

Anton hesitated, then, 'You have my word. We shall leave for court tomorrow.'

'As you wish, sir.' Marietta turned away. She needed to be alone so that she could weep. Pride would not let her show weakness before this man, but the need was great.

'Stay one moment. Your husband had a special ring he wore often—a large ruby set in heavy gold?'

Marietta was puzzled, but answered truthfully. 'Yes, he never took it from his finger. He said a good friend gave it to him some years before. Why do you ask?'

'Do you have the ring?'

'No.' Marietta frowned. 'I took some gold and my jewels when I fled, but his ring…it was not on his finger or in his chamber. Someone else must have taken it before I saw him.'

'You are telling me the truth?' Anton's gaze narrowed.

'I swear it on my life—and my son's.'

'Then I know you do not lie. Very well, lady. You must rise early, for I wish to set out soon after first light. My uncle will send some of his men with us as an extra guard, though I think we shall not be attacked again for we routed the rogues who planned to murder us in the night.'

'I am sorry for what happened to your man, sir.'

'So am I,' Anton said. 'He died for your sake, lady. If I ever discover that you have deceived me—I shall kill you with my bare hands.'

Marietta looked into his hard eyes, gave a sob and fled up the stairs to her own chamber. How could he say such things to her? How could he think it? He was cruel, and she should hate him, but he was breaking her heart!

She locked the door behind her, flinging herself on the bed to weep.

Would she never know happiness again? Her husband had been so much older, but at least he had loved and trusted her. There were times when Anton of Gifford looked at her as if he hated her.

Marietta could not rest. Her mind was in torment. She wished that Claire had given her some task—something she could do that would keep her mind from the morning. She had felt safe here, but now she was to be taken to London, as Anton of Gifford's prisoner. Her dreams had been shattered. The hero she had loved from afar was merely the product of a young girl's imagination. She knew nothing of the true man, except that he was determined to do his duty. He would take her to London, where she would face the King and be judged, though there was no proof of her guilt or otherwise.

How could she prove her innocence? She had held herself proudly, telling Anton that she cared only for her child's safety—and that was true. Yet she did not wish to die as a witch. It would be a cruel death and she would face it alone, for she had no one who truly loved her.

It was so unfair! Why should the jealousy of an evil man be believed? She knew that many would take the Bastard of Rouen's word above hers. It was her medicine that had killed her husband—everyone believed it.

Marietta washed her face in cold water from the pewter ewer on her night stand. She had not changed for the evening, and she did not think she could face the others at dinner. Anton would have told them that he had been sent to fetch her—perhaps even Claire would think her guilty now.

She crept downstairs. She could hear voices and laughter in the hall. Turning away, she slipped out of the house by a little door at the rear. The light was fading from the sky but she was too restless to stay indoors. She hardly knew what she wanted. Crying would not help her. She could take Charles and run away, but how far would she get? Anton would find her wherever she went. He would come after her, force her to go to London with him—and then he would be certain of her guilt.

She had his promise that her son would be cared for. Perhaps that was enough. The thoughts churned endlessly in her mind. Perhaps the King might believe her…or be lenient.

Marietta knew that she must stay and face her punishment, whatever that might be. At least her child would be safe, because despite his stern looks and the way he made her want to weep she trusted Anton of Gifford. He might be cold and harsh to her, but he would protect an innocent child. He might even try to regain a part of what had been stolen from Charles, for even if she were condemned as a witch her son was innocent.

Realising that she had wandered farther than usual from the house, Marietta turned back towards it. She shivered because the air had turned cold. It was time to return and prepare for the journey. Farewells must be made, thanks given for all the kindness she had received in this house. Perhaps if God were merciful she might be allowed to return. It was all she could hope for.

She was walking towards the house when she heard the

slight noise behind her. Pausing, she looked back just as the shadow loomed up at her. Something struck a blow to the side of her head and she fell, dropping her kerchief on a rose bush at the side of the path.

Blackness had descended. Marietta felt nothing as she was lifted over a man's shoulder, carried some distance and then thrown carelessly into a cart. She did not hear the coarse laughter and the cruel remarks made as she was driven away into the night.

'Have you seen her, Annabel?' Claire asked her daughter. 'It is not like Marietta to stay in her chamber all day. When I enquired, her maid told me that she dismissed her earlier. She thought she was in her chamber, but when we looked she was not there.'

'I believe I saw her go into the gardens an hour or so ago,' Annabel said. 'I would have called to her, but she seemed distressed and I thought—' She broke off. 'She must be frightened. It is a terrifying thing to be summoned by the King.'

'Yes, it is—but she is innocent. How could anyone think her guilty of murder? To look into her eyes is to know that she is innocent.'

Claire glanced up as her husband and Anton came into the hall. They had been searching the house and grounds, but from their looks it was obvious that Marietta had not been found.

'Annabel thinks she may have gone for a walk in the garden.'

'Until this hour?' Anton's brows rose. 'Has she taken anything with her?'

'You think she has run away?' Claire was startled. 'Surely she would not go alone? Her child is here; also her maid. I know she ran away from her home in France, but her life was at risk. Besides, she must know that we care for her. You promised to plead her case and surely the King will listen?

No, do not look so sceptical! I am convinced the King would see that she is innocent.'

'I shall search for her outside the grounds,' Anton said, and frowned. 'She may have strayed into the woods, but she cannot have got far on foot…'

'I'll have my people join in the search. If those rogues managed to follow you here she might be in danger.' Harry Melford, newly made Earl of Rundle, looked at his wife with compassion. 'Try not to worry, my love. I know you are fond of her, and I shall send a letter to His Majesty pleading for your cousin.'

Anton stared at him, his gaze narrowed, thoughtful. 'If she has not run away someone may have snatched her. She may even now be dead.' His voice grated harshly. 'God forgive me. I was harsh to her and I shall blame myself if she is harmed.' His skin looked grey as the colour washed from it.

'No! Do not say it,' Claire said. 'Why should anyone want her dead? She is surely less important than her son to her enemies. While he lives that evil man can never be certain that Charles will not one day take back all that is his…'

'Yes, that is true,' Harry said, looking at his wife with approval. 'If they have snatched her, the Bastard needs her for some purpose.'

Anton was already striding from the hall. If Marietta were dead or taken it was his fault. He had been harsh to her—unnecessarily so. It was not her fault that his wife had betrayed him. The more he thought about his behaviour towards Marietta, the more he blamed himself. He had tried to keep a distance from her because he was afraid of giving his heart, afraid that he might lose her. It had been cruel and heartless of him to treat her so coolly when she needed his help. She must be terrified of what might happen to her! He must find her—or punish the man who had taken her! Anton might never forgive himself for the part he had played in his wife's death, but he did not think he could bear the added burden if Marietta died because he had not offered the comfort she needed.

Because of his harshness she had gone into the garden to seek solitude and she had disappeared. He was reminded of his jealous rage, which had caused Isabella's death. What a fool he was! Because he feared to be hurt he had been cold to Marietta, when all his instincts had been to take her in his arms and kiss her.

Marietta's head hurt so terribly. She did not know for how long she had lost consciousness, but it must have been some hours. Her body felt bruised, as if she had been beaten. Her captors had treated her roughly and she had lain too long in a cramped position. She tried to move but discovered that her legs had been tied, as had her hands. She opened her eyes, but discovered that it was too dark to see anything.

Where was she? She strained to hear, and gradually became aware of movement and the lap of waves against the side of the ship. Her abductors were taking her back to France! Fear coursed through her, because she knew that she would be given no mercy. The Bastard hated her. He would see her dead—and her son! No, Charles was safe inside the Earl of Rundle's house, where she ought to have stayed.

Anton would think she had run away. Would he honour his promise to care for her son, or would he decide that she had broken her word and set him free? What would happen to her poor child? Claire would care for him, but he would never regain his inheritance for her kinswoman had no influence at court. Anton had given his word that he would do what he could, but could she trust a man she hardly knew? She had thought him honourable and generous, but he was no longer the sweet youth she had dreamed of. What had changed him to the cold, stern man he had become? Was it because he suspected she was guilty of murder and witchcraft, despite his declaration that he believed her innocent?

Tears stung her eyes as she lay in the darkness. How could she have been so foolish as to walk alone when darkness was falling? She should have known that the Bastard might try to get her back. Her safe arrival in England had lulled her into a false sense of security these past weeks and she had no one but herself to blame.

She could hope for nothing. Claire and her family had been kind, but why should they bother to search for a woman who was to be tried for murder and witchcraft? Why should anyone bother to save her when King Henry's justice might condemn her to death? The only person that might have saved her had looked at her so coldly when they last met.

Bitter tears ran into her mouth as she wept. She was alone, and the future held only terror and pain.

'I found this on a bush,' Anton said, holding a kerchief for Claire to see. 'Is it hers?'

'Let me see… Yes, I gave Marietta this myself.' Claire looked fearful. 'It proves she was in the garden. I do not think she has run away.'

'She would not go without the child,' Anton agreed. 'There were signs of a struggle, footprints in the earth near where we found the kerchief. I think she has been abducted.'

Claire gave a cry of distress. 'Those wicked devils! What will they do to her?'

'If they meant to kill her we should have found her body,' Anton said, his mouth pulled into a grim line. 'She has been kidnapped and taken to her husband's bastard, which means that she will be kept alive at least until they reach the Castle of Montcrief. I shall leave at once, and we must pray that I am in time to save her.'

'You will go after her?' Claire looked at him in relief. 'You will try to save her?'

Anton inclined his head. 'She went walking alone because I distressed her. My honour compels me to find her and bring her back if possible.'

He turned and left the hall. Outside, he summoned his men.

'They have taken the lady Marietta, Comtesse Montcrief.

She was accused of witchcraft and murder, but I believe her innocent and I intend to bring her back to England if I find her alive. Some of you may not wish to follow me on this mission. If you wish, you may wait here for my return or leave my service. The choice is yours. I am leaving for France now.'

Anton swung himself into the saddle. He did not glance back as he rode off. If they all chose to leave him, he would go alone. Honour demanded it. He could not bear the death of another young woman on his soul!

'We are with you,' Miguel said, his horse coming along-side. 'For pity's sake go a little slower, for the sake of those who cannot keep pace with you. The lady is in God's hands. If she be the innocent you think her, He will protect her.'

Anton's mouth was tight, his eyes bleak as he glanced at his friend. 'I thank you for your company, Miguel. Pray God you are right. For I cannot bear the stain of another sweet lady's death on my soul…'

Marietta opened her eyes as the cabin door swung forward and two men entered. They stood over her, grinning evilly as they saw that she was awake. She knew them as men who had once served her husband, but had transferred their allegiance to the Bastard.

'Untie me,' she demanded. 'How dare you do this to me— your master's wife? You will be punished for this!'

'We serve the Bastard of Rouen, not you, lady,' one of them growled. 'He commanded that you be returned to him.'

'He has no right to command you. My son is the rightful heir—and I am the chatelaine of Montcrief until he comes of age. When the King hears of this, you will all be punished.'

'Shut your mouth, woman. You are a witch and a murderer and will die in the flames.'

'Be quiet, Pierre,' the second man said. 'She is not yet proven. Show some respect.' His dark eyes went over her. 'Forgive us, lady. We but do our duty. I shall untie the bonds if you give me your word that you will not run away. If we do not take you back, the Bastard will kill our children and us.'

Marietta closed her eyes for a moment, then inclined her head. 'I thank you for your courtesy, Boris. You have my word.'

'Do not trust her,' Pierre warned, but Boris bent and sliced through the ropes with his knife. 'Fool! If she escapes you shall bear the blame.'

'Thank you.' Marietta rubbed her wrists. They felt sore and numbed. When she tried to stand she almost fell. Boris steadied her, then lifted her in his arms. 'Forgive me, the ropes have taken the feeling from my legs.'

'You will ride with me,' he told her gruffly. 'Remember that my son's life is forfeit if you run from us.'

'I shall not forget. It was for my son's life that I ran. I do not care what becomes of me...'

Marietta closed her eyes as she was taken on deck and then on shore. She was numbly aware of the horses, and being lifted to a saddle. Putting her arms around Boris's waist, she entwined her fingers in his leather belt so that she would not fall. Her head ached, but the fresh air was rapidly clearing the feeling of faintness, though her sense of despair grew stronger with each league they covered.

She dreaded the moment when she came face to face with the Bastard once more. He would make sure that she suffered for defying him. She imagined that he would enjoy inflicting pain on her.

She must bear it as best she could, for she knew that she could expect no help. She could only pray that death came quickly. If her son was safe she could leave this life without regret. She had nothing more to live for...

Anton stared out into the darkness. It was one of the longest nights of his life, almost as terrible as the night he had sat by his wife's dead body and wept for her. Then he had been helpless, for death was final, but now he burned with the fires of impatience, his sword-hand itching for work. Marietta's abduction was his fault. He should have watched over her more closely. His instincts should have warned him that she was in danger. Why had he not placed guards in the grounds? Why had he been so harsh to her that she had sought solace by walking alone in the gardens?

The truth hit him like a sword-thrust in his stomach, sending a shaft of pain curling through him. His anger had been because he was afraid that she might be condemned as a murderess—and he cared for her! He had wanted her on the ship, but he had fought his feelings of desire. Romantic love was a trap, a source of bitter pain. To let himself be caught by it a second time would be stupid. Isabella had sworn her child was his but he could never have been sure, and the maggot of jealousy had eaten deep into his soul.

Anton did not want to care for another woman. He did not want to feel the agony of loss again—but he was already feeling it. Marietta was in grave danger of losing her life.

If she died at the hands of that evil Bastard, Anton would not be able to bear the guilt.

Marietta allowed Boris to help her down from the back of his horse. She glanced up and thought she saw sympathy in his eyes, but it was quickly hidden. Even if he felt sorry for her plight, his son's life meant more to him. She could not blame him, for in his place she would have felt the same. The Bastard of Rouen was ruthless. He ruled by fear and example, and would not hesitate to kill or maim any of his servants if they displeased him.

Fear was making her tremble inside, but she managed to hide it as she turned and saw him. The Bastard was a handsome man in a coarse, harsh way. Tall and strong, he had eyes the hue of blue ice, his hair worn long, hanging in greasy strands. His clothes looked as if they needed washing, and his beard was in need of trimming, stale food caught in the thick hair. Revulsion coursed through her as she saw the way he stared at her; the heat in his eyes burned her. He seemed to strip away her clothes so that she felt naked, vulnerable.

'So, the witch returns…' He grinned, vastly pleased with himself. 'Where is the brat?'

'We snatched her as she walked alone,' Boris said. 'The child was nowhere to be seen.'

'Fool! I need them *both*.' The Bastard struck him across the face, making him stumble. 'I do not suffer fools, nor failure.'

'We brought you the woman…' Pierre said, and fell to his knees as the Bastard swung round, glaring at him. 'Forgive me…'

'Take these blundering idiots away and whip them,' the Bastard ordered. 'Think yourselves lucky that I don't have you and your families killed.'

'You will never get my son,' Marietta cried, pride making her forget her fear. 'He is cared for and protected and…' Her voice trailed away as the Bastard towered over her. He raised his hand, striking her across the face. She stumbled but did not fall. 'Yes—hit me, kill me—as you killed my husband. I know the truth. You were his murderer, not I. You are a coward and—' Her words failed as he struck her once more and sent her to her knees.

'Take her to her chamber and lock her in,' the Bastard roared. 'If she escapes again I'll hang every last man in the castle.' His eyes glittered with fury. 'I'll speak to you later, witch. You will be sorry you dared to defy me.'

Someone grabbed hold of Marietta's arms and dragged her away.

'You are a bully, a murderer and a thief!' Marietta screamed as they forced her into the castle. 'One day I shall be avenged. My son will be the master here and he will not spare you…'

'Be quiet, lady,' the man who had her arm whispered. 'He is a devil when roused. You would be wise to do as he wants, and then he may let you live.'

'I would rather die than live as his whore,' Marietta said.

On the voyage she had been close to despair, ready to die

if she must, but now she was angry. Her feeling of apathy had gone. She would fight him to the last! The Bastard had no right to rule here. Surely God would strike him down!

'If there is any justice he will die first…'

Locked in her chamber, Marietta paced the floor restlessly. Her faithful servants were in England. She had no hope of escape this time, unless she could find a way out of here…

She swung round as a key turned in the stout lock that guarded her door and a woman entered. She was a beautiful woman, with long pale hair and narrow cat-like eyes. Her mouth was thin and hard as she looked at Marietta with dislike.

'So you are the woman he would wed,' she said. 'What have you done to him, witch? Have you put your spell on him? He was mine, but he never spoke of marriage. He thinks of nothing else but you. You must have bewitched him.'

'I swear to you that I have put no spell on him. He wants me only so that he can be sure of my husband's lands and fortune.'

The woman's gaze intensified. 'If he marries you he will forget me—and he owes me much. I bear his child and I should be his wife.'

'If I could change places with you I would,' Marietta said. 'I mean that I would wish for you to be his wife, not me. Believe me, if I could leave this place again I would not wait to be forced to wed him.'

'You say that, but how can I believe you?'

'I swear it on my life, lady…I do not know your name?'

'It is Claudette. I was but fifteen when he took me from my parents and made me his whore. At first I hated him, but then—' She broke off, eyes glittering. 'If I could think of a way to set you free—would you go?'

'Yes, I swear it.' Marietta moved towards her eagerly. 'Please help me. I have nothing to give you, but…'

'I want nothing from you,' Claudette said, stepping back. 'Speak of this to my lord and you are dead.'

'I swear I shall not...' Marietta's heart sank as the woman went out and locked the door again. 'Please help me...'

She had thought the Bastard would kill her, but it seemed that he still planned to wed her—why?

Had he discovered that he needed her? She was sure that he had expected to rule here, whether she lived or died, but something must have happened to make him realise that he couldn't do it without her.

Marietta clenched her hands, her nails cutting into her palms. She would prefer to die than live as the Bastard's wife, but she might not be given the choice. He could force a priest to do his bidding—and he could force himself on her once she was his wife, for she was not strong enough to prevent him.

She had seen anger in his eyes as he looked at her, but also the gleam of lust. He wanted her. And he needed her. The will her husband had lodged at court must have upheld her husband's wish that she should be in charge of his fortune until his son was of age. Rouen had taken the castle by force, but he could not touch the vast fortune in gold that her husband had lodged with the King's goldsmiths for safety. It seemed that the Comte de Montcrief had outwitted his bastard after all. Much of her son's birthright was safe—but to keep it that way Marietta would have to pay a terrible price.

She fell to her knees beside the bed, head bent as she prayed for help.

If only Anton of Gifford had believed her innocent! She was certain that he would have come to her aid.

'Please, please help me,' she whispered, and it was no longer to God that she prayed.

Now she was remembering the face of the charming youth who had rescued her from certain death, and despite the way he had looked at her the last time they met she was comforted.

Chapter Five

Anton's men were close enough behind the abductors to discover that a party of men and one woman had taken a ship for France the previous morning, but the tide was against them. It would not turn again until the evening.

'Damn them! If he harms her I swear I shall kill him!' Anton's frustration at being held in port was tearing him apart. He stood looking out across the sea, his face like thunder. 'I cannot bear the thought of her at his mercy.'

'Courage, my friend,' Miguel said, clapping a hand to his shoulder. 'We shall bring her back if she lives. If she is dead, by his hand or theirs, they shall all pay for it.'

'There are but ten of us, and he must have a hundred fighting men,' Anton replied in clipped tones. 'I shall not let you all die trying to storm the walls of such a fortress. We should give our lives for nothing.'

'The man Sandro says he knows a secret way into the castle.'

'Is he with us? I had not noticed.' Anton glanced round at the men who had dismounted and were waiting for his orders.

'You have been too preoccupied. The lady's maid stayed

behind, to care for the child, but Sandro followed you from the start. We would all of us give our lives to serve you,' Miguel said.

'But I shall not waste lives in vain. If there is a secret way into the castle some of us will go in when the enemy sleeps…' His face twisted in an agony of remorse. 'I must find her alive. I must. If she died because of my neglect I could not forgive myself…'

Marietta lay fully clothed on her bed. She had not undressed, even though one of her own nightgowns had been brought to her and the serving woman had offered to help her. The woman's name was Veronique, but she was new to the castle and Marietta did not know her.

'Thank you, but I can manage alone.'

She dismissed the woman and drank the cup of wine she had been given. A piece of coarse bread and some cold bacon had been sent with the wine. Her hunger drove her to eat what she could, even though it sat uneasily on her stomach.

The walls of her chamber were still hung with the tapestries she had worked herself. All the possessions she had abandoned when she fled were as she had left them, though her lyre had been smashed. She had thought the Bastard might have rent her belongings to pieces, but he had left them undisturbed—all but the lyre, which he must have known was her prized possession.

She touched the silken surface of the wood, which had been smashed apart, then shook her head. What did such things matter? She had left the lyre behind when she fled because her thoughts had been only for her child. His safety and well-being were still of paramount importance.

She paced her chamber, torn between hope and despair. Where was Charles? Did Claire still have charge of her baby? Had he been taken from her—perhaps to become the King's ward, as often happened when there were lands and money involved? The King of England would know that Charles was the rightful heir to a fortune and he might do something for her son—speak to the King of France on his behalf. She herself was beyond help, but it did not matter if her son was safe.

Marietta's lips moved in prayer. She could bear anything if her son were safe!

She stiffened as she heard a key in the lock, and then the door of her chamber opened. She saw a large shadow enter and froze, because she knew instinctively that it was the Bastard. He came towards the bed, the sound of his steps heavy and uncertain. The smell of strong wine hung over him and she guessed that he had drunk deeply at table.

Marietta kept her eyes closed as she sensed and smelled him near. He was looking down at her. Would he throw himself on her? Ravish her? Her stomach churned as the fear curled inside her. She would fight him, but she knew that he would take her for he was too strong for her.

'Thought to escape me...' The Bastard's words were slurred with drink. 'Mine now...always wanted...beautiful but a bitch...'

Marietta tried not to move as she felt his breath on her face. Her only chance was surprise. If he thought she was sleeping he might be careless, giving her an opportunity to escape. She felt the touch of his hand on her hair. He lifted strands of it, sniffing it as if to inhale the perfume.

'Witch...' he muttered. 'I'll make you pay. Not tonight... must be wed...only way to get the gold. Need your signature... won't give me the gold without it...'

He was moving away, unsteady on his feet. She heard him knock into a stool and curse, then the door opened, closed again, and a key turned. Marietta had her answer. It was as she'd suspected. The Bastard needed her to get his hands on the Comte's fortune. He believed that once she was his wife he could force her to do anything, but she would rather die than marry him! She was locked in for the moment, but somehow she had to escape...

Anne Herries

* * *

'The lord says you must come down—and you are to wear your best gown,' the serving woman said the next morning. 'He is waiting for you in the hall, lady.'

'Tell your master that I cannot come,' Marietta replied, giving a little moan. 'I am sick and must rest. My head aches so much that I can scarce stand.'

'If I tell him that he will beat me.'

'Then tell him I will not come.'

'Are you truly sick, lady?' The woman looked at her uncertainly.

'Look in the pot. You will see that I have been sick.'

The woman fetched it out, recoiling at the sour smell. 'You are sick, lady. I will show him this—but if he comes you must lie on your bed and groan, or he will blame me and I shall be punished.'

'I am too ill to get up today.'

Marietta lay back as the woman took the pewter pot with her. It was true that the coarse food she had been given had turned her stomach, but she had made herself sick by mixing some powders from her medicine chest with water and swallowing them. She was surprised that her herbs had not been taken as proof of her witchcraft, but perhaps the Bastard feared her powers? She had used the mixture before. In the case of poisoning, sometimes the only remedy was to make the patient sick. Sometimes the remedy worked, at others it did not—healing was not a precise form but a matter of trial and error, at least for her.

The mixture had made her feel unwell, and her stomach heaved as she felt bitter bile in her throat. If the ruse worked it would be worthwhile—but would the Bastard accept her excuses?

After some minutes had passed she heard a commotion outside her door, and then it was thrust open and the Bastard entered. She saw that he had shaved and was wearing his best clothes. For their wedding, she suspected.

'What ails you?' he demanded.

'I am sick. Your men hit me too hard and I have been feeling ill.'

'You were sleeping well enough last night.' He looked at her and bent over her, but caught the rancid smell of vomit that she had taken care to spill on her covers. Recoiling in disgust, he glared at her. 'Very well, you may rest today—but tomorrow I shall wed you. You are mine. If you please me I may let you live for a while…'

Marietta gave a little moan and made a retching sound, pressing a cloth to her mouth. She lay with her face buried as she heard the sound of the door slamming.

He was angry, but he could not force her to rise and go down to be married if she was ill. However, the reprieve might not last more than one day. She glanced up as the serving woman approached her.

'Will you ask the lady Claudette to come to me, please?'

'That one is a haughty bitch and will do only as she pleases.' The woman sniffed. 'I shall ask, but I do not know if she will come.'

'Please ask…'

Marietta lay back and sighed as the woman left her. Her head ached, though she could have risen and gone down to the hall had she wished. If Claudette truly wanted to be the Bastard's wife she must realise that she needed to act quickly to prevent his marriage to Marietta, for he was determined to have his way. Marietta had managed to delay the ceremony but he would not be thwarted. Next time he would drag her from the bed and take her with him!

'Please come for me…please…'

Her only hope of salvation lay in the faint hope that Anton would feel it his duty to bring her back to face King Henry's justice—unless she could persuade Claudette to help her…

'Our scouts have spoken to local people. There are still some that remain loyal to their true lord's wife, and they say she is a prisoner in the tower. She has her own rooms and has been given clothes and food. It is rumoured that she would have been wed today had she not been ill.'

'Marietta is ill?' Anton seized on the statement fiercely. 'Damn him to hell for this! He deserves to be hanged for the way he has treated her.'

'It is as well she was ill, for at least it has saved her from worse,' Miguel said. 'If Sandro delivers a way into the castle we may be able to get her out tonight.'

'I pray that we are in time to save her…' Anton's expression darkened. There were worse fates than death, and he could imagine what the Bastard planned for the woman who had humiliated him. 'It is a chance we must take. If she is too ill to walk I shall carry her.'

Miguel nodded, looking thoughtful. 'It is said that the Bastard drinks heavily. We must pray that he will indulge at the table this night, and his men with him.'

'I noticed that there were few guards the last time we visited. His men are ill-disciplined, and it may well be that they are in the habit of drinking too heavily at night…'

Anton's eyes glittered. He had come after Marietta because it was his duty to rescue her and deliver her safely to the King of England—and he would do all in his power to outwit the Bastard of Rouen.

'You asked me to come?' Claudette looked sulky as she entered the chamber. 'I am not yours to command, even if my lord weds you. My obedience is given only where I choose.'

Marietta met her challenging look. 'I asked if you would come. I know I cannot command you, lady. If you would see me gone from here, I beg you to help me.'

'My lord will kill me if he learns you have fled.'

'He need not know you helped me. Come tonight, when the castle sleeps, and unlock the door. I ask nothing more of you.'

'If he knew I was having his child he might wed me—if

you were gone…' Claudette looked thoughtful. 'But he will send for you in the morning, and if you do not come he will order men to look for you. They would find you and bring you back. Nothing would be gained and I might be blamed.'

'If I have enough time I might be far away by the time he realises I am gone.'

'I do not see how that could be…unless…' Claudette's eyes gleamed suddenly. 'I could change places with you—wear your gown and a veil to cover my face.' She looked excited. 'I shall wed him in your place. When he discovers the truth it will be too late. I shall be his wife and you will be far away.'

'Are you certain you wish to do this?' Marietta looked doubtful. The Bastard would undoubtedly be furious when he discovered that he had been duped. 'What will he do to you when he discovers that you have taken my place?'

'He may hit me and shout, but it has happened before. I do not fear him. He knows it, and that is why he loves me. Even if he wed you he would sleep in my bed, for you could not hold him.'

Marietta made no reply. She did not wish to have the Bastard in her bed even on her wedding night, but she would not tell this woman for it would anger her.

'How can you make sure that he does not discover what we have done too soon?'

'I shall put a sleeping draught in his cup when he grows careless. He will sleep late, and when he wakes he will hardly know what he is doing for hours. By the time he realises what has happened you should have a good start.'

'Thank you. I believe you are a brave woman, Claudette.'

'I do this for me, because I love him. He took me when I was but a child. I should be his wife.' Claudette looked her in the eyes, her expression one of pride. 'If he catches you again he will kill you. You are no good to him unless he is your lawful husband. He wants your husband's gold, and you are the key that will unlock the goldsmiths' coffers.'

'I expected him to kill me this time,' Marietta replied. Claudette had confirmed what she had suspected. 'I must think of a way to disappear so that he can never find me again…'

After Claudette had left, Marietta paced the room. She was restless, impatient to be gone, but common sense told her that she must wait for night to fall. The Bastard was eager to make her his wife, and once he had her he would not spare her. He would not kill her immediately. She was useful to him for the moment. But once he had the gold he craved he would find a way to humiliate and destroy her. It would be a slow death and she would prefer to die quickly. If his men recaptured her she would die rather than be brought back alive.

'Anton…' She mouthed the word softly, not realising she spoke aloud. 'Please help me…'

Tears trickled down her cheeks. She was foolish to think of Anton. He had rescued her before, but he now believed she was a murderess. Why would he bother to look for her?

He would not think it worth the trouble. Why should he? She must forget him and think of what she could do once she had left the castle. This time she would have no money, and no one to help her, but somehow she must make her way back to England.

'Bring the witch down to me!' the Bastard demanded. 'I would have her sit by my side this night. I want her to join the celebrations for her wedding…' He laughed and drank deeply from his cup, then wiped his mouth on the sleeve of his robe and belched. 'More wine, dolt! What are you staring at me for?'

'The lady says she is too ill, my lord…' the luckless servant began, and received a blow that sent him staggering sideways.

'Damn her! Damn her black soul to hell…' The Bastard grabbed the wineskin from the serf who presented it and drank straight from the neck. 'Bring her, I say!'

As the frightened servant ran off, Claudette ran her fingers over his cheek, smiling at him. 'Why do you send for that puling creature when you have me, my lord?' She pouted her red lips at him. 'Let us go to your chamber, and I shall please you so much that you will not want her.'

'My sweet whore,' the Bastard said, grinning at her. 'Your turn will come soon enough, but you must learn to share me with my wife. She brings a fortune in gold. Besides, a man grows tired of too much complaisance. She will fight me, and the thought pleases me…'

'I can fight if you wish for it. I will whip you and scratch you…'

The Bastard caught her wrist as her nails scored his skin, his look suddenly threatening. 'Be quiet, whore! When I want you, I'll tell you.'

Claudette drew back, smarting from his insults. If she was a whore he had made her so. He wanted the gold the late Comte's wife could bring him, but she would do her best to see that his plans came to nothing.

Keeping her smile in place, she took the wineskin he had laid down and filled his cup, slipping the potent liquid that would make him sleep into it while his head was turned. She placed the cup by his hand, and in a moment he reached for it and drank deeply, but he did not finish the contents.

Claudette turned her head to look as she heard shouting, and a scream of anger. The servants had brought the Comtesse to the hall, but she was struggling and protesting, trying to break free of them. All eyes were on her as she was dragged to the high table, and no one but Claudette noticed when the Bastard drained his cup.

'Witch…' he muttered thickly. 'You cannot defy me. I shall teach you a lesson…'

He got to his feet and walked unsteadily along the back of the table where his chief men were seated, then negotiated the steps to the dais unsteadily, finally reaching Marietta. Towering over her, he thrust his hand out and grabbed her by the throat. Bending his head, he forced his mouth over hers.

Marietta struggled wildly, and he gave a cry as her sharp teeth sank into his bottom lip. He roared with pain and anger and slapped her, making her stagger back.

Marietta faced him defiantly. His fist curled, as if he would strike her again, then he muttered something and rubbed his hand over his face. A strange strangled sound came from him, his eyes rolling upwards. Sagging to his knees, he stared at her stupidly, and then fell flat on his face.

For a moment there was a stunned silence. Claudette broke it by laughing.

'My lord hath drunk too much,' she announced. 'Take him to his chamber and see that he sleeps well. He will need his strength for the morrow if he is to tame this one!'

Laughter and some coarse remarks greeted her words. Several of the men moved to gather him up and carry him off; they grinned and winked at each other, clearly amused by what had happened.

Claudette came quickly to Marietta. 'You must return to your chamber, lady. I shall lock you in myself.' She hurried Marietta away from the hall before anyone could deny them, her voice soft as she whispered, 'I gave him a strong dose. He will sleep well into the morning. You must lock me into your chamber, so that if he is angry I can blame you. I shall say that you overpowered me and escaped.'

'He will be very angry.' Marietta looked at her in concern. 'He may vent his anger on you.'

'If I am his wife I shall tell him that I bear his son—and that it was for my child's sake that I took your place after you locked me in your room.' Claudette smiled confidently. 'Once you are gone he will forget you. But remember that if you return you will certainly die…'

'I know it,' Marietta said. 'Thank you. We must hurry, for the sooner I am on my way the better…'

Claudette went into the antechamber ahead of Marietta. The next moment she was seized from behind, a hand over her mouth.

'We have come for your lady,' a voice said in her ear. 'Scream and it will be the worse for you.'

'What is this?' Marietta cried as she too was grabbed and held. 'Who are you? What are you doing?'

'Marietta?' A shadow moved towards her out of the gloom. 'We thought you were locked in the bedchamber. Are you at liberty to leave your room?'

'Anton?' Marietta's heart leapt. 'Is that you? I cannot see you…'

'We snuffed the tapers, for we did not wish to alert the castle. We came to take you away from this place—if you wish to go?'

'Oh, yes! Of course I wish to leave. I was about to make my own escape. Claudette was to take my place here. Let her go, for we must lock her in my bedchamber…'

Anton had struck a tinder. Lighting one small candle, he held it high so that he could look at Marietta's face. 'Where is the Bastard?'

'In his chamber. Claudette drugged him, and he will sleep for long enough.'

'Why do you ask?' Claudette was on her guard. 'If you mean him harm I shall scream and bring the guards down on you. You may take her and go in safety, but you will not harm my lord.'

'He may have something I need—a ring.' Anton's hard gaze went over the girl. 'He took it from the Comte de Montcrief as he lay dying. It is fashioned of heavy gold with a large cabochon ruby. Have you seen such a ring?'

'He wears it on a chain about his neck,' Claudette said. 'If you give me your word that he will not be harmed I shall take you to him.'

'He deserves to die for what he has done.'

'She loves him,' Marietta said, and touched his arm. 'Claudette bears his child—for her sake let him live.'

Anton's mouth was a hard line as he looked at her, then he inclined his head. 'Very well.' He turned to Miguel. 'Take the Comtesse and ride for the coast at once. I shall join you as soon as my business is done here.'

'You are not coming with us?'

'I must have that ring.' Anton did not smile as he glanced at Marietta. 'You will be safe with my men. If I should not follow Miguel will take you back to Lady Claire.'

Marietta looked for some sign of warmth in his face but found none. He had come for her, but it must have been at Lady Claire's bidding or because the King had ordered it. For a moment she had thought he had sought her out because he loved her.

She moved towards him urgently, laying a hand on his sleeve. 'I beg you to take care, sir. I would not have you die in my cause.'

'I am commanded to find that ring. You are merely delaying me. Please go with Miguel as I bid you.'

She turned away, fighting her tears as she allowed Miguel to hurry her back down the stone steps of the tower. Near the bottom they heard the sound of voices, and Miguel pulled her back into the shadows until the men had passed.

'There is a secret way beneath the outer walls,' Miguel whispered. 'Your servant is waiting in the stables to guide us through the passage. It is dark, and there are rats and cobwebs, but you must not scream lest someone hears. Remember, Anton is still in the castle.'

'I shall not scream.'

Marietta glanced at his face and saw a strange expression in his eyes. She sensed that he was hiding something, but could not tell what was in his mind. He had come with his friend to help rescue her, but he did not like her. He was hiding it, but she felt strong resentment, even hatred. Perhaps he thought her the witch she had been named?

They slipped out of a side door and ran swiftly across the inner bailey. Reaching the solid stone block that was the stable, Marietta went inside, closely followed by Miguel.

'Sandro?' she called softly. 'Are you there?'

'God be praised, you are alive, my lady.' The groom came towards her, looking beyond her to Miguel. 'Where are the others?'

'Anton and Fitch follow,' Miguel said. 'We are to ride for the coast at once. Anton will do as he thinks best.'

'Then I shall wait for him,' Sandro said. 'He may not be able to find the secret way without me. Take my lady to safety, and may God go with you, sir.'

'If you wait for him then so do I,' Marietta said in a determined tone.

Miguel glared at her. 'You must come with us. Anton ordered it, lady, and he will be angry if you disobey him.'

'I shall not leave without him.' Marietta set her face stubbornly. 'Go on ahead and prepare the ship. I shall wait here with Sandro.'

Miguel's eyes narrowed. He looked furious but, seeing that her mind was set, he turned on his heel and left her with Sandro.

Anton looked down at the Bastard as he lay snoring on his couch. He stank of stale sweat and wine, his hair was lank with grease. Had he been awake, it would have been a joy to kill him, but there was no honour in killing a helpless enemy. There would be a reckoning for the evil that this man had done, but not this night.

'Here is the ring.' Claudette took it from the chain the Bastard wore about his neck and brought it to him. 'Take it and go quickly, but you must lock me in the tower room. I shall tell my lord that you overpowered me. It will be so much better than the story we planned, for he might not have believed that she could do it.'

'Why should I believe you? You will raise the alarm as soon as we leave.'

'You may tie me and gag me if you choose.'

'It might be safer,' Fitch said. 'I will make her secure without hurting her.'

Anton nodded his assent. 'Come then, lady. We have no time to waste, for I would be on board my ship by the time the Bastard wakes…'

Anton pocketed the ring. It was the twin to the one he had seen on the King's finger.

Wondering at the significance of the matching rings, Anton was thoughtful as he left the Bastard's chamber. What was so important about a ring that the King of England needed it returned?

Anton might never know, for he was bound to serve the King but not entitled to an answer. He must concentrate his thoughts on getting out of here alive!

They had been lucky so far, but could be discovered at any moment. If the alarm were raised it would be almost impossible for two men to fight their way out of this castle. The Bastard of Rouen allowed his men to drink and neglect their duty, but if roused their numbers would be overwhelming.

As they made their way back to the tower where Marietta had been imprisoned Anton heard the sound of raucous laughter coming from the hall. Twice he stopped, motioning to the others to keep back as he heard voices and someone approaching, but each time the men passed without noticing the figures in the shadows.

They gained the tower room safely. Claudette was bound. Before the gag was placed about her mouth, Anton asked if there was anything she needed.

'For your help this day, I would offer my protection in the future if it is asked.'

'I need nothing from you, sir. Go on your way.'

Bowing his head, Anton signalled that she should be gagged. When it was done they locked her in the room and threw the key into a corner. Let it be searched for!

Running down the steps, they were soon outside in the night air. It was as they approached the stables that Anton heard raised voices. One was Sandro's, the other unknown. As he hesitated, he heard a woman scream.

Marietta! Why was she still here? Had they been caught? As Anton prepared for the worst, he heard a man speaking.

'What are you doing here? Answer me or by God I'll have your tongue—but not before my lord has his fun with you.'

'Do your worst, scum,' Sandro said defiantly. 'Your master will burn in hell for his sins.'

There was the sound of a struggle and a shout of pain. As Anton entered the stable he saw that one man held Sandro's arms behind his back while another struck him about the face. Marietta was being held by a third man; there was no sign of Miguel or his other men. Anton nodded to Fitch and they moved as one. Fitch drove his dagger into the side of the man holding Sandro, just as Anton sprang at the man who had been hitting him, grabbing him by the throat and jerking his arm back until he gave a cry and fell senseless to the ground. Turning to look at Marietta, Anton saw the third man had a dagger at her throat.

'Come any nearer and I will slit her throat,' he warned.

'If you spill one drop of her blood you are a dead man. Let her go and I shall spare you.'

Anton advanced, sword at the ready. The man tightened his arm about Marietta's waist, but she suddenly jerked back, then kicked his shin, and at the same moment shoved her elbow hard into his stomach. He gave a grunt and released his hold sufficiently for her to break free of his grasp. Anton grabbed her, thrusting her behind him. The man dropped to his knees, face pale as he begged for his life.

'Spare me. I was simply obeying orders.'

'Tie him up!'

Fitch moved to obey instantly. The man made no attempt to resist as he was bound and gagged.

Sandro was still on his knees, gasping. His nose was bleeding, and more blood ran from the side of his mouth.

'Why are you both still here?' Anton's gaze went from Marietta to Sandro. 'Where are Miguel and the others?'

'Sandro stayed to make sure you found your way through

the secret passages,' Marietta answered him. 'I stayed with him. I could not leave while—'

'You foolish woman! When I give an order I expect to be obeyed! If I miss the tide I can look after myself until I find another ship. You will only hamper me!'

'I beg you, do not be angry with my lady,' Sandro said. 'It was my fault. If I had not waited she would have gone with the others.'

'Are you able to walk?' Anton's attention returned to him. 'You should have persuaded your lady to go with the others— but I know well she is wilful and heedless. I shall not blame you. We must leave at once, for I do not want to miss the tide.'

Anton took hold of Marietta's arm. His strong fingers bit into her flesh, his grip uncomfortable as he thrust her ahead of him into the tunnel. Her throat felt tight, and tears were very close, but she would not shed them. He was so angry with her! She was a burden to him that he would rather not have had, and his harsh words were like the lash of a whip, wounding her deeply.

The journey through the tunnel was a nightmare for Marietta. There was an unpleasant smell, and cobwebs hung from the low ceiling brushing over her face and into her hair. She could hear rustling sounds, and sometimes the squeak of a bat, which made her want to scream, but she held her nerve, the nearness of Anton giving her courage to bear her ordeal.

At last they were out into the open. She gulped the night air, breathing it in thankfully. One of Anton's men had stayed behind to guard the horses. But there were only enough for the men, which meant that she was expected to ride with one of them.

'Come, lady!'

Anton held out his hand imperiously. She took it and he swung her up into the saddle, mounting behind her. Marietta shivered as his arms went about her and she felt his body at her back.

'There is no need to be frightened now.' Anton's voice was softer. 'We shall be safe once we reach the ship.'

She could not answer him. Being so close to him made her feel safe, and yet she was aware that he was still angry with her despite his words of comfort. She had prayed that he would come to help her, and her prayers had been answered, but she knew that he had not come to Montcrief for her sake. Anton had come for the ring. Claire had asked him to bring her back and he had rescued her—but it was obvious that the ring was more important. She would be foolish to imagine that she meant more to him than duty.

The wind stung her face, getting into her eyes. She wasn't crying. It was just the wind. Anton would take her to his king and abandon her to her fate, whatever that might be. She had escaped the Bastard, but she would not escape the King's justice.

Marietta held herself proudly. It would be foolish to cry for a man who did not love her but she could not help herself. Despite his coldness, he had stirred something deep inside her.

Dawn was breaking when Marietta first smelled the tang of the sea. They had begun the descent of a steep cliff to the secluded cove below. She could barely make out the shape of a ship anchored just off shore, waiting to take her to England. She felt no sense of joy. Anton had saved her from the Bastard's spite but she still had to face the King of England's justice.

He cared nothing for her. Even if the King were merciful the years ahead held nothing for her above the pleasure of motherhood. Yet if she were spared to care for her beloved son she would count herself blessed.

Looking back over her shoulder, she could see nothing but dark shapes and shadows, but knew that people would soon be stirring in the cottages they had passed as they rode. In another hour or so servants would be stirring in the castle. They would take Marietta food, believing her to be locked in the tower. When they discovered she had fled once more they would be frightened. Someone would have to wake the Bastard and tell him. No one would want to be the messenger, and that might give her more time.

Marietta regretted that a servant might be made to pay for her escape. Claudette was sure she could placate him…and she planned to take Marietta's place and wed him.

God protect her! Marietta prayed that the Bastard would not make her suffer too much.

Anton had dismounted. He offered his hand to help her down.

'Praise God, we are in time. The ship has sent a boat for us. We must go aboard at once, for we leave with the tide.'

'Yes…'

His tone was so cold, his manner distant. He was still angry with her. She raised her head, holding the tears inside.

The wind from the sea was cool. It whipped about Marietta, blowing her cloak and her hair. She shivered, but it was not so much the wind but her thoughts that had turned her blood to ice water.

Marietta's stomach turned as she felt his fingers grip her arm. He pushed her towards the water and she stumbled, almost falling. Sailors had got out of the rowing boat and were waiting to take their passengers on board.

'You are tired,' Anton said, and bent to sweep her up into his arms. He waded through the shallow water to where the boat waited.

Marietta's tears were very close. The softer note in his voice had almost broken her, and it was taking all her strength to keep from weeping.

A sailor helped her into the boat. She murmured her thanks, staring back at the beach. The light was strengthening with every stroke of the oars but still there was no sign of pursuit. Claudette's potion had worked well.

Marietta climbed the rope ladder to the deck of the ship, Anton's presence behind her giving her the strength to pull herself up. For a moment she stood facing the shore, the wind whipping her hair into her eyes, her cloak hugging her body. She felt so cold, so lonely and afraid.

'You must go below,' Anton told her. 'You are exhausted. Rest, and we shall talk later.'

Marietta inclined her head. As she moved away from him she saw Miguel watching her. For a moment his eyes held some smouldering emotion, and she knew that she had made him angry by insisting on waiting for Anton. She shivered, feeling cold, lonely and lost.

Left alone in her cabin, Marietta lay on the hard cot, listening to the sound of the water lapping about the ship. The light from the small porthole was dim, and it seemed cold and dark, almost like a prison cell. Her skin was prickling with goosebumps. She might soon find herself incarcerated in the King of England's prison.

Marietta closed her eyes, forcing herself to rest. She was exhausted after the long ride, for she had hardly dared to sleep at the castle lest she was attacked. Her eyes flickered and closed as she drifted into a restless slumber, tossing and turning and crying out in her dream.

Though she did not know it, her cheeks were wet with tears.

'I thought you might miss the tide,' Miguel said as the ship weighed anchor.

'It was as well you waited until the last moment, for had we missed the tide I should have been hard pressed to protect the Comtesse until I could find another ship.'

'She would insist on waiting with Sandro! I tried to force her to come with me but she is proud and wilful.' Miguel's gaze narrowed. 'You should be careful of her, Anton. A woman like that is dangerous.'

'Surely you do not believe these stories of witchcraft and murder? Proud and wilful she may be, but the rest is false.'

'There is no smoke without fire…'

'They are but foolish tales. Believe me, Marietta is no more a murderer than she is a witch. The murderer remains at Montcrief.'

'You did not kill him?'

'He lay in a drugged sleep. Had he been awake I should have found satisfaction in making him confess his guilt—but I had a more important mission.'

'You found what you wanted?'

'Yes.' Anton was thoughtful. 'Excuse me. I have something to do below. We shall talk more of this later.'

He walked away, descending the iron ladder to the cabins below. Apart from the incident in the stables, and Marietta's foolish decision to wait for him, everything had gone almost too well. Anton would have preferred a reckoning with the Bastard of Rouen, for he suspected that the man's rage would know no bounds when he woke and discovered what had happened.

He hesitated outside Marietta's cabin. She had suffered badly on her last voyage to England, but there had been a terrible storm that night. This day there were good winds, but no huge waves to toss the ship from side to side. Almost reluctantly, he opened the door and went into the cabin. He hesitated as he saw that she was sleeping.

Her arm was thrown out, her hair spread on the pillows, but she was not peaceful. She was dreaming and it seemed her dream disturbed her.

'Forgive me… I love you…' Marietta cried, and moved restlessly. 'Please do not hate me… I love you…'

Anton frowned. Who was it that she called to in her dreams? Did she have a lover? Was she dreaming like this because she was guilty of some crime? His heart rejected the idea, though his mind told him that women could be faithless. He had believed that he loved Isabella but she had not returned his love. If the letter he had received were true, his wife had betrayed him with another man: the child she had carried when she died would not have had his blood. She had come to his bed that night so that he would not guess the truth. If Isabella could be so false, how could he trust any woman again?

Anton approached the bed. Marietta looked so beautiful. Something inside him reached out to her, despite his resolve not to let her into his heart. He wanted to take her into his arms, to hold her close and kiss away her fears. The temptation to touch her was strong, but he resisted. He should let her sleep, because once they reached England he must take her to London. Anton wished that he could save her the ordeal of facing the King's justice, but he had no choice in the matter. He had been ordered to bring her before the King and must obey. Only if she were cleared of this crime would she be free of the shadow that would otherwise follow her wherever she went.

As he stood staring down at Marietta, her eyes opened.

'What is it? Have we been followed?' She pushed herself up against the hard pillows, her eyes wide with fear.

'We are at sea. You are quite safe now.'

'Are you still angry because I disobeyed you?' Marietta's voice caught with emotion. 'I know you must think me foolish, but I could not leave while you were in danger for my sake.'

'It was foolish, but I am no longer angry. If I spoke harshly it was for your sake, Marietta. Alone, I should have had little trouble finding a ship, but with you...some captains might have refused to take you. I am certain the first thing the Bastard will do would be to send out messengers offering a reward for your capture.'

'I did not mean to cause you so much trouble. If I had stayed inside Lady Claire's home in the first place I should not have been captured. It was foolish to walk alone, but I thought I must be safe at the house.'

'And so you should have been. That was my fault. I should
have guarded you better. It was perhaps a little foolish of you
to go out alone in the circumstances, but I am not angry.'

Marietta swung her legs to the side of the bed and stood up.
She gazed into his face uncertainly. 'Are you not? I did not
expect that you would come for me...'

'You should have known I would. His Majesty ordered me
to bring you to court. I was merely following orders.'

'Oh... I see...' Her voice trailed away. 'I thought when
you came...but that was foolish. You came for the ring, of
course.'

'Do not look like that!' Anton said hoarsely. His need at
that moment was so great that he hardly knew what he did as
he reached out to take her in his arms. 'I would have searched
for you if it took me the rest of my life...' He groaned as he
held her pressed to his chest, burying his face in her hair. Why
did she always smell so sweet? 'I swore that I would never let
another woman near, but you have bewitched me...'

'No!' Marietta pushed away from him. 'Do not say such
things. I have used no spells to bind you to me, Anton.'

'I did not mean with witchcraft.' Anton bent his head and
kissed her. At first his lips gently brushed hers, and then the
kiss intensified, becoming demanding, drawing a response
from her. Her body arched into his, her arms about his neck,
her fingers moving at the nape. 'Only the magic that binds a
man's senses and makes him want a woman so much that it is
agony to deny that need.'

'Anton...' Marietta breathed. Her eyes opened wider as she
sensed his desire. Her body throbbed with need, but she was
afraid to believe. 'Do you truly want me? You want to lie with
me?'

'Yes, more than you will ever know.' He drew away from
her, his mouth loose and soft with aching desire. 'You are
tearing me apart, Marietta. I must take you to the King, but I
will do everything in my power to persuade him that you are
innocent of all the crimes laid at your door. I would not have

you die. You must know I would give my own life to save
yours.'

'No, I should not want that...'

'I will do everything I can. I give you my word.'

'You can do no more...' Marietta touched his face with
her fingertips. Her body seemed to dissolve with wanting and
need, moisture trickling between her thighs. Her lips parted
on a soft sigh. 'Do not torture yourself for my sake. If you are
with me I shall not flinch. I am innocent. Please believe me. I
would never have harmed my husband, though I did not love
him.'

'Did you have a lover?'

'No...' Marietta faltered. Her eyes met his steadfastly.
'There was once someone I loved, but he did not notice me.'

'And now?'

'There is only you. You saved my life. I am grateful.'

'I do not want gratitude...' Anton moved away from her,
turning his back. Her words had broken the spell that bound
him. 'I have things to do. If you need my cure for seasickness
come to me...'

'Anton...'

Marietta watched as he left the cabin. Why had she not
told him that he was the only man she had ever loved? He
had kissed her, told her he desired her—what more could she
ask?

She shook her head, for the answer was foolish. Anton desired her. He might make her his mistress if the King did not
have her condemned as a murderess, but love was merely a
dream.

Chapter Six

Marietta slept for some hours before going on deck. It was close to nightfall when the shores of England came into view, and a cool wind had blown up. She thought there might soon be a storm and was glad that it had not struck while they were still in mid-sea.

Anton's remedy for seasickness had not been needed this time. He had not returned to the cabin, and she would not allow herself to go in search of him. However, he came up to her now, as the ship anchored a short distance from the English beach.

'You look much better, Comtesse Montcrief.'

'Please…my name is Marietta. You called me by my name last night. I would rather you used it always, at least when we are alone.'

'As you wish. We shall go ashore as soon as the boats are launched. This evening we shall stay at the nearest inn. I know of a decent one where we may safely lodge for the night. In the morning we shall leave for London. We shall be two days on the road and will spend least one other night at an inn, perhaps more.'

'Thank you for telling me, my lord.'

'If I am to call you Marietta, you must use my name in return.' He smiled at her ruefully. 'Do not fear me, lady. I mean you no harm, believe me.'

'I have always felt safe with you—even though I did not tell you my name at the start. I was afraid you might think me guilty of murder. I think at first you did?'

'I was not sure,' Anton admitted. His gaze was intense, seeming to search her very soul, 'When I found you on the road I took your part, as I would that of any lady who was being attacked. I have tried to keep an open mind, but now I believe it was the Bastard who murdered your husband. He took the ring the Comte always wore, and must have done so as he lay dying. If it was not there when you were called to your husband's bedside only he could have taken it—and so the finger of suspicion points at him.'

'I am certain that you are right. My husband feared that his bastard might try to kill him and steal all that should belong to my son. For that reason he took precautions meant to protect us. The Bastard of Rouen needs my signature to release my husband's gold from its guardians. He thought that once I was his wife he could force me—or perhaps he would not have needed my agreement then, for a husband's will takes precedence.'

'I do not know how French law stands, but in England your fortune would pass to your husband's care. However, if your husband made you trustee for his son, your signature will be needed until Charles is of age. Without it, Rouen will find it difficult to persuade the goldsmiths to give up what is in their charge. They could be called to account by your son when he reaches his maturity; they will not lightly part with gold trusted to their charge.'

Marietta nodded her agreement. 'Then that is the reason I am still alive. I refused to marry him, clung to my bed and pleaded sickness. I know my ruse made him very angry, but it gave me more time. Claudette promised to help me...' She

Anne Herries

glanced back across the water towards France. 'I pray that he
does not take too harsh a vengeance on her.'

'We left her bound and gagged. She need only plead that
she was overcome.'

Marietta nodded. She remembered Claudette's mad plan to
be married in her dress. Perhaps she had thought better of it.
She hoped so, for she would not be in Claudette's shoes when
the Bastard of Rouen discovered the trick.

'You scheming witch! I swear I'll beat you to a pulp! How
dare you trick me so?'

The Bastard towered over Claudette, his eyes bulging. His
neck was red with rage. He struck her a heavy blow across the
face, sending her staggering back.

'I am your wife…' Claudette cried defiantly. Her eyes were
very bright but she would not weep for mercy. 'Beat me if you
wish. It makes no difference. You have married me, and only
my death can free you—for the church will not let you put me
aside in favour of that witch.'

'Damn you!' The Bastard threatened her with his fist. 'I'll
see you in your grave before I'll let you ruin all my plans.'

'Will you kill your own son?' Claudette asked, facing him
proudly. She placed her hands on her belly. 'My son will be
a legitimate child, and heir to all you have stolen from your
fa—' She got no further for the Bastard rushed at her, seiz-
ing her about the throat. She struggled, putting up her hands
to try and force him back, but he was too strong for her. Her
eyes widened in horror as his grip tightened and she knew
that he meant to strangle her. Her mouth moved in a plea for
forgiveness but no sound came, only a sighing breath. It was
her last.

The Bastard let her lifeless body fall to the ground. He
stared down at her for a moment and then laughed, lifting her
with the toe of his boot and kicking her aside.

'So end any that seek to defy me,' he told the silent, watchful servants. 'Steward, have my things packed and tell fifty

of my men to be ready. We leave for England within the hour.
They will have taken her back with them. This time I shall go
after her myself, and she will follow that whore to hell!'

Marietta looked about the inn bedroom. It was sparsely
furnished, but clean, and would serve her well, the bed softer
than that on board the ship. She imagined it was more comfortable than the cell that might soon be her resting place—
but she would not think of that! If her life was forfeit, so be
it.

Kneeling, Marietta closed her eyes and prayed. Anton had
promised to help her as much as he could, but the King's word
was law. She knew that Anton felt something for her, but was
it merely the kind of passion that men often felt for an attractive woman? If he loved her he would surely help her to run
away instead of taking her to the King? He had said little on
their journey to the inn, seeming lost in his thoughts. Had she
done something to anger him again?

Her thoughts went round and round in circles. God must
know that she was innocent—but would He spare her? She
had just risen to her feet once more when someone knocked
at her door. Having asked that she might be served supper in
her room, she thought it must be a servant.

'The door is not locked...' She turned as it opened and
Anton entered. 'Oh...I thought you were a servant with my
supper.'

'Forgive me. I came to ask if you would sup with me
instead?'

'I am tired. I shall do better alone.'

'Are you angry with me, Marietta?' His gaze was intent on
her face. 'I should not blame you if you were—but I must do
my duty.'

'Why should I be angry? I thought I had angered you once
more. You said little on the way here.'

'I have much on my mind. Perhaps we could talk at
supper?'

'If I asked you, would you let me go back to Claire's house? Would you let me take my son and go away—perhaps to Italy?'

'Do you think it is easy for me to escort you to the King, knowing that he could condemn you to a terrible death?'

'I do not know…' She watched his eyes take fire. 'If it distresses you why will you not help me to run away somewhere I am not known?'

'This is what I wished to talk to you about…' Anton's gaze was intent on her face. 'If Henry clears you of both crimes you will be free of the stain of murder and able to live as a woman of your standing should. Your son will be entitled to make a claim for his inheritance—which means I shall do it with your blessing and in your name, so that you are his guardian.'

'You would do that for us?'

'Yes, of course. If you run away again it will confirm your guilt in the eyes of the world.' Anton's voice was soft, caressing. 'You would never feel safe, Marietta. You would spend your life looking over your shoulder, afraid that someone would recognise you.'

'Yes, that is true,' she said. 'But supposing the King does not find in my favour?'

'This is what we must discuss. Believe me, if judgement goes against you I shall not just stand by and watch you hang. Come down now and we shall make plans…'

'Very well. If you wish it I shall come down.'

'I do wish it. I believe we need to talk in private.'

'We are private here.'

'If I stayed here too long I should think of other things rather than talking.' Anton smiled at her, but the flame in his eyes told her that he wanted her. 'I do not think you are aware that the scent you wear arouses a man's senses.'

'I am not wearing perfume. I washed at the castle. Perhaps the perfume of my special soap lingers in my hair.'

'It does…' Anton's eyes went over her hungrily. 'Come down to supper, Marietta.' He held out his hand to her, a smile on his lips. 'I would not dishonour you, but being here alone with you tempts me beyond bearing.'

'If you want me...' Marietta's cheeks burned but she forced herself to speak. 'I should not deny you. I have been married. I am not a shy maiden to run away from the truth of men's desires. My husband did not often trouble me, but I do not fear physical union. I do not seek to turn you from your duty. All I ask in return is protection for my son...that if I am dead you will try to recover his inheritance.'

'I have already given you my word on that,' Anton said, his voice hoarse. She was so beautiful, and the scent she claimed not to wear was inflaming his senses. 'You do not need to offer me anything, Marietta.'

'Yet I have—I am offering more...' she said, and moved towards the door, turning the key in the lock. 'This is not just for you, Anton. Tomorrow or the next day may be my last day of freedom. I have just two nights left before I must face the King's justice, and I would not spend them alone.'

'You are certain?' Anton moved towards her, taking her into his arms. 'I do not want gratitude, Marietta.'

'It is not gratitude I offer.' She lifted her face to his, her tongue smoothing over her lips, wetting them. They were moist and soft, tempting. 'I want to spend tonight in your arms, and tomorrow night. I want the pleasure I know you can give me...a pleasure I may never know again.'

If she told the truth she would spend every night of her life in his arms. Perhaps he would never love her, but she would be happier as his mistress than she had ever been as her husband's wife.

'God forgive me, I cannot resist...' Anton bent down, scooping her up behind the knees and carrying her to the bed.

He had the smell of horses on him, and his own masculine musk, and it sent her senses spinning. Her body cried out to him, wanting, needing this gift. Perhaps it was not love, but his desire was strong. She felt his heat and it warmed her to the core.

'You are so beautiful…so lovely…'

'Take me, love me for as long as we have,' Marietta whispered. She felt his lips at her throat and arched towards him, her body begging for his touch. Her mouth opened to the delicate flicking of his tongue. She met him, teasing and duelling in a dance of pure pleasure. Drawing him down to her, she gave herself to him, moaning softly as his hands sought out the most intimate places of her body. Heat pooled low in her and moisture ran as she welcomed his touch.

'You are so hot and wet for me,' Anton murmured as he entered her. 'I have burned for you almost from the first.'

Marietta gave a cry of pleasure as he thrust deep into her. Her body arched to meet his, taking him deeper and deeper. Never once had she felt such pleasure in the act of love. He was young, strong and well made, his manhood filling her, stretching her despite the fact that she had borne a child. White heat licked its way through her body. She sighed and screamed, her fingers digging into him as the climax took her.

Anton looked down at the woman as she lay in his arms. He was not sure at what period they had shed their clothes. Was it after the first time he took her or the second? His need had been great, for it was many months since he had lain with a woman. The first time had been too swift, and his desire nowhere near slaked. Even now that he had loved her thrice he still burned with desire, wanted to feel the moist heat of her silken sheath enfolding him once more. At the moment she slept, her lips parted a little. She looked so beautiful, so soft and sweet, that he could hardly keep from kissing her body.

He had thought that once he'd lain with her the need would go, but it seemed stronger. It was almost as if he were bewitched, for he did not remember a night such as this with his wife. He had believed he loved Isabella at the start, but she had not set him on fire as this woman did. Isabella had been a shy virgin. In the beginning she had flinched from him, and he knew that his loving had hurt her at first, but even after their first child was born she had not welcomed his attentions in bed.

Isabella had rejected him, and the few times they had made love it had been cold and passionless. On the other hand Marietta was a passionate woman, her kisses warm, her body willing and welcoming. She aroused feelings in him that he had never known were there.

Anton rose from the bed. Marietta had no bad dreams to disturb her this night. Instead she smiled as she slept, one hand beneath her face. Was she a wanton? She had given herself to him fearlessly—but was he the first besides her husband to receive her favours? If he let down his reserve and took her into his heart would she break it? Jealousy turned inside him like a handful of maggots, eating at his stomach.

He was a damned fool to care! He should simply take what she offered and then move on. Yet he knew that she had found a way to penetrate his being; she was inside him, whether he willed it or no, and he would not be able to forget her as he had intended.

Anton wanted to wake up and find her by his side every morning! He wanted to lie by her side each night and make love to her until they both slept. He was not in love with her. Desire was not love. He wanted Marietta with a passion that surprised and even frightened him, but he would not let himself love her.

Yet if Marietta died it would tear him apart.

She would not die! Somehow he would persuade the King that she was innocent. He must, because he could not lose her.

He felt for the ring in the inner pocket of his jerkin. The Bastard of Rouen had taken it from Comte de Montcrief and the King wanted it returned. Why? He looked at it carefully, turning it over to examine it from all angles. The back of the stone was not open to the light but encased in gold. Anton had

seen rings like this before, and knew that sometimes there was
a little compartment behind the stone. The trick was to open
it, and that was not always easy. He could see no obvious signs
of a catch…

'Anton?'

Hearing Marietta's voice, Anton slipped the ring on his
finger and turned to her. She was smiling at him sleepily, and
as he hesitated she pushed back the covers, inviting him to
return.

'Do not leave me yet, I beg you.'

'I shall not leave you,' he murmured against her ear. In his
heart he knew that he would never want to leave her. Love was
not necessary when she could give him such pleasure!

He breathed in her perfume, the wonderful scent of her
skin, her essence. She needed no other, for her own scent was
intoxicating. Already he could feel himself hardening, feel the
heat building, pooling deep in his belly. He wanted her again.
He would never have enough of her.

'I shall never leave you, little one.'

'Anton…make love to me,' Marietta cried as he began to
kiss and suck at her breasts. Her body arched towards him as
he slid his hand between her thighs. She was ready for him
instantly.

'My precious, wonderful woman,' Anton said, hardly
knowing that he spoke. 'So warm and lovely. I want you more
than I can tell you.'

He plunged deep into her, feeling her wetness as she took
him in. She arched and whimpered beneath him, abandoned
and wild with desire as they moved together. He had never
known such pleasure in a woman. She was beyond anything
he had ever dreamed.

Marietta woke again and saw that Anton was dressing. It
was dawn, and the first rays of light were beginning to creep
into the room.

'I slept so long,' she said. 'I did not mean to sleep at all.'

'We both slept,' Anton told her, and bent to kiss her once more. 'If I stay longer everyone will know I spent the night with you. I must leave, or you will have no reputation left.'

'Do I have any to lose?' Marietta asked, and sat up. Her long hair tumbled over her breasts and fell across her face. Her skin was flushed, her body pliant and sensuous, a feeling of well-being stealing over her. 'It matters little to me, Anton. If the King spares me I shall be proud to be known as your mistress—for as long as you wish.'

'My mistress…' Anton looked at her. 'You have the right to more, Marietta. You are of gentle birth.'

'I was the wife of a nobleman of France, but it brought me little happiness. Last night you gave me more than all the jewels my husband heaped on me. I shall be content as your mistress—and when you tire of me I shall ask for nothing more than a place to live. For my son I ask much more.'

'You love the child, and would see his fortune and rank restored to him.' Anton nodded. 'You have my word that I shall do all I can for him. As for the rest…we shall speak of this when the King has made his judgement.'

Marietta saw the ring on his finger. 'You wear my husband's ring?'

'I was trying to discover its secret. He did not show you?'

Marietta knelt up in the bed, her body pink and warm from sleep. 'Does it have a secret? He never spoke of that to me, though once he said a good friend gave it to him. I wondered why he chose it above all others.'

'Perhaps it is merely sentiment,' Anton said, and tugged at the ring. 'It went on easily but now it will not come off.'

'You must wet your hand with soapy water. If the water is cold it will make it easier, and the ring will slip over the knuckle.'

'Yes, I shall do so when it must come off. For the moment it is safe enough on my hand.'

'Why is it so important?'

'I do not know,' Anton told her. 'I am leaving now, to

order breakfast and prepare the men for our journey. You should dress and come down for we must be on our way soon.'

'Yes, of course.'

Marietta sighed as he closed the door after him. He was still determined to take her to London to the King. Had she hoped that he might change his mind after spending a night in her arms? She had given him pleasure, but his will was still strong. A little chill slid down her spine.

Anton desired her, but his duty to the King still came first.

Anton glanced at the woman riding just ahead of him. She sat her horse well, and pride was in every line of her body. What would he do if the King condemned her to a terrible death?

Wild thoughts of delivering the ring but not the lady had been running through his mind. He could send her to Spain, where he had friends and she would be cared for until he came for her. Surely he had done all that his royal master had asked of him?

Yet it would not sit well with his honour to lie. If he told Henry the truth he could well find himself in the Tower, his head on the block. Marietta would be alone, with no one to help her, and she might be sent back to England to face justice, or worse still to France. Even if they managed to escape the King's justice, others might somehow hear of it and condemn her. Only with the King's pardon could she be free.

No, he would not disobey his King, for that way lay dishonour and despair for them both.

He would plead Marietta's case, use all his influence. Perhaps his father and uncle would add their voices to his if he asked it of them. Henry must listen, for Marietta was innocent of any crime. Anton would never believe her guilty of murder. She was too warm and beautiful to harm anyone.

Had she bewitched him? A smile tugged at the corners

of his mouth as he remembered the night he had passed in her arms. She was beautiful, warm and desirable. He had felt things that he had thought dead in him...desire, warmth... love?

Anton's smile dimmed. No, he would not give her his heart. He had been hurt once, and only a fool offered himself to the fire twice.

The feeling of despair swept over him, causing his expression to become severe, his mouth to set in a hard line. Even when Marietta turned her head to look at him Anton could not smile in response. He had good cause to know that women were faithless. When he lay with Marietta he had come close to giving her his heart and soul, but now the doubts were creeping back into his mind.

Why had she invited him to lie with her? Was it because she hoped that he would help her escape the King's justice? Would she have lain with any man to gain her own way?

He tried to rid himself of the unworthy thought, but it worried at him like a wild dog at a dead sheep, tearing at his guts. Somehow Marietta had got beneath his skin. Even though the doubts had returned to torment him, he could not wait for the night, when they would lie together once more.

Marietta had seen the harsh expression on Anton's face. How could he look at her so if he cared for her? Had the night they spent together meant nothing to him?

Holding her head high, she fought off the tears that threatened. She would not let anyone see that she was unhappy. Anton had made love to her so sweetly, yet now he looked through her, as if their night of love had never been.

Pride came to her rescue once more. She had learned to bear so many things. Anton's indifference was just one more. Perhaps he believed that she had bewitched him...that she was a witch. He desired her, but she had not touched his heart.

Turning her head to glance at Miguel, she surprised a look

that came close to hatred in his eyes. Why did he look at
her so?

On the ship she had sensed that he was angry. What had
she done that he should look at her that way? Miguel became
aware of her gaze and smiled. Perhaps she had misjudged his
look? Perhaps her fear made her see shadows everywhere?

She turned her head away, her heart aching. The journey
seemed long and the day was cold, wind blowing into her face
and whipping her hair into tangles. She pulled the hood of her
cloak over her head, as much to hide her face as to keep out
the cold. It would shame her if Anton realised that she was
breaking her heart for him. Let him think her a wanton if he
would!

When at last they stopped at an inn to take refreshment, it
was Miguel who came to assist her from her horse. His hands
were firm about her waist as he lifted her clear, his fingers
bruising her flesh beneath the thin gown. She looked into his
eyes and saw a spark of something she did not at first understand.

Breaking from his hold, she moved towards the inn, her
head held proudly. She had recently seen that look in another
man's eyes—the Bastard of Rouen had looked at her with a
mixture of desire and resentment.

Surely Miguel did not feel anything of that nature for her?

Could a man want a woman and yet dislike her at the same
time?

Marietta shuddered. She had known what her fate would be
at the mercy of the Bastard. Was Miguel another such man?

No, surely not! He was Anton's friend and his confidant.
He would not lust after her because he must know that Anton
had spent the night with her.

Was that the reason she had seen anger in his eyes as they
rode? Was he jealous because he wanted her for himself? Or
was there another, deeper reason for his hatred? He must believe her a witch!

Perish the thought! A man like Miguel would not hesitate

to see her put to the test. She dared not think what might happen to her if Anton abandoned her.

Perhaps it was all imagination? Miguel had treated her with nothing but the respect due to a lady. Her experience at the Bastard's hands had made her too suspicious. He was Anton's friend and he had helped rescue her from the Bastard of Rouen. She must stop seeing enemies at every turn.

Marietta's thoughts were confused and fearful as she forced herself to eat a little of the bread and meat, and drink the ale provided. The future loomed dark and dangerous. Her instincts told her that even if she escaped the King's justice she would not be safe.

Why was she so cursed? Would she never find the happiness she craved?

When they finally stopped for the night, Marietta was bone-weary. Alone in her room, she brushed her long hair and undressed, getting into bed. She had locked her door, because she was not sure that Anton would come to her and she did not wish anyone else to walk in as she slept.

She lay for a long time, listening to the wind in the eaves. Somewhere a shutter was loose, and every now and then it shut with a bang. Her eyelids seemed heavy, closing even though she tried to stay awake, listening for Anton to come. For a long time Marietta struggled against the weariness but in the end she fell asleep.

She did not hear the soft knock at her door, or Anton's voice as he asked if he might enter. The latch was lifted but the door did not open, and after a moment or two he walked away.

Waking with a start as a loud knocking brought her from her strange dreams, Marietta jumped out of bed and went to the door. It was morning. She must have slept all night! A tavern wench had brought her water to wash, and some bread and honey to break her fast.

'The lord said that he wants to leave as soon as you are ready, lady.'

'Thank you. I shall not keep him waiting long.'

Marietta dressed quickly, washing her face and hands. She combed her long hair back from her face, securing it with jewelled clips. Eating some of the bread and honey, she hastily gathered her things.

Had Anton come to her room after she had fallen asleep? She had meant to stay awake for him, but the journey had tired her too much.

She went downstairs to the hall and saw that Anton was standing there, talking to Miguel. Both men turned to look at her, but neither of them smiled. They looked so serious! She feared that they both expected the worst—that she would be hanged as a murderess.

'Forgive me if I have kept you waiting,' she said. It took all her pride and courage not to give way to tears. 'I was tired and slept deeply.'

'No matter,' Anton said, and his tone was harsh, his manner shutting her out as if that night of passion had never existed. Why did he not smile at her? Did he think she had locked her door against him—or was he accepting that she would soon be a prisoner in the Tower? 'We should reach London this evening—unless we are delayed.'

Marietta looked from one to the other. 'Is there some reason why we might suffer delay?'

'Miguel thought he saw men lurking in the woods when he went to the stream to wash. I do not think it can be Rouen's men, for I doubt he could have caught up with us so soon, but it is a reminder to be on our guard. There are always rogues and bands of roaming beggars ready to set upon the unwary traveller.'

'You think he will come after me?' Marietta studied their faces, wondering at their grim expressions. Was it because they were expecting to be attacked that they looked so grim? The hurt inside her eased a little as she realised that Anton was not angry, but anxious. She had misjudged him.

'He needs you if he is to gain control of your husband's

fortune. I expect he will come.' Anton's expression softened. 'Do not fear him, Marietta. We are a match for the Bastard's men—but we must keep a strict watch lest he take us by surprise.'

'I see…' Marietta's pulse raced. 'What am I to do?'

'First we must get you to court,' Anton said. 'Come, lady, we must leave. It is possible that Rouen's men might catch up to us if they had a fast ship and rode all night.'

'I am a great deal of trouble to you, sir. You must wish that you had never set eyes on me.'

'You speak foolishly,' Anton replied. 'I deal in what is real. Whether I wish it or not, you are here and my responsibility. I must get you safely to court.'

'And then?'

'I have told you I shall plead your case. You must have faith, lady.' Marietta swallowed hard, because the closer they got to London the more anxious she became. 'I am a man of my word, Comtesse. Whatever happens, I shall do my best for your son.'

'Then I am content…' Marietta hesitated, then, as he came to help her mount, 'Forgive me. I meant to stay awake but you did not come.'

'The hour was late. I had much to do.'

A little pulse flicked in his throat. Marietta was not sure if he was angry or the victim of some strong emotion.

She smiled tremulously as he lifted her effortlessly to the saddle, and for a moment he smiled at her, making her heart lift.

'Do not give up all hope. Henry is a fair man, and he likes beautiful women. He may find in your cause—and then he will bring his influence to bear on your son's behalf.'

'Thank you…' Marietta's voice was no more than a whisper.

She glanced at Miguel. He was standing close enough to hear what had been said, and as he returned her look she saw something in his eyes that worried her.

Why did he look at her that way? She could not decide whether he disliked her or felt some resentment because she preferred Anton. Perhaps it was just imagination. Miguel had given her no reason to believe that he felt either desire or hatred for her.

Anton was striding away, mounting his own horse. His manner to Miguel showed that he trusted and relied on him, thought of him as a friend. Marietta was misjudging him, just as she had mistaken Anton's mood earlier, thinking he was angry when he was merely anxious.

Her fear about what would happen in the King's court had made her too sensitive. She must trust Anton and his friends, for there was nothing else she could do.

London was a sprawling and dirty city. The narrow streets were choked with filth: rotting food, excrement and dead rats lying at the side of the road. No one cleared the rubbish away, and consequently the smell in some parts of the city was foul, disease carried in the air. The houses were mostly of timber, with overhanging top storeys that made them look as if they might topple over and fall down. Some of the larger houses belonged to merchants; they had brightly painted signs that showed which guild they belonged to—the guild of shoemakers, metalworkers, cloth merchants, bakers, tailors, goldsmiths or physicians.

There was so much noise, and the roads were clogged with wagons and horses, the iron rims on the wheels clattering over cobbles. Men drove sheep to market, costers plied their wares, calling out to the people who passed by on foot or on horseback. Dogs barked and fought over the offal they found lying in gutters, and the fashionable ran to avoid the slops tossed out from bedroom windows; many held pomanders to their nostrils to block the foul odours.

When Anton's train finally came to a halt in the courtyard of an impressive house, Marietta looked about her curiously. It was far more modern than her husband's castle or her father's

manor in France. There was an undercroft for the horses and
servants, but the upper storeys had paned windows of dull
grey glass crossed with lead.

'You must be tired,' Anton said, as he came to her. His
hands clasped her waist, lifting her from the saddle effortlessly. For a moment her breath caught, for she sensed strong
feeling in him, but he suppressed it ruthlessly. 'I shall send
word to the King that you are here, but I do not think he will
see you until tomorrow at the earliest.'

'Is this your house?' Marietta asked, looking about her.

'It belongs to my grandfather, Lord Melford. You will be
safe here and may rest in peace.'

'Thank you. I am tired, but not—' She broke off as she saw
Miguel staring at her. 'I must spend the night in prayer. If God
has mercy, I shall be exonerated of all the accusations made
against me.'

She turned away and went into the house. A woman in a
grey gown and white cap came to greet her.

'My master sent word. Your chamber is ready, my lady.
I dare say you would like some good hot broth after such a
journey.'

Marietta thanked her. The woman seemed kind and uncriti-
cal. Perhaps she had not been told that Marietta was to face a
trial for her life.

Marietta found the house welcoming and comfortable. The
furniture was good solid English oak, as was the panelling on
the walls of the bedchamber she was shown to. At once she
noticed how much warmer the wooden house was than the
damp stone walls of the older inns. Her husband's castle had
always been cold, even on a summer day, but this had a comfortable feel.

The crimson velvet hangings about the tester bed matched
those at the window, edged with gold braid and draped back
with twisted threads of gilded rope. The floor was also of
wood, and partially covered with a red and gold carpet.
Marietta had always thought carpets too precious to be used

on the floor, for they were costly and often used to adorn tables or hang on walls. She thought that the Melford family must be very wealthy.

She had learned something of Robert Melford's history from Claire. He had been with Henry Tudor when he took the throne of England, and his family had served the monarch since that time, rising from humble beginnings to great power and wealth.

'I will send hot water and food, my lady,' the housekeeper said, and bobbed a curtsey.

Marietta explored the room after she had gone. There was a large armoire, carved and polished, coffers and a padded stool, also a lyre and a music stand. She opened the armoire and saw gowns of costly silk lying on the shelves. They must belong to a lady of the house. Marietta touched one with reverent fingers. As the Comtesse she had owned gowns almost as fine as these, but they had been left behind. All she had was the dress she was wearing. It was travel-stained and looked creased after so many days of being constantly worn. She would ask the housekeeper if something could be done to freshen it, so that she might be presentable when she was brought before the King.

What did it matter what she looked like? A wave of despair swept over Marietta. She clutched the silver cross she wore on a chain about her throat and kissed it, then sank to her knees.

'If I have sinned, forgive me,' she whispered. 'I ask only that the truth be believed...'

Hearing a knock at the door, she called out that the servant might enter, but when it opened she turned to see that her visitor was Anton. She rose to her feet, heart pounding. She wished that he would take her in his arms, kiss her and tell her that he could not give her up—but she was dreaming again! He would not risk his King's anger for her sake.

His dark eyes went over her, his expression grave.

'I came to see that you have all you need. I hope your chamber is comfortable?'

'Yes, quite comfortable. Is this Lady Melford's chamber?'

'Once it may have been. She does not come to London these days. My grandparents stayed here often in the past, I believe, but now they allow my parents to use it. My cousins and uncle stay here too, when attending court. Uncle Harry is most often here, I believe, for he is called to attend the King several times a year.'

'Will the lady whose chamber this is mind that I am using it?'

'This is a guest chamber. It is not a family room these days.'

'I thought…the gowns in the armoire…'

'Are for you. I commissioned them before I left London to return to my uncle's house, for I knew that you had none of your own. If the King allows you to return to my cousin's home, you may take them with you.'

'They are very costly. I cannot repay you…'

'I ask for no payment, Marietta.' He moved towards her, his gaze suddenly intense, burning her with its heat. 'Forgive me for bringing you here. I should have fled to Spain and taken you with me…I could do it still…'

'You fear for my life…' Her eyes opened wide and she gasped, because she sensed his urgency. 'I thank you for the thought, sir—but I shall not allow you to put your own life at risk for my sake. If you disobeyed His Majesty he might punish you—he could punish your family too. Besides, you were right when you said that I should never be free if I did not face the King's justice.'

'Henry is just. I believe he will treat you fairly.'

'Then why do you fear for me? Do you still doubt my innocence?'

Anton stared at her, his face working with passion. 'I do not wish to think you capable of any wickedness, Marietta. However, life has taught me not to trust a woman's smile.'

She felt chilled as she saw the look in his eyes. 'I think someone has hurt you, sir. You are at times bitter…angry. All women are not faithless. My father married me to a man many years my senior. I did not love him as I might a young, passionate lover, but I tried to be a good wife. I denied him nothing he asked of me—and I nursed him faithfully when he was ill. If that makes me faithless or a witch, then so be it.'

'Marietta…I have promised I shall speak to the King in your favour, and I shall keep my word.'

'Even though you do not trust me?' Her clear eyes met his. 'Tell me, do you think I lay with you so that you would help me to evade justice?'

He hesitated, then, 'I do not know.'

'If you do not know there can be nothing more to say, my lord. If you will excuse me, I need to wash away the dust of the road—and then I should like to be alone.'

Anton stared at her, then inclined his head. 'You are angry, and justly so. I am little better than the man you ran from in terror, for I took advantage of your vulnerability. Yet I *do* care…'

She shook her head, unable to bear more of this. 'Please go now.'

Marietta was fighting to hold back her tears. How could he not understand that she loved him?

Someone had hurt him so badly that he could not love or accept love. She had fallen in love with a bright-eyed young man, eager for life and its pleasures. This man was not the man she had enshrined in her memory for so many years. He was honourable, and he would help her, but he could not love her.

Someone had robbed him of the power to love.

Chapter Seven

Anton stood staring out of the window at the long garden that ran down to the river Thames. It had begun to rain, the wind howling through the trees that fronded the river's bank. He felt as if he were being torn apart, little by little. His body ached to know the delight he had found in Marietta's arms, but still his mind would not let him accept her for what she seemed. Her beauty beguiled him, and her smile turned his insides to molten fire, but was she honest? If he trusted her, asked her to be his for ever, would she betray him?

Miguel had made it plain in little ways that *he* did not trust her. He had said nothing outright, couching his words in innuendo and suggestion rather than saying outright that he believed her a witch and a murderess.

Was Anton a fool to feel as he did about her? Despite his doubts and his caution, the scent of her haunted him. He longed to snatch her up on his horse and ride away with her, to keep her safe for the rest of her life. Yet he knew that if he disobeyed the King in this it might mean that his whole family would be slighted and shut out—his own liberty forfeit if he ever returned to England. It was foolish to think of such wild plans. Marietta would never be safe until she had the King's pardon, and with it his protection.

'Your message has been sent.'

Anton turned as Miguel entered the parlour. He knew that his friend hoped they would be rid of the Frenchwoman once she was taken before the King. Miguel was no coward, but he saw no point in spending lives to keep her safe. Indeed, Anton strained the loyalty of his men by asking it of them, for she was no kith or kin to any of them. Only if he offered her the protection of his name could he expect the men to give her their wholehearted loyalty.

'You sent word to His Majesty in my name?'

'It was the reason you brought her here—or has she bewitched you?'

'Yes, perhaps she has,' Anton replied, his eyes thoughtful as he returned his friend's stern gaze. 'I have almost felt that I could find happiness with her.'

'You were betrayed once. Do not put your trust in women, Anton. If you let her rule your heart she will destroy you—as Isabella did.' Something flickered in Miguel's eyes as he spoke Anton's wife's name.

'I swore I would never love again, but this woman…'

'She uses witchcraft to bind you to her. Do not trust her, or you may rue the day you saved her life.'

'Perhaps you are right. I have been wondering…but you did what I ought to have done as soon as we reached London.' Anton's expression softened. 'I do not know what I should have done had you not been my friend when Isabella died.'

'I shall always be your friend. You should marry again, Anton—but choose wisely, a good woman you can trust. The Frenchwoman is too beautiful. Her kind take a man's heart and bring him to his knees. You should choose a plainer, gentle lady.'

'You dislike her very much, do you not—the Comtesse?'

'I do not trust such as she. I fear her magic for your sake.

After Isabella was killed I thought you might lose your mind for a time.'

'Was killed? What do you mean? She tripped and fell to her death...' Anton's eyes narrowed. 'Do you know something I do not? Have you kept something from me all this time?'

'It was a slip of the tongue, Anton. As you say, Isabella slipped and fell...' He made as if to turn away, but Anton crossed the distance between them swiftly, catching his arm.

'What do you know?' he demanded. 'You must tell me!'

'It will do no good...' Miguel faltered, and then inclined his head. 'The servants whispered that she had been pushed. I kept it from you, because it was nonsense...'

Anton's eyes narrowed. 'What else did they whisper?'

'Nothing.' Miguel's mouth tightened as the pressure on his arm increased. 'If you will have it...they thought that you had killed her in a rage when you discovered her faithlessness. Raised voices were heard by a gardener—a man and your wife's, he said. I questioned him and told him he would be dismissed if he continued to slander your name. He ran away and the whispers stopped.'

'I wish that you had told me. I should have liked to question him myself. I did not follow Isabella into the garden that day. I was too angry, too hurt—but she may have been pushed by someone else...' His eyes became flinty. 'If the gardener heard a quarrel it could have been with someone else—her lover. Perhaps he wanted her to run away with him.'

'There was no one in the garden. The man imagined it all.' Miguel's eyes slid away. 'I should not have told you. You will brood on it and the pain will send you mad.'

'No.' Anton frowned. 'I thought I had driven her to her death because I was cruel to her—but if she argued with someone, if she was pushed, it means that he and not I was responsible for her death.'

'The gardener ran off. You could not have questioned him. At the time you were in such despair. I did what I thought right.'

'I know that you acted out of concern for me, and I thank you for it,' Anton said. 'However, in future I want to know everything. I shall send to Spain when this business is over and see if the man can be found.'

'I had a search made for him. I doubt you will find him, but you must do as you see fit.'

'Yes…' Anton nodded. 'Your advice has served me well in the past, Miguel, but in this you were wrong.' He turned back to the fireplace, taking a glass of wine from the mantle. 'I shall not rest until I have the truth…'

Anton remained staring into the fire. He did not turn as the door closed when Miguel left the room.

Marietta was ready when the summons came. She had chosen a dark blue gown, very plain, with a squared neckline and a band of gold braid beneath her breasts. It suited her well, making her look what she was—the widow of a wealthy nobleman. She had only the silver cross she had been wearing the night she was abducted, for her other jewels and possessions were still with Lady Claire. Her hair was dressed simply and allowed to fall onto her shoulders, covered only by a black French cap.

She went downstairs to find Anton waiting for her. He was dressed finer than she had ever seen him, in black and silver, a jewelled sword at his side. She made him a curtsey and he smiled.

'You look very well, lady. I am glad that you did not spurn my gift.'

'I did not wish to wear a stained gown to meet the King of England. It was thoughtful of you to provide gowns for me, sir.'

'I have done no more than was owed you. Everyone is entitled to a fair hearing—and you should wear clothes befitting your rank.' Anton's face was expressionless.

Marietta inclined her head. 'You sent for me. I am ready.'

'Then we should leave. Today you will ride pillion with me.'

'Do you think I might try to escape?'

Anton smiled briefly as he saw the flash of pride in her eyes. 'Many might in your position, but it would be useless. I shall deliver you to the court, as I must—but I have promised to speak for you, and I shall see His Majesty first.'

'I thank you for your goodness, sir.'

Anton hesitated. 'I would do more for you...' It was on the tip of his tongue to say that he wished to offer her his hand and fortune, but at the last he drew back. 'Do not fear too much. I have a little influence, and I shall use it on your behalf.'

'Thank you.' She glanced at his hand. 'I see you no longer wear my husband's ring. Did it come off easily?'

'With some effort. It is in my pocket. I shall give it to the King before he speaks to you.'

'I do not know why it is so important.'

'Perhaps that is a secret known only to your husband and the King of England.'

Marietta's eyes widened. 'My husband went often to court in France. Do you think...?'

'I think it is not for us to speculate.' Anton held out his hand. 'Come, we must leave, for if we are late the King's temper will not improve.'

'Anton of Gifford. We are glad to welcome you back to court, sir.' Henry looked at him. 'We are pleased that you have succeeded in both the commissions we gave you.'

Anton bent his head. 'I hope this is the ring you sought, Sire.'

He held it out to Henry, who took it, twisted the gold-encased cabochon and took something from the cavity inside. He glanced at the small piece of parchment, seemed to read something, and then threw it into the fire with a grunt of satisfaction.

'You did not discover the secret, then?'

'If I had, Sire, I should not have disclosed it to anyone else—but I was unable to solve the mystery.' Anton's tone was bland, his expression unchanging, but there was a hint of something in his eyes.

Henry's gaze narrowed, an expression of anger mixed with appreciation about his mouth. 'We thank you for your loyalty, sir. There are things I would not have my ministers know concerning certain negotiations...if you understand me?'

'How should I understand, Sire? I have heard rumours that you seek an annulment of your marriage to the Queen from the Holy Father, but that is not my affair...'

'Indeed—though others seek to make it theirs. I shall not be thwarted, Gifford. In this I shall have my way—the future of England depends upon it. I need a son!' Henry had dropped the royal *we* to speak plainly.

'Yes, Sire. A King must have a son to follow him.'

'Then you understand that this business must remain within this room?'

'You have my word as a gentleman and nobleman of England.'

'Then this is done...' Henry's gaze narrowed as he slipped the ring inside his jerkin, returning to his royal stance. 'You have served us well, sir. Have you a request of us?'

'Yes, Sire.' Anton met his eyes. 'There is something I would ask of you...'

Marietta looked around the small chamber where she had been told to wait. The walls were hung with rich silk tapestries, perhaps from France, she thought, for the work was very fine. There was but one small table in the room, and a Bible lay on its surface.

Had it been placed there to comfort or to threaten? The priests threatened the pain of everlasting hell for the crimes of murder and witchcraft. Marietta wished that she might sit down. Her throat was dry, and she would have liked a cup of water or ale, but there was no one to ask. She felt like running away, but she suspected there were guards outside the door. She would not get far, and it would seem to prove her guilt. She must wait and pray.

She walked to the window to look down, and saw several ladies walking together. They were laughing and talking, clustered about one very beautiful lady who seemed to be the centre of attention. The sun had decided to shine and the rain of the previous day had gone.

How much longer was she to be kept waiting? Marietta paced the floor, her nerves as tight as the archer's string. Anton had been with the King for so long. When would it be her turn—and would His Majesty listen?

She turned in sudden fright as she heard footsteps, and her heart raced when she saw the servant. He did not smile as he beckoned to her and she feared the worst.

'Will His Majesty see me now?'

'You are to come this way, lady.'

Marietta followed him down the narrow passage. He stopped in front of a pair of large doors, which were gilded and embossed with symbols of royalty. The man pushed open the doors and indicated that she should go in, closing them behind her with a sharp bang that made her jump.

At first glance she thought that the room was empty. It was richly furnished with hangings and heavy furniture; some pieces were fashioned of walnut and carved, the legs twisted in the Dutch manner, some oak, plainer, and clearly English. Then, as she hesitated, a heavy curtain moved at the far end of the room and a man entered.

She knew at once that this must be the King of England. He was a tall, well-built man, handsome, with red hair and beard, his clothes richly embroidered with jewels. As he came nearer she was aware of his eyes on her. For a moment she met them, then she sank into a deep curtsey, her head bent.

'So you are the Comtesse Montcrief. Your husband was our good friend, *madame*. We are glad to have been of service to you. Sir Anton tells us that he snatched you from the bastard who stole your son's inheritance.'

'Yes, Sire. I owe everything to Sir Anton.'

'He has performed a service for us. In return he asks that we give you a fair hearing—which we are inclined to do. Tell me, *madame*—did you cause your husband's death?'

Marietta's head came up, her face proud. 'No, Sire. I was a good and faithful wife to the Comte, and nursed him through more than one illness. Without my nursing he would have died last winter. Why should I take his life? He was good to me, and I had no reason to want him dead.'

'We know he appreciated your skills and your worth as a wife,' Henry said. 'There have been charges of witchcraft made against you, *madame*. Some say that you could not have saved your husband's life if you had not used the black arts—what do you say to this charge?'

'If the use of herbs and devoted care is witchcraft, Sire—I am guilty. I used nothing that cannot be readily found in the hedgerows or the woods.'

'And you did not use incantations to aid his recovery?'

'Had I known one that would save his life I would not have hesitated, but I am not a witch and I have no magic—just a little skill with herbs and healing.'

'It is as we imagined. Your husband was no fool, *madame*. He praised you in his letters to us. We thought you innocent, and that was the reason we asked Sir Anton to find you and bring you here. Your husband, the Comte of Montcrief, has done service for us in the past. Tell us how we may serve you. Sir Anton tells us the Bastard of Rouen has seized the castle and will take your son's inheritance if he can.'

'I would have justice for my son, Sire. My husband lodged his gold with the Jews, who are court goldsmiths in France. Rouen seeks to gain control of it, but it belongs to my son.'

'And it shall be secured to him if England's influence weighs with our brother of France. Your home is another matter. We do not approve of fighting amongst the barons, and to instigate a siege at Montcrief would cost many lives. However, we shall see what can be done.' Henry held out his hand to her. Marietta curtsied once more, and kissed his ring—very like that her husband had worn, she noticed.

'You are gracious, Sire.' She hesitated. 'Am I acquitted of all charges?'

'There were none to face. We had you brought here for your safety. You may remain at court if you wish—unless you have somewhere to live?'

'My father's cousin, Lady Claire Melford, would take me.'

'The choice is yours. You are free to leave, but we would see you again in the future—and the lady you claim as cousin. The Earl of Rundle and his wife are always welcome at court.'

Marietta curtsied deeply. 'I am so grateful, Sire. I shall hope to visit the court with my kinsfolk another time.'

Henry waved a hand at her. 'Go, then. You may attend the banquet with Sir Anton this evening if you choose.'

Marietta thanked him again, curtsied, and left the chamber. Outside the door, she found Anton waiting for her. His eyes searched her face and he nodded.

'Henry has used his good sense. You are acquitted.'

'I am free to stay at court or go.'

'And you choose?'

'I shall go back to your uncle's home. My son is there, and I am anxious for his safety. Before that…' She shook her head. 'His Majesty said there was a banquet at court this evening.'

'I am to take you with me?' Anton inclined his head. 'If you wish to attend?'

'Yes, I should like that,' Marietta said, suddenly shy and unsure. 'If you would wish to take me?'

'We accede to Henry's wishes,' Anton said, his expression giving her nothing. 'He has been gracious, and it would be foolish to ignore his command.'

Marietta looked at him. 'Afterwards, you will take me to the Lady Claire and my son?'

'Of course. Why should I abandon you now?'

'I thought…I have already been a great deal of trouble to you…' Her eyes searched his face, but she could not read what was in his mind. 'You spoke once of your daughter. Do you not wish to go to her?'

'In good time. Madeline is safe with my mother for the moment. In the other matter, I have but done my duty. Henry commanded me to bring you to court. I acted in his name. You have nothing to thank me for, Comtesse.'

'My name is Marietta.'

'It would not be fitting now. His Majesty has seen fit to restore your good name. You are the Comtesse de Montcrief and must be treated as your rank deserves.'

'I see…' Marietta shot a glance at his profile as they left the palace. She sensed a barrier between them. Anton looked stern, a little pulse flicking at his temple. It was quite clear to her that nothing had changed. The King had declared her innocent because of his friendship with her husband—but that did not mean that Anton Gifford believed it. She knew that he desired her, but did he feel anything more?

She sighed inwardly. If he cared for her his reaction would surely have been very different.

Anton refrained from looking at the woman who rode her horse so proudly. He had wanted to sweep her into his arms and shout with joy when she told him she was acquitted, but his conscience had held him back.

She was innocent of murder, but he was not. His anger had driven Isabella to her death that day—at least that had always been his belief. Miguel's suggestion that she might have been pushed down those steps had set him wondering. If Isabella had been pushed, it meant that he was not directly guilty of her death. Yet there must have been a reason for her murder…

* * *

Marietta glanced round the large room. It was filled with richly dressed courtiers, light flashing from the magnificent jewels they wore about their person. She had been seated with some other ladies at a table close to the high board, where the King and his favoured nobles were seated. Anton had been so honoured, as had the striking woman Marietta had noticed in the garden earlier that morning.

She touched the arm of a young woman sitting next to her. Bertha had been friendly when they met, and she felt able to ask a question.

'Who is that lady sitting two places from the King? He seems to look at her often, and she is beautiful—her face is lit up from inside when she smiles.'

Bertha giggled. 'Do you not know that she is Anne Boleyn? She is His Majesty's favourite of the moment. Some say that he will marry her.'

'I thought he had a queen?'

'He does, but…' Bertha shook her head. 'You should not ask such questions.'

Marietta looked at the young woman sitting at the high table. She was beautiful, but also proud. Did she think that the King would put his wife aside to marry her? The church forbade such things. Marietta did not see how it could be done, though it would be easy enough for the lady to become his mistress. Perhaps she was too proud for that. But a divorce might rock the security of the English throne.

It was not for Marietta to judge what the King did. She put the thought aside and glanced round the room once more, becoming aware that she was being watched. Miguel's eyes were on her. His expression was so severe that she wondered if he hated her—yet why should he?

Had he hoped that she would be imprisoned and condemned as a witch? Was he angry because she had been released?

Marietta turned away. Course after course of rich food had

been brought to table as the evening wore on. Feeling it wiser not to touch some of the richer dishes, Marietta had supped but lightly. She enjoyed the entertainment, laughing at the antics of the jugglers and the fool. He was a dwarf, and ran about the room hitting people with a pig's bladder that was tied to a stick and filled with air.

Towards the end of the evening musicians began to play, and some people got up to dance. Marietta declined one offer with a young, rather handsome gentleman, preferring to watch. In her heart she hoped that Anton might ask her, but he was in deep conversation with His Majesty. At one point he left the hall with the King.

Marietta felt uneasy. Had he forgotten her? What ought she to do? She was not sure that she could manage to find her way back to Lord Melford's house alone. She wandered over to a window and glanced out. The view was of a secluded courtyard. In the moonlight it looked mysterious and peaceful. However, her reverie was interrupted as a young page approached her.

'You are the lady Comtesse de Montcrief?'

'Yes. Do you have a message for me?'

'Sir Anton Gifford awaits you in the courtyard, *madame*. I am to take you to him.'

'Thank you…' Marietta smiled her relief. She had been foolish to worry. Anton would not forget her. 'Please lead the way. I shall follow you.'

The page started off, and Marietta followed. She had thought he might mean the courtyard overlooked by the Great Hall, but it seemed he did not for he led her down a long dark passage which seemed to go on endlessly and take several twists and turns. Eventually they reached a door, which the page indicated.

'The courtyard is beyond, *madame*. You will find the gentleman waiting.'

As he turned away, Marietta noticed a smirk on his face. Did he imagine she was meeting a lover in secret?

She opened the door and peered through it. The night air was very cool, but the moon was full. Somehow reassured because of the light, Marietta ventured outside.

'Anton…are you here?' she asked, for although there was a small fountain, a stone bench and what looked like beds of rose bushes and lavender, as yet not in bloom, she could see no one. The courtyard was bordered with high walls. 'Anton… I have come…' She took a few steps into the open space and then heard the door slam behind her. Suddenly fearful, she rushed to the door and tugged at the latch; it would not budge. Someone had locked it from inside. 'Open this at once!' she cried, and beat on the door with her fists. 'I am locked out here and it is cold…'

No answer came. Marietta felt an icy trickle down her spine. She was trapped, because she could see that there was no other way out of the courtyard. Someone had sent the page in Anton's name to lure her here—but why?

She shivered, feeling the cold of the night air begin to seep into her flesh. Who had trapped her here? Was it the Bastard of Rouen? A moment or two of reflection told her that had it been he she would already have been dead or his captive. Someone else had done this—but who could it be?

Marietta began to walk around the perimeter of the small courtyard, hoping that she might find a gate, or some other way of leaving it. However, there was none. Someone had planned this well, but why shut her out here? Was it merely to frighten her, or were they hoping that she would remain here all night? She shivered, crossing her arms over her breasts, hugging herself to try to keep warm. She must move about or she would not be able to bear the cold. If only she had found a servant to send for her cloak—but she had not given it a thought. Usually Anton did these things for her. He had taken care of her and she ought not to have doubted him.

Tears caught in her throat. Anton was often stern, and sometimes harsh, but he was a man of honour. Surely he would look for her when he realised that she was missing?

She went back to the door and banged on it again and again, calling out for help.

'Please help me. I am locked out…' she cried. 'Please help me…'

'I shall wish Your Majesty goodnight,' Anton said. 'The hour is late, and the Comtesse will wonder where I am.'

'Forgive us, Gifford. We have kept you too long. The lady will begin to think that you have deserted her.'

Anton bowed and left him. He was thoughtful as he returned to the Great Hall to look for Marietta. He had made up his mind that he would ask her to marry him. She needed the protection of an honourable man, and their night of passion had shown him that she would be a wonderful wife. His hesitation had been because he was afraid to trust again, but now he decided that he must take the chance. No other woman would satisfy him. He must have Marietta or no one.

Glancing round the huge hall, he saw that it was almost empty now, for people had begun to drift away after the King's departure. A brief glance told him that she was not here, but he saw Miguel talking to one of the ladies and went up to him.

'Have you seen the Comtesse?'

'Not for some time,' Miguel replied. 'Perhaps she tired of waiting and went home?'

Anton's gaze narrowed for a moment, then he shook his head. 'She would have no idea of how to get there. She would have waited for me to take her.'

'Perhaps she went to meet someone—a lover?'

'She knows no one here. You wrong her, Miguel.' Anton frowned. 'She may have wandered off looking for me and got lost. This place is a rabbit warren if you do not know it well. We must search for her. I shall question the servants. Someone must have seen where she went…'

'I can do that for you if you have more important business.'

'You can search outside the palace with some of my men.' Anton looked round. 'I shall start with that serving woman over there. She looks to be ordering the others and may have some sense...'

He left Miguel and went over to a woman dressed in a grey gown made of good cloth, who seemed to be ordering the servants as they began to clear away the debris and discarded wine cups left lying about by the courtiers.

'Good evening, madam. I need to find a lady. This is her first visit to the palace and I think she may have got lost. Can you help me to search for her?'

'Yes, sir,' the woman said. 'I will summon the pages that have not yet retired. They are always about, and see much that happens. One of them should have seen her. Can you tell me the lady's name?'

'She is Comtesse de Montcrief and she is under my protection.'

'I shall help you all I can, sir.' She beckoned to a young woman and spoke to her, then turned back to Anton. 'Bethany will take you to the room where the pages wait until they are required or given leave to go to bed. I am certain one of them will know something.'

'Thank you.' Anton took a silver coin from his jerkin. 'I am grateful for your help.'

He was frowning as he followed the younger woman. Why had Marietta left the hall? Surely she had known that he would return for her?

How long had she been here? Marietta hugged herself to keep out the chill wind. She had walked round and round the courtyard a hundred times, every now and then going to try the door and call out for help. No one had come, and she thought that perhaps this courtyard was seldom used. She might be here for a long time.

Supposing no one came tonight? Supposing no one came for days?

Fear rippled through her. She was close to tears, but crying would not help her. If the walls had not been quite so high she might have tried to climb them, but there was nothing to help her gain a foothold.

She was trapped! She might die here!

Fighting her fear, Marietta went back to the door and tugged at the latch. It moved, and the door opened. She stared at it in disbelief. Why had it not opened before? For a moment she hardly dared to go inside, fearing that someone might be waiting behind the door to pounce on her.

But she must go in or she would freeze to death! Venturing in, Marietta found that the torches which had lit their way here had guttered in their sconces on the wall and gone out. She had been locked outside for what seemed a very long time. She was shivering as she felt her way along the passage, touching the rough stone of the walls. At the end of the hall were some stairs. Had they come this way? She could not recall stairs, but she could see no other way to go.

At least now there was a window and more light. At the top of the stairs there were passages to the left and the right. She took the left. Inside it was a little warmer than outside in the courtyard, but she was still so cold that it was all she could do to stop her teeth chattering.

At the end of the passage there were more stairs, this time leading down. Marietta stood undecided, and then heard the sound of voices from below. Perhaps she could find someone who would tell her the way back to the Great Hall.

She ran down them and saw that she had come into a chamber that was full of men. They were drinking and laughing, some of them in a state of undress. As she entered they turned to stare at her and fell silent.

'I am lost,' she said. 'Can you please tell me the way to the Great Hall?'

'I can show you more than that, lady,' one of the men said in a ribald manner, and made a gesture that made Marietta recoil in horror. As he moved towards her she gave a scream of dismay and ran back the way she had come. As she fled she could hear the drunken laughter of the men. Did they think she was a whore, come in search of some sport?

She ran back along the passage, feeling close to tears. How was she ever to find her way out of this maze? Hearing voices, she stopped, her heart racing. Lights were coming towards her, but this time she was nervous of calling for help.

She stood poised for flight, though she hardly knew which way to turn. The lights were very near now, and she saw that a man and a pageboy were approaching her.

'Please…' she began, and then faltered as she saw the man's face. 'Anton—thank God. I was lost and…'

'Marietta?' he cried. 'Where on earth have you been? I have had the palace searched for you. Why did you not wait for me?'

'I was told you awaited me in a courtyard and I went to meet you. But you were not there and the door was locked behind me.'

'The door was locked behind you? How could that be?' Anton's disbelief was in his eyes. 'Was someone with you?'

'A page took me there, but left before I went into the courtyard. The door shut with a bang and I could not open it. I was trapped for a long time—and then…it was suddenly no longer locked.'

'You panicked and could not open it at first,' Anton said with a frown. 'You say a pageboy told you I had asked you to meet me—but when I spoke to the pages none knew of this…'

Marietta lifted her head, looking into his eyes. Why did he always doubt her?

'I speak the truth, sir. I was summoned to meet you, but when I got there you were not waiting for me. The courtyard had high walls and I could not leave it…' Her eyes sparked with temper. 'It was bitterly cold. Do you think that I would linger there longer than need be? The door was locked. I paced the courtyard because I was so cold, but I tried the door many times. It was always locked, and then suddenly it was not.'

Anton reached out and touched her arm. Discovering that she was icy cold to the touch, he took off his cloak and wrapped it around her shoulders.

'I sent you no message,' he said, and his eyes were narrowed, thoughtful. 'If you were trapped, as you say, someone played a silly trick on you, my lady.'

'Perhaps—though why would someone play a jest on me? I hardly know anyone at court.'

'I cannot think why anyone would do such a thing. It was a dangerous jest, for if you had remained there much longer on such a night you might have died. We must hope that you do not take harm, Comtesse.' He took her arm, his thoughts of asking her to be his wife pushed to one side in his concern. 'Come. You are shivering with cold. I must call off the search and get you home…'

Safe in her bed, with several quilts to keep her warm, Marietta fell into a deep sleep. She slept despite the disturbing dreams that caused her to cry out once or twice, and she did not wake to see the man who watched over her. She was not aware that he stretched out on a coverlet at the foot of her bed, leaving just as the first light began to creep in through the shutters.

Waking some time later, to find a maid had brought her warmed ale, hot rolls, butter and honey, Marietta was aware that she had a sore throat. She had not escaped completely unscathed from her ordeal of the previous night, and knew that if she had not been released when she had been, she might well have taken a chill that would lead to a fatal illness.

She put two spoons of the honey into her warmed ale and drank it. The drink was soothing and eased her throat, though not completely. When she tried to get out of bed she felt a little dizzy. The unpleasant feeling passed in a moment or two, and she decided that she would ignore her feeling of being unwell.

She was not certain that Anton believed her story. He probably thought she had been to meet one of the courtiers in the courtyard and turned cold, for he did not seem to have a high opinion of her.

Perhaps because she had given herself to him on the journey here he thought her a whore?

Tears stung Marietta's eyes but she blinked them away. Short of confessing that she had fallen in love with him the first time they met on the Field of the Cloth of Gold, she could not explain her feelings. He would probably think it the fancy of a foolish girl. Besides, to confess her love for a man who clearly despised her would shame her. She was shamed by the wantonness she had shown as they travelled to London. Had she not genuinely believed that she was to die as the murderess of her husband, she would never have done it.

However, she could not take back what had happened. She must simply retain her dignity and hope that once Anton had returned her to her kinswoman she need never see him again.

Chapter Eight

'The Comtesse de Montcrief says that she was sent a message that was supposed to come from me,' Anton said, his eyes meeting Miguel's across the room. 'She claims that she was trapped in a courtyard with no means of escape for a long time—and then the door was suddenly unlocked.'

'The wind must have blown it,' Miguel said. 'It stuck, as doors will at times. What else could it be?'

'But who sent her the message?'

'Can you be certain anyone did?'

'You think she went to meet someone—a man?'

'I do not think anything about the lady, Anton. She is not my concern.'

'No, she is mine. I brought her here, and until she is safe with my uncle and her cousin I must care for her. Had she died it would have been a stain on my soul. I cannot bear the guilt of yet another death.'

'You blame yourself too much. Isabella fell to her death that day. You were not there to see it, but she ought not to have been careless in her condition, for she carried your child.'

'If the child was mine...' Anton's eyes darkened. 'You

know of the letter that claimed she was faithless…that her child belonged to another?'

Miguel looked at him, seeming almost wary. 'You asked the truth of her—what did she say?'

'She denied it, and ran from me in distress. You know this, Miguel. I have spoken to you of my guilt, for you are my closest friend. If I cannot confide in you, who may I confess my sins to—other than the priest?'

'You know I am always here for you.' Miguel's dark eyes were unfathomable as he looked at Anton. 'Do you believe her innocent or guilty—I speak of Isabella?'

'For a while I thought her guilty, and it tore the heart from me, but when I saw the stricken look in her eyes I thought I had misjudged her. She ran from me in such distress. I was never sure if she had deliberately thrown herself down those steep steps.'

'I am certain it was an accident.'

'Then you do not believe that she quarrelled with someone and was pushed to her death—whether by design or accident?'

'Who would she quarrel with—and why? The servants adored her. You were the only one to think ill of her—and you were not there.'

'Do you believe that, Miguel?' Anton's gaze narrowed. 'Or do you think me guilty of yet another sin?'

'Have I given you cause to think so? I told you that I had the gardener searched for. Had he been found I would have brought him to you. If someone else killed her they should be found and punished.'

'I loved her. Even though I believed she had betrayed me, I loved her. My words were cruel that day, but I could never have harmed her—do you believe me?'

'Yes, of course.' Miguel could not quite meet his eyes. He brushed a speck of dust from his black velvet jerkin. 'When do we leave for the Earl of Rundle's house?'

'Tomorrow, if the Comtesse is well enough. It will be a

wonder if she has taken no harm from her ordeal. If I should discover the perpetrator of this evil trick I shall punish him, Miguel.'

'I think you should be careful how much you believe of what that lady says. She has been cleared of murder, but she is not as innocent as she would have you believe.'

'What makes you say that, Miguel?'

Miguel stared at him for a moment and then shook his head. 'I have no proof. I merely sense that she is trouble. Do not ask me why. Men have already died for her sake, and they won't be the last.'

'In that you speak truly,' Anton said. 'I have requested an escort from His Majesty when we leave the city. I expect that Rouen may try to waylay us on our return. He is unlikely to give up without a fight. He wants her, dead or alive. Mayhap I should have killed him as he slept. No matter—I shall guard her well. I do not intend to have her snatched from my care again.'

'And when we reach our destination?'

'I am not certain,' Anton said. 'There is much to consider. My duty ends when she is safe in my uncle's care, but the future is not clear. I mean to settle here in England, but I think that you may wish to return to Spain?'

Miguel looked at him oddly. 'Are you telling me that you no longer have need of my service?'

'You are my friend, Miguel. I merely suggest that it may not suit you to continue in my household if I remain in this country. I mean nothing more.'

Marietta went downstairs when she was dressed and ready. She wandered about the house, feeling restless, and finally settled in the back parlour overlooking the garden. She would have liked to go out, but her throat was still sore and she did not wish to risk making herself worse. They would soon be leaving for her kinswoman's home, and she wanted to be ready when Anton gave the word.

She was sitting lost in thought when the door opened and someone entered. Turning, she saw that it was Anton and rose uncertainly, wondering what he would say to her.

'How are you, *madame*?'

'My throat is a little sore. Otherwise I think I have taken no harm. I was fortunate.'

'Yes…' Anton's dark eyes were on her. 'Have you given much thought to the future?'

'Claire told me that I should be welcome to stay with her. I do not know what more I can expect. His Majesty promised that he would do what he could for me, but I am not sure it would be safe to return to France. Even if Rouen were no longer at the castle there might be others who coveted my son's possessions.' She hesitated, then, 'My husband told me that I should find an honest man to marry, a man who would stand guardian to my son and see that he prospers. Perhaps I shall find such a man, but I am not sure it is possible. Some will think me tarnished by scandal, no matter what the King says…'

'It is possible that you may find some still have doubts,' Anton told her and looked grave. 'That cannot be changed. I am sorry for it, Marietta, but there is little I can do.'

She raised her head proudly. 'Why should you do anything more than what you have promised? I am already too much in your debt.'

'You owe me nothing, lady.'

'I owe you my life. The King may help my son regain his fortune, but had you not come to my rescue I might be dead.'

'I do not ask for gratitude.'

'What *do* you ask of me?' Marietta held her breath, hardly daring to look at him.

'There might be something…' Anton's gaze narrowed. 'I have had it in mind for a while to offer you marriage. As your husband I should be the guardian of your son and his fortune—and I would make it my business to recover his inheritance and to protect it for him until he came of age.'

'You are asking me to marry you?' Marietta stared at him, her heart beating wildly. 'Why do you offer me marriage? You have already promised to protect my son's inheritance. I cannot expect more of you.'

'You ask me why?' Anton frowned. 'I believe we should deal well together, Marietta. I know you are a good mother, for I have seen you with your child. I believe you might find it in your heart to offer love to my daughter. She has been too long without a mother…'

Marietta looked into his eyes. Was his concern for his daughter the only reason he wished to wed her?

'You are generous, sir…' Her heart raced, because a part of her longed to accept his offer. It was what she wanted more than anything in the world but she was uncertain of his feelings. If he could never love her she might find it too painful to be his wife. 'I am honoured that you should ask me, and grateful for your promise to help my son recover his inheritance, but…I am not worthy of such a marriage. Even though the King has pardoned me the shadow of accusation hangs over me. There will always be those who think that I am a witch and that I murdered my husband.'

'Only fools or bitter minds will think it.' Anton took her hand. 'Let me make you safe, Marietta. As your husband I can protect and care for you so much more easily than if we live apart.'

'Would it help you with your daughter if I agreed?'

'I believe you might bring a smile to her face again. She is too serious these days.'

'You must give me a little time to decide. I had not expected this, Anton.' She lifted her eyes to his face. 'You must know that I feel…kindness towards you…'

'I know that you are warm and beautiful, and it would make me happy to spend my life protecting you and our children.'

'I shall give you my answer when we reach Lady Claire's home—if that is agreeable to you?'

'Yes, of course.'

He looked disappointed, and Marietta wanted to tell him that she had changed her mind and would marry him this instant but something held her silent.

'I am content to wait for your answer.'

'Thank you. When do we leave London, sir?'

'Tomorrow morning, soon after first light—if you are well enough to begin the journey?'

'I shall be well enough. The sooner I am back with my son the better.'

'Yes, I imagine you must miss him?'

'I love him dearly.' Marietta smiled. 'He is all I have in the world.'

'Yes, I dare say he is. I believe you are a good mother, as well as a good wife.' Anton's thoughtful eyes studied her. 'Is there anything you wish to purchase in London before we leave? His Majesty gave me five hundred silver pieces for you—so that you might purchase clothes and replace those possessions you were forced to abandon in your flight.'

She stared at him in shock. 'Five hundred… That is a fortune. I cannot take so much.'

'You would not offend His Majesty by refusing his gift?'

'Oh…no…' Marietta looked anxious. 'Do you think I should accept such a gift? I have jewels I could sell.'

'You must keep them for the future, Marietta. Accept what has been given you. I am sure there must be things you would like to order? We could visit the merchants this afternoon, and anything you purchase can be sent on with goods I have ordered myself.'

Her cheeks were faintly flushed, her look oddly shy, making her, had she known it, more beautiful than ever.

'I do not think I thanked you adequately for the gowns you provided for my use. If I may keep them I need little more for the moment—though I would like a lyre. Mine was destroyed, and it is my pleasure to play and sing when I am alone.'

'Then we shall purchase a fine instrument, and anything else you see that takes your fancy. The few gowns I had prepared for you are a mere trifle.' Anton smiled oddly. 'Please do not refuse my poor gift.'

'They are beautiful. I could not have chosen better myself. If you will wait while I put on my cloak, I shall be ready in a few minutes.'

'Wear a fur muffler to keep your throat warm. I believe you will find one amongst your things. I do not wish you to catch a chill.'

'No, for then we should be forced to stay in town longer.' Marietta smiled at him. 'Excuse me, sir. I shall not keep you long.'

Her heart felt lighter as she ran up the stairs to her bed-chamber. It was years since Marietta had been taken to visit the shops of merchants; her husband had always ordered anything she needed and had it delivered to the castle. To be able to choose what she wanted was a rare treat and she felt a little thrill of excitement.

She might buy some silk for embroidery, for then she need not sit idle, and material to make clothes for her son, combs for her hair, silver trinkets that would replace the others she had left behind—and of course a lyre. All of a sudden she could think of so many things she needed.

'You must be weary of shopping,' Marietta said when they returned to the house late that afternoon.

They were both carrying some parcels, though the bulk of what she had ordered would be sent on a wagon with goods Anton had ordered for himself and his family. He had taken her to all the best merchants in Spitalfields and Cheapside, encouraging her to spend recklessly. At first she had been afraid that she might spend more than she had, but Anton had laughed and said he would advise her if she became too

reckless. He had said nothing more, merely watching her pleasure with a look of indulgence that made her feel almost shy.

'It was so generous of you to give up your time, for I think
you must have more important matters. The Comte always
ordered my things and had them sent to the castle.'

'Is it not more amusing to choose what you want?' Anton
asked, arching his brows. 'You could not decide between the
colours you admired easily, so how could anyone else know
which you preferred?'

'I was pleased to have new gowns. I did not mind that
my husband chose for me—though my father always let me
choose before I was married.'

'Your father was a nobleman?'

'Baron Villiers. He was not a rich man, and lost much of
what he had in unlucky investments, I believe. It was fortunate
that Comte de Montcrief offered for me, or my father might
have lost all.'

'So it was a marriage of convenience?'

'My father thought it a good one.' Marietta dropped her
eyes. 'I believe I was fortunate.'

'The Comte treated you well?'

'He was kind to me.'

Anton nodded, looking at her thoughtfully. 'Marietta
Villiers… I have sometimes wondered if we met before that
day I won the silver arrow?'

'Yes, we did. I remembered you even then, because you
saved my life, though you had forgotten me…' Marietta's eyes
challenged him. 'It was some years ago. The day two kings
met on the…'

'Field of the Cloth of Gold…' Acceptance dawned in his
eyes. 'How could I have forgotten? I knew that I had seen you
before, but the memory eluded me. I thought once you might
be that girl, but so much had happened in the years between,
and you have changed, Marietta.'

'I am older, and my waist is a little larger…' she said ruefully. 'You should not remind a lady of her age, sir. It is not gallant.'

'I meant no disrespect. You were a pretty girl then, but you have become a woman—a very beautiful, desirable woman.'

Something in Anton's eyes at that moment made her heart leap. She felt heat pool inside her, and desire trickled through her veins like molten lead. Her lips parted on a sigh. She longed for him to give her some sign that he felt the same way…to take her in his arms and kiss her. If he truly cared for her she would be so happy to be his wife!

'I…thank you,' she said a little shyly. It was on the tip of her tongue to say that she would wed him, but the words would not come.

'Marietta—' Anton began, but broke off as he heard foot-steps and Miguel entered the hall. 'You should go up now, lady. We have a long journey, and I do not wish to waste time in the morning. You should see that the servants have packed all you need.'

His words were a curt dismissal that made Marietta turn away. How could he go from gallant lover to the reserved man she hardly knew so suddenly? She met Miguel's cold stare and wondered what was in his mind. He had told her that he was glad the King had pardoned her, but she was not certain he meant it.

'Yes, I would not wish to keep you waiting,' she said to Anton. 'Excuse me, gentlemen. I shall dine in my room this evening, for I wish an early night. I am tired and I would rest.'

Marietta found that she slept better than she had expected that night. In the morning she woke refreshed and ready for the journey. When she went down to the courtyard she discov-ered that Anton's men were assembled, also some ten others that she did not know who all wore the King's livery. His Majesty had sent the escort he promised.

Anton was engaged in conversation with the captain of the

royal guard, and did not see her as she approached her palfrey. Instead, Miguel came up to her. She was reluctant, but could see nothing for it but to accept his help. He stood for a moment looking at her, his expression telling her that he was angry, and resentful about something.

'You have been fortunate, lady. Do not imagine that Anton's attentions mean more than mere courtesy. He has no love for such as you. His wife was a beautiful angel and his heart lies in her grave—where he put her.'

The words were spoken in hushed tones that only she could hear, but in a way that sent shivers down her spine.

'I do not understand you…'

'He mourns her because he killed her. He may use you as a whore, but he can never love another woman. His sin will haunt him for his whole life, as he deserves. Be warned for your own sake.'

Marietta shuddered as he took her and threw her into the saddle none too gently. For a moment she looked down at him. Miguel's intense look sent shudders through her. She had thought previously that he disliked her, but he had never spoken out like this—did he hate her or was he jealous?

Could he be jealous of Anton? Surely not? She had always thought they were the best of friends, and she was sure that Anton trusted him.

Why had he said such things to her? Marietta did not truly understand what lay beneath the warning. Was he warning her against Anton? He had claimed that Anton had killed his wife…almost accusing him of murder.

There was some mystery here. She sensed that there were things she could not know…things hidden in the past that cast a long shadow and would affect the future.

Anton was mounting himself. He glanced at Marietta and nodded his head, then turned and smiled at Miguel. The friendship between them was plain to see. For a moment Marietta had thought she should speak to Anton, tell him what Miguel had said to her, but his smile made her change her mind. He would not believe her. He would think she had made it up.

Marietta thought she understood Miguel's outburst. His manner had always puzzled her, but now she thought she had solved the puzzle. He wanted her himself, and because she had shown her preference for Anton he had tried to turn her against him.

She could not tell Anton because he would think she was being spiteful. Besides, she did not wish to cause trouble between them. If she decided to accept Anton's offer of marriage, Miguel would have to accept it or return to Spain.

They had been riding for the best part of the day before Anton finally called a halt. He had chosen to stay at a different inn from the one they had used as they journeyed to London.

'I am trying to stay away from the high roads,' he told her as he came to help her dismount. 'If we were followed to London our enemy may be waiting for us to return the same way. At the moment we are too many for Rouen to risk falling on us in open countryside, but in woods the advantage might lie with him.'

Marietta looked at him anxiously. 'Do you think he will try to snatch me again?'

'I think he might kill you this time.' Anton's expression was grave. 'If you were dead he might try to claim guardianship of your son. He does have a claim, for he is Charles's half-brother.'

'He would kill him!' Marietta's eyes opened wider as she stared at him in horror.

'If the claim was made Henry would take the boy as his ward. He has told me that I would be appointed Charles's guardian until he came of age.'

'So the Bastard must kill us both...'

'I am sure he would wish to be avenged on me for more than one reason,' Anton told her. 'I know that the reckoning must come, but I want it to come on my terms. Once you and the child are safe with my uncle I shall seek him out and settle this thing.'

'You will risk your life again for my sake?' Marietta felt her throat tighten. 'I…do not wish you to die in my stead.'

Anton laughed softly. 'Have you not forgotten I bested him once before, lady? This time I shall kill him.'

'Can it not be settled some other way? I would not be the cause of any man's death—and I do not want you to risk your life.'

'You should not concern yourself, Marietta. These things are best left to men.'

'Yes, perhaps…' She sighed. 'I am tired and my mind sees too many terrors.'

'You need to rest. I sent ahead to secure rooms for us at the inn. Go to yours and lock your door. Open it only to someone you know, or the host's wife. I think it would be best if you supped alone again.'

'Yes, perhaps you are right.'

Marietta felt tired after so much travelling. She wanted to see her son again, to feel safe and relaxed in Lady Claire's home. Perhaps then she would be able to think clearly about the future.

Marietta turned her head as Anton brought his horse alongside hers the next day. She had hardly spoken to him since they had left the inn that morning, but she knew that he had to be alert to all the dangers they might face on the journey, and did not expect to be noticed. He had more important matters on his mind.

'We shall spend one more night on the road,' he told her. 'Tomorrow at dusk we should reach my uncle's house if we continue to make good time.'

'I shall be glad of it. I must confess that I begin to feel weary.'

'It is not to be wondered at,' Anton said, looking at her in concern. 'We have been constantly on the road since we returned to England. But I thought you would wish to be with your son as soon as it could be achieved.' He lifted his brows in enquiry.

'Yes, I long to see him. Thank you…' She met his searching gaze. 'Last evening, if I seemed to question your judgement…please forgive me.'

'It is forgiven. You know little of me, Marietta. I took you to London, where you might have met your death, and I have sometimes been harsh with you. How should you know what kind of man I am?'

'You have saved my life and pledged to help my son. Believe me, I trust you no matter what…'

'You have heard something ill of me?' Anton's eyes darkened. 'I believe I may guess. Please accept my word that I regret sincerely what happened. If I could bring Isabella back to life—' He broke off as one of his men shouted to him. 'Excuse me. I must see what is going on; there may be a trap up ahead…'

Marietta watched him as he rode on with two of his men to investigate a small commotion. The rest of the party was told to halt, and she saw that the men had their hands on their sword-hilts lest this was a diversion to mask an attack on them. However, a shout that all was clear started the train of men moving again, and as Marietta came up to the little cluster of wagons and horses in the clearing ahead she saw that they were travelling players.

She greeted Anton with a smile as he rode back to her. 'Is all well, sir?'

'They are a band of travelling players, Marietta. I have asked them to join with us. When we stop for the night they will perform one of their miracle plays for us.'

'A play?' Marietta's laughed. 'It is a long time since I saw a play. Sometimes the players and mummers came to my father's house, but at the castle we had our own troubadours who played and sang for us. The Comte did not encourage bands of players for he thought them vagabonds.'

'Some undoubtedly are, but others are honest entertainers. You will enjoy the performance, and so will my men,' Anton said, looking more cheerful than he had when he'd left her. 'We are almost at the inn, Marietta, and then tomorrow we shall reach our journey's end.'

And then she must give him her answer, as she had promised. The only trouble was that she was still not sure he wanted her for herself and not just as a mother for his daughter.

Marietta joined some other ladies who had assembled in the inn yard to watch the players set up their scenery. Torches blazed in every corner of the yard, concentrated around the stage so that everyone could see the actors. A mood of excitement had descended, because it was not often that such a treat was offered.

Anton had set some of his men to patrol the yard so that others might watch in safety, but still the feeling was relaxed. Marietta had begun to hope that perhaps Rouen had stayed in France. Perhaps he had decided to be satisfied with what he had—though she knew that the revenues he could extract from the peasants would not long pay for his extravagances. The Bastard must get his hands on her husband's gold, or he would have to find some way of earning more for himself.

The entertainment opened with a display of tumbling, juggling and fire-eating, which brought some gasps from the watchers. Then the play began. It was the story of the adoration, telling of how the three kings and the shepherds heard the news of Christ's birth and came to worship him in a stable.

'Only one more night and then you will be safely with your cousin.'

Anton's voice made Marietta turn to him. His face was in the shadows and she could not read his expression.

'Shall you be glad, Marietta?'

'I shall be glad to rest for a while,' she said, 'and to hold my son in my arms. I have missed him, and I am anxious that he has fretted for me, even though I know he has been well cared for. I have always nursed him myself. Even when my milk dried I spent hours holding him and singing to him each day.'

'You are a loving mother—and will, I think, make a good wife to some fortunate man.' A wistful expression was in his eyes. 'I think of my daughter often.'

'You must be missing your daughter. You have left her too long for my sake.'

'She is safe with my mother, but I shall send for her as soon as we reach my uncle's. I intend to stay for a while, and I want you to meet Madeline as soon as possible.'

'Yes, I should like to meet her. I should enjoy seeing you together. You are so good with Charles. I think you are a good father.'

'You are a generous and loving woman. My daughter would be fortunate to have you as her mother—and I to have you as my wife.'

'Anton...' Her lips parted on a soft breath of need. 'I have been thinking...'

'You need not answer yet. Wait until you are with Claire and your son. Tell me your answer then...' He smiled. 'Look, the play reaches its end. Come and meet the players and tell them you enjoyed their work.'

'Yes...' Marietta smiled up at him. When he behaved like this she was certain of her answer. Indeed, she felt foolish to have doubted, for he had shown her that he was an honourable man in so many ways.

She turned her head, feeling that she was being watched. A man was standing in the shadows, staring at them. Was it Miguel? Had she been right to think he was jealous? Or was she letting her imagination run away with her?

For a moment she was tempted to tell Anton that she was disturbed by something Miguel had said to her at the start of their journey, and yet she did not want to spoil this evening. She felt happier than she had for years. There would be time to tell him another day. After all, Miguel was unlikely to do anything to harm his friend or her because of a little jealousy…

Marietta lay sleepless for a while after she retired. She could still hear noises from the inn yard, people laughing and talking. Some of them had drunk too well of their host's good ale and were celebrating noisily.

She had almost made up her mind to accept Anton's offer of marriage. Perhaps he did not love her as she loved him, but he felt passion for her. She recalled the tender way Anton had loved her that night, the exquisite feeling that had taken her to the heights of pleasure. The touch of his hand on her cheek in the yard had sent shivers running through her, making her ache with the need to lie in his arms once more.

Snuggling down in her feather bed, Marietta drifted into sleep. Something at the back of her mind was vaguely troubling her, but she could not put her thoughts into words. Perhaps it would come to her in time…

Chapter Nine

'Marietta, my dear! I am so glad to see you home again.' Claire Melford drew her into a warm embrace. 'I was devastated when they snatched you from us, and I feared for your life.' She drew back to look into Marietta's face. 'You have suffered no harm?'

'None save for a few bruises when they bundled me into the wagon and I fought them.' Her eyes were anxious as she looked at Claire. 'My son is well? Has he fretted for me?'

'He was a little miserable at first, but I have spent time with him and he seems content. I am sure that he will be glad to have you home, Marietta. Come, let us go up to the nursery. Ease your mind concerning his welfare and then we shall take some refreshment, for I am sure you are hungry and tired from the journey.'

'A little weary,' Marietta confessed. 'I am much better now that we are here.' She hesitated for a moment and then turned to Anton. 'I must thank you for bringing me here. When shall I see you again?'

'You will see me in the morning. I too have travelled much, and I do not intend to leave again for a few days at least.'

'Oh…I am pleased…' For some unaccountable reason her

heart leaped. She smiled at him, then turned and followed Lady Claire from the room.

'So, do you think you've heard the last of Rouen?' Harry asked as the ladies disappeared from view. 'Did you have any trouble on the way here?'

'The King sent an escort of his own men. I think it would have been a bold man who attacked us. We were too strong a force, and to attack men wearing the King's livery would be treason. If the rogues were taken alive the punishment would be harsh for such crimes.'

'Yes, I know it.' Harry looked thoughtful. 'So you think the Bastard is waiting his time?'

'What would you do in his place?'

'Wait my chance to strike. You were expecting him to move against you. He will seek to take you by surprise.'

'I have ordered my men to patrol outside the estate. I do not think they will try to storm the house, for that would bring the King's wrath on them—but they will try to snatch her again if they can.'

'So what do you plan?'

'He will not expect me to go looking for him. I shall send out scouting parties. If we discover they have a camp nearby, we shall make a surprise attack. The Bastard of Rouen is a vindictive man and a bad enemy. This will not be settled until he is dead.'

'Henry does not approve of the Barons fighting amongst themselves. If you seek Rouen out you risk the King's displeasure.'

'I know Henry would have us all live in peace with one another. His father called a halt to the old way of settling quarrels, and he has followed—but there are times when only blood will settle an affair such as this.'

The Earl nodded. 'I know you speak truly, Anton, but I would still advise you to tread carefully.'

'I thank you for your good advice, but I must do what is necessary to keep her and the child safe.'

'Yes, I see you must.' Harry smiled oddly. 'You know you may call on me for anything you need?'

'Yes, indeed,' Anton smiled at him. 'You are my mother's brother, sir, and she has told me that I may always count on you.'

'Catherine and I were close when we were young, as twins often are,' Harry said. 'I think of her and enjoy her letters, though we do not meet as often as I should wish.'

'Perhaps you will do so soon.' Anton lifted his gaze. 'For I hope that you will attend my wedding?'

'You are to marry?' Harry's gaze was thoughtful. 'Ah, yes, I see—have you spoken to the lady?'

'This business with the Bastard must be settled first—and there is something else I need to sort out. I am expecting news from Spain, though it may not arrive in time…'

'If you have a problem you may share it with me, Anton.'

'My problem is that I am not certain. Something hovers at the back of my mind, but I am not sure enough to speak of it…'

Marietta spent an hour sitting by her son's cradle. He was sleeping peacefully, his fist curled against his mouth, his skin pink and warm. Her heart wrenched with love. The worst part of her ordeal had been the fear that something might happen to her beloved child, but here he was, safe and sound, and now she could begin to put the terror behind her.

She could not help wondering if the Bastard of Rouen was still out there, perhaps hiding in the thick woods that bordered the estate on three sides. On the fourth side were open meadows, where sheep grazed and a river wound its way lazily through the lush valley. The Earl of Rundle's home was a stout building, more comfortable and warmer than the castle where she had lived with her husband. She thought that she could live happily in a house like this, but she was not certain where her future lay.

Lady Claire had said that she might make her home with her, but Marietta knew that she ought to marry if she could—a good man who would help her son to grow strong and learn all the things he should know. Charles had scarcely known his father. She had a duty to provide him with another—a man who would care for him as if he were his own. However, she was not sure that she was worthy to accept Anton's offer of marriage. And could she truly be content to be married to a man she loved so desperately, yet who had never shown that sort of love to her?

Sighing, she left the child to the care of a servant and went to her own chamber. Rosalind greeted her with glad cries, embracing her warmly.

'We feared for you, my lady.'

'I think I should have died had Sir Anton not come for me. The Bastard would have forced me to wed him, and I would have cut my wrists rather than lie with him.'

'Sir Anton is a good man. You should think of wedding *him*, my lady.'

Marietta looked at her for a moment, then smiled. 'He has made me an offer, Rosalind, but I am not sure why he wants to marry me. My future is still uncertain, and I fear that he may only have asked because he is a man bound by honour, not by love.'

'I have seen the way he looks at you. Besides, Sandro told me he was like a madman when he first discovered that you had been abducted. I do not believe that he is indifferent. You should give him some encouragement, my lady. He would make you a fine husband.'

'Perhaps…' Marietta felt warmth spreading through her like molten treacle, thick and comforting. To be Anton's wife would be more happiness than she could ever expect. 'You must not speak of this to anyone else, for I would not have him feel obliged to wed me for honour's sake.'

'I would not breathe a word, my lady.' The serving woman grinned at her. 'But he is a fine man, and would not leave you to lie lonely in your bed at night…'

'Nor should I wish him to,' Marietta replied, and gurgled with laughter. 'I admit it would pleasure me to wed him—but not unless he truly wishes it…'

Anton was in the hall when Marietta came down the stairs. She was wearing a gown of green silk that clung to her slender waist, flaring out at the hem. Around her waist she had a girdle of silver threads, and a plain silver cross hung from a ribbon at her throat.

She wore her simple clothes with such style that she might have been a queen. Her hair had been left loose, and fell upon her shoulders in rich red-gold waves; her eyes were more green than blue. For a moment his breath caught in his throat, and he could scarce breathe for the racing of his heart. She was so beautiful! Magnificent. Beside her, Isabella would have seemed pale and slight.

How had he ever forgotten such a woman? Anton knew that the memory of the child he had pulled from beneath the flailing hooves of a frightened horse had remained at the back of his mind—but he had never dreamed she would grow up to be a woman like this…

Hearing an indrawn gasp behind him, Anton turned, surprising a look on Miguel's face that shocked him. He realised that Miguel was jealous—but why? Was he jealous of Anton because he wanted Marietta, or jealous of Marietta because he thought she would come between them? There had been a special relationship between the two of them since Isabella's death.

Anton waited as his friend came up to him.

'What are your plans now?' Miguel asked. 'I have been thinking that I may return to Spain in a month or two…'

'If it is your wish,' Anton said. 'I shall be sorry to lose you, though I knew you might wish to return to your home in time. We have been good friends, Miguel.'

'It may be for the best if I go. I should only remind you of things you wish to forget.' Miguel's eyes looked through him. 'I will stay until you have settled with the Bastard of Rouen if you wish it.'

'I shall need all my men for that,' Anton replied, feeling puzzled by his manner. 'Please, accept the hospitality of my uncle's home and enjoy yourself this evening. We have all earned a rest.'

Inclining his head to Miguel, he walked to greet Marietta as she stood at the bottom of the stairs, hesitating a moment. Her eyes seemed to question him and he made her an elegant bow.

'You are beautiful, lady. That gown becomes you.'

'It is one that you chose for me. I believe the style is flattering to me.'

'You look like a queen.' Anton offered her his hand. 'Your son does well?'

'He has been cared for with all love and attention. He was sleeping, and I dare say he has hardly missed me at all.'

'I do not believe that for a moment. Any man would miss you, Marietta. I think that most must love you from the moment they see you.'

'I do not wish for the love of just any man.' Her eyes met his steadily.

Anton inclined his head. 'The man you love will be fortunate indeed.'

Marietta waited, hoping for more, but then Sir Harry came up to them and Claire beckoned. She excused herself and went to her kinswoman.

'I have had a letter from Lady Melissa Melford,' Claire told her. 'She is Anton's grandmother. Melissa has heard about you, my love, and she wishes to meet you. My husband's mother suffered a great deal at the hands of her uncle before she was

wed. When she learned your story she wanted to know if there
was anything she could do to help you.'

'We stayed at Lord Melford's house in London,' Marietta
said. 'I should very much like to meet her.'

'She knows that you are our guest, and I believe she may
make the journey. Lord Melford is well enough at the moment,
though he does not go far from home these days. He will not
accompany her, but she may come and bring Catherine with
her, and Anton's daughter at his request. Lady Catherine is
Anton's mother, of course, and my husband's twin. I believe
you met their younger sister, Anne de Montfort, in France?'
Claire laughed softly as Marietta nodded. 'I dare say that
most of the family will choose to visit us soon for Annabel's
wedding—though perhaps not the de Montforts. I shall enjoy
seeing all my family under my roof for once.'

'You will have much work to do. Perhaps you will allow me
to help you prepare.'

'I dare say you would like to be busy.' Claire nodded and
looked thoughtful. 'Once you have had the running of a large
house idleness hath little to recommend it. We shall oversee
the preparations together, but you must have time for leisure.
You will wish to spend a little time with Anton before he
leaves us.'

'Has he spoken of leaving?' Marietta's gaze flew to her.

'I believe he means to stay a few days, or perhaps longer.
I am not certain. I shall prevail on him to tarry, at least until
his parents are with us. However, his visits are not usually of
long duration. I know that it is his intention to look for land
that would provide him with a good estate—and to employ
builders to construct him a sound dwelling.'

'You believe he wishes to settle near here?'

'He likes the area well, I think. I understand Harry has
been making enquiries concerning a manor that may come for
sale after the death of its lord. It would be pleasant if he were
to settle within a few hours' distance of Rundle Park, would
it not?'

'Yes…' Marietta was watching Anton as he laughed with his uncle Harry and some of the other men. 'Very pleasant. You would often have his company, for you might dine with each other.'

'Yes, and I should also have the company of his wife.'

Marietta glanced at her. Claire was smiling at her in such an odd way. Could she have guessed that Anton had asked her to be his wife?

Marietta retired soon after supper that night. She was tired from the journey, and wished to rest, but she was feeling content and drifted into sleep moments after her head touched the pillow.

In the morning she woke feeling refreshed and ready to face the day. As soon as she was dressed in a sensible gown she paid a visit to the nursery. Her son shouted and cried when he saw her, but once she had played with him and given him some sweetmeats he quieted and sat on her lap, snuggling up to her contentedly.

It was as she was nursing him that she heard someone enter the room, and turned her head to look. Anton was standing just inside the door, looking at her.

'You both look happy,' he said. 'It is clear that your son knows his mother is home.'

'He cried when he saw me, but he has settled now. I have never left him for more than a day before. I believe he thought I had abandoned him.'

'You would never do that in this life.' He smiled at her. 'I shall leave you, for I must speak with my uncle. We shall meet later.'

'Yes, of course.'

Anton went away. Marietta nursed her son for a while longer, then he grew restless and clamoured to be put down.

Marietta left him playing with a wooden horse that the Earl had commissioned for him, and went down to Claire's still-room. They were to take stock of what stores were available, so that the Earl could send to Shrewsbury for anything they needed.

After an inventory was made, a list of ingredients was written out, and the ladies began a tour of the house, making notes on what needed to be done. Servants were set to cleaning, and the linen was checked so that it could be washed and beds made up with fresh-smelling sheets in the guest chambers.

In a castle only the most honoured guests and ladies were given chambers of their own. Men of the lower ranks slept in the Great Hall, or in little cells that were only big enough to hold a truckle bed that was stored away during the day. It had been the custom in Medieval times, and persisted even now in older houses. Only the more modern houses had separate chambers, and many of those led into each other, which could be inconvenient.

It was not until after they had stopped for refreshment at noon that Lady Claire declared herself satisfied for one day. She went to her chamber to attend to some private business, and Marietta was left to herself.

She was staring out at the gardens when she heard something behind her, and turned to see Anton enter the room.

'Oh…' She smoothed her gown. 'You have found me in all my dirt, sir. We have been working all the morning and I should change…'

As she turned to leave Anton caught her wrist. She glanced back at him and her heart raced.

'We have scarce had a moment alone,' he said. 'You look charming to me, Marietta. Do not leave so soon.'

'If you wish me to stay, I shall.'

'Please sit down. I have something to say to you.'

Marietta sat in a chair with wooden arms and looked at him.

'I have tried to be patient, but now I wish to speak to you. You said you would give me your answer when we reached my uncle's house, but first I must tell you something you should know. Because I believe you may have been told something, but perhaps not quite the truth.'

'Very well. I am listening.'

'You know that I was married to a Spanish lady I cared for?'

'Yes, I know that, sir. You have spoken of your wife.'

'She was lovely…very different from you. Isabella had black hair and pale skin and she was gentle. I thought her an innocent…an innocent angel.'

'You loved her very much?'

'I believed so at the start, and I thought she loved me. I was content with my life. Our daughter was born and all seemed well. Then one day Isabella told me she was to have another child, and I thought my happiness was complete…' Anton's eyes darkened, became hard as black diamonds. 'Isabella did not carry the second child easily. She was ill and troubled, often complaining, and unwilling to be near me. I thought her manner was simply because she felt ill, and then…then a letter came to my hand. It was unsigned, and I tried to dismiss it as lies from the pen of a coward. The writer said that my wife had betrayed me with another man—that the child was his, not mine.'

Marietta started up. 'How shocking and hurtful that must have been. I am so sorry…'

'I was devastated. I felt that my life was shattered, my trust betrayed. I tried hard to ignore it, telling myself that only a coward would send an unsigned letter—that what it contained must be lies.' Anton turned away from her, his back stiff with tension. 'In the end I could not bear it any longer. In a jealous rage I accused her of betraying me. I asked her if the child was mine…'

'What did she say?' Marietta caught her breath as he turned and she saw the agony in his eyes. It was costing him much to tell her this story.

'Isabella denied the accusation. She looked stunned, hurt… afraid…' A nerve flicked in Anton's cheek. 'I was terrible in my anger. She ran from me in tears and fear—and in the sunken gardens she fell down some steep stone steps and hit her head. She died, and the child died with her. I knew I was being punished for my outburst.'

'Anton!' Marietta stood up, looking at him with a mixture of horror and sympathy. 'How terrible! You must have felt so guilty—as if you had killed her and the babe…'

'Yes. I see you understand me.' Anton ran restless fingers through his hair. 'Some months have passed now since her death, but at first I could not forgive myself for what I had done. I hardly knew how to live. I think I might have taken my life if it had not been for a friend. He was my comforter—the only one who understood what I suffered…'

'You are speaking of Miguel?'

'Yes…' Anton sighed. 'We were as brothers—or so I believed.'

'You have doubts now concerning his loyalty?'

Anton's eyes sought hers. 'Do you wish me to speak plainly?'

'I think it best.'

'I have asked you to wed me. You know that there is something between us? You have felt it, as I have?'

'Yes, I feel it.'

'I saw Miguel's face when you came down last night. I believe he is jealous, but I do not know why—whether it is because he wants you, or because he believes you will destroy the friendship we have had these past months.'

'Why should I come between you and your friend?'

'I do not know. I saw jealousy in his face as he looked at you—it may be that he wants you for himself.'

'Yes, perhaps…there is something…'

'You have sensed it yourself?'

'I know there is something, but I do not know if he desires me or hates me.'

'He gasped when he saw you, and the look on his face shocked me.' Anton shook his head. 'I shall not allow Miguel's wishes to distract me. I must ask you for my answer now. Will you be my wife, Marietta? I do most sincerely wish it, if it will please you.'

'Marry you…' Marietta caught her breath, and then she was smiling, her doubts fading as she saw the look in his eyes. 'Yes, I will marry you, Anton. I should be honoured—if it truly pleases *you*?'

'Marriage to you would please me well,' Anton said. He stood up and offered her his hand, bringing her to her feet. 'However, we must be careful. I am not sure how Miguel will react to the news—and we still have to face the possibility that Rouen will come after you again. Miguel speaks of returning to Spain after we have dealt with the Bastard. I think that perhaps we should keep this agreement private for the moment.' He gazed down at her. 'I wanted to settle this between us. You know it is possible that I may be killed…'

'I beg you not to say it! I do not think that I could bear it…' Marietta caught back the words that would betray her heart. He had still not told her that he loved her. Only that he had cared for his wife and been devastated by her death. Perhaps he sought a marriage with a woman who had been married before, a woman who was well versed in the needs of a man, both in his bed and his home. She knew he needed a mother for his daughter. 'I would have you live and be my husband, sir.'

'It is my true wish,' Anton told her. 'Now, I must tell you something more. I have had word that there may be soldiers in the west woods, and I suspect they are the Bastard's men. I am taking a party to search them out…'

Marietta's nails curled into her palm, but she did not beg him to stay. It grieved her that he must leave so soon, but she knew that the future depended on what happened now.

'Take care, Anton. I shall pray for you.'

'Think of the future. It is what sustains me…' Anton moved closer. He reached out and drew her into his arms, looking down at her for a moment before he bent his head to claim her lips. His kiss was soft, tender, deepening as he clasped her hard against him. For a moment the hunger and need was in his eyes as he looked at her. 'Forgive me. I do not wish to leave you—but I must…'

'God go with you…'

Marietta released him as he tore himself from her arms and walked away. She blinked as she felt the sting of tears. She loved him, and if they both lived she would wed him, but she was still not certain of her place in his heart.

Marietta spent some time playing with her son. When she went down to join the others for supper in the Great Hall it was almost dusk. She asked Claire if the men had returned from their search but she shook her head.

'We have heard nothing,' she said. 'Harry went with them, because he said that if the rogues were on his land he wanted to deal with them. I thought they would have returned before this, for they cannot search in the dark—' She broke off as there was a commotion in the hall and then Sir Harry came striding in. He had blood on his clothes and Claire gave a scream of fright, running to him, his name on her lips.

'Stop,' Harry commanded. 'The blood is not mine, but Anton's. He has been wounded in the side and has lost much blood. I came on ahead to warn you. The men are carrying him home…'

'Anton is wounded?' Marietta approached hesitantly, her face deathly white. 'How did it happen? He is such a skilled warrior…'

'They came upon us suddenly, about thirty of them out of the trees. We held our own easily and drove them off. The Bastard of Rouen was killed by Anton's own hand, but somehow in the melee he was wounded.' Harry frowned. 'From the angle of the wound I think a sword was thrust into his side from behind. I doubt he knew his enemy was there. When all is confusion these things sometimes happen, but it is a cowardly way to strike a man—from behind, when he is fighting another.'

Marietta hardly heard his last words for they were bringing Anton. He was being carried on a gate taken hurriedly from its hinges, and his garments were soaked in blood.

Holding back the feeling of terror that swept over her, Marietta hurried to her chamber. She had healing herbs that would be needed, and she would use all she knew to save him—because if he died she did not care what became of her.

When she went to Anton's chamber, Claire was already there. Anton was naked, for they had stripped away the bloodied raiment and the servants had brought water to wash the wound.

'Let me help,' Marietta said, and went to Claire's side. She took the cloth and soaked it in the bowl, wringing out the bloody water and bathing the area around the wound. 'The cut is deep, but I do not think it had penetrated a vital organ. See—the flesh does not open far. If we cleanse the wound and apply salves it will heal...'

'Yes, that is what I thought,' Claire agreed. 'But wounds like this can turn bad so quickly, Marietta. Perhaps we should use the iron on him? The danger will come if the pus turns green.'

'Sometimes the iron can do more harm than good with a fresh wound like this. I could sew the flesh together with silk thread. And I have some herbs that may help. I need to make an infusion to pack the wound. Have I permission to use your stillroom—and to apply the poultice?'

'Do you understand what you do?' Claire's eyes were upon her. 'If he should die...'

'I care little what becomes of me if Anton dies. Please let me try, Claire. He will suffer so if you cauterise his wound, and I think my way will work better in this case, for there is no putrefaction to burn away.'

Claire looked at her oddly for a moment, then inclined her

head. 'I know your heart is good, Marietta. Fetch all that you need, and I will send the servants out of the room when you are ready.'

Marietta thanked her and hurried away to the stillroom. She soaked the herbs in water that had been boiled, for it was often contaminated, then strained them into a vessel. The mulch would be packed around the wound after she had sewn Anton's flesh together, and the infusion drunk a little at a time.

Returning to the chamber where Anton lay, his eyes closed, she found Claire alone.

'I sent the servants to boil more water and heat the cauterising iron,' she said. 'It is best if they do not see what you do, Marietta, for it would be thought strange—and servants talk. I would not have your goodness taken as something different.'

Marietta nodded. Her skill with healing was at times controversial, and had been learned from various sources, but mostly it came from within. Her instincts were strong in this case.

The wound had been bleeding again. She took a clean cloth and wiped the skin dry, then threaded her needle with white silk. She gathered the open wound, pulling it so that the gap closed, and then pushed her needle through the flesh, pulling the thread behind. Claire made a gasping sound but said nothing, holding the candle nearer so that Marietta could see to work. It took several minutes to complete the seam. Satisfied that only a dribble of blood was seeping through, Marietta packed the mulch of herbs over the wound and laid a patch of clean linen on it. Then she and Claire wound the bandage about him, letting him back gently on the pillows when it was done.

He had cried out a few times as Marietta did her work, but now he merely lay still, his eyes closed, beads of sweat on his brow.

Claire went to the door and took the iron from a servant, sending the girl running to fetch more clean linen. She brought the red-hot poker back and laid it in the grate, then stood looking down at Anton.

'He does not suffer as he would had we used the iron.'

'I once spoke to an Arab doctor. He told me that he had seen cases where the iron killed rather than saved life. It was his belief that stitching was the best way if the wound was clean, and he showed me how to infuse the herbs to guard against infection.'

'Was this when you were at the castle?'

'Before—at my father's house. My father believed in herbs and medicines. As a young man he studied to be a physician, but when his father died he had to take over the ordering of the manor. I think he made a better physician than a baron, for he liked nothing better than studying—and he taught me much of what I know.'

'So it is not witchcraft but the study of medicine?'

'I am not a witch, Claire. If I were a man the methods I use would cause no raised eyebrows. 'Tis because I am a woman, and women should not know these things. Apothecaries have always been men, as have doctors. They are jealous of their privileges and will not share them. My father was frowned on because he accepted new ideas and was friendly with men of Arabia, for they are often not trusted—perhaps because they push the limits of known medicine and dismiss old methods as crude and useless.'

Claire's gaze rested on Anton. 'Will he take a fever?'

'It is possible, indeed likely. He must be made to drink the infusion, though it is bitter and he will fight us—at least until he comes through the worst.'

'Supposing the wound turns putrid?'

'If it does we shall pack it with maggots so that they eat the infection.'

'No!' Claire looked at her in horror. 'That is horrible. How could you think of it?'

'I saw my father use the method on a lad whose arm was badly infected, and his wound healed when everyone thought he would die.' Marietta met her questioning look. 'I shall do whatever is necessary. Anton saved my life more than once—do you think that I would let him die from neglect?'

'I know you love him.' Claire said. 'I will help you to nurse him. But please do not ask me to touch maggots!' She pulled a face of disgust and shuddered. 'I cannot abide the creatures.'

'Have you never fished with them?' Marietta smiled. 'That is another thing my father taught me—to fish with a pole, thin string and a bent pin.'

'It is no wonder you are different from other women. Your father was unwise to teach you so much, Marietta. Did your mother not object?'

'She died too soon. My father had no son. I became his friend, son, and chatelaine of his home. We were happy until he lost all his money—and then I had to marry to save him from the debtors' prison. I did not wish to marry a man so much older than myself, but I obeyed my father so that he might live out his days in comfort.'

Claire nodded. 'I shall leave you to sit with Anton for a while. If you need me, call me. I shall take your place while you sleep.'

'I shall not leave him until I know he will live. I may sleep at the foot of his bed until then.'

'It is hardly proper…' Claire began, and then shook her head. 'You know best. Call me if you need me…'

Marietta waited until the door had closed behind her, then brought a chair close to the bed and sat in it, so that she could watch over her patient. There was no point in Claire taking her place, for if she went to bed she would not sleep a wink.

Anton's fever started in the early hours of the morning. Marietta had been half dozing in the chair when the cry woke her.

'Isabella! Forgive me. I beg you to forgive me. Come back to me. Please come back to me…'

Marietta fetched a cool cloth and went to stand over him.

She washed his face and his shoulders, then his arms. His hair was damp with sweat. Smoothing it back from his forehead, she bent to kiss him.

'It is all right, my love. I am here. Isabella is with you. She forgives you. I forgive you…' She stroked his head with her hand. 'My death was not your fault. You must forgive me for hurting you. I did not mean to hurt you. Isabella did not mean to hurt you. Do not grieve for her.'

Anton's eyelids fluttered. For a brief moment his eyes opened and he seemed to look at her, then he closed them again, sighing and settling.

Marietta felt the ache about her heart intensify. He had loved his first wife so much. She could not expect that he would ever feel as much for her. He would wed her, and she would make what she could of her life, but she must not expect too much.

Anton's fever lasted two days, but he was a strong man, and though he gagged on the bitter medicine Marietta spooned into his mouth he swallowed it. On the third morning, he opened his eyes and looked at her.

'Have you been here long?'

'Since they brought you home.'

'You should sleep. I shall do well enough now.'

'Your wound is healing fast and should not take harm. The fever lasted but two days. I believe all will be well with you, sir.'

Anton sighed, his eyes closing. 'Thank you…'

Seeing that he had slipped into a peaceful slumber, Marietta sent for Claire and told her that their patient was through the worst.

'His wound appears healthy. It seems he has been fortunate.'

'More fortunate than anyone guesses, I dare say.' Claire smiled at her. 'He owes his life to you, Marietta.'

'It was the will of God,' Marietta said. 'Please do not give me the credit. I but nursed him as any woman would.'

'You should rest now. Lady Melissa Melford will be here this evening, and Lady Gifford, Countess of Malchester, may be here even sooner. I shall tell them that you nursed Anton, but nothing more.'

Marietta smiled, and left her to watch over Anton for a while. Now that she was sure he would not die of a fever she was prepared to leave him in Claire's capable hands. His wound might yet become infected, but she would watch, and pray that he took no harm.

When Marietta returned to Anton's bedchamber she saw that another woman had taken Claire's place. She was of a similar age to Claire, and beautiful, but when she looked at Marietta there was a flicker of hostility in her eyes.

'Who are you to enter my son's bedchamber without so much as a by your leave?'

'Forgive me. I have been nursing Sir Anton. I did not know you were here, my lady.'

'You are the Comtesse Montcrief?' Catherine Gifford's eyes held the glitter of anger. 'He was wounded in a battle to protect you, I think?'

'Yes, I fear that is so. I am sorry for it, but nothing would sway him. He would go to search for Rouen. He said that we should never be at peace until my enemy was dead.'

'Indeed?' Catherine's brows rose. 'What are you to my son, *madame*? I know only what Lady Claire has told me.'

'I am someone who hath reason to be grateful to Anton of Gifford. He has saved my life more than once. I believe that I have in part repaid my debt. Anything more must come from your son, *madame*.'

'Is there more? You are a widow, and stood accused of your husband's murder—is that not so?'

'Yes, it was so. I was unjustly accused, for I did nothing to harm my husband and nursed him through illness many times—but someone hated me and craved what rightly belongs to my son.'

'I thank you for your care of Anton. However, I am here now, and I shall nurse him myself.'

'That is your privilege, my lady,' Marietta said, and smiled. 'I hope you will continue to use the herbs and infusions I have prepared, for they have seen him through the fever but he still needs them.'

'My mother will be here soon. She is skilled in the use of herbs. I shall ask her advice on this matter.'

Marietta inclined her head. Lady Catherine was hostile to her. She might try to influence her son to turn away from the marriage he had proposed. Marietta would not hold him to his promise if he told her that he had changed his mind.

Would the stigma of murder and witchcraft hang over her all her life?

Marietta was close to tears as she went to her bedchamber. She would begin to make clothes for her son with the cloth she had purchased in London.

Perhaps it was just as well that Anton had told no one that they planned to marry.

Marietta had been at her stitching for three hours when someone knocked at the door. She called out that they might enter, looking up in surprise as a woman she had never seen before came in.

This woman was older, but had a gentle beauty, her once flame-red hair lightly streaked with white, though her face had few lines.

'Madame la Comtesse Montcrief?'

Marietta got to her feet and curtsied, for she knew at once who the lady must be. 'Lady Melford, forgive me. I thought when you knocked it must be a servant come to call me. Had you summoned me, I would have come to you.'

'I have come to thank you for your excellent care of my

442   *Anne Herries*

grandson, *madame*—or may I perhaps call you by your name?'

'I am Marietta, my lady. I did only what was necessary, just simple nursing.'

'You do not need to pretend with me,' Melissa, Lady Melford, said, and smiled. 'I saw your work. It was excellent, my dear, and I believe his wound will heal well now. The herbs you used are much the same as I would have chosen—as I told my daughter. Catherine was distressed. If she was a little harsh to you, please forgive her.'

'She had the right to question me, my lady.'

'She loves her son dearly. I am sorry if you felt slighted. You are of course welcome to return to Anton's chamber whenever you wish.'

'Perhaps it would be best if I left him to his mother and you. I am merely a dependant, living on Lady Claire's bounty.'

'I think that is not quite the case. My grandson asked for you twice. You will oblige me if you will visit him, for unless you do I fear he may try to leave his bed too soon.'

'Oh…the foolish man…' Marietta blushed. 'It is always so. Men are the worst patients. They will never be sensible.'

'I have often found it so,' Lady Melissa replied, and laughed. 'As soon as they feel a little better there is no bearing with them. So you will visit him soon?'

'I shall go immediately. I thank you for coming to me.'

'It was my duty and my pleasure. I have not lived this long without knowing the signs of a man in love.'

'Oh…' Marietta blushed. 'I am not sure… He feels a kindness towards me, I know, but—' She broke off as she saw the amusement in Lady Melissa's face. 'Do you truly think?'

'I know my grandson, even though I have not seen him for some years. He has not changed much: impatient, a little arrogant, quick to temper and sometimes he sulks. At those times he looks grim and will not speak for hours on end.'

'You *do* know him!' Marietta gave a little chuckle.

'I should, for I have been married to a man of the same

temperament for some years.' She nodded to Marietta. 'You must go to Anton now, but one day, when you have leisure, I shall tell you my story. I think you may understand a little better then.'

Marietta thanked her and hurried away. She was feeling confused and uncertain, for Anton had cried so pitifully for Isabella in his fever. He must have loved her dearly, but perhaps it was possible to love again?

When she entered the bedchamber, Anton was lying with his eyes closed. He opened them as she approached the bed, giving her a look of reproach.

'Why have you abandoned me?'

'You were better, and your mother and grandmother are here. You no longer need me.'

'Perhaps I do not need your nursing, but I shall always need you.'

Marietta looked down at him, her heart racing. 'I have not told anyone of our...arrangement. If your family do not approve...'

'They may go to the devil,' Anton said, and gripped her wrist. 'I want you for my wife. You have promised me and I shall not let you break your word.'

'I do not wish it. I merely offered for your sake.'

'Then rest easy. I am not a man who changes his mind lightly.'

'I did not think it, but I should not wish to cause a breach...' Marietta smiled as his grip tightened about her wrist. 'Very well, it is settled—now, tell me how you came to be wounded like that. It looks as if you were struck from behind.'

'Have you seen Miguel since the day I was wounded?'

'No...' Marietta stared at him. 'Was it he that wounded you? But he is your friend...'

'He was once my friend,' Anton corrected. 'I do not know it all, but I believe he blames me for Isabella's death.'

'Yes, he said something that seemed to indicate you were at fault as we journeyed here.'

'You did not see fit to tell me?'

'He was your friend. Besides, I thought it was merely a little jealousy. I did not want to sound spiteful, because you were so fond of him and I never thought he would harm you. He seemed to dislike me—but you were his friend.'

'Damn him!' Anton's eyes darkened. 'He waited his chance and this was his way of murdering me. Miguel knows that he could never best me in fair fight, so he struck me from behind as I fought the men who sprang on us from the trees. I killed your first enemy—he will trouble you no more—but I fear we both have another.'

'Was he…was Miguel Isabella's lover?' She saw a flash of pain in Anton's eyes. 'Forgive me. I should not have asked.'

'You have the right to ask what you will of me. I had no suspicion of it until very recently, but I believe you may be right. Miguel has deceived me all this time. It was only when I saw the look on his face that I began to suspect him of something, but even then I did not realise how much he hated me. He cried out that it was for Isabella as he thrust his sword into me. I may discover the whole truth, perhaps, when my enquiries in Spain are done. I suspect that someone witnessed what happened the day she died. If the gardener can be persuaded to speak we may have the answer at last.'

'I am sorry Miguel did this to you—not just the wound from behind, which was a coward's way, but all the rest.'

'Isabella's death has played on my mind for a long time.' Anton's gaze narrowed. 'In my fever it seemed to me that she was with me—that she forgave me.'

'I am certain she would if she could. Besides, if she had a lover, she should have begged for *your* forgiveness.'

'Perhaps. However, her father wanted our marriage. I may have pushed too hard. If Isabella obeyed her father while her heart was given to another…' Anton sighed. 'Miguel has little fortune, and no hope of a title. I shall be a marquis one day—a long time into the future, I hope, but it is so. My father holds the titles of earl and marquis…'

'You think that Isabella was obliged to obey her father…as I was?' Marietta looked thoughtful. 'She should have refused, or if she chose to obey remained faithful to her husband…but that is not for me to say. I never knew her.'

'She was not like you. I do not think she would have dared to defy her father.'

'Then I am sorry for her. It is not easy to marry where there is no love.'

'There was love on my side—at least at first.' Anton frowned, holding Marietta as she would have turned away. 'No, do not run away. You must hear me out. I loved Isabella in a way, but she was like a child. She never gave herself to me as you did that night, Marietta. I have come to believe that in time I should have found that we did not suit…though I would always have honoured her as my wife. I might, however, have taken a mistress once we had our sons.'

'But you grieved for her so much…' Marietta was not sure what to think.

'I grieved for her and my unborn child, and I shall never cease to regret the way she died—but I believe I am ready to move on. I wish to make a new life with you, my love.'

Marietta bent down to kiss him on the lips. He caught her hair, tangling his fingers in it to hold her as she would have moved away, deepening the kiss, his tongue demanding entrance to her sweetness.

When he let her go at last, she shook her head at him. 'You are not strong enough for such things, Anton. I meant just a sweet kiss to seal our bargain.'

'Tell me you love me,' he demanded. 'Tell me you want to be my wife, as I want you.'

'Do you not know it?' Marietta smiled. 'I have loved you from the very first time we met…when you held me safe in your arms after you rescued me from the horse's hooves and looked down at me. I wish that the years between had never happened. I would have come to you untouched, a virgin bride—but fate decreed that our ways should part.'

Anton's passionate gaze held her fast. 'We shall never be parted again. I vow it on all I hold dear. I have done with waiting. We shall be wed as soon as I can walk down the aisle with you.'

'First you must get well and strong again.' She laughed as she saw the impatience in his face. 'Do not look so, my beloved. I am as impatient to be your wife as you to have me—but if you do not take care your wound may open again. You might take another fever, and sometimes that leads to death.'

'My grandmother says that you used a method of sealing the wound that she had heard of but never dared to use. She was all admiration for your skill.'

'It is best not to speak of such things. My father taught me the skills of a surgeon, and he studied in Italy and the East— but as a woman I should not know these things. I fear that it would be frowned upon, for the guilds of medicine and healing are the province of men and they guard them jealously. It was my husband's apothecary who grew jealous of my skill at the castle and began rumours that I used witchcraft. He and others had grown jealous of my influence with my husband.'

'And the Bastard saw his chance to seize what was yours.' Anton frowned. 'I thank God that we have seen the last of him, though I do not know what has become of Miguel…'

'Hush, my love. The Earl of Rundle has men searching for the rogue. If he has not already fled to Spain he will be found.'

'You will not be safe while he lives.' Anton frowned. 'He tried to kill me and failed. He may try for you next time.'

Chapter Ten

Entering the nursery some time later, Marietta saw a child standing next to her son's cot. As she watched, the little girl reached out and touched Charles's face, patting him with her hand. This was surely Anton's daughter, though she had a rather exotic look which must have come from her mother. This little girl would no doubt be beautiful one day.

'Baby…' she said, and, turning as Marietta came up to her, she smiled. 'Pretty baby. Maddie like…Maddie want nurse baby…'

'You want to hold Charles?' Marietta asked, a little surprised that she should speak English rather than Spanish—though perhaps her father had taught her. The little girl nodded and sucked her thumb, her eyes widening. 'I see no reason why you shouldn't. Come and sit down on the cushions and I shall give him to you.'

Maddie did as she was bid, her chubby legs crossed as she perched amongst the pile of cushions on the floor. Her dark eyes were wide with wonder as Marietta lifted her son and brought him to join her on the floor. He was free of his swaddling clothes and beginning to find his balance. For a moment he was content to perch on Maddie's lap, but then he wriggled off and began to crawl about the floor, with the little girl copying him. Clearly she had fallen for the golden-haired boy, and seemed fascinated by his every move, while Charles, pleased with the attention, lost no time in asserting his place in the nursery hierarchy.

Maddie seemed to understand his needs, for it was enough for Charles to point at something to send her running after it for him. Marietta laughed as she watched them playing; they might have known each other all their lives!

She was so intent that she was not immediately aware of someone watching her. She glanced up and saw Lady Gifford standing on the threshold.

'May I come in, *madame*? I do not wish to disturb you.'

'I was just watching them. They have made friends.' Marietta smiled down at the children. 'Charles has been restless, for he is teething, but he seems happy with his new companion...'

'My granddaughter is a charmer. I think she will break hearts one day—but for the moment she seems to have met her match...' Catherine hesitated as the door opened and a woman entered. 'Ah, Lily—this is the Comtesse Montcrief. As you see, her son has met your charge. We shall leave them to your care.' She caught Marietta's eye. 'Perhaps we could talk?'

'Yes, of course.' Marietta looked at the nurse. 'I shall return later, Lily.'

'Yes, my lady.'

'I wondered why Maddie spoke such good English, but clearly she has an English nurse.'

'I believe Anton thought it best, as he always meant to return to England.'

The two women left the nursery, closing the door softly behind them. Marietta looked at Anton's mother, feeling a little puzzled.

'Is there something I may do for you, my lady?'

'You may begin by calling me Catherine. I fear I did not start well with you. I felt you threatened my son, but he tells me that it was not your enemy that wounded him so sorely, but his. I have wronged you, lady. I am sorry for it.'

'Make me no apology, Catherine. Anton was only in the woods because they were hunting the Bastard of Rouen to protect me. However, I believe Miguel was waiting his time. He would have made his attempt sooner or later—and perhaps it was as well that the Earl was also present.'

'I am sure my brother did all he could to assist Anton. We are a close family and I hope we shall continue so—which is why I would make my peace with you. Am I forgiven?'

'You sought to protect your son. In your place I should have done the same.' Marietta smiled. 'I have no wish to quarrel with Anton's mother. I believe he has told you we are to marry?'

Catherine nodded. 'My son tells me that he wishes for the wedding very soon. Can you not persuade him of the need to recover his strength?'

'I have tried, but he is impatient.'

'Anton is much like his grandfather. You will meet Lord Melford when you go to my father's home. Unfortunately he does not travel often these days, but he is more than three score years and that is a great age—especially for a man who fought so valiantly in the Wars of the Roses.'

Marietta smiled. 'Your mother also wears her years lightly.'

'Yes, my mother is as young in spirit as ever, and she will not admit to her years, even though she was unwell in the winter.' Catherine smiled. 'We are a fortunate family, Marietta.'

'Indeed, and powerful. The Earl told me that he has doubled the men searching the woods and countryside. I think it cannot be long before Miguel is found.'

'I pray it may be so,' Catherine said. 'Now, my dear—what do you plan for your wedding gown? My mother has some lengths of ivory and gold-embroidered silk that might look well on you, and if we all help with the sewing your dress can be ready within two weeks.'

'If Anton will wait so long then I should be glad to wear such a gown, but I may have to be wed in a gown I have, for he grows stronger with every hour. I do not think he will be put off for such an excuse.'

'Your mother and grandmother want me to have a special gown for the wedding, Anton. It will take but two weeks to make...' Marietta saw the look in his eyes and smiled. 'Can you not wait that long to please them?'

'Will it please you to wait?'

'Yes, for it will give you a chance to recover your strength. I know that you have healed well, but you are not yet as strong as you were.'

'I know it,' he growled. 'But it is too long to wait, Marietta. I burn for you, my love. I want to make love to you.'

'You know I would not deny you,' she said, and smiled. 'Say the word and I will lock the door and join you in that bed.'

She leaned forward, kissing him lightly on the mouth. His hand held her locked to him, their tongues tangling in a sweet dance of delicious play. Marietta moved closer and he placed his lips to her throat, moving down to where the swell of her breasts was revealed by a dipping neckline. His tongue teased between them. He pushed the material lower, seeking the rose nipples that peaked beneath his tongue, sending tingles of pleasure running through her. Then he cursed and leaned back against the pillows, looking rueful as beads of sweat formed on his brow.

'Damn it, you are right. I am weak as a kitten.'

'Your strength will return soon. Tomorrow you can get up and come downstairs. I believe you will soon see an improvement once you are on your feet.' Marietta got to her own feet and his eyes narrowed.

'Where are you going?'

'To make a potion that will put iron in your limbs.'

'More of that foul-tasting stuff?'

Marietta made a wry face at him. 'Your grandmother advised me to mix it with wine and sweeten it with honey—since you make so much fuss about taking it without.'

'Both of you should try drinking it,' Anton complained, and then laughed. 'You are a lot alike, you know. I have always admired my grandmother. Perhaps that is why I am so drawn to you.'

Marietta smiled. 'The sooner you regain your strength, the sooner we may be married…'

She laughed as he pulled a wry face, and went out. He was making huge strides in regaining his health, but he grew bored with lying in bed. She was certain now that his wound would not reopen or take harm. Once he left his bed he would soon feel more himself again.

Anton found his way to the nursery later that afternoon. The door was open, and he heard the sound of children laughing as he paused outside. That was Maddie, but he had not heard her laugh so freely before.

Pushing the door open, he paused. Marietta was down on the floor, lying amongst a pile of cushions. Both children were climbing over her, and she was tickling Maddie, making the little girl shriek with laughter.

His throat caught with emotion and his eyes stung. He could not recall Isabella playing with her daughter once, though she had loved her.

Something shifted in his mind, the shadows falling away. A part of him wanted to join the children playing with their mother…*their mother*. Yes, Marietta had already taken Isabella's place in Maddie's heart, for the child had hardly known her true mother.

He smiled, turning away so as not to disturb them. Marietta did not know she was watched. One day he would join them in their play, but not just yet. He had been told that Miguel had been seen in the woods but not yet apprehended. He must save his strength until he was truly well again.

'So, tomorrow we shall be wed,' Anton said, and reached out to touch Marietta's cheek. 'You were right to make me wait until your dress was finished, my love. I am feeling much better. I should not have wanted to come to your bed and find myself unable to consummate our marriage. I am almost back to my full strength, thanks to your disgusting potions.'

'I doubt there was much chance that you would fail to consummate our marriage,' Marietta teased. 'You would have performed your duty as a husband if it killed you.'

'Wretch! You have teased me back to health, Marietta. I do not know how I shall manage you once we are wed—am I to be petticoat-led?' His eyes challenged, and dared her to answer.

'I am not sure,' she responded in kind, knowing that he enjoyed this banter. He was just as she had seen him in her dreams, the shadows seeming to be banished from his eyes. She felt now as if the years apart had never been. 'I may demand more than you can give…'

'Witch,' Anton muttered, drawing her to him. He bent his head, kissing her lips with such hunger that she melted into him. 'My beautiful, lovely woman…'

'I love you so…' Marietta lifted her eyes to look at him, melting with desire. She felt the press of his aroused manhood as he held her crushed to him, her heart racing as hot liquid desire built in her. She wanted him, needed him more than words could express. He was her life, her love—her destined lover. 'I can hardly wait for tomorrow…'

'Nor I, my love—but we shall, now that I have waited so long…' He slipped the shoulder of her gown down, kissing her soft flesh. 'You are so beautiful—and you are mine.'

'For ever,' she murmured, moving her fingers into the hair at the nape of his neck. 'I thought when they condemned me as a witch and a murderess that my life was over, but now I have so much to look forward to.'

Anton caressed the sweet curve of her breast. 'I envy the babe that sucked at these sweet jewels, and I hope that your son will have a brother or sister one day.'

'I long to hold your babe in my arms.' Marietta pressed against him, her need to lie with him as great as his to take her. 'Are you sure that you wish to wait one more night?'

'Temptress!' Anton smacked her rump. 'Off with you now. This time I shall let you go, but watch how you tease me in future.'

Marietta laughed and ran from him. All the shadows of the past seemed to have faded away. There had been no sign of Miguel, at least as far as she knew. The Earl was of the opinion that he had taken himself off back to France to lick his wounds. Perhaps Miguel had decided that honour was satisfied and returned to Spain.

She could only hope that it was so…

'You make a beautiful bride, Marietta,' Lady Melford told her. She handed her a small silver casket. 'I brought this with me just in case. Anton was my first male grandchild, and I saved this for his wife.'

Marietta gasped as she opened the casket and saw the beautiful cross set with cabochon rubies and pearls.

'This is lovely! I have my own silver cross, but this is magnificent. How can I thank you for such a gift?'

'Be a good wife to Anton.' Melissa smiled. 'I know that you will—and I wish you both happiness.'

Marietta thanked her, then kissed her cheek. 'You are so good to me—' She broke off as the door opened and a young girl entered. Marietta had recently employed her to help Rosalind with nursing her son. 'Eleanor…is something wrong?'

'No, my lady. Lily is to take Mistress Madeline to church—

and Rosalind told me to ask if you wished for your son to be present in the church when you are wed?'

Marietta hesitated. 'I am not sure. He may cry if his gums hurt, for his teeth are coming through…but I suppose you may take him home if he starts to fret.' She smiled. 'Yes, bring him to the church. He should be there.'

'Children often cry in church,' Lady Melford said as the door closed behind the girl. 'But I agree that your son should be there to see you wed.' She looked thoughtful. 'The girl is very young to have charge of the boy. Have you long employed her?'

'I took her on when Anton was ill. She is from the village. Her brother works for Sir Harry, and she asked Claire for work. Claire thought that I might like her to help with my son. She seems a pleasant, careful girl, and I have been satisfied with her work, but of course Rosalind is always there to keep an eye on things. And there is Lily too. She has had the care of Madeline, and must continue to look after her because it would upset the child to part from her nurse. I want us all to be happy together.' Marietta smiled. 'Anton is so good with the children. He says that I am a good mother but he is gentle and patient and they both love him.'

Anton turned his head to look as Marietta walked up the aisle towards him. He caught his breath as she halted at his side and turned to smile at him. She was so beautiful! Almost regal as she walked, her head held proudly. He could hardly believe that so much happiness was his. After Isabella's death he had felt that his heart was dead, but Marietta had wakened it, bringing him back from the dark place that had claimed him.

A ray of weak sunshine had managed to break through the clouds, piercing the stained glass window high above to shower the stone flags with a rainbow of colour. As she took her place at his side, Anton looked tenderly on his bride. For a while he had wondered if this day would ever come, fearing more mischief from Miguel, but nothing had been seen of him.

From somewhere in the church he heard the high, thin wail of a child, and then the sound of movement. Marietta turned her head for a moment to look. He raised his brows as she brought her gaze back to meet his, but she shook her head and smiled.

Anton reached out to take her hand as the priest began the marriage ceremony. Marietta would be his wife, and tonight he would claim her for his own…

The bells were ringing joyfully as they came out of church. Marietta stood on the steps with her husband and smiled as the cheers of village people greeted them. Children came forward with tokens of friendship and small gifts for the bride, which she accepted gracefully.

'Are you happy, my love?' Anton's voice brought her thoughts back to him. She laughed as he drew her to him and kissed her, in full view of their friends and family. 'It is too late to change your mind now, for you are mine—my wife.'

For a moment she saw jealousy and possession in his eyes, and understood his mind. He could not quite rid himself of the fear that she might betray him, as Isabella had.

'It is all I have ever wanted to be,' she told him, her eyes meeting his. 'I love you, Anton. I shall never look at another man.'

'We should go, for they will be ready to begin the feasting.' He took her hand and they ran down the steps together, laughing as they were deluged with dried rose petals and rosemary. 'Come, for the sooner the feasting begins, the sooner it will be over.'

A giggle of delight bubbled inside her as she saw his hot eyes. She had made him wait for this day so much longer than he had wished, and she did not doubt that he would make her pay for it that night.

The Great Hall was filled with people. The Earl and Lady Claire had invited all their friends to this joyous occasion, and they were assembled to greet the bride and groom. Marietta was feted by the other ladies, and given so many gifts and good wishes that she felt she must be dreaming.

Were all these beautiful things for her? Anton's gifts had been lavish, and included a wonderful string of huge creamy pearls that wound twice round her throat and fell to her waist. She had not expected to receive so many gifts of silver, costly cloth, and precious glass which came all the way from Venice and was rare and expensive. His family had almost over-whelmed her with their generosity, and the Earl's neighbours had also brought gifts that were magnificent.

Anton came to her as the toasts were drunk and everyone began to find their places so that the feasting could begin. He led her to the place of honour, sitting at her right hand while the Earl sat at her left. Lady Claire sat to Anton's right, and his parents were a little further along the high board.

The entertainment began with minstrels singing love songs, and the first dish to be brought to table: carp swimming in a rich wine sauce with tiny onions. After this came the boar's head, capons, a huge side of beef, pork, venison, wood pigeons and sweetbreads, plums, tarts of quince, custards and almond comfits.

Marietta tasted each dish but ate only a morsel, though she could not resist the marchpane and ate two that were stuck with walnuts and dates. Quantities of wine accompanied the food, also mead and sweetened ale.

She drank a little of the wine but kept a clear head, notic-ing that Anton did the same. His eyes were constantly on her, throughout the feasting, and she knew that he was waiting for the moment when they could leave.

As the afternoon wore on the guests began to call for danc-ing. Anton stood up, offering his hand to Marietta. She took it and they walked behind their guests at the high board, de-scending down the steps at the end to the centre of the hall. As the music began she made her curtsey, and Anton led her through the steps of a stately pavane. For a while they danced alone, but then their guests began to join in, and soon the floor was filled with smiling, happy people.

'Are you enjoying yourself?'

'Of course. This is our wedding…' She gazed up at him, catching her breath as she saw the heat in his eyes. 'Anton…'

'I want to sweep you up and—' He broke off as Lily came up to them, looking distressed. 'Something troubles you?'

'Forgive me for disturbing you at your wedding feast, sir. Maddie seems to have taken a fever, and Lady Melford said that I should ask my lady to come…'

'Surely my grandmother can manage—?' Anton began, but Marietta smiled and put a finger to his lips.

'If the child is ill I shall tend her. We shall be together later, my love.'

'I shall come with you,' he said, looking anxious now. 'It is not like Maddie to take a fever.'

They hurried up to the nursery, where they found Lady Melford bending over the little girl's cot. She was stroking Maddie's forehead and looking anxious.

'What ails her?' Anton said. 'Is she truly ill?'

'I thought at first that it was simply a fever, but she does seem very hot and unwell,' Melissa said. 'I wanted to ask Marietta what she thought. It isn't a teething rash—have you seen anything like this before? I do not think it is the pox…'

'Let me see. I have treated the pox before…' Marietta bent over the child, stroking her damp hair back from her forehead. She examined her arms and her neck and face, and then straightened up. 'I do not believe it is the pox. Maddie was taken into the garden earlier this morning. I think she has touched something that has brought out this rash. She may have eaten something she ought not. I can make a mixture to help with the fever, and a lotion to spread on her arms and legs. Stay here with her and I shall go down to the stillroom…' She smiled at Anton. 'Stay and comfort her, my love. Talk to her, for your presence may calm her…'

He nodded. 'Yes, I will stay. Though I think you are the one she needs. I believe she already thinks of you as her mother...'

Reaching the stillroom, Marietta set to work with a will. She took down various jars as she sought the herbs she needed. Maddie was not in danger but she was undoubtedly feeling ill, for she had a nasty rash and might have eaten berries that had made her unwell.

'I wonder if I should make her sick or simply ease her...'

Marietta did not realise that she had spoken out loud until she heard a sound behind her and turned. Her eyes widened in shock and fear as she saw the man watching her. Miguel was looking at her in such a way that her blood ran cold. She was not imagining it this time! He *did* hate her.

'What are you doing here?' she asked, her hand going to her throat as she sensed his evil intent. 'We thought you had returned to Spain. You tried to kill Anton...'

'May his soul rot in hell! You saved his life with your potions and your spells, witch—but I shall kill you, and then him.'

Marietta stared at him. 'Why do you hate me so? Why do you hate Anton? What have we done to you?'

'*You* took away his guilt and his pain. He was supposed to suffer for what he did to her...*my* Isabella. I saw her lying there, all the life gone from her. Her eyes looked at me...such accusing eyes...'

'Anton told me what happened. He merely asked her for the truth that day. She was his wife, and he was afraid that she had betrayed him with another...was it you...?' Marietta saw his face twist with agony. 'Yes—she was carrying your child. But you wanted more, didn't you? You wanted her to run away with you, and she would not, so...' A gasp broke from her. 'You were there when she died... What did you do, Miguel? What did you do to her?'

'I loved her. She was always mine. He stole her from me...'

Miguel's eyes glittered as he moved closer to Marietta. 'I was her friend, and then her lover. She came to me when she was unhappy and told me she did not love him. We made love, and she conceived. She was terrified that he would know the child was not his because she had not slept with him, so she went to him and asked him to love her. I tried to make her understand that it was me she loved, to persuade her to flee with me...' His hand was shaking and she saw beads of sweat on his brow. 'It was his fault, not mine. He was her murderer, not I...'

'You?' Marietta saw the truth in his eyes. 'What did you do to her that day, Miguel? She ran from Anton because he was angry. But she didn't fall, and she didn't take her own life... *You* pushed her down those steps. It was you that killed her, not her husband.'

'I never meant to kill her,' Miguel said, and he was trembling. 'She told me that her life was over, that she must go into a convent to atone for her sin. She did not enjoy marriage and felt that she had failed as a woman. Even when she lay in my arms she was afraid of giving herself. That day she was weeping, and I tried to comfort her. I tried to take her in my arms but she pushed me away, and then...she just fell...'

'You grabbed her and she pulled away, losing her balance... and you watched her fall. You could not save her, and instead of blaming yourself you blamed Anton...'

'It was *his* fault! She was mine. He stole her from me...' Miguel cried, and then made a move to grab Marietta. 'He took my love from me and I shall take his from him. Before he dies he will learn what it is like to lose everything.'

Marietta backed away from him, her eyes on his face. 'You cannot bring her back. Vengeance is empty. You will still be guilty of her murder.'

'Be quiet, witch! I intend to have my way—but first I will taste you. You will have *my* kiss on your lips when you die, feel the humiliation of—'

He broke off as Marietta picked up the sharp knife she

had been using to peel roots and strip bark from a branch of willow. She held it in her right hand.

'Come near me and you will feel this blade in your flesh,' she said, and made a threatening stabbing movement. 'The blade has been used to squash the berries of deadly night-shade. If it enters your flesh you will surely die…'

'Witch! They were right to name you murderess. You should burn in hell for what you have done…'

'I did not harm anyone. What little skill I have is used for good, not harm. *You* are the murderer. You killed Isabella by knocking her off balance so that she fell down the steps…'

'Damn you!' Miguel drew his sword, advancing on her menacingly. 'I shall not drink at your poisoned well. It is enough to see you dead…'

'Stay away from me!' Marietta screamed as he lunged at her with his sword, jumping back, retreating to the other side of the bench where she had been working. He was between her and the door. She could only draw him on and hope to get past him as he followed. 'Your soul is doomed to burn in hell. You cannot wash away your stain by taking my life…'

'If I burn in hell so be it—but you will be there first!'

Miguel lunged at her again. She screamed and jumped back once more. If she could just get past him and make a dash for the door…

He had seen her intention, and moved back to cut off her flight. He laughed, his eyes glittering with hate.

'You cannot escape. Your knife is of no use against my sword—'

'But my sword will match yours,' a voice rang out, and Miguel swirled round to face his new adversary. 'It seems that you are too much a coward to face me. You prey on defence-less women, and you make sure that I am not near. Are you a coward, or will you fight me?'

'He killed Isabella. He caused her fall, not you…' Marietta cried.

Anton gave no sign that he had heard her. His eyes were

fixed on Miguel. Suddenly the Spaniard lunged at him with his sword. Anton sidestepped, drawing him on further into the room.

'Run, Marietta—rouse the house…'

Marietta ran towards the door. Opening it, she screamed for help, but she did not leave. Her eyes were glued to the men who were joined in battle. The chilling sound of steel on steel was echoing through the room. She could see at once that they were evenly matched, for Miguel was also a skilled swords-man, and they were of much the same weight, though Anton was a little taller.

Marietta's heart was in her mouth as the fight swayed one way and then the other. Anton drew the first blood, his sword-tip catching Miguel's left arm, but then Miguel struck back, his sword sliding across Anton's shoulder but failing to pierce his heavy leather jerkin. He swore and slashed wildly, catch-ing Anton's arm with the tip, making the blood run. Marietta screamed again.

Anton parried, bringing his sword round with a movement that swept Miguel's blade from his hand. Miguel's eyes were wide with fear as he looked at Anton. For a moment Anton hesitated, then lowered the blade of his weapon.

'I shall not kill you, for it would be to take foul advan-tage,' he said. 'You will be taken into custody and tried for attempted murder—and may God take pity on your soul.'

Anton turned towards Marietta, his eyes seeking hers. 'Are you hurt, my love?'

As Anton turned his head, Miguel swiftly bent and re-trieved his sword with his left hand. Even as he thrust it at Anton's back, Marietta threw the knife. It pierced Miguel's neck and he fell to the ground, a thick crimson tide bubbling as he tried to speak and failed.

Anton looked down at his fallen enemy and frowned.

'Have I killed him?' Marietta asked, and crossed herself. 'God forgive me! I have murdered him…'

'What nonsense is this?' Anton tipped her chin, gazing

down into her tear-drenched eyes. 'Do not cry, my love. You have been brave and strong. You have done no wrong to any being—had you not thrown the knife, he would have murdered me.'

She swayed against him, her senses swimming as the terror of the ordeal came over her. Anton swept her up in his arms, the watching servants parting as he walked towards them, leaving the way clear for him to carry her upstairs to the chamber they were to share that night.

He lay her down on the bed and stood watching her as the colour slowly came back to her cheeks.

'You have done too much,' he said, in a harsh voice that hid his anxiety. 'You nursed me for weeks and then this…'

Marietta pushed herself up against the pillows as her head cleared. 'No, I have not exhausted myself,' she said, and smiled at him. 'It was just so…overwhelming. He wanted to kill me.'

'And would have done so had I not come in time.' Anton looked grim. 'It is little wonder that you felt dizzy just now…'

'It was just for a moment. I shall be better now.' She swung her legs over the bed. 'Your arm is bleeding, Anton. Let me bind it for you.'

'It is but a scratch. I can do it myself. I have had worse and survived it without nursing. Stay where you are, Marietta, and rest.'

'I do not need to rest, and Maddie needs me…' She bit her lip as he prepared to leave the room. 'Will you not stay with me?'

'My grandmother will care for the child. Rest for a few hours or you will make yourself ill,' Anton told her. 'I need to rest myself. I shall see you later…'

Marietta lay back against the pillows as he went out, then she shook her head, refusing to give way to tears. She was tired, and she would sleep later, but if Anton did not wish for her company she would go to the nursery and see if Maddie responded to the potions she had made.

'I came to take my leave of you,' Lady Catherine said the next afternoon. 'My husband hath business that will not keep. I hope that Anton will bring you to us soon. I do not know where you plan to settle now that your enemy is dead.'

'Miguel *is* dead…?' Marietta swayed and gave a little moan, sinking down onto a padded stool. 'Anton would have spared him. Forgive me, I am feeling a little faint. Mayhap Anton is right and I am ill…'

Catherine looked at her for a moment, her eyes narrowed in thought. 'Is there any chance that you might be with child?'

'With child?' Marietta stared at her. 'It is possible…' She blushed as she remembered the night she had given herself to Anton as they travelled to London. 'I had not thought…one night…is it possible?' It had taken years of trying before she had been able to give her husband a son.

Catherine laughed. 'You were married to a man much older, perhaps an invalid?' Marietta nodded her head, looking bemused. 'Anton is young and strong. If you lay with him before your wedding then there is every possibility that you carry his child.'

'I believed that I might die in prison, or at the rope's end,' Marietta said, her cheeks hot. 'You will think me wanton…'

'I was young and hot-blooded once,' Catherine told her with a smile. 'I was forced to marry a man I was not sure loved me. If he had made love to me before we were wed I might not have suffered so much doubt or wept as many tears.'

'Oh…' Marietta laughed. 'I believe you are right concerning my condition, for now I think of it I have not seen my courses since before that time. I had not noticed, for there has been no time to think of myself.'

'I am no physician, but if you need confirmation ask my mother. She will know if you are with child.'

'I do not think I need to ask. I had not considered it, but

now…' Marietta laughed. 'I am not sure what Anton will think of my news…'

'If I know anything of my son he will be delighted. He has a daughter he loves, but I am certain he longs for a son.'

'Thank you…' Marietta was suddenly glowing. She put her hands on her stomach. 'Our child… Yes, perhaps it will be a son…'

'You will come to us when you can?'

'Of course.' Marietta moved to kiss her cheek. 'I have no idea what Anton plans for the future. We have had little time to talk…'

'You must ask him when he comes to you—and tell him your news. I dare say the news that he is to become a father will sharpen his thoughts. It would please his father if he were to buy an estate that borders ours and has recently been offered for sale.'

'It would be pleasant to have you as neighbours, but Anton must decide…'

After Lady Catherine had gone, Marietta went to sit on the bed, piling the pillows up behind her. She was not tired, but she wanted to relax and think. She had already visited Maddie that day, and knew that the girl was recovering well. There was no need to be anxious for her. All Marietta needed to do now was think of the future.

She was carrying Anton's child! It was a blessing from God, and the shadows that had hung over her melted away as she realised how fortunate she was. She slipped back against the pillows and closed her eyes.

When Anton entered the bedchamber an hour later, he found Marietta sleeping. She looked so lovely! He stood watching her, resisting the temptation to touch her. If she woke he would want to make love to her, and it was obvious that she was still tired. When she had almost fainted in his arms he had been terrified that she was ill; the fear of losing her had made him harsh. He had spoken sharply and it would not do.

He must learn to speak softly to his beautiful wife, because he did not wish to see shadows in her eyes.

He would leave her to sleep. They were due to leave the next morning. He had agreed to escort his grandmother back to Melford, and stay with her and his grandfather for a while.

Anton had been told of two estates that might suit him. One was close to his father's house, the other a little closer to Melford but with more land. He wanted to see both manors for himself before he came to a decision.

Marietta might prefer to return to France. Anton frowned as he turned away. He could not blame her if she wanted to claim her son's inheritance. Unless a strong man was put in charge of the castle, it would fall into neglect and ruin.

Had Miguel not proved to be the traitor he undoubtedly was, Anton might have trusted *him* to hold the castle. Without someone who could be trusted not to try to steal the manor from the young Comte de Montcrief it might be better to sell it—but would Marietta agree?

'Anton…' Marietta's sleepy voice stopped him as his hand moved towards the door latch. 'Are you going? Why did you not wake me?'

He turned and smiled, coming back to her as she pushed herself up against the pillows. 'You looked so peaceful. I did not want to disturb you, my love.'

Marietta yawned, and then swung her legs over the side and stood up. She gazed up at him, her lips soft and moist, slightly parted.

'I was dreaming of you. Are you angry with me, Anton?'

'Why should I be angry?' He gave her a rueful smile. 'Yesterday I may have spoken harshly. You looked tired and pale. I was anxious that you had made yourself ill looking after others.'

'I am not ill, Anton…' She hesitated, her eyes searching his face. 'I think there may be a good reason for my faintness—and the tiredness…'

'You have worked too hard—' he began, but she put her fingers to his lips and smiled. 'Then what—?'

'You remember that night…when we travelled to London?'

'Yes, but—' He broke off staring at her. 'What are you telling me?'

'I am not yet certain, but I think it very likely that I am carrying our child…' She saw his face darken. 'Oh, no, please do not look at me so. Why are you angry? I know it is too soon, but…'

'Too soon?' Anton looked into her face. 'Not too soon, my love—but I wanted to have you to myself for a time…before you face the agony and danger that awaits you.'

'Childbirth is painful, and at times it can be dangerous,' Marietta admitted. 'However, I carried my son easily, though I lost others. My husband blamed himself, for he was not strong enough to give me more children, but *we* are both young. There is no reason to think we shall lose our babe.'

'It is not of the babe I think…though I should be loath to lose a child…but of you, Marietta…' He reached out to hold her close, his face buried in her hair. 'Isabella was always so sickly… If I lost you…'

She drew back, looking at him. 'I am not Isabella. I shall not draw back when you touch me, or run from you. We can only trust in God that I shall be safely delivered of a child, Anton—but I do not fear it.'

'You are so brave…' He touched her cheek. 'I love you more than life itself. I am a coward compared to you, my love.'

'You? A coward?' Marietta laughed mockingly. 'You won the silver arrow against all comers. You fought my enemy face to face and killed him—yet you would have spared Miguel. Why would you have spared him?'

'Because I felt pity for him. He loved Isabella and I took her from him. I wish that I had never seen her. Had I not asked for her, her father would have let her marry Miguel and both of them might still be alive.'

'Do not blame yourself for their deaths, Anton. Isabella's was an accident—for Miguel acted in haste, sending her to her death without understanding what he did—and he brought his own death on himself. I blamed myself at first, but I see now that I had no choice.'

'You speak truly. When he tried to murder me there was no other choice.'

'Miguel was mad with hate for you, Anton. He would have killed you if he could. We must neither of us feel guilt over his death.'

'I shall not, and nor must you, though we may pity him...' Anton looked down at her. 'I had thought to lie with you this night, but now...'

Marietta laughed softly. 'And so I should hope, my husband. We missed our wedding night. You have much to make up for...'

'Wicked wench!' he murmured. 'But should we not be careful?'

'We need not take care for a few months yet. I am hardly sure I carry the babe, but I have missed my courses and I feel it.' She reached up to kiss him on the lips. 'I see no reason why we should wait for the night, Anton. Secure the lock and come to bed with me.'

He hesitated, then, 'You are sure?'

'Yes, I am sure. I want to lie with you, my beloved. I want to seal my marriage vows. I am yours and I long to be in your arms...'

Anton smiled and moved to the door, turning the key in the lock. When he returned he saw that Marietta was trying to unlace her gown at the back.

'Come here and I shall do it for you,' he said, lifting her hair to kiss the back of her neck. She looked round and smiled at him. He kissed her lips and she moved against him. Anton wrenched the laces free and pulled the bodice over her head. Marietta swiftly untied the ribbon at her waist and let her overskirt fall to the ground. She stood before him in her thin

undergown, holding out her hands. He took them, pulling her
hard against him, suddenly fierce with need. 'I want you so
much…'

'Your arm?'

'A mere scratch…' Anton said, bending his head to kiss
her. 'Nothing that will keep me from your bed…' He reached
out, gathering her up in his arms. 'I have waited so long for
this…'

Marietta smiled and kissed him.

'You long for it no more than I,' she whispered. 'I have
waited for you far longer than you know, my love…'

It was dark save for a chink of light from the small window
when Marietta woke to find herself snuggled close to her husband. She could hear his even breathing and knew that he still
slept. She stretched and moved away from him, getting up and
going to the closet to relieve herself.

She could still taste his kisses on her lips, and feel the tingling between her thighs where he had loved her well. She had
wondered if the excitement and pleasure she had known the
first time in his arms could ever be repeated, but if anything
this night had been better. Anton's tenderness, his care for her
pleasure and her comfort, had carried her to new heights of
ecstasy. All her dreams had been surpassed. She knew that
she was the happiest, most fortunate of women.

A little cry came from the bed. Marietta went to see what
was wrong. Anton was having a dream—and a bad one,
it seemed. He threw his arm out and kicked as if he were
fighting.

'No! Do not leave me… I cannot bear it… You must not…'
he muttered.

Marietta's smile dimmed. Did he still think of the woman
he had lost? Even after the night they had just spent in each
other's arms! He had sworn he loved her, but if he still called
for Isabella…

'Stay with me…' Anton pleaded, tossing restlessly. 'Marietta… my love…'

He was dreaming of *her*! Marietta climbed on to the bed and bent over him, pressing her lips to his cheek and giving him a little shake.

'Wake up, Anton. Wake up, my love. I am here with you. I love you.'

Anton opened his eyes. He stared at her and then smiled. He reached out to touch her cheek, his hand moving in her scented hair.

'I was having a bad dream. I dreamed that you had the child, but then you—' He choked back the words. 'No! It was just a dream. A stupid, foolish dream. You are strong. I am a fool to burden you with my fears. Forgive me, my beloved wife.'

'Of course I forgive you,' she said, and kissed his mouth. 'I love you. I promise that I shall not leave you. I shall not die. When my time comes to have the child I shall be well cared for and nothing will happen. You must believe me.'

'Yes, I believe you,' he said. 'I shall forget this nonsense. Forgive me for waking you.'

'You did not wake me.' She held her hand out to him. 'Come, my love. Slip on your robe and come with me.'

Anton rose and put on the loose chamber gown that lay beside the bed. He looked at her oddly.

'Where are you taking me?'

'Just take my hand and wait…'

She led him along the passage to the nursery. Going in, they saw a candle still burned atop a chest some distance from the child's cot.

Marietta drew her husband close to the cot, gazing down at the boy as he lay sleeping, his arm curled about Maddie. He must have climbed in with her, mayhap to comfort her. His skin was soft, touched with pink, one fist curled under his head the other arm across her body. Maddie was sleeping peacefully, her face against her companion's curls. They looked so perfect together that it brought a lump to the throats of the man and woman who watched.

'Is that not beautiful?' Marietta whispered. 'Our children. Think of the other children I shall give you, Anton. Is it not worth a little risk for a son of your own?'

Anton looked down at the boy and smiled. 'He is beautiful, and I shall love him as a son. We are lucky to have these two...' He touched her face. 'I care not what our child is—a son or a daughter. I know that you will bear it without fear. You will not weep and curse me as she did.'

'Isabella blamed you for her discomfort?' He nodded, and Marietta smiled. 'All women complain and weep sometimes when they are with child, but it does not mean that they truly blame the father—it is just that they grow weary of feeling fat and ugly. Once it is over the pain and discomfort is forgotten.'

'You are so wise and lovely,' he said. 'Do you mean to absolve me of all blame, Marietta?'

'Isabella could not enjoy marriage as you might have wished, but that was not your fault. You must let the past go—as I have.' She led him from the nursery back to their chamber. 'Only then will you be free of the nightmares that haunt you.'

'Yes, I know.' He smiled and stroked his fingers down her cheek, placing a kiss at the little hollow at the base of her throat. 'Shall you be content to live in England? Or do you wish to return to the castle?'

'Could we have a house such as this?'

'I hope to find something as comfortable—is that what you would like?'

'Yes. I was never truly comfortable at the castle. It holds no fond memories—only those that I can create here with my son, Maddie and our children. I think I should be pleased if you could sell Montcrief and invest the money here in England for my son.'

'Then you have solved my problem.' He grinned as she

raised her brows. 'My father wishes me to buy an estate next to his—and my grandfather sent word that there was an excellent manor near to Melford. I was not sure which to choose. If we bought both we should between us own a huge area of land—all of which is held by members of my family. It would make our family one of the most powerful in England.'

'Then purchase both and sell Montcrief,' Marietta said. 'If you need more gold I will sign so that you can use the money from the Comte's deposits with the goldsmiths at the French court.'

'I think the money would be better invested here,' Anton said. 'Your son will be raised as an English gentleman. Better that his land is here and well cared for than he inherit a neglected castle in France.'

They had reached their bedchamber. Marietta reached up to kiss him on the mouth, pressing herself against him.

'Do it with my blessing,' she said. 'Build for the future, for all our children—and now, my love, I want you to come back to bed with me...'

Anton gazed down at her. 'I almost passed by that day I saw the notice for the contest for the silver arrow. Had I never seen you, I might have refused when the King commanded me to take a message to the Comte de Montcrief. Had I not come, the rogues who tried to capture you might have killed you that day. I had decided that I would retire from court life, and would have liked to refuse the King, but it was the memory of your face as you gave me the arrow that drew me back to France, though I knew it not then. It has taken me a long time to let go and allow myself to love again, Marietta—but now that I have I shall love only you until I die.'

'It was fate, our destiny,' she said. 'You saved me from certain death beneath the hooves of that horse, and when the dog attacked me—and you have saved me many times since. Yes, I am certain it was fate that drew us together at the last, my brave and gallant husband...'

Afterword

'You must wait a little longer, my son.' Anton's father smiled as he motioned to him to sit down. 'Come, drink some wine and exercise patience. You are not wanted in Marietta's chamber for the moment. At times like these we must leave matters to the women. Your wife is strong and has already borne a living son. Your mother and grandmother are certain she carries a boy child, and they are usually right.'

'How am I supposed to just sit here while she is in such pain?' Anton demanded. He looked round as he heard another piercing scream. 'I cannot bear it a moment longer. If she dies…'

'There is little you can do, Anton.' The Marquis of Malchester looked sympathetically at the Earl of Rundle. Both were strong fighting men, powerful and influential in their circles, and both felt helpless. 'Catherine will call us when you can go up to your wife.'

Hearing another scream, Anton started for the door. He did not look round as his father called to him. 'I must go to her. Perhaps I can help…'

Anton pounded up the stairway to the little solar where the child was being birthed. His heart was racing wildly, for

Marietta had been in labour some hours and he was terrified that she would die. Would to God that he could bear the child for her! She had become such a huge part of his life that he would not want to live if he lost her, even for the sake of the children.

As he reached the door of the chamber he hesitated, and in that moment he heard a thin, wailing cry. That was not Marietta! It must be the child. His throat tightened and he felt his eyes sting with unaccustomed tears. Suddenly his feet were rooted to the ground, and he felt as weak as a kitten, unable to take another step. He was not sure how long he stood there, but after what might have been minutes or hours the door opened and his mother came out. She was carrying something wrapped in a fine wool shawl and smiling.

'Your son is born, Anton.'

'My son?' He looked at her, almost stupid in his relief. 'My son… But Marietta? Is she…?' He was too fearful to ask the question.

'Marietta is tired, but well. She was very brave, and bore her ordeal as she ought.'

'Marietta is always brave,' Anton said, and glanced at the red face of his son. 'He is beautiful. Give him to me, Mother. I want to hold him when I see Marietta.'

Catherine handed over the babe. Anton took him carefully, then went into the birthing chamber. Marietta was lying against a pile of pillows, her eyes closed. She opened them as he approached, and smiled.

'You have the son I promised you,' she said, and held out her hand to him.

Anton bent to kiss her on the mouth. He sat down on the edge of the bed, holding his son carefully and looking down at the babe. 'I think he looks like me. Charles looks like you, but that is as it should be. We have two sons and a daughter now, Marietta. Our family is complete.'

'Oh, I don't know. Maddie is such a darling. I might like to have another daughter.'

'I am not sure I could bear it,' Anton said. 'The birth of my son was almost too much for me…' He saw the mischief in her eyes and laughed. 'I know that you had to bear the pain, but it hurt me more than you will ever know.'

'My poor darling,' Marietta teased. 'Next time I will have you here with me, so that I can hold your hand.'

'Be careful, woman, you go too far,' he replied. 'Wait until you are well, and remember that I have the power to chastise you…'

Marietta was saved from replying by the arrival of her mother-in-law, who had brought Madeline and Charles to see their new brother. They were closely followed by the arrival of their grandfather, who was impatient to see the heir to his estates.

As Catherine took the babe and placed him carefully in his cot, Marietta felt her hand captured by Anton's. She smiled up at him, then closed her eyes, drifting into a peaceful sleep. Her happiness was complete, and the future would be all that she had ever dreamed of and more…

* * * * *

0411/09/MB330

She was his last chance for a future of happiness

Fortune-teller Jenny can make even the greatest sceptic believe her predictions just by batting her eyelashes. Until she meets her match in Gareth Carhart, the Marquess of Blakely, a sworn bachelor and scientist.

Broodingly handsome Gareth vows to prove Jenny a fraud. But his unexpected attraction to the enchantress defies logic. Engaging in a passionate battle of wills, they must choose between everything they know…and the endless possibilities of love.

Available 18th March 2011
www.millsandboon.co.uk

REGENCY
Collection

*Let these sparklingly seductive delights whirl
you away to the ballrooms—and
bedrooms—of Polite Society!*

Volume 1 – 4th February 2011
Regency Pleasures by Louise Allen

Volume 2 – 4th March 2011
Regency Secrets by Julia Justiss

Volume 3 – 1st April 2011
Regency Rumours by Juliet Landon

Volume 4 – 6th May 2011
Regency Redemption by Christine Merrill

Volume 5 – 3rd June 2011
Regency Debutantes by Margaret McPhee

Volume 6 – 1st July 2011
Regency Improprieties by Diane Gaston

12 volumes in all to collect!

MILLS
BOON

www.millsandboon.co.uk

REGENCY
Collection

*Let these sparklingly seductive delights whirl
you away to the ballrooms—and
bedrooms—of Polite Society!*

Volume 7 – 5th August 2011
Regency Mistresses by Mary Brendan

Volume 8 – 2nd September 2011
Regency Rebels by Deb Marlowe

Volume 9 – 7th October 2011
Regency Scandals by Sophia James

Volume 10 – 4th November 2011
Regency Marriages by Elizabeth Rolls

Volume 11 – 2nd December 2011
Regency Innocents by Annie Burrows

Volume 12 – 6th January 2012
Regency Sins by Bronwyn Scott

12 volumes in all to collect!

MILLS
BOON

www.millsandboon.co.uk

WEB/M&B/RTL3

Discover Pure Reading Pleasure with

Visit the Mills & Boon website for all the latest in romance

🌹 **Buy** all the latest releases, backlist and eBooks

🌹 **Find out** more about our authors and their books

🌹 **Join** our community and chat to authors and other readers

🌹 **Free** online reads from your favourite authors

🌹 **Win** with our fantastic online competitions

🌹 **Sign** up for our free monthly eNewsletter

🌹 **Tell us** what you think by signing up to our reader panel

🌹 **Rate** and review books with our star system

www.millsandboon.co.uk

 Follow us at twitter.com/millsandboonuk

 Become a fan at facebook.com/romancehq